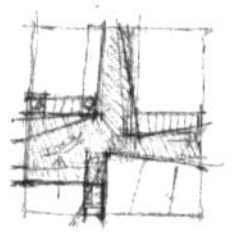

Secret Paths Editions presents

Girl & Boy

The Boy & Girl Saga - Book One
Revised 2020 edition

Alan McCluskey

First published in May 2012
Second edition 2014
Third edition 2020
Secret Paths Editions, Mureta 2, CH-2072 Saint-Blaise
Copyright © Alan McCluskey
Cover illustration by Alan McCluskey

ISBN 978-2-940553-25-9

Other books by the author

The Boy & Girl Saga
In Search of Lost Girls - Book Two
We Girls - Book Three

The Storyteller's Quest
The Reaches - Book One
The Keeper's Daughter - Book Two
The Starless Square - Book Three

Chimera
Stories People Tell

Coming soon
Local Voices

Thanks

Thanks go both to the Geneva Writers' Group in particular Susan Tiberghien and to the Basel Writers' Circle for critiquing parts of this novel. Thanks to Fred Leebron, who led a master class in fiction in Geneva during which the first three chapters of this book were critiqued. Special thanks to my young beta-readers Sarah Hathorn and Kaya Jumbe. Thanks also to Nancy Fraser and Sylvia Petter for their advice. Thanks go to my children Zoé and Iannis for their comments and suggestions about the book cover. To Caramel, who sadly just passed away at the ripe old age of seventeen, thanks pussy for being such a wonderful model for the cat in Boy & Girl

Above all, my gratitude goes to my wife, Huguette, for putting up with the strange, unreal conversations when I was so engrossed in the writing this book that much of what I said came from Peter's world.

1.

Peter glanced at the school notice board: Friday, May 13th 1960. For a Friday 13th, he'd escaped the worst so far. He looked over his shoulder as he broke into a run. There must be a clock somewhere. He was going to be late.

The next thing he knew he was tumbling forward. His hands flew out to break his fall, his fingers locking onto a girl's skirt, yanking it up as he did. The girl, who must have been kneeling in the middle of the corridor, let out a high-pitched squeal and rolled on top of him, her knee digging into his stomach, winding him.

Letting go of her skirt, he struggled to get free. To his surprise, she fought to hold on, straddling him, her skirt trussed up around her waist, her legs bare and her pants in full view. Seizing his arm, she dug her nails deep into his flesh.

"Ouch!" he cried out.

She rolled off him and clambered to her feet, pulling down her skirt and tucking in her blouse. Walking away without a word, she left him sprawling on the floor, staring at her retreating back. Who was she?

Peter gingerly fingered his arm. Blood seeped from four gashes staining his shirt. He prayed the girl had clean nails, because there was no time to tend the wounds. He picked up his satchel and got up. Frowning, he turned into the bustling corridor and saw his form waiting for a noisy group of third formers to free the classroom.

The boys were the first to leave, several of them from the third-form rugby team. They were the worst. They pushed and shoved as if they were on the pitch. Several first formers were sent flying. He'd learnt to keep out of their way. That didn't stop one trying to stomp on his toes. Peter flattened himself against the wall, narrowly escaping, but not quickly enough to avoid an elbow in his stomach, just where the girl had got him earlier. Arrogant swine, he thought, bent over double trying to breathe. How he hated rugby!

The third form girls huddled around Mrs Greengage, the English teacher, jockeying for her attention. He glimpsed his sister's girlfriend, Fi, amongst them. Despite the school uniform, she always looked different, brighter, more colourful, so full of life. His pulse quickened. The sight of her had him wishing he could be like her. Maybe then she'd pay attention, she who only had eyes for girls.

When the girls finally released the teacher and left, Peter's class filed in. Seeing Mrs. Greengage, he suddenly remembered his homework. Blast! He'd forgotten it again. His frown deepened. It wasn't that he disliked English, it was one of the least boring subjects, apart from maths that is. Rather, it was English that disliked him.

How many times had teachers told him he was clueless? His spelling was atrocious, his compositions wild and incoherent and when he tried to read out loud, he stumbled over even the most common words. At such times his guts shrunk to half their size in humiliation.

As he searched for his textbook, a tense hush stole over the class. It was so out of place he pulled his nose from his satchel in search of the cause. He groaned. The new girl. She strode into the room, back straight, head held high, chin jutting forward. She was taller than the other girls and looked to be slightly older. Her blond hair was tied back in a knot making her look severe, as did her sharp, angular features. Even if he hadn't already had a skirmish with her, he would have disliked her.

"I'm Priscilla Wit," the girl said, addressing the teacher, her upper-crust accent sounding out of place in a state school.

"You are in the wrong class, Miss Wit," Mrs Greengage informed her, having run her finger hastily down the attendance list.

"I am to attend this class, the Headmaster said." The girl's unswerving self-confidence did nothing to make her likeable.

Not Miss Wit but 'misfit', Peter thought, concealing a grin.

"Take a seat, Miss Wit," the teacher said.

There were a number of free desks, but the dim wit - what a useful name - bagged the one next to his. He caught a whiff of her new uniform, a smell that recalled both pleasant and unpleasant memories.

Turning his back on her, he stared resolutely at Mrs Greengage who was writing: Animal Farm - 1945, on the blackboard.

"Hands up those who have read Orwell's book," she asked.

Hands shot up around the class, including the eager hand of the new girl. He glanced at her waving fingers out of the corner of his eye and shuddered at the sight of the sharply pointed nails. His own hands, with their chewed nails, remained resolutely hidden in his lap, hoping no one would notice. He had no idea who Orwell was and knew nothing of a book about animals on a farm unless it was Shadow the Sheepdog.

Shuffling sideways to get her overlarge frame through the narrow spaces, the teacher shifted between the desks till she reached his.

"Have you not heard of Animal Farm, Mr. McCloud?" she asked.

He shook his head.

"What was the last book you read?"

The new girl leaned closer, no doubt hoping to catch his reply. There was no escaping. If he answered, he'd be crowned with derision. If he didn't, he'd be just as much a fool.

He hesitated between the only two novels he'd ever read and opted not to mention J.M. Barrie's book. "Shadow the Sheepdog," he mumbled, hoping only the teacher would hear. Miss Wit clearly did because she burst out laughing. Others sniggered. He was mortified.

"Your laughter is not helpful, Miss Wit," the teacher said, her tone icy. "We'll talk about this after class, Mr. McCloud."

He glanced up briefly, wondering if that might be a sympathetic smile etched between the many creases of her face. Wonderful! Now the whole class would think Greengage was playing nanny to him.

"Who can tell me what Animal Farm is about?" the teacher asked, moving away.

To his relief, at no time did Greengage call on him to read. She did ask Miss Wit, who read impeccably, of course. Greengage didn't ask him any questions either and made no comment when he failed to hand in his homework. He was beginning to believe he could slip away unnoticed, but when the bell rang the teacher motioned for him to stay.

Miss Wit lingered at least five minutes, peppering Greengage with questions about books he'd never heard of. When she finally turned to go, the girl glanced back over her shoulder at him and smirked, mouthing a word he couldn't understand, before going out and leaving the door wide open.

Mrs. Greengage sighed and got to her feet to close the door. "Take a seat, Mr. McCloud," she said over her shoulder. It was morning break. No one would disturb them.

He sat at the front desk. It felt odd to be sitting in Susan's seat. She was the girl whose blouse always looked too tight. The world was quite different from her place. He tried unsuccessfully to think himself into Susan's head. She would surely know how to deal with Greengage. She was one of the best in English and wrote such lovely stories. Not that he had much to do with her, apart from enviously studying the growth of her breasts, but when they did speak, she was kind enough. Most of the other girls made him feel uncomfortable or poked fun.

To think he'd welcomed the idea of going to a mixed school. Girls had been a recent addition at Tallford Grammar. Odd that such a change could have taken place in a conservative town like Tallford. Many parents threatened to transfer their precious boys elsewhere but there was no alternative. Peter's mother had been one of them. "Girls are an unnecessary distraction," she'd said.

He hugged his satchel as if it could shield him. The satchel was not new, but it still smelt strongly of leather. Resting his chin on its handle, he savoured the smell as he looked up at Greengage. She sighed. When grown-ups sighed that generally meant trouble.

"I don't know what to do with you McCloud."

Neither did he.

"Do you have any friends in the class?"

He shook his head. He had very little to do with his fellow first formers. He always hurried home after school, living out in the country, a long bike-ride away. Even if he'd wanted to hang around, there was nothing to do except watch pensioners shuffle around or listen to mothers chattering about their babies as they did their shopping.

Mrs. Greengage frowned as she picked up her copy of Orwell's book. "How often do you read?"

"From time to time." Rarely would have been a more honest answer. He liked stories, didn't he tell himself stacks of them, but reading books wasn't the same.

"Do you have any books at home?"

"Two."

"Apart from Shadow the Sheepdog, what's the other one?"

"Peter Pan."

"You could go to the library." She sounded sceptical.

He shrugged. How could he tell her it wasn't personal? He just didn't enjoy reading.

"I have an offer to make. At home I have a great many books covering a wide range of subjects for boys and girls of all ages. Why don't you come and pick one? You can read at my place, if you like. No one will bother you. Try it and we'll see how that works out."

That there were books written specially for girls appealed to him. He might read them without anyone poking fun. He glanced up at the clock. Break was almost over and he didn't want to get caught with Greengage. The boys would make fun of him for staying behind with the teacher. "Ok."

She wrote her address on a scrap of paper, adding a phone number and handed it to him. "How about this Saturday afternoon at three? Unless of course you want to watch the rugby."

"No!" The thought horrified him. "Saturday is fine." He got hurriedly to his feet, muttering "Thanks" and fled.

Relieved to have escaped, he was about to set off for his next class when a female voice stopped him.

"So, not only are you a pansy, you're illiterate too!"

He spun round to find Witless leaning against the wall, her arms crossed over her chest, her lips curved in a sneer.

"Do you steal your sister's knickers?" she asked, delight and disgust in her voice.

Peter shifted from one foot to another, his face on fire. How could she possibly know?

She nodded at his tacit admission.

"I can always tell." She made a show of sniffing the air. "People like you always smell bad." She stepped back, her nose wrinkled in disgust.

"You are one of God's oversights. The imperfect ones that slipped by when he had his back turned."

Peter was riveted to the spot, terrified. The girl was mad!

Priscilla lashed out and grabbed him by the tie, jerking him forward. "Don't worry," she grinned. "I'll set God's mistake right. When I'm finished, there'll be one less imperfection in the world."

Her hold tightened and he coughed as he began to choke.

"Miss Wit!" he heard Greengage call out, her voice cutting. "May I have a word with you. Now!"

The girl released him, but not before hissing: "I'll get you later."

2.

Peter pushed down hard on the pedals until he breasted the crown of the hill on which their house was built, a solitary, single-storey building. After the long ride, he was glad to get off and walk. Pushing aside the gate, he wheeled his bike along the gravel drive and round the garage. He leaned it against the porch and unlatched the kitchen door.

Halting in the doorway, he breathed deeply savouring the specialness of the moment. His stomach fluttered. Excitement, anticipation, but anxiety too. Like a faithful but shy friend, such a feeling only surfaced when he had the house to himself or was on one of his lone bike rides.

He dumped his satchel on the kitchen table with a thud, surprising the cat that slept beneath. He poured himself a glass of cold milk, adding some in a bowl for the cat, and sat down to watch the animal stretch and yawn. "You can't imagine how lucky you are not to have to go to school," he told the cat.

It ignored him.

Shafts of light streamed through the glass openings in the ceiling. It had been his father's brain child. "My home cathedral," Dad had called it. When his father abruptly fell ill and died shortly afterwards, the architect, one of his father's best friends, insisted on finishing the job. Peter had been five and the fuss with the inquest and the funeral and "all the damn wrangling with insurance companies", as his mother put it, had skimmed over his little head as he ducked into his own world.

Peter rummaged in his pockets looking for a toffee, but found none. He must have eaten them on his ride. Instead, he found a scrap of paper. He crossed the kitchen to throw it in the bin when he realised it was Greengage's address. He'd been so busy avoiding the terrifying Miss Wit, he'd given the English teacher's invite no more thought.

Witless! He shuddered. Her sharp angular features reared up in his mind, her eyes flashing, her lips curved in a sneer. What a monster! That she was a complete stranger had not stopped her threatening to kill him. She'd been so sure of her god-given right. But why him? What had he done? He scurried to the kitchen door, promptly locking it.

His arm hurt at the thought of Witless. Carefully rolling up his sleeve, he uncovered four red gashes that were beginning to swell and fester. Curse the girl! It would be just like her to give him blood poisoning. He fetched the Dettol and meticulously cleaned the wounds, before clumsily wrapping a bandage round his arm.

Back at the table, he scooped up the cat that had finished lapping the milk, and cuddled it in his arms, reassured by its friendly warmth. He rubbed his nose against its muzzle causing the animal to purr noisily and whispered in its ear: "Tell me, Jenny..." It was their joke that they'd named the cat after one of Peter's aunts. "Why does Witless want my hide?" The cat purred in response. "You're so helpful." He held the cat at arm's length above his head, its paws splayed in every direction.

Swinging the cat in a wide arc, he lowered it to the floor, where it swiped at him but he dodged. He picked up his jacket, slung his satchel over his shoulder and wound his way between the armchairs in the living room to the door that led to their bedrooms, Jenny trailing after him, miaowing plaintively.

To the left was his mother's room, the door shut tight, probably locked. He'd never tried it and had no desire to. The thought of riffling through her belongings made him shudder. Her bedroom had its own bathroom, that much he knew. Mum called it her "life-saver" because Sis spent hours in the only other bathroom. Not that it bothered him. He rarely used the bathroom. Thank heavens there was a separate toilet.

To the right, a narrow corridor led to their two bedrooms. Sis's room came first, separated from his by their shared bathroom. Sis's door was slightly ajar and from it came the characteristic scent of soap. Lemon, was it? Or some exotic fruit whose name he didn't know. It urged him to step inside.

"Not yet," he whispered to the cat that wound its way between his legs. Such apparent self-control was mere pretence. There was no way he could resist the attraction of Sis's clothes once it took hold. He dumped his satchel on his bed, shook off his shoes and socks and hung his school jacket in the cupboard. He swapped his school trousers and shirt for shorts and a t-shirt.

He went bare-foot to the toilet at the end of the corridor. The tiny room with its frosted glass window and its ice-cold seat was one of his favourite places. It was there he conjured up fantasies peopled by girls from school. He thought of Fi, his sister's girlfriend. She was in all his tales. If he were lucky, she'd drop by that evening. Not that he'd see much of her, she was Sis's girlfriend, not his.

The underground city he'd invented was some consolation, peopled as it was by girls he selected. It was a modern-day harem powered by new-fangled atomic power. He'd even invented a substance that transformed photos of girls into the real-life thing. It had the added property that the girls it created did what he said, which he found very convenient. Experience showed that girls had an irritating way of having a mind of their own.

Outside his sister's room, he didn't hesitate this time. Pushing open the door, he stepped inside and immediately dug his toes into the fluffy mass of Sis's thick carpet. The cat followed him, rubbed itself against his bare legs in encouragement, then jumped up onto Sis's bed and curled up on her discarded nightdress where it buried its head under its paws and slept.

Peter made sure the door was tightly closed and turned the key. It wouldn't do to have someone burst in on him. He wanted to pull the curtains too, but anyone watching outside would notice. God! What if Witless were there! The thought filled him with horror. He shoved the idea aside, refusing to let her spoil the moment. Peering cautiously out, no one was in sight. Only his sister would notice the drawn curtains and she was still at school. He pulled them shut, trying to reassure himself.

His sister's real name was Maryse, but she was just Sis to him. They might have been twins, were it not that she was two years older and several inches taller. Both were slim and had the same slender face, the same pale skin with a hint of freckles, the same high cheek bones that underlined their blue eyes, the same straight, narrow nose and light brown, wavy hair, although hers was considerably longer.

Sis spent the greater part of her considerable allowance, "one of the positive things about Dad's death," the girl would say with typical candour, on clothes, clothes and more clothes.

He opened wide the cupboards and pulled out all the drawers to lay bare row after row of dresses and skirts and blouses and neatly piled underwear: pink, white, blue, yellow and bottle green for school and even some black for Fi's visits. As he did so, a tidal wave of his sister's scent rushed out to greet him. He would have loved to curl up in one of the wardrobes and lock himself in. What a scandal! He imagined the newspaper headlines: boy dies in closet, suffocated by girl's scent. Let his mother and sister explain that away!

He pulled out a long white dress that Sis rarely wore. Holding it up against himself, it reached almost to his ankles. The silky material was cool and soft against his skin. He admired himself a long moment in the mirror before returning the dress to the cupboard, taking care to place it exactly as he'd found it. Sis had an uncanny eye for detail and was quick to accuse.

One cupboard remained unopened. He always left it till last. This was where Sis hid the special clothes and toys she kept for Fi's visits. It was locked, of course, but he knew where she hid the key.

The moment he pulled open the door a heavy object fell out hitting him over the head.

"Ouch!" he cried out, before he could stop himself.

A booby trap! His sister had perched a broom against the inside of the door. The broom rebounded onto the bed, startling the cat that sprang out of the way, hissing. The frightened animal landed in the middle of Sis's dressing table, scattering pots of cream and lipstick and nail varnish and talc as well as curlers and sundry other gadgets, sending them tumbling to the floor.

What a disaster!

Peter hurried to the door to listen, his chest heaving. All was quiet. He cautiously replaced the broom and locked the cupboard door. Those pleasures would have to wait for another time. He picked up the terrified cat, gave it a reassuring cuddle and laid it back on the bed. Then he got down on all fours and began gathering up his sister's make-up.

It wasn't easy to return the things to what he hoped were their rightful places. When he'd finished, he lay on the floor and stretched one arm below the dresser in search of anything that might have rolled underneath. Sure enough, his fingers latched on to a small tubular object the end of which was soft and sticky.

It turned out to be a pink lipstick without its cap. He gingerly sniffed the greasy mark the lipstick had made on his finger. It smelt good. Fruit? Or was it flowers? It made him hungry. He wondered if it would taste as good. He dabbed the bevelled tip against his lower lip, but could taste nothing.

He looked at himself in Sis's mirror. The single pink dot begged for more and the lipstick dared him to go further. He glanced at the cat oblivious on the bed, then strained to listen, but no one was there. He lifted the lipstick to his mouth and carefully applied it to the rest of his lips then rolled them together as he'd seen his sister do.

He took a long look at himself in the mirror, turning his head left and right, pleased at what he saw. He dabbed a bit of Sis's powder on his cheeks to conceal his freckles. Then he puckered his lips as if blowing a kiss and smiled at himself as he stroked his hair.

"Your hair is far too long for a boy," his mother reminded

him several times a day. She kept nagging him to get it cut. If she had seen him with the lipstick and powder, she'd have had a fit, even if having pink lips and pale cheeks didn't make him a girl.

It was difficult to put words to the feelings that filled him when he was alone; girlishness, maybe. It was all embracing with a feather-like touch, almost caressing, and warm and soft and made him feel good inside. Being in his sister's room was like being in a sanctuary. It was the closest he could come to that girlish essence. At the same time, it had a formidable force. It brimmed over with energy, breathing life into his every cell, setting each one vibrating wildly. The feeling was so strong it could be unbearable, as if he might shatter into many tiny pieces.

He glanced one last time at his sister's mirror, memorising the face that stared back at him, then lay down on her bed next to the cat, sharing Sis's nightdress as a pillow. He closed his eyes, breathed deeply the delicious scents that surrounded him and let go, giving in to the full force of the girlish magic.

3.

"Kaitling!"

An unfamiliar voice, deep and male, startled Peter. On the table in front of him, a book lay open in a language he didn't recognise. Where was he? He tried to look around, but had no control over his head. Could he be paralysed? The thought had him on the verge of panic.

No! No! He must be dreaming.

Then his hand moved to brush the hair from his eyes. To his amazement his fingers were long and slender and his hair hung in shiny brown ringlets.

"Kaitling, the cook's daughter needs a remedy for monthly cramps."

Now his head looked up and there in the doorway stood a tall Asian dressed in a long flowing black robe. He wore his hair, which was shoulder-length and greying, tied back in a ponytail. His nose was strong and his chin wilful. His face appeared intelligent and kindly.

"Yes Father," a girl's lilting voice replied in a timbre so rich and enchanting, he was enthralled. "Should I make the potion immediately?"

To Peter's amazement, that delicious voice was coming out of his mouth. Good lord! Had he become a girl?

"As soon as you have finished your reading. You can also make a cream and a potion for Master Ting. He's suffering from gout."

Peter was confused. Was it so easy to become a girl? Surely not! If he had become a girl, he was a stranger to the world the girl lived in.

"Master Tyzi," a tiny man greeted the first man, bowing gracefully. "Kaitling," he said bowing to Peter.

Like the other man, the tiny man's features were Asiatic but, unlike him, he was completely bald and his arms and legs were bared in a loose-fitting costume cut off at the shoulders and knees. He might have been small, but his limbs bulged with muscles.

"Master Zhuru," the father said, bowing and, to his surprise, Peter bowed too.

"I bring bad news," Zhuru said. "The Syvan army has invaded Drailong and is marching on the capital. You are summonsed to an emergency meeting of the Twelve."

"Bad news indeed, although not entirely unexpected. Those blasted Syvan priests have been massing an army for a while." The man frowned, lines of worry forming around his slanted eyes. Their deep green colour astonished Peter. "If we can't stop them in the next few days, the country will be overrun."

A wave of anxiety flowed over Peter, leaving him sick with worry. He tried to reason with himself, to no avail. He had no more control over his emotions than his head.

"Keep to the house while I'm away," Tyzi told him, placing a heavy hand on his shoulder. "And step up your combat practice with Master Zhuru."

"But Father, do you really have to go? You will be in danger. Can't the Twelve be eleven for once?"

It was then that Peter realised that the voice was not saying his words. They were someone else's. When the man leaned forward, it was someone else that he kissed on the forehead, although Peter felt those warm lips press against the skin as if it were his own. How troubling! He was in somebody else's body. A girl's!

In one lithe movement Zhuru disappeared out the door at the centre of the room, followed immediately by the girl's father.

The girl closed her book with a sigh and ran to join them, climbing the central stairs two at a time. Her nimble movements were exhilarating. Then he realised it was her pleasure, not his. He could sense all her feelings even a slight stiffness in the small of her back from sitting too long. When she brushed her hair from her eyes again, he wished he could see her face.

Like the floor below, the one they reached was a large circular library with the spiral staircase in its middle continuing up to a floor above. The walls were full of shelves piled high with books and manuscripts. Kaitling gave it only a cursory glance as she hurried out and followed her father along a wide corridor to what must have been the front door. He hugged her, enveloping Peter in a cloud of pipe smoke and the pungent smell of assorted chemicals and herbs.

"Don't worry, Kaitling. We'll defeat those Syvan scum and I'll be back soon." The man kissed her again on the forehead and was gone.

The full brunt of her sadness and worry lashed Peter making him want to cry, as tears began to form in her eyes. She angrily brushed them away and ran to the library from where she hurried up the stairs.

She darted into what must have been her room. It was even bigger than their living room at home; only here the walls were curved following those of the library. The outer walls, draped with fine lace, were largely made of glass, revealing a splendid view over a small lake and rolling hills beyond.

Kaitling opened one of the windows and stepped out onto a wide balcony. She hurried around what must have been half the house until she could go no further. Stretching out over the rail, she searched till she caught sight of movement where the track plunged into the forest. It was her father galloping away.

She pursed her lips and cupped her hands, making the sound of a birdcall. Kaitling's father must have heard because he rose in the stirrups and waved in her direction, then galloped out of sight.

Long after her father had gone, she lingered on the balcony, draped in sadness, unmoving, watching the empty road. Had he been able to, he would have snuggled up close and held her hand to comfort her. Instead, all he could do was suffer her pain in silence. Only when the wind got up and she began to shiver, did she turn away and enter her rooms. He expected her to fling herself on her bed and cry. That's what he would probably have done. Instead, she took another stairway down two floors to the kitchens.

"My Father will not be with us for dinner this evening," she told a plump woman wearing a white apron over her charcoal coloured dress and a large chef's hat on her head. "I will entertain the guests in his stead."

The girl sounded so serious and grown up, Peter was intimidated.

The cook bowed, saying: "Very well, Mistress Tyzi."

It was only when Kaitling returned to the kitchen door that Peter saw her for the first time. She paused a moment to look at herself in a darkened window giving him a better view as if she'd read his thoughts. Despite a faint resemblance to her father, her face was almost equine, bordered on both sides by shoulder-length brown hair that hung in large ringlets. He had imagined she would be cute, rather like Fi. He didn't generally like horsey girls, as he called them, but her face was deeply attractive in a way that troubled him.

Her skin was pale white, not yellow like her father's, and she had freckles, just like Peter. Despite a couple of extra inches in height, she couldn't have been much older than him. She had the same wilful chin he'd seen in her father and her eyes were a bright mixture of grey and green and blue. The shadows under her eyes made her look weary. One thing was sure; she had an infectious smile.

She wore no black robe like her father. Instead she was wearing an ankle length charcoal skirt with brightly coloured dragons crawling over it, held up by a wide grey belt buckled tight about her waist. Judging from its smoothness against his skin, the skirt must have been made of silk. She was also wearing a white, silk blouse. It did not fit as snuggly as those of some of the girls at school, but he could still see she had a sizeable chest for a girl of her age.

Zhuru stopped her at the kitchen door. Bowing, he said, "With the Syvans nearby, we need to call the gamekeeper back to the house. Will you come with me?"

Peter could feel her pleasure at the prospect of getting out, but she dutifully replied, "My father ordered me to stay in doors."

"The exercise will do you good."

Kaitling ducked into a small antechamber, stripped off her skirt and blouse and donned a pair of knee-length shorts and a short-sleeved blouse.

Zhuru handed her a bow and a quiver of arrows. She slung the quiver on her back and grasped the bow in her hand. The little man had a bow too. They ran side by side along the same track her father had taken. The air flowed cold around her bare limbs, but they quickly warmed at the brisk pace Zhuru was setting.

Once inside the forest, in the shade of the tall oaks, the man had them stop. "There may be enemy scouts," he whispered and cocked his head to listen. Peter could hear nothing but the rustling of leaves and the occasional bird song. Zhuru signalled for silence and pointed along a narrow pathway that headed off to the left. He took the lead and Kaitling ran close behind him, constantly darting nervous looks left and right and behind her. Neither seemed out of breath. Peter was amazed at the soundless way they ran.

The little man came to an abrupt halt near a clearing and took cover behind a large tree. Kaitling did likewise.

Two enemy scouts, Zhuru said, his voice startling Peter because the man had not opened his mouth. It was as if he had some way of speaking directly into Kaitling's head, mind to mind.

Kaitling pulled an arrow from her quiver and set it to her bow.

Peter was terrified. What would happen if the girl died while he was in her body? Would he die to?

Kaitling peered cautiously around the trunk and, sure enough, two men with swords drawn lounged on the far side of the clearing.

I'll take the one on the left, the little man spoke in her head. *You take the other.* Both took aim and on a faint whispered *Now* in her head they fired together. Peter heard the whistle of the arrows cutting through the air followed by a distant thud. Neither man let out the least cry. He was relieved to think the arrows must have hit their marks, but he was horrified that he'd had a hand in wounding or even killing someone.

Neither Zhuru nor Kaitling moved. Why didn't they hurry to see how well they'd shot? Instead, concealed behind their respective trees, they reloaded their bows and waited, listening. All was silent for a long moment. Then Kaitling abruptly turned her head at the sound of a bird cry off to the right across the clearing.

Is that the gamekeeper?

Yes, Zhuru replied in her head.

The two still did not shift from their hiding place. Peter itched to move forward and see what had happened. He had to admire Kaitling's skill and calm. He'd have been dead long ago at the hands of the enemy. It was a sobering thought.

4.

Something rough and wet rubbed Peter's nose bringing him to his senses. Several people had been shot! Had Kaitling managed to escape? And the gamekeeper? He kept his eyes closed, delighting in the feeling of being Kaitling, but as he stretched his arms and legs his body felt all wrong.

When a door slammed, he jerked upright, alarmed. It must be Sis. She'd kill him if she found him in her room. He pushed away the cat and glanced around. What a disaster! The cupboards and drawers were wide open. He could hear Sis raiding the fridge. Struggling to his feet, he shut the cupboards and drawers and pulled open the curtains.

It was then that he glanced in the mirror. To his horror he still had lipstick on his lips. Sis was singing as she crossed the living room. He fumbled with the key trying to unlock the door, then dashed for the bathroom, almost tripping over the cat, and locked himself in just as Sis opened the door to their corridor. Instead of going to her room, she came straight to the bathroom. Surely she couldn't know. She would catch him red-handed.

"Hey! Pete! Get a move on!" she said, hammering on the door. "I need to get in there quick."

"Can't you use the other bog?" he asked, searching for something to remove the lipstick.

"No! Hurry up!"

He frantically scrubbed his lips with toilet paper then flushed the toilet and washed his hands and face with soap. When he opened the door, he held one hand over his mouth, just in case. He needn't have bothered, she pushed past, knocking him against the doorframe, and locked the door, paying him no heed.

He could hear her rummaging through the cupboard as he went to have a quick look in her room, making sure he hadn't forgotten anything. Everything was closed correctly, but her nightdress had slipped to the floor. He picked it up wondering if she'd be able to tell he and the cat had slept on it. A quick sniff revealed nothing. He laid it carefully on her bed and returned to his room.

He pulled out his homework and tried to calm down. It wasn't easy, blood was pounding wildly in his ears. He plunged into the intricacies of quadratic equations, hoping that would help him forget. He'd just solved the second one when Sis burst in without knocking.

"What's this?" she shouted, waving her nightdress at him.

His face burned as he tried to bury himself even deeper in the textbook for fear she'd see his embarrassment.

"I don't know what you're talking about."

"Here! Look!" She held the thing inches from his face. There was a stain of pink lipstick smack in the middle. "You did it deliberately. I'm sure you did. You knew I was having Fi over tonight and you wanted to spoil it."

Fi, who's full name was Fiona, was short and slim, not any bigger than him, and had short, spiky, dark hair, a finely chiselled face and delicious brown eyes. Whenever she was at their place, which was often, he spent most of his time trying to catch a glimpse of her, but generally the two girls were holed up in Sis's room with the door firmly closed.

He liked it best when she stayed for dinner, then she couldn't escape his scrutiny. Not that she ever paid any attention to a boy who was two years younger. She only had eyes for Sis. Despite her lack of interest, he had elected her one of the privileged girls who, unknown to them, resided in his imaginary underground world.

"Surely you have other nightdresses." He was relieved she

hadn't found him out. "You have so many clothes."

"But this is Fi's favourite," she said, clutching the night-dress to her chest, almost in tears.

"Can't you wash it before she gets here?" Of course, he knew full well that wouldn't be possible.

The whole episode was finally forgotten when Fi arrived minutes later. She'd ditched her school uniform and was sporting dark green, knee-length shorts under which she wore those new fangled, brightly coloured tights that were all the rage. Hers were an outrageous mustard yellow. He couldn't help imagining how good they'd feel to wear. Over her red and green chequered blouse with a yellow kerchief tied loosely around her neck, she wore a black blazer that might have belonged to her brother, if she'd had one. As usual, she sported a green beret. Just looking at her and her clothes made his mouth water.

Fi was short for her age. That and her slimness maybe explained why she looked younger than she was. Not that she was a weakling. On the contrary, all the volleyball –she was in the school's second team– and running made her fit, not to mention the hiking and tree climbing he knew she did at Guides.

Ah, Guides! He would never forget the weekend he'd spent with them earlier that year. His mother was to go away for a weekend on business and was at a loss what to do with a twelve year-old, wayward son. He had no close friends to stay with and his mother refused to let him stay home alone with his sister.

Luckily, one of her friends, who ran the local troop of Guides, had offered to take him along to the Spring camp. The only boy, surrounded by all those girls, it had been paradise. It was there that he'd seen Fi in her Guides uniform swarming up trees like she'd spent her life in them.

Fi's announcement that she had permission to stay the night set off a bout of wild hugging and kissing. As he watched the two girls whirl around the kitchen in each other's arms, he had an odd impression. Fi looked almost boyish, a boy like none he had ever seen before.

His sister tried to shoo him away, once they'd calmed down,

but Mum rang. She was going to be late and asked Sis to prepare the evening meal with Fi, insisting Peter help. He quietly blessed his mother for giving him a chance to hang around.

He laid the table, taking as long as he could.

Fi helped Sis prepare tomato soup and pasta with cream and mushroom sauce. "Here pretty boy," Fi said, causing Sis to scowl at the name. "Help me chop these mushrooms."

What a joy! He was back at Guide's camp as he worked alongside her.

The moment Mum arrived they sat at the kitchen table to eat.

"Who's Wolfenden?" Peter asked, seeing the name in the oversized headline on a newspaper that lay discarded on the table. His mother read the Telegraph each day on her way to work. She always brought it home, but he never looked at it, except occasionally for the radio programmes.

"It's complicated," his mother said wearily, spooning tomato soup into her mouth.

He saw Sis give Fi a meaningful look. When she saw him looking at her, Sis shook her head almost imperceptibly.

"It says here he's a Lord," Peter pursued, deciding it might be fun to annoy Sis.

His mother had finished her soup and Fi was removing the plates as Sis bustled about the kitchen serving the pasta.

"Yes. He's a member of the House of Lords. He wrote a report about queers." The way she said the word, it sounded as if it disgusted her.

"What's a queer?" he asked, not knowing the word. Sis kicked him under the table as she bent to serve him pasta. It hurt and he would have complained, but mother was talking.

"It's not really a subject to talk about while we eat," she said, turning over the pasta on her plate.

"For once I'm interested in words," Peter complained, trying every ploy to get an answer, especially as he was sure Sis didn't want the subject discussed. His mother was always telling him he should read more, saying his father would have been ashamed at how little his son read.

As he looked at his mother, he was surprised to see dark shadows under her eyes. Were they new or had he simply never noticed them? She must be missing Dad even after all these years.

"The report is about men who take other men as lovers. That's what a queer is," she finally conceded, clearly uncomfortable with the subject. "There's pressure on the government to draw up a law to make it legal, in private. I just hope Mac-Millan will not give in to all those city men with their foreign fashions. It's not right. Thank heavens we live in a small town that votes Conservative and where religion and tradition still have a sway. That sort of thing doesn't happen here."

"How's the pasta?" Fi asked, much to his mother's relief, and that was the end of that.

After they'd washed the dishes and were on their way to their rooms, Fi nudged him, something she'd never done before, and asked: "So now you know what a queer is, you can go out and find yourself a nice boyfriend."

To be touched by Fi was in itself troubling, but her comment left him even more disturbed. He glanced at her face. He rarely saw her so close. She had tiny crinkles around the corners of her eyes as if she were amused, but she didn't seem to be making fun of him. She meant it, which was even more worrying. He'd never been interested in boys. "I prefer girls," he said, trying to appear sure, but sounding defensive even to his own ears.

"A pretty boy like you would have lots of success with boys," she said as she ran her fingers lightly across his cheek. Her mouth was so close he could feel her breath on his face. He was completely flummoxed. Was she flirting with him?

"Leave him alone," Sis snapped, pulling at Fi's arm. "He's too young for such things."

The two girls disappeared into Sis's room and he heard the click as they locked the door.

He stood there, unable to move, trying to recall what it felt like to have Fi's fingers caress his face. She'd said he was pretty.

Was that a compliment? She certainly sounded sincere. Maybe she was just playing with him.

From inside he could hear muffled giggling. They must be laughing at him. He got down on all fours and peered through the keyhole, but the key was in the lock and someone had hung something over it.

Not to be defeated, he went to the bathroom. Under the sink was a small gap next to the drainpipe. The hole went all the way through to Sis's room. He pulled out the tiny wad of paper that blocked it.

At first he could not understand what he saw. Then he realised it was Sis's hair. She must be lying on the carpet. When she shifted he saw Fi too. The girls were lying next to each other. Then both their faces were in view and their lips joined as they kissed.

5.

Early evening light slanted through the windows, soft and sensuous, as Kaitling peeled off her blouse and pulled down her skirt. A mental tremor ran Peter through. Standing in only her underwear, she pushed back a chair and a table and began a series of movements. It might have been a dance or some form of unarmed combat, Peter wasn't sure. A window stood ajar letting in a cool breeze, causing goose pimples to form on her arms and legs.

Her body felt different from his in many ways. He hadn't noticed before. There was an unfamiliar tension between her feet firmly planted on the ground as if they were about to grow roots and the crown of her head that pushed upwards trying to reach the ceiling. When she moved her hips, tracing circular patterns in the air, he felt a freedom of movement that he'd never known. It filled him with joy, her joy, no doubt, but his too. There were also her breasts, bared now, that had her balancing differently as she stretched up on her tiptoes. Even her shoulders seemed to move in ways he had never experienced as she raised her arms sideways and turned her palms upwards...

A hand shaking his shoulder wrenched him back to his body, which promptly shrivelled to its original size. All the freedom of movement he'd been enjoying evaporated. He opened his eyes to find himself lying on the bathroom floor, a sharp pain on the side of his head.

"Are you all right?" Fi asked, her voice full of concern,

as she knelt next to him, her knees only inches from his face. His mind must have been befuddled because he wondered if he stuck out his tongue, whether he could lick her knee. Her closeness was overwhelming. He shut his eyes and breathed deeply, only to have his lungs flooded by the smell of her soap. He felt assaulted in the most delicious of ways, as if she were forcing a passage inside him by whatever entrance possible.

"What happened?" he groaned, flailing mentally as he struggled not to drown in her.

"You must have fainted. I think you hit your head. Let me have a look."

When he turned his head, a sharp pain stabbed just above his ear.

"It's bleeding." Fi announced. At the mention of blood he almost passed out. "Where do you keep the first-aid kit?"

Fi was efficient in her ministrations. "I did my advanced first-aid badge in the Guides." She had the gash cleaned in no time. "What's wrong with your arm?" she asked, touching the bandage. When he winced, she unravelled the dressing. "God Lord! How did you get that? It's infected."

"A charming new girl at school decided she wanted to get her claws into me."

Fi shook her head. "You need to be more careful, pretty boy." She sat opposite him, her back leaning against the bathroom wall, cleaning the scratches on his arm.

Fi was much more like a pretty boy than he could ever be. He wasn't sure boys were meant to be 'pretty'. It sounded like it might be an insult, a bit like Mother's 'queer'.

"Why do you call me pretty? I thought the word was used only for girls."

"Because you are pretty." She laughed softly as she ran her finger along his cheek. "You'd make a very pretty girl..."

"You'd make a pretty boy," he countered.

He was afraid she might be offended, but she grinned instead.

"Fi, where are you?" Sis called out sounding irritated.

"What the hell is going on?" she asked, pushing open the bathroom door.

"Your brother fainted," Fi replied, unruffled by Sis's anger. "I tended the pretty boy's wound."

"Stop calling him that!" Sis said angrily. "Are you coming? We still have things to do." On which, she stomped off to her room in a huff.

Fi got to her feet and helped him stand. "If I were you, I'd lie down for a while. And keep putting this cream on your arm."

"Thanks. Sounds like Sis needs some more of your kisses." Fi gave him a startled look, tweaked the end of his nose playfully then turned and hurried away, leaving Peter astonished, watching her go. He rubbed his nose where she'd touched it.

In his bedroom, he drew the curtains on the night and went to examine his head in the mirror. The wound was surprisingly small and almost concealed by his hair. He looked at his face trying to figure out what could be pretty about it. It was paler than usual, making his freckles stand out. Could it be its slenderness and the high cheekbones or the narrowness of his nose?

The features taken together did seem doll-like. Maybe it was the wavy hair. If he were pretty, did that make him a queer? He remembered the distaste with which his mother pronounced the word.

Drawing back, he tried to imitate the movements Kaitling had been doing, but he wasn't nearly as good as her. Amongst other things, his hips didn't move the same way. Maybe he would improve with practice. After several minutes of swirling round the room, he collided with the cat that hissed. It had been stretched out on his bed watching him with wide eyes and must have decided to join the dance. Peter scooped it up and collapsed exhausted on his bed where the cat struggled to get free. It jumped off the bed and settled lazily on the bedside carpet, folding its front paws under its chest.

As the throbbing in both his head and his arm increased, all desire to finish his homework fled. Instead, he adjusted the dial on the radio and lay back to listen to what remained of the news.

Thursday evening, the presenter announced, a group of people calling themselves the Homosexual Law Reform Society had organised a meeting at Caxton Hall in London with over a thousand people in attendance.

Peter had the impression the presenter had a sneer in his voice as he talked about the Wolfenden Report, the very same report his mother had mentioned in relation to queers. When the subject changed to football, he turned the radio off and closed his eyes.

"No. My Father has been called to an urgent meeting of the Twelve in Navigon," Kaitling said, her voice startling Peter. They were in what must be her dining room. A young woman was clearing away used dishes, while the cook brought in a large cake. Several men were gathered around the table with Kaitling, all wore robes like her father, although not all of them were black.

"The island of Drailong has been invaded by Syvan warrior priests and they are marching on Navigon," Kaitling informed them, her voice trembling as she spoke.

Shocked, everyone clamoured for more details.

"That's all I know. Ask Master Zhuru, he brought the news."

"Ever since those priests arrived in Syvatoy and took control, war has been a possibility," Ting said. By far the eldest of those present, he was a short stocky man, who had quite a paunch. His face was wrinkled and kindly, with thick bushy eyebrows above his slanted eyes, a large bulbous nose and a tiny pointed beard on the tip of his chin. For all his facial hair, his head was bald.

He seemed to have considerable sway as all listened attentively when he spoke. Unfortunately, he had an irritating habit of licking his lips between words that made him look like a lizard.

"As their god is said to have made the world and has the sole right to create and take away life, they have always seen our work as a sacrilege."

"You should hope those priests never rule here, Kaitling,"

a young man said. He was taller than the others, and had long black hair woven in a ponytail that reached to the small of his back. His skin was sallow, but despite looking tired and sick, he spoke with fervour. "They hold that women are inferior beings without a soul. They would never let you learn to read and write, let-alone do the work you do."

"Thank you for your concern, Karr." Peter sensed Kaitling's irony, although Karr didn't seem to notice. Turning to Zhuru, Kaitling said, "Surely there is no chance they can defeat the Twelve." Her hand trembled as she raised a glass to her lips. Peter was acutely aware of her worry and fatigue. It washed over him too.

"The situation is complex," the tiny man said. Peter got a better look at him than he had earlier in the library. Like Ting, he too was bald, but he had no beard and his face was slim and full of energy. It was difficult to tell his age. Peter guessed he must be younger than Ting but considerably older than the lanky Karr.

"Navigon is easy to defend against a sea attack," Zhuru said, "but they have landed elsewhere and are travelling inland, through Gao, which makes it more difficult to drive them back. They are fanatics who hold and defend their beliefs with zeal, fighting to the death without the slightest respect for anything other than their own ideas."

"Their island was not always called Syvatoy, you know. It used to be called Yudao, which meant the Island of Fish in the old tongue," Ting explained. "Syvan priests first arrived in small numbers from a large country far to the north. Once they'd settled, they began converting the people to their Syvan religion. Little by little, they shipped in more priests who brought with them not only their religion but also their language and way of life, till many things changed on what they then called Syvatoy."

"Women were treated as inferior, little better than slaves and had no choice in the man they were to marry. Only priests could learn to read and write. The indigenous population was expected to labour to feed the priests, most of them tilling the land or fishing from small boats close to the shore. Those who did not submit to what rapidly became the terror of the Syvan priests, tried to fight back, but they rebelled too late. Many were slaughtered. Those who escaped, fled to the island of Drailong across the Xiatian Sea...”

“Another reason why the priests are trying to run the magicians from Drailong,” Karr said.

Ting coughed at his young apprentices rash comment. “The meal was excellent and the discussion extremely stimulating, but you look tired, Kaitling,” he said, getting to his feet with some difficulty. “We can discuss our work and progress another day.” Following his suggestion, the men all rose, as did Kaitling. They bowed to her and bid her good night.

“I will try to contact Navigon to know the state of things,” Zhuru said as he prepared to leave. “If I get news, I will let you know immediately. All of you would do well to pack one or two essential belongings, just in case we need to flee. Kaitling, could you have the staff do the same and ask the hostler to prepare horses.”

“I will.”

She stopped Ting as he was about to leave. “With all this fuss and bother, I didn’t get a chance to ask you how your research is progressing?”

“This morning I found a manuscript that must date from the early days of Drailong. I have never seen such a script before. I was concentrating on deciphering it.” The discovery clearly excited him, but as he continued talking, excitement was replaced by defeat and weariness. “Of course, the past no longer holds much sway when the present clamours to be heard.”

Kaitling bowed her head in agreement. “This is for you.” She handed him a small jar of cream. “It should help the swelling of your feet and ease your joints, especially if we have to travel.”

When he looked at her questioningly, she said, “My father didn’t have the time, so he asked me to make it for you.”

“I see your father has taught you well.” Ting accepted the

jar, bowed deeply and left.

Kaitling smiled at the compliment and then turned to the girl who was clearing the table. "Tessa?"

"Yes, Mistress Tyzi."

"Ask your mother, the hostler and the gamekeeper to join me in the library immediately. You should come with them." Pulling a packet from a pouch on her belt, she said: "My father told me you were suffering from monthly cramps. I have made some tea for you. If you still have cramps, drink some as soon as you can. We might have to travel and it would not do to ride with cramps."

6.

Fi slunk into the kitchen, her eyes heavy with sleep, and slumped onto a chair at the table across from him. Peter tentatively pushed a bowl and a packet of cereal in her direction and went to fetch milk from the fridge. She sat with her head rested on her hands, her shoulders rounded, her eyes closed. She was wearing Sis's nightdress, with the lipstick stain prominent between her breasts.

"Hard night?" he asked, hoping he sounded considerate.

"How did you guess?"

"Sis still asleep?"

"Yeah! She doesn't have the joys of Guides to look forward to."

"Give me Guides any day. You wanna take my place at the hairdresser's."

"Don't tell me your mother finally won."

Was that concern in Fi's eyes? Peter nodded, despondent.

"Shame. Pretty boy's going to loose his curls."

He didn't actually have curls. His hair was too short for that, but it did tend to form waves.

He felt miserable. "I couldn't talk her out of it."

"You look tired too. Pretty boys need their beauty sleep. What kept you awake? I hope it wasn't me and Sis."

Peter shook his head. He couldn't help smiling. "No. I didn't hear you."

It was true, though, he had slept badly, constantly awoken

by fears for Kaitling, but he wasn't about to tell Fi. She'd think he was making it up or worse, that he was crazy.

"Must've been the blow on the head."

"Never mind, pretty boy. If you're good I have a treat for you. But first you have to pass a test."

He looked at her, surprised. In one day he'd gone from spying on her through the keyhole to talking to her over breakfast and now she wanted to test him.

"Test?" The word evoked school and a bunch of unpleasant memories.

She grinned. "Yes. I ask a question. You answer to my satisfaction. Then you get a treat."

Whatever her idea was, it had shaken the sluggishness from her. There was a sparkle in her eyes that smacked of mischief.

"OK."

"Why did you say I should kiss Sis?"

So that was the test. Maybe he shouldn't have said it. "You are always hugging each other and..." He hesitated. "...I saw you kissing."

"You can't have."

He blushed and looked down feeling sheepish. "I spied on you. Please don't tell Sis."

He expected her to be angry, Sis would have been, but Fi smiled instead. "Why spy on us?"

"I heard you giggling and I thought you were making fun of me. Girls often do."

"That's because they don't know how to handle a pretty boy. And no, we weren't laughing at you."

He was relieved and glad he'd dared be honest. He hadn't been sure he could trust her. She could well have run to Sis. That seemed the sort of thing girls would do.

"So will you tell everyone you saw us kissing?" she asked, serious.

"Why should I? I don't tattle."

"And what do you think of two girls who kiss?"

He hadn't thought about it. "I like it."

"Lots of boys get excited when girls kiss."

He wasn't sure if 'excited' was the word for it. "It just seemed right."

She gave him a quizzical look. "Right?"

"You fit together so well."

She leaned her head on her hands and fixed him with her dark eyes. He hadn't the slightest idea what she was thinking.

"So what's my treat?"

She grinned mischievously. "That's a surprise. Come to my place at five and you'll get it." Only to add: "Better not tell Sis, she might get the wrong impression. Let it be our secret, my pretty boy."

He didn't miss the 'my'. Another little gift she'd given him. What with Kaitling and Fi, things were going so fast he felt himself reeling.

"Peter!" his mother called out from across the living room. "Are you ready?"

Of course he wasn't! He was still in his pyjamas and hadn't washed. "What's the hurry?" Maybe if they were very late, the hairdresser wouldn't be able to take him.

"You're hopeless," his mother exclaimed, arriving in the kitchen. "Oh, hallo Fiona. Sleep well?" Mum sounded surprised, if not a little irritated at finding her there. Peter wondered why. Fi was a frequent visitor. Mum shooed Peter off to the bathroom to "wash at least once a week." He gave Fi a withered look and left.

When he returned, to his disappointment, Fi had gone.

Mum drove along the back roads. He knew them well. He cycled that way every day to school. He wound down his window and watched the hedgerows flash by, caressing his hair distractedly as it blew in the wind. The morning air was cool. He wished he'd brought a hat to wear once the barber had done his worst.

"Stop running your fingers through your hair, Peter!" his mother insisted, slamming on the brakes as a tractor came round a corner in the other direction. "It's a nasty habit. People will think you're a pansy."

Peter shrugged. This was why he avoided being alone with Mum. He'd heard it all before. "What's a pansy?"

"Good Lord, Peter! Some times I wonder if you're not a bit dim. If one of the young people in the companies I work for were to behave like you, he'd have been out on his ears long ago."

Was a dim pansy a fading flower? The absurd idea had him grinning.

"Wipe that grin off your face. It's not funny at all. If you were older, I'd be tempted to send you to the army. Don't you have army cadets at school?"

Sure they did. He'd seen them prancing around school on Monday afternoons stiff necked in their khaki uniforms. If anyone was dim, it was that band of pinheads. They were the worst offenders when it came to shoving younger kids around. He never went anywhere near them.

"You have to be sixteen." Hopefully she wouldn't start on about him going to Outward Bound. Sending boys out into the wilds to toughen them up was one of her favourite solutions to what she saw as the Peter problem. He was far too young, luckily.

"You shouldn't make fun of the army."

He wasn't aware he had.

"They do an important job. Like keeping communism at bay. What with the Russians and the Vietcong."

Peter wasn't interested in politics, but the subject was hard to avoid. Vietnam had been constantly in the news since the Americans entered the war.

"Your father was in the Air Force, you know. That's where we met, during the War. He looked so dashing in his uniform."

Fortunately he was spared her nostalgia as they arrived in Tallford and she had to manoeuvre the car down a narrow alley to her parking spot behind the office block.

"I can manage and I'm sure you have a lot of work to do." If only he could convince his mother to let him go alone.

"I wasn't born yesterday, young man. You won't have enough cut if I'm not there to insist."

"Good morning Mr. Harris," she said, greeting the barber. "How's your wife since her operation?"

"Much better, thanks. Is this your son? My has he grown."

"His hair too. Could you see that you cut it really short?"

The barber chuckled. "I don't hold with this new fashion of boys wearing their hair longer. It's doing me out of a job." He laughed as he swung a cloth around Peter's neck and fixed it behind his back.

Peter stared at his reflexion in the mirror and gritted his teeth as the first locks fell to the floor. Satisfied, his mother turned to go. "Meet me in my office." She didn't see the tears that brimmed up in his eyes and rolled silently down his cheeks. He tried to stem the flow, but there was no stopping it. The barber continued snipping his way round to the back of Peter's head.

"Come on, sonny. You're too old to be cryin'. People'll be callin' you a sissy and we don't want them thinking that."

The man meant well. He patted Peter's knee, then offered him a handkerchief to dry his eyes and blow his nose. He even gave him a toffee from a large box. It was as if he were five again and his father had just died. People had been kind then too.

Once the barber had finished, Peter headed down the main street towards his mother's office. There was no hurry. His mother probably had a ton of work and they didn't need to be back till lunchtime. He paused in front of a woman's hairdresser's where wigs were on display.

"Thinking of buying one?" a familiar voice asked.

He spun round to find Priscilla Wit behind him, her unblemished face twisted in an ugly sneer. She was wearing a smart pleated skirt and a blouse buttoned up to her neck over which she wore a tweed jacket. The ensemble looked like it came from the best tailor in town.

"Getting your haircut won't fool anybody. Everyone knows you're a pansy."

He shifted nervously from one foot to another, feeling extremely vulnerable. No Greengage was at hand to protect him. If being a pansy meant he was about to die, he certainly didn't want to be one. His mother had used the same word, although more out of disgust than hatred.

Witless prodded him with her index finger. It hurt, but he didn't react. She prodded him harder. He still said nothing.

"People don't like pansies," she told him, trapping him against the shop window. "Pansies go to hell, did you know?" She prodded him again on the same spot with all her force.

He could feel his knees trembling and he wanted to cry, but he wouldn't, not in front of her. She's just a dim wit, a misfit, he told himself. His not reacting seemed to drive her mad. She lunged forward and grabbed his jaw between her fingers and pushed his head with a crash against the window.

"I hate pansies." Spittle formed on her lips only inches from his face. "I hate them. Do you hear me?" Then she spat in his face. "I'm going to make hell of the little that remains of your life."

"Oie! You! Stop that!" an angry voice called out from the doorway to the shop. "If you break my window, I'll have you pay for it."

Witless shoved Peter to the ground and walked away, her head held high, her back stiff.

A slimy gob of saliva slithered thickly down his cheek, mingling with his tears that he could no longer hold in check. He crawled on all fours to a nearby alley, not wanting to be seen in such a state. In the shadows, he sat hunched up, his back against an up-turned dustbin. Using his sleeve, he wiped the filth from his face and dried his eyes. Hell, she'd said, and she meant it.

7.

Mrs Greengage greeted him at the front door of her terraced house. "I'm glad you came," she said, with a quizzical smile as if she were in some doubt about him keeping the appointment.

A long corridor lined on one side by shelve upon shelve of books led past steep stairs that climbed to the floors above. She steered him through a door to the right into what must once have been the living room, but that now had all the walls piled high with books. It looked very much like a library with a couple of small tables and chairs to work on.

"Most of these books are for adults. Here..." and she went into a connecting room, "... are young people's books." The spines of the books were far more colourful in the afternoon light. The tables and chairs had been replaced by large cushions.

"If you agree, I'd like to take you on an unconventional tour of my library. But first, tell me how much time we have."

"Two hours." How could he possibly spend so much time on books? At least he had Fi's treat to look forward to.

"Good. Now I'm going to put this blindfold on you," she said, producing a scarf from her pocket.

"How can I possibly read if I can't see?"

"I told you it was unconventional." She chuckled. "You need to make friends with the books first. The blindfold will help you get to know them better."

She folded a silk scarf till it made a narrow band and tied it round his head, obscuring his eyes. The material was soft and smelt faintly of perfume.

She led him across the room by the arm and then, taking his hands, she placed them on what must be the spines of the books.

"Just run your hands along the back of the books. Try to read them with you fingertips."

Some bindings were flat and cold. Others bulged with their curved backs pressing outwards. Then there was the embossed lettering that climbed the length of the spine. When his fingers strayed, he caught a taste of the pages that lay behind, rough under his fingertips. Moving along a shelf, his index trailing across the spines, he was aware of the difference in size of the books. Some lasted forever, like fat old men planted on a branch. Others were thin and aerial, like fairies that might flit away at any moment.

"Good." She startled him. He'd completely forgotten she was there. "Now explore with your nose."

He had had no idea Greengage was so odd. She was not like that in class. He moved closer, cautiously, till his nose touched the spine of a book. He tried rubbing his nose up and down and promptly sneezed.

"Sorry about the dust."

He tried again, not moving this time. What struck him was a sharp smell not unlike wood. Not pine. It was more delicate and distant. Oh! And there was also a faint smell of glue at the uppermost edge of the spine. He was surprised there was no trace of ink.

"Can you smell the stories?"

He leaned in, straining to sense them with his nose, but nothing was forthcoming. He shook his head.

"Doesn't matter. It will come. Now reach out to your right and choose a book you like the feel of."

He did as he was told, glad that no one else, was watching.

"Good. Take off the blindfold and read out the first sentence of the book. I'll try to guess which it is."

"Mother, have you heard about our summer holidays yet?"

"That one I know." Greengage sounded pleased with herself. "It's the first of Enid Blyton's Famous Five series. What do you imagine happens in the book?"

The answer seemed obvious. "They go on holiday and have an adventure."

"Correct. Now close your eyes and pick another one and then read out the first sentence."

"Once there were four children whose names were Peter, Susan, Edmund and Lucy."

She chuckled. "That's too easy. It's the first of C.S. Lewis's books about Narnia."

"Sounds like another group of children off on a holiday only to have an adventure."

"You are right, except that it is set during the world war and the children travel to another world called Narnia. Try another book."

He closed his eyes once again and stretching higher this time, he pulled out a thicker book. "'The Bottoms' succeeded to 'Hell Row'." That should stump her, he was sure.

"Ah yes. Now there's an interesting book. The author has been in the news lately although he's been dead for over thirty years. Penguin want to publish the full version of another of his books, but the authorities say it is obscene."

"What does 'obscene' mean?"

"Obscene is used for things that are said to be offensive or disgusting according to accepted moral standards, especially related to sexuality. Just one or two more, then we'll stop for tea."

"Alice was beginning to get very tired of sitting by her sister on the bank..." This was a far longer first sentence that lasted the length of a paragraph. He read it all the same. "... And what was the use of a book, thought Alice, without pictures or conversations."

"Now there's one for you. It's about a girl who gets lost and..."

"...has an adventure," Peter completed.

"Exactly, but this young girl's not very interested in reading books without pictures or dialogue. Sounds like you might get on well with her, except that she was a rather haughty child...”

“Haughty?”

“Arrogantly superior and disdainful.”

The description fit Priscilla Wit like a glove, except that she read a lot. The thought of the girl dragged up all the earlier unpleasantness that the book game had made him forget.

“Let’s have a cup of tea.” She showed him into the kitchen, which was out back overlooking a narrow garden that stretched away from the house.

He was surprised there were no books lining the walls of the kitchen, but there was one large bound manuscript lying on the table. As Greengage heated water and prepared biscuits, he flipped open the manuscript and read: The Trial of Oscar Wilde by Madeleine Greengage. So his teacher had written a book. Browsing through the pages he found it wasn’t at all like the books he’d looked at earlier.

“Who’s Oscar Wilde?”

“Ah! You’ve found my thesis. Oscar Wilde was a well-known author who lived in the second half of the 19th century. He wrote a book called The Portrait of Dorian Gray.”

“Was it obscene?”

“Why do you ask?”

“Because of that story you mentioned about Penguin.”

“No. Wilde was put on trial because he was a homosexual. Do you know what that is?”

Peter nodded.

“Wilde made a silly mistake. When a high-ranking man, the Marquess of Queensberry, accused him of homosexuality, Wilde took him to court for disgracing his name in public. In order to defend himself, the Marquess hired detectives to pry into Wilde’s private life and prove he really was a homosexual. Unfortunately Wilde was involved in many activities that were unacceptable, some of them illegal, including homosexuality. The press made a great scandal of the whole affair and when Wilde lost the case, he was arrested, tried, found guilty and finally imprisoned. He died in prison shortly after.”

“I don’t understand. What’s wrong with being...” Peter searched for a suitable word. He felt uncomfortable about using the word ‘homosexual’. “... a pansy?” he asked, trying to sound casual.

“Well, if you are referring to the flowers, I’m sure they are quite happy with their lot.”

Peter gave her a withered look. He was glad she hadn’t laughed, he was in no mood for laughter.

“But I suppose you are referring to the disparaging use of the word to mean an effeminate man. That’s not quite what Wilde was accused of. Some men like other men, that’s what being a homosexual is and some men like to dress up or act like women, which is what you called a pansy.”

Peter nodded, embarrassed. He wished he hadn’t asked.

“Some people, a lot in fact, take exception to boys or men who are not how they expect males to be.”

He pictured Priscilla’s face twisted in hatred as she called him a pansy. He shuddered at the thought, brushing away an unwelcome tear. Wit had been so angry, she would readily have killed him. She’d already tried twice. He couldn’t help it, he glanced nervously around to make sure she wasn’t spying on him.

“A lot of men put on a tough face and play the strong guys because that is what they think society expects, when in fact they might be much happier being a little more, how can I put it, rounder at the edges.”

It was his turn to laugh, albeit nervously. “Rounder at the edges?”

“Not all brawn and pushing and shoving in the corridors...” Peter could see exactly what she meant. “... but more attentive to others and to their own emotions.”

“Surely people expect them to be rough, don’t they?”

“You are right. Our society does expect males to be tough and not cry.” She gave him an encouraging smile. “If you were to ask a muscle-bound member of the rugby team, he probably wouldn't understand." She chuckled. "But if he did, I'm sure he'd be convinced that was how he really was."

He couldn't believe he was having such a conversation with a grown-up, let alone a teacher. He only ever talked to teachers when he had to. He hardly ever talked to grown-ups, not even his mother.

"Are other children giving you trouble at school?"

"No, no!"

"Just wondering." She leaned her head to one side and looked at him questioningly but, thank heavens, didn't insist.

"Is that the time?" he asked, glancing up at the kitchen clock. He was going to be late for Fi. "I have to go."

"So, did you enjoy the guided tour of my library?"

He was surprised to find he had. "Very much."

"Would you like to come back next Saturday at the same time?"

"Yes, I would."

8.

Peter rang the bell but no one answered.

Fi lived in a detached house not far from the centre. The house was not as new as his, nor was it as big. It lay at the end of a drive lined with oak trees that looked age-old. Peter pictured Fi clambering to their uppermost branches, exhilarated by the climb.

He glanced to see if anyone was watching then tiptoed between the roses and peeked through one of the windows. The dinning room. A large painting hung over the fireplace depicting a swirling mass of colours that shifted and changed as he watched.

The clock on the mantlepiece chimed five. He was on time. He rang again. Still no answer. So much for promises. Disappointed, he turned to pick up his bike when he saw Fi running up the drive, her rucksack joggling up and down on her back. She must have come directly from Guides for she still wore the navy blue uniform. The skirt met her long socks just below her knees, but the shirt was rolled up above her elbows, stopping short of the badges that adorned her sleeves.

"Sorry," she said. "One of the girls broke her wrist. We had to take her to hospital."

She shrugged off her backpack and fished out a set of keys. He stood watching, perplexed. No kiss, no handshake, no greeting. Was this how it was done? She pushed open the door and gestured him in.

"I'm parched," she said, dumping her sack on a table. "Can you believe it, there was nothing to drink at the hospital."

She grabbed him by the hand and dragged him into the kitchen. Her hand was firm and strong, her skin smooth and soft. Her touch set off a wild fluttering in his stomach.

The kitchen was small, new-fangled gadgets taking up much of the space. His father would have been fascinated, unlike his mother who didn't hold with such things. "No labour-saving device ever saved anyone anything," she always said. So their house was free of contraptions. Looking around, Peter could only guess at their uses.

"Tea?" Fi asked. He nodded. "Put some of those biscuits on a plate." She pointed to a packet of chocolate digestives, his favourites.

Now that he was alone with her, he was tongue-tied. Apart from Sis, he hadn't much experience talking to girls. His silence didn't seem to bother her. She happily syphoned off hot water from the steaming spout of a shiny metal device, singing a scout song as she did.

She had him sit in one of the chairs in the dinning room and placed tea and biscuits in front of him. "I'll go get changed. Back in a sec. Help yourself."

He could hear her shifting around upstairs. From the dull thuds, it sounded like she was moving furniture. When she didn't come down by the time he'd poured tea, he got to his feet and went to examine the painting he'd seen through the window. The swirls of colour were even more astounding close up. The artist must have dipped his fingers in the paint and smeared the stuff on the canvas.

"You like it?" she asked, startling him.

"It's beautiful. Who painted it?"

"I did."

He stood staring at it, absorbed, for a long while. When he finally turned away, he was surprised to see she'd changed into grey trousers, a white shirt and a smart grey waistcoat. Had it not been for the bright yellow kerchief she wore around her neck, she looked like a young man ready for work.

"You like it?" she asked, spinning round on her heels so he could see her from all sides.

"You look so..." He began, but his voice trailed off.

"...stunning!"

Breathtaking, he'd wanted to say.

"Do I look handsome?" she asked, moving closer.

Words again. Pretty? Handsome? They were such tricky things. People were constantly cheating with them.

"Isn't handsome supposed to be for boys?"

"Forget the rules. Look at me. Am I handsome?"

"Yes. Breathtaking."

"Good. You've earned some tea and biscuits."

He was beginning to wonder if she'd forgotten the treat. Perhaps him being there was the treat. Or maybe she was playing with him, holding out till the last minute.

"So, pretty boy has been to the hairdresser's?" She ruffled his hair. "How does it feel?"

Good to have your hands in it, he wanted to say. "Shorn like a sheep, and cold around the ears."

"I have the solution," she told him bounding away up the stairs.

"Close your eyes," she said when she reappeared. She fixed something snuggly on his head then spent a moment adjusting it before he was allowed to look. His mouth fell open when he saw his face in the mirror. Gone was his short hair, instead he had shoulder-length, light brown hair.

"So, are you a pretty boy?"

He had often dreamed of having longer hair, but as he stood there in front of Fi he felt guilty. "It's not right," he muttered.

Fi adjusted the wig slightly, misunderstanding what he meant.

"How about that?"

"I mean boys shouldn't have such long hair."

"That's what your mother says. That's why she insisted on taking you to the barber."

All barbers are barbarians, he thought, struggling to understand. "But boys are boys and girls are girls." Their conversation unsettled him, as did what he saw in the mirror.

"For most people boys and girls is all there is. But there are loads of other possibilities."

She sounded so sure that he began to doubt what had otherwise been self-evident. Maybe there was something he hadn't understood. "You mean like pretty boys?"

She grinned. "And handsome girls."

"But if I'm a pretty boy, like you say, does that make me queer?"

"Do you dream of kissing boys?"

"No." The idea repulsed him.

"Then you're probably not queer. Although many boys might want to kiss you if they saw you like that."

"But you're queer," Peter said, suddenly understanding something that had been troubling him. "You like kissing Sis."

"That's true. Although queer is not a nice word. It means strange and there's nothing strange about it. I'm what they call a lesbian. I like kissing other girls. But I also like to dress as a boy and behave like one, that makes me what I call a handsome girl."

"But isn't that wrong?"

"Why should it be wrong?"

"Cause people say it is."

"Who says so?"

"My Mum. The police. The Vicar. The newspaper. The man on the radio last night. I'm sure the Headmaster would to. And what about your parents?"

"My Mum is very easy-going. As for the others, maybe they don't understand or are afraid."

Afraid? That seemed improbable. They were important people. Could important people be afraid?

"What could the Headmaster or the Vicar be afraid of?"

Fi didn't reply, instead she munched on a biscuit. "I'm not sure," she finally said. "Maybe if there weren't just boys and girls, but instead the choice was much bigger, maybe they'd feel unsure what they were. Imagine you had always thought you were a boy then one day you suddenly realised you might be something else, something that was not so clear-cut, something that some people would be attracted to, while others might shy away or even get violent. Wouldn't that be frightening?"

Peter felt uncomfortable. Had that not just happened to him? Did he not now have to live with the knowledge he might not be a boy like the others? That was scary enough.

He glanced at the clock. It was six and he had to get home. "I have to go."

"What about your treat?"

He'd forgotten about it. "So?"

"It's upstairs waiting for you. First bedroom on the right."

He climbed the stairs, noting the family pictures that lined the staircase. Just the three of them, to begin with, two happy parents and a very normal looking little girl between them, then mother and daughter, older now, alone.

The bedroom to the right was Fi's. He knew immediately. It smelt of her soap. He glanced around the room looking for his treat. She'd given no clue as to what it could be.

Her room was as small. Bookshelves vied with cupboards for rare space. Clothes on hangers hung from anything that offered the slightest hold. Dirty underwear lay strewn in one corner along with her discarded Guides uniform. In the centre of the room was a single bed. On the bed Fi had laid out a pretty white dress. He could see nothing else.

"Fi," he called out, "I can't find it."

She came bounding up the stairs and stopped in the doorway, a broad smile lighting up her face. "Even pretty boys can be dim some times!" she exclaimed theatrically. "It's on the bed, silly."

He looked back at the bed. All he could see was the dress. He lifted it up to see if she had hidden something underneath. There was nothing.

"Do you like it?"

Suddenly he twigged. She was giving him a dress, one of hers. He looked at her astonished and not a little worried.

"I can't take this. Won't your mother notice? It's so beautiful. Surely you'd miss it."

"It's for you, a present from me to my pretty boy."

He lifted it up and held it out so he could look at it better. The cuffs and the hem of the dress were boarded in white lace and there was a fine petticoat sewn inside the skirt part.

"I can't. Where would I put it? If Mum found it, she'd go spare. She'd call me a queer and run me off to the shrink. If Sis found it, she'd kill me. She'd think I stole it from you. And if she knew you gave it to me that would be the end of the world."

Fi was crest-fallen.

"You're right. How come I didn't think of that? Pass me that pen," she said pointing to one that lay on a tiny desk. She took it and wrote on a label sewn to the hem - PETER. "There. Now it's got your name on it." She hung it up back in the cupboard. "It's waiting for you, any time you want." She leant forward and kissed him on the end of his nose whispering: "My pretty friend."

9.

Peter lay back on his bed, staring up at the ceiling. The cat had curled up next to him purring noisily as he absent-mindedly massaged the back of its neck. He liked to stroke the cat. The slow circular movements helped him relax, as if he were the one being caressed.

Fi had offered him one of her prettiest dresses! He couldn't get over it. She'd wanted him to be a girl for her. He often toyed with such fantasies, but he never imagined it might happen. The thought of being dressed as a girl holding hands with Fi in her suit, sparked off weird flutterings in his stomach. He wanted to prolong the feeling, even if it was almost unbearable, but the face of Priscilla Wit surged unbidden, twisted with hate, spitting at him as she called him a sissy.

He shuddered and stopped caressing the cat. It immediately complained, digging its claws in his hand. He shoved it off the bed and sat up. The pleasant bubble in which he had been floating burst, leaving a bitter taste and a headache.

Why should Priscilla hate him so? It was true she'd noticed something in him that few others spotted, apart from Fi. Putting the two girls in the same thought didn't seem right. Fi saw his feminine side and did everything she could to encourage it, even taking the risk of getting them in trouble. Whereas Priscilla hated him for being a feminine boy, what she called with so much distaste, a pansy.

His door abruptly flew open and Sis barged in. "Mum says

you're to go to bed." Their mother had gone out to the club with a friend, leaving Sis in charge.

"But it's Saturday," he pleaded, wondering how Sis might force him if he refused to obey. She could be downright nasty when she put her mind to it.

She was still standing in his doorway but instead of paying attention to him, she was sniffing the air.

"You have been playing with my perfume."

Of course he hadn't, but he always felt guilty, even when he'd done nothing. She strode across the room and grabbed him by the arm and lifted his fingers to her nose, almost wrenching his arm from its socket.

"You have! I can smell my perfume on your fingers." She tossed his hand away and prodded him in the ribs. "If ever I catch you messing in my room again, I'll make you pay for it." She jabbed him in the ribs again as down payment. "Go wash your hands and face, they're filthy. I want to see you in bed in ten minutes." On which, she left, her chin held high. A perfect little mother!

Peter massaged the dull ache in his ribs. Then he brought his hand gingerly to his nose and sniffed. It was true, there was a faint smell of perfume, but it wasn't Sis's, it was Fi's. Thanks heavens Sis hadn't recognised it.

Peter sniffed his hand one more time, inhaling the essence of Fi, then hurried to the bathroom. It took him more than ten minutes to get ready, but Sis didn't seem to care, she was on the phone in the living room. It felt odd to know she was probably talking to Fi. Now Fi was just one more secret that made up the wall between him and his sister.

To get his own back, he said goodnight, interrupting Sis's call. "Tell Fi I said goodnight." Then he hurried away before Sis could hit him. Buried in his bed he expected to lie sleepless for hours, but he promptly fell asleep.

A heavy hammering awoke Peter at the same moment it awoke Kaitling.

"Bad news, Kaitling," Zhuru said, once she'd opened the

door. In the light of the candle he was carrying, Peter could see the old man had slung a dark gray cloak over his usual robes. "The Syvan army has reached Navigon. The capital is besieged."

"My father...?" Kaitling asked, gripping the doorframe for support. Her apprehension tied Peter in knots.

"The Twelve are defending the capital and all the magicians present are working together."

Ting had followed Zhuru into the room and was listening to the news with consternation. "This is bad indeed. I must leave for the capital."

Their discussion was interrupted by an urgent knock at the door. When Zhuru pulled it open, a sturdy man dressed in green stood on the threshold.

"Do come in Yuan," Kaitling said.

Yuan held a bow in his hand and a quiver of arrows was slung over his shoulder. Peter guessed he was the gamekeeper.

"Mistress Tyzi," he said bowing, his weathered face grave. "An enormous army of Syvan soldiers is marching through the forest not more than four miles from here."

"Where are they headed?" Zhuru asked.

"They took the shortcut to Navigon. They must have help from local traitors. How else could they travel through the forest without getting lost?"

"They will have landed at Feng Bay," Zhuru speculated. "They must be planning to attack Navigon from two sides. I have to warn the Twelve." He bowed to Kaitling and turned to go.

"Do not leave," Ting ordered. "I will warn the Twelve. I can communicate at a distance. You will not get through on horse, not if the enemy are in the forest. Should you wish to go round the forest, you'd arrive too late. No. You must stay with Kaitling and protect her and the rest of us."

"I can protect myself," Kaitling said, making an effort to sound convincing. Peter was not dupe. He could feel the fear and uncertainty that flowed in her veins.

"Master Zhuru has taught you well, Kaitling, but you cannot

take on a whole army. We are in grave danger. If the Syvan army have traitor guides, they will know a member of the Twelve lives nearby and will want to take his daughter captive. We must leave immediately. I suggest we go inland and head for the War-si Mountains. They are wild and of little interest to the Syvans. We should be able to hide there.”

“With all due respect, Master Ting, you are forgetting that once the Syvan army have taken Navigon, they will follow the river Chu and march on the mines in the Kasum Mountains. That’s their real goal. That is why they came, to take the gold and silver. If we try to cross the river, we are likely to be inter-cepted.”

“Exactly!” Ting exclaimed. “That’s why we must leave im-mediately, to beat them to the river.” Turning to Kaitling, he asked if everybody was packed.

“Yes, except Karr, who was sleeping. We have supplies for five days. We couldn’t carry more.”

“Things have changed,” Zhuru said. “We need to take tools for survival.” Turning to the gamekeeper he said, “Bring bows and arrows and traps and hunting knives and tell the cook to bring pans that can be used on an open fire and solid cups and bowls. Abandon some of the food, if there is not enough room.” To Kaitling he added: “Gather up the basic healing remedies and minerals to purify water.”

Peter could not watch what was happening with indiffer-ence. It was not a film he’d paid to see from which he could walk away at any moment. Not only did he feel every emotion Kaitling felt, but he also felt a part of their story, even if they were unaware he was there.

He couldn’t help marvelling at Kaitling’s calm. Had it been him, he would have been paralysed at being overrun by an ene-my army and having to flee to unchartered mountains.

It took nearly no time for Kaitling to collect the remedies and instruct the staff. The cook who’d been unflustered earlier, was now on the verge of panic, but her daughter, Tessa, came to Kaitling’s aid and helped her mother. The hostler had the horses saddled when Kaitling arrived. Handing her saddlebags to the hostler, she went from person to person checking what they'd brought.

Karr had been difficult to wake. A hot stimulating beverage had not sufficed. Zhuru had had to shake him violently. Finally, they managed to get the lanky young man on a horse, loosing precious minutes doing so.

Their cavalcade moved forward into the night with the gamekeeper in the lead. The staff followed, with the hostler leading the horse on which Karr slept slumped in his saddle. Peter would willingly have dumped the young man in a ditch and left him to rot. Kaitling followed in the rear with Zhuru.

All had donned the same gray cloaks, as they travelled along the path skirting the forest. Their cloaks turned them into shadows that flitted at the limit of his vision. It was so cleverly done, Peter wondered if there might not be some magic to it. They followed the forest south for an hour then, when it turned east, so did they, following it for about a further hour before they branched off across the fields.

The ride seemed to go on for hours leaving Peter exhausted. He desperately needed to sleep, but there was no way he could force himself to return to his own body. It didn't help that he was also subject to Kaitling's weariness. Finally Zhuru ordered a halt in a small wood where they could conceal the horses and get some rest. Kaitling kept awake till everyone was settled and a small meal had been handed out. Only when everyone was catered for did she lie down and close her eyes.

10.

"Not again," Peter groaned as hammering awoke him.

"Peter. Get up. It's Sunday. You have to go to church." It was his mother's voice, not that of someone from Kaitling's world. He let his head slump back on his pillow, closed his eyes and promptly fell asleep.

"Hush!" Zhuru said in a forced whisper.

Kaitling halted. Like all the others, she was on foot, leading her pony forward through a clump of trees that overlooked the river. As she strained to make out the danger in first light, Peter was able to see row after row of men marching along the road that ran parallel to the river.

"How did they get ahead of us?" Kaitling whispered.

"The second army must have marched directly south heading for the Kasum Mountains," Zhuru replied.

"What news?" he asked Ting who was crouched on the ground, his eyes closed. Peter was worried the man might be ill, but when Ting stood he looked refreshed and full of vigour.

"The Twelve have managed to keep the Syvan army out of the city, but the enemy have inflicted much damage in the fields and buildings around Navigon," Ting reported. "Most of the people of Homchi have fled further south, taking refuge in Kasum where the population is preparing to defend their mines."

As Kaitling looked around the group, she noticed Karr slumped on the ground asleep. "What are we going to do with him?" Peter was glad she asked.

Ting bowed his head. "I am ashamed of my apprentice. I had no idea he was using opium. Maybe I am too old to have an apprentice." Both Kaitling and Zhuru objected, but the magician continued. "These apprentice magicians require so much time and attention. I was responsible for him but instead I was caught up in my studies."

From time to time Kaitling glanced at the road across the river. The flow of soldiers continued unabated. Peter wished they wouldn't waste time on Karr. There were more pressing problems to handle.

"We are forced to rest," Zhuru said. "But we can't stay here. They will have scouts out on either side of their army and we will soon be discovered."

The party turned noiselessly back and followed a path towards a deserted farm. They had just stabled the horses in one of the barns when a group of Syvan soldiers breasted a nearby hilltop, marching directly for the farm...

"Wake up Peter," his mother shouted. "What's wrong with you? Are you ill? You look very pale."

Peter fought desperately to ignore his mother and return to Kaitling. His body shuddered uncontrollably at the thought of the soldiers as he worried what they would do to her.

"Stay where you are!" his mother said, hurrying away, no doubt to fetch a thermometer, her first line of defence against illness.

Stay where you are, he thought. How ironic! He had no choice. He tried closing his eyes but all he could hear was his mother rummaging through the medical supplies in the bathroom.

"Here!" she said, handing him the thermometer. "Put it under your tongue." Then she hurried away promising to be right back.

He lay back with the thermometer sticking out of the corner of his mouth and closed his eyes.

The shouts and clash of arms were deafening. Peter was giddy, Kaitling too. She swung her arm, her fist connecting with a jarring crash against the nose of a Syvan soldier. The man collapsed to the ground, blood spurting from his nostrils. A second soldier dashed at her brandishing a curved sword. He fell at her feet, one of the gamekeeper's arrows piercing his throat.

Rough hands grabbed Kaitling's neck from behind, her assailant growling like a wild animal. She struggled to rip the fingers from her throat. To no avail!

What if Kaitling were to die, would he die too?

Dark patches swam before Kaitling's eyes as she struggled to breathe. With an immense effort, she flung an arm behind her and grabbed the man's ear, jerking it forward as she knelt. The man grunted with pain and toppled forward. Caught off balance, he flew over her shoulder, relinquishing his hold on her neck. He crashed to the ground, winded. Whipping a knife from her belt, Kaitling slashed the man's throat causing blood to spurt over her...

"Sis!" his mother called out, alarmed. "Call the doctor. Peter's having a fit."

Peter lay on the floor by his bed, a strong taste of blood on his tongue. His hand flew to his mouth. Had they been wounded? His mouth was wet and sticky. Blood! He crumbled to the ground, blacking out...

"Kaitling?" Zhuru called out. "Are you all right?"

Kaitling opened her eyes. She was lying in a pool of blood, the corpse of a Syvan soldier next to her. Zhuru helped her to her feet. She felt unsteady but was not hurt, just bruises round her neck and a cut on her mouth. She took stock of the fight. Several Syvan soldiers lay dead, arrows sticking out of them. Others had been stabbed. None had survived.

"Has anybody been hurt?" Kaitling croaked, looking around for her medical supplies.

"Only you and Master Ting. His wounds are not serious. Cook is tending to him."

"Where's Karr?" Kaitling asked.

"He fled when the soldiers attacked. We've found no signs of him," Zhuru said. He cleaned his knife and sheathed it before

turning back to Kaitling. "Let me have a look at your mouth."
And he cautiously prized her lips apart...

Peter felt fingers on his own lips.

"Oh Peter! What possessed you to bite the thermometer? It's cut your mouth," his mother said. "I hope you haven't swallowed the glass or the mercury. Spit in here!"

She held up a small bowl into which he spat blood and tiny splitters of glass. He closed his eyes, hoping he wouldn't faint. His mother rinsed his mouth with warm water then she examined his lips, his gums, his tongue and the roof of his mouth in search of glass. Blood flowed anew as she dislodged several pieces. She staunched it with improvised swabs of cotton wool.

The doctor arrived shortly afterwards.

"I was close by," he told Peter's mother.

Their family doctor was a short, chubby man who always looked unhealthy. His hair was lank and uncombed, his face spotted with pockmarks and he was constantly coughing.

"So what have we here?" he said staring at Peter.

"He had an attack," his mother's voice trembling. "I was taking his temperature and he bit the thermometer. I think I've removed all the glass..."

The doctor wiped his hands on his trousers then knelt down. Taking hold of Peter's chin, he forced the boy's lips apart. A fishy smell mingled with the taste of blood had Peter struggling not to throw up. The doctor leaned even closer; his face inches from Peter's and peered into his mouth. The man's hot breath blowing down Peter's throat reminded him of Fi's talk about men interested in other men. He couldn't help it, his stomach erupted in violent spasms spraying the man with bilious vomit. The doctor struggled backwards, not quick enough to get out of the way.

"Oh Peter!" his mother exclaimed. "How could you?"

As if he had done it on purpose. His stomach continued to churn but there had been very little to throw up.

"Let me show you to the bathroom," his mother was saying, more concerned about the doctor than him.

Peter clawed his way back onto his bed. He felt so shivery that he pulled the blankets tight round himself and drifted off to sleep.

"We should leave," Zhuru was saying. "Can you travel, Master Ting?"

The man nodded in response, a bright red gash above his ear.

"And you, Kaitling?"

"I'm fine." Her croaking voice belying her words. "What about Karr?"

"He's the reason we need to flee," Zhuru said. "He will have been taken prisoner and will tell the enemy who we are and where we are."

"Surely not," Kaitling said.

Peter disliked the way she defended the useless apprentice.

"I am sorry Master Ting, but your former apprentice is a coward and an adept of opium. I have no doubt he will tell the enemy all they want to know," Zhuru replied.

As there was no more to be said, they went to fetch their horses. It was then that they discovered Karr had fled with a horse. So much for him seeming intoxicated.

"We'll ride back towards Navigon in the hope of getting behind the army then we'll cross the river. The enemy will not expect anyone at their backs, not yet. So we should have a good chance."

They saddled up and rode away from the farm and its dead men, much to Peter's relief.

11.

"What are you doing up and about, freak?" Sis greeted Peter, not bothering to look up from the maths problem she was trying to solve. Her homework was sprawled across the kitchen table, so he guessed his mother wasn't around. Mum hated them doing their homework in the kitchen. "That's what you have your own rooms for," she always said.

"Looking for someone else to spew up on?" she asked, putting up a hand in mock protection. "The doctor's going to charge Mum to have his clothes cleaned. No doubt she'll deduct it from your pocket money."

He ignored her jibes and went to fetch a pint of milk from the fridge. Realising that food might be available, the cat wound itself around his ankles purring ostentatiously until he gave it some milk.

He pushed aside one of Sis's books and cleared himself a small corner of the table to eat his cereal.

"Still hungry after all that glass?" she asked, finally looking up from her work, her lips curved in disgust. "You might get a job as a fakir in a freak circus."

"You need to transfer that to the other side," he said. She looked at him blankly. "The 'x' should go on the other side of the equation."

She glanced down at her book and grunted. "It's not because you're good at maths that you're any less of a freak. On the contrary."

They lapsed into silence as Peter hurried to finish his breakfast. The church choir was singing a piece by Elgar at Communion. They'd been practicing for the past weeks and Peter didn't want to miss it. He was one of the oldest boys and was now lead chorister. The voices of almost all the other boys of his age had already broken. His turn would come soon enough, the choirmaster had warned him. He was not looking forward to it. He loved his treble voice. What's more, he found the unpredictable pitch of boys whose voices were breaking unnerving and once their voice had settled he had the impression there was a little man talking out of a boy's body.

"I'm off to church," he told Sis as he washed his bowl.

"Don't be an idiot. Mum said you were to stay in bed," Sis replied. She was always inventing excuses not to go to church. Maybe she begrudged him not using a legitimate one.

He just shrugged and went to get washed and dressed.

He got off his bike at the back door to the church just as the ringers reached the end of a series of changes and began ringing rounds. He was late, but there would be just enough time if he hurried. He shrugged off his jacket as he entered the vestry where the other boys were already lined up for the procession into the nave. Peter hastily donned his cassock, fixed the ruff around his neck and pulled his surplice over his head, straightening it till it was just right. Taking the medal of St. Nicholas, patron saint of choirboys, from his cassock pocket, he hung it around his neck and made his way to the head of the line of boys, nodding to the others as he did. Just then, the organ struck up the first notes of the introit, time to open the door and lead the choir into the sunlit nave.

It was one of his favourite moments. All heads turned in their direction as the congregation stood. He walked, his head held high, swinging his hips slightly in time with the music so his cassock swayed from side to side as he walked. He let himself be absorbed by the music till it buoyed him up. Behind him he could just make out the footfalls of the other choirboys when the organ played pianissimo. Above, light was streaming in through the stained glass windows, flooding the church with warmth and colour.

His soul fluttered into wakefulness and flew up to join those of all the others flirting with the rays of light as they floated on the organ music. What better moment to burst into song as he sang solo the first verse of the opening hymn. The notes of the organ softened to give his voice the room to soar and join his soul. A solitary tear of relief and gratitude rolled down his cheek and it was time for the others to join him and his voice could once again take refuge in the body of the choir.

As it was a special occasion, with all honours going to the choir, the boys did not change out of their choir robes after the communion, but lingered at the west porch receiving the praise of parishioners, most of whom were elderly. Several people congratulated him on his voice. "You ought to make a career in singing," one old man suggested. Peter enjoyed the singing but he liked the praise less.

As the mingling crowd began to move off in the direction of the parish hall and parish breakfast, Fi joined him.

"You look like an angel," Fi said, leaning so close he could smell the telltale fragrance of her soap. She was dressed more soberly for church in a loose-fitting, dark blue dress that came to a frilly stop just below her knees.

"That's no angel, it's a pansy," Priscilla said, coming up behind them, unnoticed.

Peter trembled at the sight of the girl, but Fi stood unflinching.

"When did they let you out, Priscilla?" she asked with a sneer. "Don't they keep people like you locked away for life?"

Priscilla ignored Fi. She tugged at his ruff, saying: "Suits a boy like you." Then she prodded the medallion that hung on his chest. "Did you know that St. Nicholas was also patron saint of prostitutes? Seems befitting."

Fi took a swipe at the girl, but Priscilla hopped out of reach and hurried after a tall, rigid looking woman that Peter supposed must be a relative.

"That girl scares me," Peter said, when they were alone. "I met her for the first time yesterday and only an hour afterwards she was threatening to kill me." He could feel himself trembling at the memory. "Would you believe, she spat in my face."

Fi hugged him, a brief contact that had him trembling even more. "Oh my poor pretty boy," she whispered. "You shouldn't be scared of her, even if there are good reasons to be terrified."

"What do you mean?" She'd left him alarmed, her attempts at reassuring him misfiring completely.

Fi laughed. "She's nuts."

"How do you know that?"

"Priscilla attended a private girls' school where my mother works as administrator." The feel of her hand as she took hold of his sent a thrill down his back that met a wave of guilt travelling in the opposite direction. Peter glanced nervously around, hoping the Vicar wasn't nearby. The man was a stickler for correctness when it came to the choirboys and girls.

Fi was engrossed in her tale and didn't seem to notice Peter's wariness. "My mother didn't tell me very much. But I know they had a lot of trouble with the Wit girl, that's what she called her, until she was finally expelled for doing serious harm to a number of younger children. They didn't realise at first. The kids were so terrified, none of them dared say a word. But a young boy, who'd particularly suffered at the hands of Priscilla, had a nervous breakdown and tried to kill herself. That's when the truth came out."

"So I'm to be her next victim?" Life was complicated enough without the witless girl turning it into hell.

"I won't let that happen," Fi said.

"I've got to get ready for parish breakfast. Come with me while I change." Being with Fi was making him reckless. No boy would ever invite a girl into the choirboys' vestry. As he changed out of his surplice and cassock, Fi studied the fading photos that hung high on the walls above the rows of robes.

"Who's that?" Fi asked, pointing to a large picture of an old man playing the church organ.

"My grandfather. He was organist and choirmaster at St. Mary's for years. He died shortly after my father did." The picture no longer made him as sad as it used to. His grandfather had been a scary man, all strict and distant, but Peter liked him. "Let's go," he said.

Parish breakfast came once a month. Local women prepared fresh bread rolls and jam. There was tea, coffee and orange juice. All had been laid out on trestle tables with several women serving. Most people were seated in small groups on benches around the tables, chattering amiably.

He always looked forward to parish breakfast. Not just for the food, which was excellent, but also because he could watch the girls, not needing an excuse to be near them. Fi had always been one of them. Now she was sitting opposite him, talking to him, just the two of them together. What a change!

"I have an idea," Fi said quietly. She saw Priscilla's words as a challenge and was debating ways to get the better of her. "We could get into my mother's work place and read Witless's school file. I'm sure there must be something in there we could use against her."

The idea of stealing into a private girl's school had a mixed impact on Peter. He'd love to sniff around the places that only those haughty girls could go to, prying into their little secrets. Like finding an abandoned shoe or a lost scarf in the forest, it could conjure up all manner of stories. But this would be different. He'd go with Fi and they'd pry into Priscilla's private record. The thought made him feel guilty.

Trust him to feel guilty just when the Vicar was watching from across the room. The man, true to his reputation, was keeping a jealous eye on the choirboys when girls were around.

"Watch out," he whispered to Fi, "the Vicar's on the prowl."

"I told you men would flock to the pretty boy," she said, grinning.

Peter scoffed at the idea only to look up and see the Vicar looming over him, his dog collar tight around his skinny neck.

The man was particularly tall and thin with short black hair standing on end. Peter's mother disrespectfully called him the 'Rake'. She didn't like him, she told Peter, because of the way he'd reacted at father's death. She'd boycotted the church ever since.

"Good morning Fiona," the Vicar said. "Would you mind leaving us for a moment. I want a private word with Peter?"

Peter wondered if Fi might refuse, but she got to her feet, giving Peter a look that was heavy with meaning. "See you," she said casually and was gone.

The Vicar sat down in the place left vacant and placed a bony hand on Peter's. Compared to Fi's, this hand was cold and hard. It was all Peter could do not to snatch his hand away.

"I know you have reached that difficult age for boys, when things begin to change," the Vicar said, patting Peter's hand as he spoke. The man glanced across the room at Fi who was talking animatedly to some school friends. "No doubt your voice will break soon and you will probably leave the choir. I hope you will continue to attend church."

Not like mother, Peter thought.

"At this time of change you will need to be particularly vigilant, Peter. Temptation is always close at hand but you should not give in. Know that I am always available should you want to talk or need comfort. The door of the vicarage is wide open."

Peter shuddered at the thought of being comforted by the Rake.

The Vicar squeezed Peter's hand one last time, looking deep and long into his eyes, then got to his feet and walked away.

12.

The town of Tallford was bordered to the south by a winding river that meandered across marshlands and into the hills beyond. The Frayne, as it was called, had once been used for barges and the rugged towpath that hugged the riverside was a vestige of that period, offering a dry passage through the marshes. It was along this path that Fi walked side by side with Peter who pushed his bicycle.

They had the path to themselves. No doubt normal people were having Sunday dinner. Peter's mother didn't hold with such traditions. "All those roasts are just an excuse to keep the butcher in business," she said. Instead each of them helped themselves to a snack and retired separately to their rooms, just one more hole in his family life.

"We've got to act quickly," Fi was saying, "before Witless gets her claws in you."

Peter shuddered, absently rubbing the wounds on his arm. The girl was so single-minded it might already be too late. "What do you suggest?"

"We need ammunition. That's why we need to find an excuse to go to her old school."

"I don't like the idea of breaking in. What if we get caught?"

"That's why we go with my mother on a day when she's alone in the office. Maybe we can offer to tidy up. She's always complaining she's plagued by masses of paper."

The idea sounded feasible. "How would you explain me being there?"

Fi chuckled. "My Mum would be delighted to see me with a boy. She might be easy-going but I suspect she's concerned about me always being with girls."

"Why do you go with girls?" The idea of two girls kissing intrigued him.

"Now there's a question," she replied, looking thoughtful.

They walked on in silence for a while, Peter recalling the two kissing as they lay on the bedroom floor. It was Fi that broke the silence. "I'm attracted to girls. I want to be with them, to hold their hands and kiss them. I enjoy it. It makes me feel alive and whole."

Peter found it difficult to imagine. He certainly didn't feel attracted to boys and the idea of holding hands or kissing them was repulsive.

The sun was high in the sky, it was nearly noon, and there was very little wind. A host of tiny flies rose from the nearby marshes and buzzed lazily around. Dragonflies flitted across their path at oblique angles in search of food. Peter took off his jacket and hung it over the handlebars, undoing the top buttons of his shirt. It was hot.

"Don't you wish you wore a dress, pretty boy? It would be much cooler. Have you ever tried one on?"

Peter looked away across the marshes, sure his face was red with embarrassment. "Once. Yes." It wasn't true, of course. He'd often dressed up, but he'd never told anyone. He couldn't bring himself to admit it had become a habit that part of him would readily be rid of.

Fi chuckled. "I bet you took Sis's clothes."

"What's so funny?"

"If your sister knew, she'd be furious. She might enjoy kissing girls, but the idea of her brother dressing as a girl would drive her nuts."

Fi was right. Sis would kill him if she caught him. In a way, Sis and Priscilla were similar in their violent dislike of pretty boys, as Fi called them. Luckily, Sis didn't know and Witless could only guess.

"So what did you wear?" Fi was clearly fired up by the subject.

He gave her a pleading look, but Fi pursued her prey unrelentingly, as if she desperately needed to know.

"One of her old dresses..." he admitted, sheepishly.

Her face coloured with excitement. "Details!"

Of course, she'd want to know! He remembered the moment well enough. He'd wanted to know what it felt like to be a girl. He'd often watched girls at school and at church. If he watched them long enough and with sufficient intensity, it was almost as if he could feel what it was like to be them. Donning his sister's dress was just a further step.

"It was pale blue and frilly and reached to my ankles. I tried dancing, but I was so clumsy I almost fell over. I was afraid I might tear the thing and someone would notice. I remember being disappointed. I think I'd expected wearing it would transform me into a girl. I kind of believed in the magic of the dress. But it didn't work. I was stuck as a boy. It did give me a thrill and I knew I would do it again just to have that feeling, but I also felt terribly guilty. It was as if a dark pit had opened in my stomach and it gnawed at me from inside. I kept thinking there was something wrong with me. Something twisted and dirty! Maybe that's why Priscilla's words hurt so much."

Fi listened, enthralled.

"Why are you so interested?"

Fi looked surprised at the question and not a little troubled. "Maybe..." she hesitated, "... Maybe for me, you dressing up like a girl is like wearing a dress for you. It's a magic potion. I have always wanted to taste it."

He saw so much longing in Fi's eyes, but also tenderness and vulnerability that it touched him deeply. He knew he wouldn't refuse her if she were to ask him. But she didn't. Instead she walked on in silence, scuffing up the dust that lay on the path. Maybe she was even more frightened than he had been when he'd first pulled a dress over his head.

He reached out and tentatively took hold of her hand. He felt as if their conversation had woven such a bond that any difference of age or background had been swept away. Fi did not shake his hand off, but continued walking doggedly forward. He pulled gently on her hand till she came to a stop and turned to face him. She looked at him, her eyes begging as tears streamed down her cheeks. He let his bike slip to the ground and pulled on her hand till she was close enough for him to put his arms around her. She laid her head on his shoulder and burst into sobs, her body shuddering in his arms.

They stood there for ages, silent and unmoving. He could hear the splash of a fish as it leaped clear of the water in the nearby river. He could hear the marsh birds calling to each other as they hunted insects. He could hear the chirping of fledglings eager for food. He could feel Fi's heart beating, her breasts heaving hard against his chest. He could taste the salt of her tears on her neck as he pressed his lips against her skin. He could feel his own heart fluttering as he sensed the thudding pulse of blood in her throat.

"Yes," he whispered in her ear, answering an unspoken question.

At first she didn't seem to understand, then she pulled away a short distance and looked into his eyes, questioning. "Yes?" Her voice trembled.

He leaned forward till their lips almost touched. "Yes."

She laughed, her breath warm and sweet on his waiting lips. Then she pulled back and he could see that her face was flushed with excitement.

"We need to find a place," she said, an urgency in her words.

"There's the disused shack," he reminded her.

It had probably been built when the river was busy with barges, but no one had used it since the river silted over and lorries and trains replaced river transport. Peter picked up his bike and Fi slung an arm around his shoulder, possessively pulling him close and they walked hip against hip.

The cabin lay slightly back from the river on a small rise.

It was flanked by a couple of trees, the only ones as far as the eye could see. The roof and walls were intact, but the windows were broken and had long been boarded over. The only door was locked, but Peter knew the trick. He'd been there before.

Inside was cool and dark and the place smelt unpleasantly of rot and damp although it was quite dry. The sole piece of furniture was a large wooden table abandoned in the middle of the single room. Fi brushed it clean with some leaves and, pulling a large scarf from her bag, spread it like a cloth in the middle of the table.

Fi turned to face him. "Are you sure?"

He nodded,

If he had been in control up to then, it was Fi that now took the lead. She shifted him so that he was standing a few feet from the table, facing it, and unbuttoned his shirt taking care not to touch his skin. When she'd finished, she pulled it off one arm at a time. She folded it meticulously as if it were of immense value and placed it ceremoniously on the table. Then she came and stood, shoulders held high, chest thrust forward, next to him in front of the table.

"Unzip my dress. Fold it carefully and place it on the table."

He unzipped the dress and pulled it over her head, taking care, like she had done, not to touch her. She stood now in front of him in only her underwear. He was surprised to discover she wore no bra. It was the first time he'd ever had a girl standing almost naked in front of him. The sight made him feel strange all over.

"Dress me in the shirt," she ordered.

He picked up the shirt from the table and shook it out then he slipped one sleeve over her arm before he threaded her second arm in the other sleeve. He took his time, executing each movement with meticulous care. Finally, he buttoned the shirt over her breasts and went to stand next to her.

"Now your trousers," she explained. She had some difficulty getting his trousers over his shoes. When she'd finished, she folded them neatly and lay them on the table where his shirt had been. As she went to stand next to him, he felt exposed and ridiculous in only his pants. If she were to laugh, he'd probably shrivel up and die. Instead she nodded. He didn't need further instructions. He helped her step into the trousers and zipped them up.

Now it was her turn to act. She stepped forward to the table, picked up the dress and shook it out. Then she slid her hands expertly up inside it until it was all bunched up around her wrists and she placed it over his head, pulling the material down till it reached his knees. She helped him thread his arms through the armholes and finally zipped the dress up at the back. Her characteristic smell surrounded him in a halo of warmth.

Once she'd finished, she returned to her place next to him. Then she placed her hands on his hips and spun him round till he was facing her. There they stood, looking each other over for a long moment until Fi moved forward and took him in her arms and hugged him. She ran her hands down his back as if to confirm he was wearing a dress. When she drew away, he saw her face was flushed with excitement and her eyes were closed.

Instead of being aroused, he felt mildly disappointed. The high point of their ritual had been an anticlimax compared to the time on the towpath. Her crying in his arms had been much more moving.

The distant sound of the church clock striking one brought her back to the present.

"Good Lord!" she said, her eyes springing open. "I have to go to Granny's"

They undressed. No ceremony this time, just haste, a good deal of clumsiness and some embarrassment on Peter's part. Once she had donned her dress and he'd zipped it up for her, he pulled on his trousers and she helped him button his shirt. That was it. They opened the door of the cabin and emerged into the blinding sunlight.

She paused a moment and gave him a quick kiss on the cheek, breathing "Thank you" close to his ear. Then she hurried off along the towpath back to Tallford, while he jumped on his bike and rode away in the opposite direction. He would have all afternoon to think about what had just happened.

13.

Peter had the road to himself as he peddled leisurely through the forest, relieved to have made it up the steep incline from the river below. The oaks were taller there and offered some shade from the mid-afternoon sun. They also sheltered him from the sharp breeze that had got up shortly after he'd left Fi. It had buffeted him all the way across the exposed marshland as he followed the river for what seemed like miles. Finally he had quit the towpath and taken a road that wound up into the hills.

He glanced in amongst the trees where rays of sunlight danced from bush to bush. He couldn't help it, his mind returned to Fi as he pictured her dressed in only her pants. It had been a magic moment, so intimate and delicate, suspended out of time, one like he might have dreamed of all his life. Yet with hindsight it seemed weird and out of place. What exactly had they been doing? Whose idea had it been not to touch each other? It made the whole scene distant and unreal.

And why the ritual? It reminded him of the church. Fi in her underwear and the church didn't fit well together. He giggled nervously. The Rake's warning sprang to mind. Temptation had come knocking much quicker than the Vicar could have imagined, although the Rake would never have dreamed it in that form. Peter played at rewriting the first book of Genesis in his head. Instead of the snake and the apple, Eve produced a flowing wedding gown and coaxed Adam into wearing it. No wonder god had been furious when he found out...

His rumination was interrupted by the sound of a vehicle labouring up the hill behind him. As it drew level, he saw it was a police car. He could never see cops without feeling guilty. Could they know about him and Fi? A rush of anxiety left him queasy.

He sighed with relief when the car continued past, but much to his dismay, it pulled to halt a short distance down the road, its wheels scrunching on the wayside gravel. The message was obvious: Stop your bike boy and get off. But he was disinclined to obey. Instead, he pulled out further into the narrow road in the hope of overtaking the car and cycling on. The policeman was clearly having no such nonsense. He pushed open the car door and blocked Peter's path with his burly body. The bike screeched to a stop inches from the policeman.

The bobby put a restraining hand on the handlebars. "Where are you going, young man?"

"For a ride."

It wasn't wise to oppose authority, but he couldn't help it. He was not courageous, but headmasters, teachers, policemen, soldiers, clergymen and experts all inspired mistrust if not antagonism. He was a little surprised the bobby didn't react to his impudence.

Instead, the policeman glanced him up and down. "Do your parents know where you are?"

Probably not. His mother never showed the slightest interest when he rode off all day. Not once had she asked where he was going.

"Yes," he lied. "I ride my bike for hours at weekends," he added, more truthfully.

The policeman pulled out a notebook from his uniform pocket and extracted a small pen from the spiral at its top. "Where do you live?"

"Tallford."

"But that's over fifty miles away!"

Peter didn't bother to answer. Adults never could understand. Life seemed to have sucked the imagination out of them.

"You wouldn't be running away, would you?"

Silly question, Peter thought. As if he'd tell him.

"Nope."

"What's your name?"

"Peter."

"Peter what?"

"McCloud."

"And what's your phone number?"

He reeled off his home number while the policeman dialled using the phone in his car.

"Mrs. McCloud? Do you know where your son is?"

There was a pause while the man listened to the answer. His mother was the sort of person who charged in and laid about her, only worrying about the injured afterwards. He couldn't help smiling when he saw the policeman move the phone away from his ear.

"Well I will tell you Mrs. McCloud, he's on his bicycle south of Winchester."

His mother would no doubt be expressing her surprise and indignation, admitting she had no idea where her son had gone. Had she known, she would have stopped him.

"No. He's not hurt."

Peter wondered if it was regret he heard in the policeman's voice.

"Should I escort him home? Or do you think he can make it back alone?"

The answer apparently took a long time coming as the policeman put away his notebook with his free hand and straightened the shabby beaded cover draped over the back of the driver's seat.

"As you like, Madam. Goodbye." The policeman hung up, replaced the phone in the car and turned to him. "You'd do well to turn back now and hurry home. Next time, let your mother know where you're going." Then he climbed into his car and drove off, leaving Peter alone by the wayside.

Something bright and eager stirred in the forest around him

the moment he was alone and, as if in response, a waiting spirit uncurled within his breast. Impatient now, he got off his bike and pushed it in amongst the trees along a faint path that led away from the road. He had to duck at times to avoid the branches that leaned in around him. The path seemed on the verge of fading out, when it abruptly slipped between two bushes and came to a halt in a small clearing tightly bounded by trees and bushes.

He abandoned his bike against a tree, pulled a small blanket from his saddlebag and spread it on the grass. Shrugging out of his sandals he took off his shirt and trousers and threw them on the ground. Glancing nervously around, he sat down and pulled off his pants, discarding them with the rest of his clothes.

A breeze rustled approvingly in the trees and swirled about him, caressing his naked body, making him shiver although it wasn't cold. He closed his eyes as he lay back and let the dappled sunlight rove over his skin.

So this is how you spend your time when you're alone! Kaitling said, her voice startling him.

He'd heard it often enough, but what startled him was that he was hearing it in his own world for the first time. He couldn't help glancing in the direction it had come from. Even though no one was there, he still blushed red to the tips of his toes and scrambled to get his pants back on. As he pulled on his trousers, amid memories of doing so with Fi, he wondered if he'd imagined Kaitling's voice as she said no more.

He couldn't help feeling disappointed. It would be good if they could talk to each other. There were so many questions he'd like to ask. Then again, if she could be in his head that might cause problems. The idea alarmed him. Imagine if she'd been with him during his exploits with Fi! He shuddered at the thought. What if she could hear his thoughts? Not that he had ever been able to hear hers. But as the daughter of a magician, maybe she could do things he couldn't. It would be worse than having the Rake, Sis and Priscilla on his trail.

He sighed in relief. Thank heavens her voice had only sounded briefly in his head. He finished getting dressed and prepared to wheel his bike back to road when Kaitling's now familiar voice said, *Sorry about that. I had to leave abruptly. We had to get round a squad of Syvan soldiers.*

Peter wasn't sure how to reply. Should he talk out loud? Or should he think the words in his head?

In your head, Kaitling replied as if she'd heard his thoughts. *Yes, I can hear your thoughts. I've always been able to, but I didn't want to frighten you or make you think you were going mad.*

Peter leaned his bike back against a tree and sat down.

Yes. Maybe it's better if you take this sitting down.

But I couldn't hear your thoughts, he suddenly realised, feeling at a great disadvantage.

Yes. I can see why that might upset you. You could hear my thoughts, if I let you. To be fair, maybe I should teach you how to veil what you think.

I should think so, he thought, feeling annoyed. But he couldn't stay annoyed for long. There were so many questions he wanted to ask, like, had they managed to cross the river?

Yes. We managed. Once we got behind the army, it was easy. All their attention was on Kasum and the mines.

Where are you now?

We are crossing the large plain that slopes gently up towards the Warsi Mountains. We should get there tomorrow evening.

Any news of that Karr bloke?

You have such a funny way of talking. I don't always understand, she said, laughing in his head. *We have heard nothing of Karr, but the fact that we have met several enemy patrols far from the main road must mean he's told them about us.*

Shouldn't you go somewhere else?

The Warsi Mountains are the only remaining wild area in Drailong. Nobody lives there and there are few paths in the mountains. It is the only place we can hide in safety.

Couldn't you sail away?

Syvatoy is the sole island nearby. We have no boats capable of making the long sea journey to the other lands we suspect lie across the ocean.

What about fighting the Syvans?

We do not maintain a trained army like them. We can only use our limited magic against them.

But you are good at unarmed combat. Master Zhuru taught you.

He did, but the Syvans are good at unarmed combat too, although not in the same way.

Maybe you could learn something here, something they don't know and use that to defeat them.

That's an excellent idea. You will have to show me what your people do. Of course, you'd have to learn for me. I have not found a way to travel to other worlds except through minds.

The idea of doing a course in unarmed combat didn't appeal to Peter at all. He never did any sports, except cycling and walking.

It would do you good, Kaitling said. *It might help you against that nasty girl who spat at you.*

You saw that? Peter was alarmed at how much Kaitling must have seen of his life. A brief image of Fi dressed in his clothes crossed his mind before he could push it away. *You really must teach me to hide my thoughts. I hardly know you and there are things I find difficult to share with anyone.*

Ok. I'll teach you how to hide your thoughts. It's not very difficult once you get the knack ...

14.

Learning to mask his thoughts proved more tiring than expected. It involved doing things his brain was unaccustomed to. In addition, he didn't always understand. Although she spoke his language perfectly, there were concepts and actions English had no words for.

Finally, once she'd let him into her mind and shown him how masking thoughts and feelings worked, he managed to grasp what she wanted and, through practice, became sufficiently good to keep her out of his thoughts unless she was determined to break through.

You're pretty good for a beginner. He could hear the smile in her voice as if emotions accompanied words more explicitly than they did in normal speech. *There are many apprentice magicians who never really manage.*

Doesn't that make them vulnerable?

It sure does. Apprentice magicians who can't mask their thoughts are a real liability. You can never trust them with a secret.

He spread a blanket on the ground and, lying on his back, folded his hands under his head. *How long have you been delving into people's minds?*

Apprentice magicians in Drailong learn a lot of things, but not how to enter people's heads.

She opened her mind for him to see some of the things they learnt. He particularly liked the way she'd healed an old man whose leg was broken.

So you can use your thoughts to heal?

Yes. Though not every magician can.

I wish I could.

Maybe you can. When I'm settled in the mountains, I'll try to teach you.

The idea appealed to him. He'd finally be able to learn something useful, not all the rubbish they filled his head with at school.

It was healing that gave me the idea of delving into people's minds, as you call it. When you heal someone, like I did in that memory, you heal from within even if you don't actually get into the person's mind. Doing so had me wondering if I might be able to enter people's heads. I quickly discovered that people had a layer of protection, a bit like a second skin that kept intruders out. For a long time it resisted, despite the force I used. I began to wonder if that wasn't the natural way of things. Maybe I should not pry into people's heads.

But there must have been some way in if you were able to heal people.

He felt her smile again. It was a real pleasure.

I know. That's what bothered me. It was as if the answer was right in front of me, but I couldn't see it. So I tried another tack. Maybe if I could understand why some people could heal and others couldn't, I might have part of the answer. It wasn't easy. I was just ten at the time and officially young people don't begin their studies to become a Master till much later.

Fortunately, my father was always very encouraging and, although I didn't tell him, or anybody else, about my project, he knew I was interested in healing and he invited several adepts. I talked to them about this second skin. Most were surprised, as if they took the act of healing for granted and never wondered about it.

In my world, Peter thought, *there are many grownups that take what they do for granted. What's more they'd never listen to a child.*

I was lucky. These Masters respected my father and they were open enough to consider my challenging questions. I suspect they learnt as much as I did.

Peter laughed out loud. He could hardly imagine teachers doing that. None of them were interested in anything new, except perhaps Mrs. Greengage, and they certainly didn't expect to learn anything from their pupils.

Our system is very different, Kaitling said. *But I must get on with my story. None of the people riding with me know I can travel to minds. All they can see is that I am dozing on my pony.*

Don't fall off!

She snorted mentally, a very odd feeling Peter realised.

I have been riding since I was little and I haven't fallen off a horse once. But you are distracting me again. Where was I?

The difference between those who can heal and those who can't...

Ah, yes. It had to do with how their protective skin reacted. Those who couldn't heal were incapable of producing the right interaction with the other person. It was as if they were blind.

His English teacher would say she was mixing her metaphors. *I know what you mean. The other person's protective layer was impermeable to those whose own layer didn't react in the right way.*

Yes. My task was to simulate the right approach at a distance so as to get beyond the protective layer and into the person's mind.

Sounds like a recipe for control and corruption. The prospect worried Peter.

You're right. Theoretically, if it worked, it could be used to manipulate. That's not so surprising really. Some people have a sway over others by simply being with them. Your horrible Miss Witless is one of those.

She isn't mine, Peter shuddered at the mention of the girl. All of sudden he felt cold and pulled the blanket around his shoulders for warmth. Time was getting on and the sun was low on the horizon, casting long shadows through the wood. *I'm going to have to go soon. I have to cycle at least three hours to get home.*

You mentioned manipulation, she recalled. *In reality, it is hard to do. People's minds and bodies naturally resist. I suspect that only willing subjects can be manipulated.*

You mean I want Witless to mess with me?

In a way, yes. You are open to her type of manipulation. That's why she singled you out as her next victim.

But I don't want her to send me to hell.

Of course you don't. Who would? But you are afraid of her and being afraid lays you open to mishandling.

So I've got to stop being afraid?

That's part of it. Now let me get to the end of my story and you will understand better. The secret lies in the way you approach the other person. If you touch him or her, it is easier because your two protective layers intermingle. If the person lives elsewhere, getting under her skin, as it were, requires quite a different approach.

But you reached me and I live in a completely different world, at least I think I do.

Did anyone ever tell you you're a chatterbox, apprentice McCloud? Both humour and frustration tinged her thoughts.

He was proud she'd called him an apprentice.

A real apprentice would know to keep quiet and listen to his master.

It was Peter's turn to snort. He had to admit, though, when it came to travelling between minds she was undoubtedly an expert.

As far as I know, she corrected, *I am the only one in Drailong who can.*

So what did you learn?

Most people's protective field naturally collides with the protection of people nearby. That collision sparks off the barrier. It is a way of knowing you exist and are separate from others. It is also a way of warning others that you are there and won't be messed with. People don't even know they are doing it.

So how do you get by?

I sneak up on it, making my presence as small and as unthreatening as possible. That way I can slip by before the barrier knows I am inside and then it can do nothing to stop me.

Does that barrier always work?

There are situations in which it is softened or removed. Love, for example. Strong mutual identification works too. Take you and your friend Fi for example, your mutual boundaries are confused, you don't know which of you is which.

Peter blushed at the thought of the ritual with Fi as he hastened to throw up a wall to keep the memories from Kaitling.

There's no need to hide that. I am aware of your games with that pretty girl. You would find it difficult to be otherwise. I suppose it's a form of love, albeit a bit lopsided, with her resolutely on top.

But there's another reason why you link up so strongly with her. It's the same reason I found you so easily. It is probably also why Miss Witless pounced on you and why your sister gives you hell. You are particularly open. Your protection is much lower than most people. That would probably make you a good healer and good at communicating mind to mind, but it might also lead you to catch everybody's illnesses and suffer from their bad moods, not to mention being singled out by nasty people as their next victim.

Peter was flabbergasted. Kaitling had spun a web of meaning around him that set his whole life in a completely new light.

I desperately need to learn to protect myself.

You do indeed, apprentice McCloud. Kaitling's tone was deadly serious. *If I am to teach you, I will need to come at it from another angle. Rather than teach you how to open your protective skin and feel the presence of others, I will have to teach you how to selectively close it so you are not the unwilling subject of other people's foibles and illnesses.*

Peter had often wished he could stay twelve years old. He wasn't called Peter for nothing. But listening to Kaitling's voice in his head brought a new breadth and depth to his understanding that could only come with age.

It's not really a question of age. But I know what you mean. The more you learn, the more your feeling of age will grow. You may well find it is difficult to be with other people of your age. You will see your sister and Witless differently. They will no longer frighten you. They will no longer concern you, lest it be as people who need healing.

Your relationship with your friend Fi will change too, loosing a lot of its naiveness and earthy pleasure. It won't be easy. You'll be frustrated. So much so you'll want to scream. You'll be hurt both physically and mentally. But if you chose to go down that road, it will be worth it. I know. I've been there.

Peter thought for a moment. Not because he hesitated, but because he wanted to savour Kaitling's words. Saying yes to Kaitling's proposal had nothing to do with the passionate "Yes" he'd said to Fi. This was his project, his life and he wanted to live it to the full.

<h1 align="center">15.</h1>

It was getting dark when Peter propped his bike next to the kitchen door. Once Kaitling had left, he'd ridden as fast as he could, not wanting to get caught by the fall of night. Even with good lights, riding in the dark along that uneven surface next to the river could be very dangerous.

The evening had been beautiful, the wind had dropped and the sun was setting in a flaming mixture of reds and yellows and golds that had the marshes and hills ablaze. He delighted in drawing up a list of all he planned to learn from Kaitling and the uses he'd put that knowledge to.

His discussion with her had been exhilarating. That excitement was still coursing through his veins, but the exercise and the many adventures of the day had exhausted him. He was looking forward to a quiet evening and a chance to recuperate.

To his horror, when he opened the kitchen door there, sitting at the table with Sis and his Mum was Witless, the crafty smile of a fox on her face. Peter wanted to turn and run. How did she get there? In a panic, he wanted to call Kaitling for help, but he had not yet learnt how to.

"Ah! There you are!" his mother exclaimed, sounding genuinely relieved. "Thank heavens that policeman found you and sent you home. What were you thinking of? Winchester!"

She'd got it all wrong, of course, but with Witless watching he wasn't going to argue.

"I'm glad to see you've recovered from your attack this

morning," his mother continued, heavy sarcasm in her voice. "You know Priscilla, don't you, I believe she's new to your class." She smiled as if she were doing him a great favour. Sunday evening was normally not a time for visits.

"Cilla and I bumped into each other in town this afternoon," Sis said, delighted to share the good news. "I invited her over for tea and she's been here ever since."

Of course she had. Poison had a way of clinging to things. He was starving, but he'd willingly skip evening meal to escape Witless.

"Priscilla bought a cake specially for you," his mother said. "You should thank her."

Peter just stared at the girl, hatred and fear vying for control. The cake was a bright pink affair that had the drawing of a girl in a long dress in icing sugar on it. Nobody seemed to notice the incongruity of bring such a cake for a boy. Apparently only Peter could see the significance. She might well have written 'pansy' on it in big, bright letters. Everyone was so enthralled, no one would have found that odd.

"We've been waiting for you to cut the cake," his mother said, picking up the knife.

"I'm still feeling queasy," Peter said, convinced the pink monstrosity would have arsenic in it, at least in his part. "I think I'll skip it this time."

Witless made a great show of being disappointed. "How odd. I could have sworn I saw you eating several bread rolls at parish breakfast."

The swine, Peter thought.

"You were sitting alone with a young girl, what was her name?" Witless innocently launched an incendiary bomb that was about to blow up in his face.

He was sure she knew who Fi was, she was just playing with him like a cat would a mouse before she sunk in her claws.

"Fiona, wasn't it?" she asked, looking at him for confirmation.

Peter wanted desperately to spit in her face like she'd done to him. Sis was winding up like a threatening thunderstorm, her face already red and her fists clenched. Witless sat there calmly, smirking, knowing full well what she'd done. He made a move for the door, praying he might yet escape.

"You stay here!" Sis said, her voice heavy with threat. "What were you doing with my friend?"

"Oh!" Witless butted in, sounding surprised. She was a devilish actor. "I thought the two were going out together. I saw them walking hand in hand along the towpath."

That was a barefaced lie, they had not held hands in public, but he didn't dare contradict her, it would be tantamount to admitting guilt. What worried him was that the dim wit knew they had been on the towpath. Had she been spying on them? What if she'd witnessed their ritual? The bottom fell out of Peter's world as fear swirled black and nasty around him in ever tightening circles. His knees began to tremble and he thought he was going to faint.

"You what?" Sis shrieked and flung herself at him across the expanse of the table, trying to claw at Peter's face. He jumped back just as Sis knocked the pink cake flying. It landed on the floor where it sagged in a sickly heap. Even the cat slunk away, wary of this unexpected offer of food.

"You bastard," Sis screamed, flailing hopelessly, unable to reach him.

"Peter. Go to your room," his mother ordered.

"But I didn't do anything. It's not fair," he complained, forgetting that all he wanted to do was get away. "Why don't you send Sis to her room. She's the one who's gone mad."

His mother swung out with her hand and slapped him with all her force. Tears sprang to his eyes as he was flung backwards against the fridge.

"Get out of my sight!"

Peter fled, nursing his cheek, which throbbed violently. As he left, he couldn't help noticing Witless smirking in her corner.

He sat on the edge of his bed, tears running down his cheeks till they fell in his lap. Hell the girl had promised and hell it was. He flung himself on his bed and buried his head in his arms, trying to contain screams of frustration and fury. It had all happened so quickly. He felt lame and helpless. He wasn't ready to defend himself. His plans with Fi or Kaitling had not even begun. Empty and exhausted, he finally drifted off to sleep.

"Keep down!" Zhuru whispered.

Can't talk now, Kaitling said hastily to him in her head. *We're under attack.* She glanced around a large rock revealing a group of Syvan soldiers spread out across the road, bows and arrows at the ready. Spotting Kaitling, one let fly but she saw it coming and withdrew, narrowly missing being skewered.

Ting lay wounded behind a nearby rock. The cook was trying to staunch the bloody gash in his chest. Judging from the amount of blood there was little hope for the old man. Yuan, the gamekeeper, had given Tessa, the cook's daughter, and the hostler bows and arrows, but they didn't seem very proficient with them. Only Zhuru, the gamekeeper and Kaitling scored the occasional hit, causing the enemy to hesitate about coming closer.

They were in a narrow gorge, at what Peter guessed must be the beginnings of the Warsi mountains. Boulders scattered around offered scant cover. If the enemy managed to scale the rocks on either side, they would be able to pick off Kaitling's group easily, but the idea didn't seem to have occurred to them.

They don't have mountains on Syvatoy, Kaitling told him between two shots, one of which killed a Syvan soldier.

You'll run out of arrows soon. You need to get out of here, fast.

Where?

Back the way you came, at least a short distance. Let them think you are fleeing in panic, then stop and pick them off when they are not expecting it.

At that moment arrows rained down from high on the right. Some Syvans must have scaled the rock face. Both Tessa and the hostler were hit. Zhuru made a sign to Kaitling to withdraw while he and the gamekeeper tried to hold off the remaining Syvans. She didn't want to run, but Peter insisted.

They are offering you a chance. Don't throw it away.

Kaitling turned and ran, head down, dodging left and right between the boulders, hoping they would offer some cover. Several arrows flew past, but the further she went the fewer the arrows that reached her. Peter urged her to keep going.

When she crossed a narrow path that led off to one side, squeezing its way steadily up between the boulders, she took it. No one seemed to be pursuing, but she forced herself to run on, despite her exhaustion.

I should go back and help the others.

No you shouldn't. Don't throw away the gift they offered.

Kaitling shrugged at his words and laboured on up, walking as fast as she could, her breath coming in painful gasps.

Suddenly a shout went up not far behind. The Syvans must have spotted her and were following. Kaitling broke into a run, hopping from one boulder to another, almost falling several times. There was plenty of shelter, but if they searched thoroughly it would be easy to find her.

She looked over her shoulder to see if her pursuers were in sight and abruptly plunged forward into a black hole. There must have been a large chasm between two rocks. Her leg twisted as she fell and snapped when she hit the ground some ten feet below sending a searing pain through both her and Peter.

She must have passed out because Peter found himself alone in her head. It was a very strange feeling. He might have enjoyed it, had it not been for the situation and the acute pain.

Kaitling, he called out, trying to rouse her. There was no response. She couldn't be dead, he realised, because he could feel her heart beating and presumably dead people didn't feel pain. *Kaitling,* he called again. Still no response! If she had broken her leg and couldn't walk, chances were she'd die anyway, alone as she was out there in the wild. He refused to accept that ending. There must be a way.

Mentally he tried to shake her and, to his surprise, she stirred. *Kaitling,* he called again. She groaned and tried to move.

I wouldn't move if I were you. You've broken your leg.

I know, she croaked. *What a stupid thing to do.*

Can you heal yourself?

I've never tried, she admitted, attempting to shift to a more comfortable position only to send pain shooting up her leg. *Let me concentrate.* He felt her attention and energy flow in the direction of her leg. From what he could judge, it didn't seem to be working, if anything, the pain got worse.

No! She moaned. *It won't work.*

Maybe I can heal you.

Don't be silly. She sounded dreadfully weary. *You're not even here and you're in no way trained.*

Well if healing is anything like talking mind to mind, I should be able to do it at a distance. As for training, now would be the very best time to start. He hoped she could feel the smile he tried to put in his voice and not the hopelessness that gripped him.

You tell me what to do and I'll do it.

He could feel she wanted to argue, but didn't have the strength.

Ok. Let's try.

So, little by little, she explained how to get close to the broken bone, and what it should look like, sharing images of her past experiences. She took him step by step through shifting the parts of the bone - it was a multiple fracture - back into their rightful place and coaxing them to knit together. He was amazed at how simple it was. It was almost as if the body wanted to heal itself. He wondered why no one in his world had ever discovered that.

Throughout the healing, he was aware that she was desperately holding her pain at bay, forcing herself to concentrate, when any normal human would have fainted long ago. He felt very proud of her, but made no allusion to her superhuman efforts. He merely concentrated on doing what she said.

Once he had realigned the muscles and healed those tissues that had been wrenched or damaged, she finally let go and slipped into sleep. As she did so he heard her whisper, *thanks.* He too was exhausted, so saying goodnight, he left her and returned to his bed.

16.

"Peter!" his mother shouted. "Get up immediately!"

What now! He'd just performed his first healing at a distance and was exhausted. He had no time or energy for a family circus.

"Leave me alone. I'm tired."

His mother dragged him brutally to his feet and shook him violently. "Don't tax me any more, boy. How do you explain this?"

He had no idea what she was talking about. When he didn't reply she shook him again and pointed to a dress Sis was holding up. His sister, who was standing in the doorway next to Witless, looked a disaster. Her eyes were bloodshot from crying, her clothes were in a mess and her hair stood wild on her head.

He still didn't understand.

"Why did you tear your sister's dress?"

"It was one of my favourites," Sis wailed, starting to cry again.

"I don't understand," Peter said.

"Surely the question is simple enough. Why did you tear your sister's dress?"

"But I didn't tear it. I have never touched it."

That wasn't true. He'd tried it on once or twice but he'd certainly never torn it. He was always so careful.

"Who else could have? Sis certainly didn't tear her own dress."

Peter glanced at Witless and the whole situation suddenly became clear. She must have sneaked into Sis's room and done it, knowing Peter would be blamed. But no one would believe him. From the look of triumph on her face, she knew it too. The girl was downright bonkers and extremely dangerous.

Once his mother had made up her mind, there was no changing it, but he tried all the same. "I tell you, I didn't do it." He could see Witless whispering in Sis ear. His stomach clenched in dread. This was not over. What else had she prepared for him?

"What about the dress he stole?" Sis accused.

One glance at Witless's face convinced him that a search of his room would uncover the missing item.

"Ask Witless," he said, furious. "She should know where she's hidden it"

"What nonsense. Where is it?" his mother asked, looking almost as furious as he felt.

"If I didn't take my sister's dress, and I insist I didn't, then there is only one person here who could have done so and hidden it in my room to have me blamed, it's her!" He pointed at Witless, whose face was a mask of innocence.

Drop it, Kaitling said. She sounded exhausted. *You can't win this battle and if you fight back you might well make things worse.*

Peter was relieved to hear her. *I wanted to call you, but I didn't know how.*

In the mean time, his mother was rummaging through his cupboards and quickly found the dress. If he had hidden it, he would have made it more difficult to find, but then Witless wanted it to be found.

"You lied," his mother accused.

"That the dress is in my room is no proof that I took it."

His mother's patience had reached its limit, which was never far away. She let fly with her right hand.

Sidestep shouted Kaitling. He did, his mother's hand flying just were his head had been.

The force of her unchecked movement had her spinning on

her heals. When she came to a halt she looked at Peter, astonished. Then she glared at him.

Get ready, Kaitling warned. *Move closer to the door.*

He didn't like having Witless at his back, but he trusted Kaitling. His mother took a step forward and aimed a second swipe at him as Kaitling shouted, *forward roll.* He did, fetching up across the far side of the bedroom just in time to hear Witless scream as his mother's outstretched hand connected with the girl's face. Sis fled, screaming too, although she was untouched.

His mother was devastated at what she'd done and flew to help Witless who lay on the floor. As Peter shifted to watch, he was pleased to see Witless scuttling on all fours down the corridor trying to get out of his mother's reach, afraid she'd get hit again.

A temporary victory, Kaitling said. *Although, I don't think she will try that again.*

She won't stop there, Peter replied. *I have humiliated her.*

Witless scrambled to her feet half way down the corridor. "This is a madhouse. You're all completely mad!"

People tend to accuse others of their own afflictions, Kaitling commented, as they waited to see what Peter's mother would do. *Breathe deeply. Try not to react, if you can.*

Someone ought to keep an eye on Witless. Goodness knows what she'll do to get vengeance.

"I'll deal with you later, boy," his mother said turning to go. Her face was pale, her lips tense, she looked strangely deflated. She locked his door behind her.

Prisoner now, he thought.

I have to go. There's something stirring in my cave. Come with me. Your mother will leave you alone for a while.

Sure. But teach me how to come on my own.

Kaitling did as he asked, telling him exactly what to do and, once again, he was surprised how easy it was.

Back in her cave, it was pitch black. He too could now hear the sinister sound of claws scraping across the rocks. His fear mingled with hers as Kaitling got cautiously to her feet and backed away as best she could.

To his surprise Peter could hear purring. Could it be his cat at home? How had the animal managed to get into his locked room? *Can you hear that?* he asked Kaitling.

What you call purring? Yes. But I've never heard the likes before.

Do you not have pets?

She didn't understand the word, so he sent her the image of his cat curled up on his bed next to him. It surprised her.

If it is anything like our cats, it could be harmless.

Kaitling was dubious and continued easing backwards till the rock wall stopped her. She bit her lip as she tried not to scream when something heavy and warm leaned against her leg. Whatever it was, she could feel the immense strength of the thing as it rubbed what must be its back against her calves.

Move your arm very slowly, Peter said, *and hold out your hand to it.* He could feel the tension in Kaitling's body as she braced herself to spring, so he tried to use the little he had learnt in healing to relax her. *If you are relaxed,* he murmured, *the animal will be too.* When Kaitling reached a fluffy mass, the animal pushed against her hand, burying her fingers deep in its fur.

Peter had a wild idea. Not stopping to think, he let himself slip from her fingertips into the animal as unobtrusively as he was able. A feeling of confusion and disorientation hit him the moment he crossed over. It was so strong he almost lost concentration. The animal tensed as it felt his presence, but when he calmed and adjusted to this new environment, the animal relaxed.

Peter wondered if he should make reassuring noises but he had no idea what sound would work. A sharp pain attracted his attention. He headed for it, realising that the animal had a broken leg.

Being in the animal, he was no longer in contact with Kaitling. He'd have to go it alone. He tentatively shifted the bones until they fitted smoothly together. Very little coaxing was needed as if the body remembered how it should be.

The healing must have hurt because the animal whimpered. Kaitling was still running her fingers gently through its pelt, her caresses helping to relax both the animal and himself. It took a long time to heal the muscles and tissues, which were extremely complex.

He was afraid he might get stuck in the animal, especially if Kaitling withdrew her hand. But he couldn't hurry his work. When he had finally finished, he sped back to Kaitling.

Where were you? I was afraid you'd had problems at home and had had to leave me alone with this beast.

No. I was inside the animal. It had a broken leg and I was healing it. He felt Kaitling's surprise at his words. *I tried and it worked.*

Well done. Soon you'll be teaching me.

Peter felt a tug at home. *I've got to go. Just keep stroking it. I'll be back as soon as I can.*

It was his mother. She was standing over him shaking his shoulder. After so much dark, he blinked at the bright lights as he struggled to focus. His mother looked gray. He wondered if his eyes were playing up, but as he became accustomed to the light, she really did look gray. Haggard, even. He had never seen her look so old. She seemed tired and unsure.

"I'm at my wits' end," she said, sighing.

His mind idly toyed with the idea of coming to the end of a wit. There was certainly one wit he'd like to do away with. Concentrate, he told himself.

"I am afraid you have very serious problems, Peter. I hesitate to think why you should steal your sister's clothes." She shuddered at whatever crossed her mind. "If your father had been here, things would have been different."

Now she was blaming his father, when the poor man had nothing to do with it. Peter was amazed at how far she went to find explanations for things she didn't understand. Of course, he could tell her how things really were, not that that would make any difference.

"I fear that the death of your father must have damaged you

in some way," she mused, raking her fingers through her hair. "I phoned a friend for advice and he has given me the address of a very good psychiatrist. I will contact him first thing tomorrow morning and get you an appointment."

All this time she'd been staring off into space, but she finally looked down at Peter and a watery smile softened her features. "Oh Peter," she sighed and leant forward and briefly hugged him. He couldn't remember the last time she done such a thing. It was so out of character.

His mother turned to leave but then stopped, hesitant in the doorway. "Your sister is ill," she said quietly, presumably not wanting Sis to overhear. "I don't want you to disturb her and on no account are you to go in her room again." It was more of a plea than an order. Her tone was so unfamiliar it startled him. The hug, her voice, the greyness, the sudden tiredness, all these changes in his mother had him worried.

17.

The moment he awoke, Peter was eager to join Kaitling. He wanted to know what had happened to the furry animal. He found her asleep on a rock with a warm mass cuddled up next to her. Well, at least both of them survived the night. Kaitling must have felt his presence because she stirred and opened her eyes. Light was streaming in through a sizable hole in the ceiling of the cave, some fifteen feet above.

The animal awoke too and stretched, its weight and strength pushing Kaitling off her rocky bed. To his alarm and also secret delight, the furry animal turned out to be a lion cub. It sniffed Kaitling and licked her face with a tongue that was so rough it chafed her skin. Both Peter and Kaitling were alarmed at the sight of its sharp teeth, but the animal sat back on it haunches, like his cat, and studied the girl through slanted eyes.

It must be hungry, he thought with a shudder, not wanting to pursue the idea to its inevitable conclusion.

I'm hungry too, Kaitling told him. *We need to get out of here.*

She stood cautiously, afraid she'd scare the cub, but it sat lazily watching her as she explored the walls. There was no apparent way out.

You might climb out, but that's not going to help him. Peter nodded mentally to the cub. *Can't you use magic to get out?* He showed her a scene from a film where a magician conjured up a rope and used it to escape prison.

Kaitling chuckled. *We don't learn that kind of magic. Though it might turn out very useful. Where can I learn that?*

Peter didn't bother explaining what a film was. Instead he asked what she had learnt. *Maybe there's something we might use.*

Well, reading and writing to start with.

That much magic we all learn at school, not that we call it magic.

There's healing and divining and shapeshifting and...

What's shapeshifting?

When you change into another form, like an animal.

Can't you change into a bird and fly out and get help?

Only advanced apprentices at the university in Navigon learn shape-shifting.

How about divining? Peter liked the word. It made him think of divine. He'd seen a man doing it on the farm near his house. *Maybe there's some water nearby. At least you won't die of thirst.*

But I've never done it before.

All three sat in silence for a long moment.

Put your hand on the cub's back, Peter suddenly said.

That won't work, she told him, having spotted the thoughts behind his request.

It's worth a try. But don't take you hand away till I'm back. I don't want to get stuck in a lion. He felt Kaitling shiver at the thought. She went over to the lion cub, not without trepidation, and began stroking its fur.

He let himself slip from her fingers into the animal, just like he had the first time. The disorientation was no less shocking, but at least he was prepared for it. He could see the cave much more clearly and was acutely aware of sounds and smells, but his thoughts were confined to a very narrow space. Without words, how could he possibly get his message across?

Maybe images would work. He pictured the cub running across a wide-open space. The animal immediately responded with a scene of lions lounging in the long grass, a memory tinged with sadness and longing. So you got separated from your parents. He imagined climbing rocks till it was possible to get out of the cave.

The cub immediately sprang to its feet, breaking the contact with Kaitling. So much for his precautions! It prowled the cave and then clambered onto the largest of the rocks, tensing its muscles. Peter knew what it wanted to do but was sceptical, a feeling he tried to hide, for fear it would hinder the animal.

The cub jumped, just managing to hook its claws over roots that snaked along the edge of the hole. It hung there for a dreadful moment, then, with an enormous effort, heaved itself upwards and out of the cave.

The animal's delight at getting free flooded Peter, as it set off at a run along the path. He, himself, was terrified, stuck as he was in the cub's head. He desperately sent the animal pictures of Kaitling sitting alone in the cave, not stinting on his own sadness and despair at leaving her. Finally the cub slowed and came to a halt.

Peter thought of a broken branch and showed the lion the thing clamped in its jaws. Maybe Kaitling could use such a branch to get out. Not that he knew if there were any trees nearby.

The cub lifted its muzzle and sniffed. Peter was astonished that the air revealed a picture of the whole area, and there were trees. Not many. But it might be enough.

The cub bounded off in the direction of the trees. Once there it was at a loss what to do. Its eyes roamed the copse, nestled between the rocks, giving Peter a glimpses of a large branch. He let his enthusiasm for that branch flow through the lion, imagining the lion grasping it between its teeth and pulling it towards Kaitling. It took a while, but he managed to coax the lion to drag the branch to the cave and push it in.

The animal sat next to the hole and began licking its paws. He could hear sounds below but it was long time before Kaitling's head finally emerged. She scrambled to her feet and walked over to the lion.

He heard her make a noise but was unable to distinguish the words. He guessed she was saying thank you. He could also sense her fear. It smelt so strong that it set the cub's gastric juices flowing and had it flexing its claws ready to strike. Peter had to throw his whole energy into reversing the effect of her fear until the animal sat back on it haunches and studied her, perplexed.

He wanted to warn Kaitling to hurry, he couldn't hold the lion cub much longer, but there was no way to tell her. If only he could travel from mind to mind without needing physical contact.

Finally, Kaitling laid a hesitant hand on the cub's back and Peter fled. He immediately threw his strength into dampening Kaitling's fear, not sparing a second to explain what he was doing. She was startled, but quickly caught the drift of his thoughts and understood.

The lion cub stood for a long moment, suspended, staring at her, a look akin to disappointment in its eyes, and then with a roar it bounded away along the path.

Is it disappointed because I was no longer in its head?

Or because you convinced it not to eat me? Kaitling added with a nervous laugh. *You must tell me what happened. I've learnt more in the last couple of days with you, than in two years with all those experts my father invited.*

I know what you mean. We have a place we call school where we are supposed to learn, but it's boring and we learn next to nothing.

When I've found something to eat, I'll come and see this 'school' of yours.

Back in his room, he was in high spirits after his brush with the lion. Shame he had nobody to talk to about it. He was hungry, so he hurriedly dressed. Grateful that his mother had not locked the door this time, he stepped out into the corridor where a wave of moroseness hit him. The rest of the house reeked of it. Had his stay with the lion changed how he smelt the world?

He tiptoed past Sis's door. It was closed and no noise came from within. His mother's door was also closed, but that was normal. She might have gone off to work. She often left early, especially on Mondays.

Nobody was in the kitchen and, as far as he could judge, nobody had been there. No telltale dirty dishes or bowls lay in the sink and the cat hadn't been fed. Could his mother have slept in? That would be uncharacteristic, but then he remembered her face the night before. She had seemed worn out. Maybe she was ill. He wondered if he should go and check, but he never went into her room and was loathed to do so.

He gave the cat some milk, much to its delight. The animal seemed so tiny compared to the lion he had to laugh. His laughter rang strange to his ears, so out of place in the dingy atmosphere that permeated the house. He forced himself to laugh again out of defiance, causing the cat to look up surprised, a drop of milk perched precariously on the tip of its nose.

"Silly Billy," he whispered, leaning down to wipe the milk away. The moment he touched the cat he felt himself slip inside it's mind. For some strange reason, the shift was less upsetting than entering the lion cub. He showed the cat a picture of itself rolled up in a ball in its basket. It purred in response. He couldn't stop himself quickly checking to see if all was OK. For such an old cat, it was remarkably well. He eased a couple of creaky joints and then withdrew.

"What were you doing to the cat?" he heard Sis ask, her voice startling him. She sounded sour and full of suspicion.

"Stroking it." He got up to face her, shoving aside the fear he would normally have felt when she challenged him. Had he not dealt with a lion?

She had slung a nightgown over her shoulders, but it hung open, revealing an old pair of pyjamas that were stained in several places. Her shoulders were slumped forward, her hands hung aimlessly at her sides and her head seemed perched precariously atop her body. Her eyes stared almost unseeing, haggard, underscored with dark patches.

Don't engage her, Kaitling warned, arriving at that moment.

So you found something to eat, he thought, as he eased himself round the opposite side of the table from his sister and headed for his room.

"Peter," Sis said, her voice trembling.

He turned to look at her.

"When you see Fiona, tell her it is over between us." She burst into tears and crumbled to the floor, sobbing.

He was about to help her up when Kaitling warned him not to. *She'll get over it and if you touch her she might hurt you, such is her pent up anger.* He turned his back on her and hurried to brush his teeth and leave for school.

18.

To Peter's relief the chair next to him in class was empty. He hoped it would stay so all day. Witless must be recuperating from her adventures, probably plotting some fiendish attack. He tried to forget her and participate whole-heartedly in his lessons. It wasn't easy. Each new class had him worried the girl might return.

Kaitling had also left him as she went looking for food. It was almost a normal Monday morning, as they corrected maths homework. Nothing like a dose of quadratic equations to keep your mind at ease.

The moment the bell rang, he went in search of Fi. He had no idea where to look. Boys of his year didn't mix with girls two years older. When he finally found her, she was seated alone on a wall overlooking the playing fields reading a book. Break was almost over.

"Hi Fi."

"Hi pretty boy," she greeted him and closed her book. "You ready for some mischief?"

He heaved himself onto the wall a few feet from her and turned to face her.

"Listen Fi, things have happened."

Her smile faded. "Tell me."

He told her about the shock of finding Witless at his home and the drama with Sis's dresses. He omitted any mention of Kaitling. That might require additional explanation.

Fi burst out laughing when he reached the part where Witless got slapped.

"So Witless told Sis we were going out together and she went crazy."

"I heard she was off ill. I thought it might be her period come early."

"I saw her briefly this morning. What a wreck!" He remembered her face, haunted by some unseen nightmare. "She sent you a message." He hesitated about going on.

He wasn't sure what reaction to expect. She might go nuts like his sister and wail and scream or attack him trying to claw out his eyes. "She told me to tell you it was over between you."

There was a moment of silence when anything was still possible, then Fi shrugged. "It would have ended soon enough. We didn't have much to say any more. Making love is fun, but it has its limits."

Did that mean things between Fi and him were over? It had been short-lived but intense. As if to underscore the impending rift, the bell rang to announce the end of break.

"Meet me here at lunch. Skip school dinners and we'll go and get something in town," Fi said and dashed off to class.

So things with Fi were still on the cards. He jumped off the wall and did a quick improvised dance hoping no one was looking.

When he arrived for Greengage's lesson everyone was already in place, except Witless, thank heavens. He was about to go to his desk when the teacher stopped him. She spoke quietly, but those sitting close must have heard.

"The Headmaster wants to see you, McCloud."

What now, he wondered, as he hurried along the corridors to the Head's office. If there was one experience he never wanted, it was being summoned to see the Headmaster.

He had no trouble finding something to feel guilty about. His adventure with Fi immediately sprang to mind. Had Witless struck again? As his stomach knotted in anxiety, he slowed his pace. There was still time to run. Maybe he could escape to

Kaitling's world and live with her in the wild.

He was standing in front of the secretary's office, his hands clasped behind his back, hesitating about knocking, when the Headmaster stepped out a couple of yards further on, his gown swirling about him. He was a tall, thin man whose gray hair made him look distinguished. Even his stately handlebar moustache was gray. Peter had always imagined him to be severe and unbending but close up the man seemed friendly enough.

"Ah McCloud," the Head said, recognising him. Peter wondered how teachers and staff managed to remember so many names. "Come in," the Headmaster said, gesturing to his door.

The Headmaster's study struck him as old fashioned and smelt like it. He was reminded of scenes from a film about a school at the turn of the century, the dark heavy desk, the bookshelves in the same dark wood with numerous books in regimented rows and a set of sturdy armchairs upholstered in tartan material.

To a nose that had just been honed by the senses of a lion cub, the thick cloud of pipe smoke, mingled with the powerful scent of aging books and the pungent odour of expensive wood polish was suffocating.

Another man stood in the study, staring out the window at a group of girls playing ball in the yard. He could have been an insurance man. His mother had several of them amongst her clients. The man wore a light grey suit, a white shirt, an equally grey tie and shiny black leather shoes. When the Headmaster closed the door, the man turned to face Peter, his piercing eyes sizing him up.

"Mr. McCloud," the Headmaster began, "this is Detective Inspector Grant from the local constabulary. I believe he has some questions for you."

The inspector turned to the Headmaster. "Would you mind if I question the boy alone?"

"I can't permit that."

Good for you, thought Peter, the Headmaster immediately rising in his esteem.

"The pupils in this school are our responsibility," the Headmaster pointed out. "In the absence of his parents or a lawyer, I am obliged to remain to ensure that McCloud's interests are protected."

"As you like."

Peter had the impression the Headmaster's stand annoyed the inspector, but the man's face remained expressionless.

"Peter, that's your name isn't it?"

"Yes,"

The man stood in front of Peter, his height intimidating.

"Why don't you sit down, McCloud," the Head said.

Peter welcomed the suggestion, choosing an armchair as far away from the policeman as possible. A flicker of irritation crossed the man's face, but it was gone in a flash.

"What exactly happened yesterday?" the man asked.

Peter broke out in a sweat, his hands going clammy. So it was about him and Fi. His stomach tightening an additional notch as his anxiety got the better of him.

Calm down, he heard Kaitling say. He was delighted to have her back. He felt himself relax as Kaitling borrowed from his techniques, throwing her weight into influencing his emotions. *Yesterday is a very vague word,* she thought. *He's trying to catch you out.*

As Peter looked up, he saw greed in the man's eyes.

He thinks he's got you. Ask him to be more precise.

"A lot of things happen during a weekend," Peter said, "did you have anything particular in mind?" He could have sworn he saw the Headmaster smile briefly at his response.

"Don't try to get smart with me, boy!"

"McCloud's request seems legitimate to me," the Headmaster said. "I suppose you were thinking of a particular event or time."

Peter sent up a prayer of thanks that the Headmaster had stayed. He had completely misjudged the man.

The inspector pulled out a notebook, flipped it open and read silently for what seemed like a long moment. "We have had a formal complaint that your mother attacked a young girl yesterday evening at your home. What can you tell me about that?"

Peter was relieved to know it was not about Fi and himself and Kaitling was doing a great job relaxing him. In such threatening circumstances, his mind often went blank. With Kaitling's help, he felt confident he could outplay the man.

"My sister was very upset. Someone had torn her favourite dress. Miss Wit, who had come to visit my sister, was goading her on, suggesting that I was responsible. She even announced that my sister's best friend was going out with me, which was not true. My mother was trying to sort things out. She's been tired lately, what with work and my father's death, and the situation got on her nerves. She tried to slap me, but I dodged and Miss Wit, who was standing just behind me, got slapped instead. My mother was so upset. I'm sure she had no intention of hitting Miss Wit. The girl threw a fit, screaming that our house was full of nutters. When my mother tried to calm her, Miss Wit scuttled away on all fours shouting abuse."

Well done, Kaitling said. *Let's see what he does with that.*

The inspector continued taking notes long after Peter had finished. All eyes were turned on the man, waiting for him to react.

"Miss Wit said it was you that damaged your sister's dress."

"I hardly see that is relevant," the Headmaster put in. "If you are here to question McCloud about the unfortunate accident with Miss Wit, one of our newest pupils, I can't see that a dispute about a dress is pertinent."

Peter wanted to hug the Headmaster. What a wonderful man. Instead he kept his eyes fixed on the inspector. He would have liked to voice his suspicions about Witless, but he had no proof.

"What you have said is substantially what your mother told me. Although she was convinced you were the culprit."

Peter shrugged. "There's not much you can do with mothers once they've got an idea in their heads." He immediately regretted having been so pretentious, but the Headmaster chuckled, albeit briefly.

"Talking about your mother, I wondered what was wrong with her?"

"Why do you say that?" Peter asked, worried.

"She wasn't at work and when I went to your home, I found her ill in bed."

Peter was shocked. He'd suspected as much, but mothers didn't just get ill like that and take to their beds.

"I thought she looked tired," he said remembering how he had found her gray. "But I didn't know she was ill. I thought she'd left for work. She often goes before we get up."

We can check on her when you go home, Kaitling said. *I'm sure between the two of us, we'll get her healthy again. In the mean time, I'm off. I want to find a good place to shelter.*

"Do you think I should go home?" Peter asked.

The inspector glanced at the Headmaster. "No. I don't think so. She said she would call the doctor. Apparently your sister is ill too."

Peter nodded, still worried.

Once the policeman had left, Peter sat back down in an armchair dazed, staring blankly in the direction of the window.

"Are you alright, McCloud?"

"Yes, Sir. Just a little worried about Mum."

"I'm sure things will work out."

"Thank you, Sir. I mean thanks for not leaving me in the grips of that man. I really appreciate it."

"I thought you handled him very well."

"I wouldn't have managed if you hadn't been here."

"Listen," the Headmaster said, his tone serious. "If you have any further trouble with Miss Wit I want you to let me know, immediately."

Peter looked up, surprised. An ally?

"She had a difficult upbringing. Although you don't need to go around school telling everyone that, not that I think you would."

"I know about her troubles."

The Head raised an eyebrow. "This wasn't the first time

Miss Wit has caused you trouble?"

Peter hesitated. He didn't want to tattle, but the girl really was crazy. "She called me a pansy and spat in my face, saying she was going to kill me. From the first moment she entered our class on Friday I had the impression she'd singled me out..." Peter's voice trailed off as he wondered if he hadn't said too much. "I'm sorry. I didn't mean to tell tales."

"You are right, McCloud. Telling tales, as you call it, is not always a good thing, but there are circumstances that require it, especially if keeping a secret will cause even more harm. Some people count on the silence of others."

"Thank you."

"I hope your mother gets better quickly and your sister too."

Now was the time to go. Peter got to his feet, thanking the Head one last time and left.

19.

The last period of the morning was cancelled. Most of Peter's classmates hung around waiting for lunch. One or two made a brave attempt at doing homework, most chattered, a few went out to the playground. Peter wanted to find a quiet spot to visit Kaitling. Locking himself in the toilets was a possibility, but he couldn't face the stink. He finally opted for the wood on the far side of the playing field. Pupils rarely went there and no class was using the fields.

Having skirted the rugby pitch and crossed the cricket ground, he sauntered into the woods. The word 'wood' was a gross exaggeration. There were a dozen trees and a number of bushes in a small area. Copse would have been a better word, but everyone called it 'the woods', so he did too. He sat with his back against an oak, hidden from view by a couple of bushes. He made himself comfortable and closed his eyes...

I've found a place to stay, Kaitling said delighted. She showed him a memory of an old shack perched high in the mountains. The building had weathered well. The roof and walls were intact although covered with lichen and there was a sturdy door with tiny windows. It was set in a small dip in the ground amongst rock faces that surged abruptly to hundreds of feet above.

I'm glad you came. I'm going to see if anyone survived the Syvan attack, but I prefer not to go alone.

Using a vantage point above the rocky battlefield, she cautiously searched for soldiers waiting in ambush. None were to be seen.

Down on the site itself, Peter was unprepared for the horror. Bodies had been ripped apart, flesh gnawed off bones, and sculls lay discarded. Only the occasional fragment remained intact. The stench was unbearable.

The lions, Kaitling said, her emotions tightly under control. She walked through the remains of the gruesome meal, salvaging bows and arrows as well as a knife. They found no survivors. Then, to their surprise, behind a rocky outcrop they found a Syvan priest, his body untouched. The scary thing was that it was floating inches off the ground.

How did he manage to escape the lions? Kaitling wondered.

Maybe they didn't like the smell of him. Peter regretted he couldn't hold his nose.

No. This is something else. Kaitling prodded the body with a long stick. The moment it was within inches of the priest, it burst into flames. She dropped it and jumped back, her heart beating wildly.

Now we know why the lions left him alone, Peter said. *But how did he get killed?*

Magic probably. There are ways to kill people at a distance.

He looks as good as new, Peter thought, shuddering. *You don't think they could bring him back from the dead, do you?*

I doubt it.

Let's get out of here, Peter suggested, affected by her apprehension.

I don't like leaving him. You're right. Maybe they have a way of bringing him back.

Peter glanced at the stick, which was still smouldering. *We could try burning him,* he said, horrified at his own idea.

Without further discussion, Kaitling began gathering dry wood. *There'll be smoke. We'll have to wait till the last moment to start the fire. We'll need as much time as possible to get away.*

When she had a heap of wood, Kaitling tentatively pushed a large branch over the body. It burst into flames, hanging inches above the corpse.

This is not going to work, Peter exclaimed.

Kaitling ignored his scepticism and kept adding more and more branches, till all the wood was burning furiously. In the middle of the pyre, the priest's body began to blister and turn black. Then suddenly the flames roared upwards as the Priest came to life and sprang to his feet. The fire had finally reached the man who screamed in pain and lashed wildly about trying to quell the flames.

Let's get out of here, Kaitling urged, both of them wrestling with morbid fascination. She picked up the pile of weapons and ran back up the mountain path. Every few yards, she looked back at the burning priest. It was a relief when he broke free and careened down the mountain, trying to escape the flames that enveloped him.

Ten minutes later, Kaitling came to a halt gasping for breath. *That was terrible,* she said once her heaving lungs had calmed.

The scorched memories rose before his mind's eye like inescapable nightmares. To think I have to eat with Fi now. Blast! He suddenly realised he was going to be late. *Can you cope here, Kaitling?*

Sure, she said as she continued up the path, heading for her shack. *Once I've put all this away, I'll come and meet that Fi of yours.*

Peter was worried that might not be a good idea.

I'll stay quiet and out of the way, she said, playfully, *you won't even notice I'm there.*

That's what worries me, he thought and hurried off.

He glanced at his watch. He still had time. Peering round the bush, he saw Fi hadn't yet arrived. Instead, a band of older boys were crossing the pitch. Noisy, jostling each other, throwing mock punches, they were the sort of trouble he didn't need.

Peter ducked behind the bush, but too late. A shout went up. He could hear them hurrying in his direction, their voices jubilant. Out running them would not be possible. This was the rugby elite.

He got to his feet, stiff from sitting so long and stretched his legs. If only he'd learnt from Kaitling, he might be able to defend himself.

He stepped away from the bush, afraid he'd end up amongst its prickly branches and stood with his back to a tree, thinking it would stop anyone getting behind him.

The group came to a halt a few feet away. There were six of them, each a good head taller than him, each with the build of a rugby player. He glanced briefly at their faces. The rough lines of emerging manhood gave them a brutal, unfinished look.

One stepped forward, the biggest, the leader. "What you doing here, squirt? Playing with yourself?"

The others laughed at Peter's embarrassment.

The boy leaned forward, his face inches from Peter's, and pushed Peter against the tree. "Hey guys! We've caught one of those precocious wankers." The others guffawed, making rude gestures.

The boy shoved him against the tree. A knot in the trunk caught Peter in the small of his back, sending a sharp pain up his spine.

Trouble? Kaitling asked.

Am I glad to hear you.

Let me see them.

He glanced at each one in turn.

Now let me take over your body.

How?

Kaitling didn't bother to explain. She shoved him mentally aside and took control. In an instant, he was a stranger to himself, watching someone else possess his body.

She made him dodge, just in time. The big boy had aimed a punch at his face. Instead his fist hit the tree trunk with a resounding crunch. He fell to the ground, grasping his hand as he writhed in agony. Kaitling stepped aside to face the others.

Two of them flung themselves at Peter, all fists and elbows and feet. Kaitling cartwheeled out of the way only to turn and swipe one of the boys' feet from under him. He crashed head first into the tree and sank unmoving to the ground.

The second recovered his balance and turned on Peter, screaming abuse. Kaitling sidestepped, bringing Peter's fist down on the passing boy's shoulder causing him to topple to the ground, his collarbone probably broken.

Three remained. He could see that one was edging round to get at him from behind. Kaitling pretended not to notice. She was enjoying the fight and was confident she would win. When the one behind tried to jump on Peter, she elbowed him in the stomach and used his outstretched hand to fling him over her shoulder.

The two others chose that moment to attack, managing to get close enough to grab Peter by the arms. One pummelled him in the ribs. The pain was excruciating. Kaitling jerked Peter's knee up into the boy's groin causing him to sink to the ground clutching his crotch. The last of the boys pushed with all his might against Peter's nose, trying to force it back into his head. He could hardly breath.

Now let's finish this, Kaitling said. She grasped the boy's wrists and rolled over backwards, thrusting Peter's feet into the boy's stomach, projecting him onwards over Peter's head. He landed screaming in the prickly bush.

How do you feel? Kaitling asked, relinquishing control of his body.

Peter slumped to his knees bruised and exhausted, like a string puppet with the strings cut.

I think they've broken my ribs. A sharp knife-like pain stab where they'd pummelled him.

Stay still, Kaitling ordered plunging inside his body. Little by little, his ribs shifted into place and the breaks knitted together. It was a very strange feeling, as if his body had a mind of its own. Despite its oddity, he watched closely, just in case he ever needed to mend someone's broken ribs.

Good, she said after a few minutes. *Your chest will be a bit sore, but the ribs are no longer broken. I could have taken time to set the tissues and muscles right, but I believe you have an appointment.*

Oh blast! He looked across the playing field where he could see Fi pacing up and down by the wall.

What about them? Peter nodded at the heap of boys.

Let them have some time to think.

You know they'll come for revenge.

Then you are going to need to learn to defend yourself.

20.

"Hey Peter!" Fi greeted him with a smile that quickly gave way to a look of concern. "Your nose is bleeding!"

He lifted his hand to his nose and, sure enough, it came away covered in blood.

Fi pulled out a handkerchief and began delicately dabbing the blood away.

"You've been in a fight!" she scolded. "Pretty boys don't get in fights. You'll spoil your lovely looks."

Remembering the hard features of the older boys her fears seemed pointless, his face would change soon enough, with or without fights.

"Naughty," she said, taping him lightly on the chest. He winced, at which she looked at him questioningly. He just shrugged, feeling Kaitling busy easing his sore rib cage.

He longed to talk to someone about Kaitling, but hesitated to tell Fi. He knew it was silly, but he was afraid she'd be jealous. What's more, he didn't want to share Kaitling with Fi, or anyone else, a thought that he was careful to hide from Kaitling. The girl was keeping a low profile, as she'd promised she would.

"So? Are you going to tell me what happened?" Fi asked.

"Just a misunderstanding. I'll explain later. Where are we going?"

"How about fish 'n chips? Then we can go to the quay."

The quay was a large cobblestoned area by the river dating from the days when the Frayne had been alive with sailboats and barges. Now, with Tallford transformed into a sleepy town for commuters, the only boats in sight were permanently moored to the riverbank. People staying at the nearby riverside hotel or dining in its restaurant used the quay as a car park, as did those who came down on day trips from London some fifty miles away. They visited the church, a local monument, which lay in the square behind the hotel.

The fish 'n chips shop was in the high street, a few strides from the quay. It was a dingy hole, its walls slick with accumulated cooking fat. Only the foolhardy and those with no sense of smell braved the cod-filled atmosphere longer than it took to get served. Fi paid for the cod and chips that they received sprinkled with vinegar and salt all wrapped in several sheets of the local newspaper. They were making their getaway when a group of older pupils from their school entered. Peter couldn't help overhearing their conversation.

"...Six of them. They all had to go to hospital..."

He tried to hang back to hear more, but Fi hustled him out, paying no heed to the gossip.

Several benches were still free by the riverside, but Fi suggested they cross the bridge and sit on the grass on the other side.

"There will be fewer people to overhear us," she said.

The bridge was built of stone from a local quarry. It was age-old and too narrow for two cars to cross. They found a grassy spot in a slight dip in the ground with a sizable rock against which they could lean. A nearby bush shielded them from passers by.

As they ate, Peter told her about the police inspector.

Fi whistled when she heard what the Head had done. "I would never have believed him capable of such kindness. Rumour has it he is severe and unbending. Sounds like you got lucky, pretty boy. Maybe he fancies you."

Peter shook his head. He couldn't understand why Fi was always imagining men swooning at his feet.

Ask her, Kaitling suggested, making him jump.

He'd completely forgotten her silent presence.

Sorry, she apologised. *I did say I'd keep quiet.*

"I don't get it," he said. "What appeals to you so much about men being attracted to me?"

Fi screwed up the remains of the fish in a tight ball of greasy newspaper as she thought. "Many men like pretty boys," she finally replied.

"But why does it matter to you?"

She was about to toss paper ball into the river, but he stopped her and stuffed it in a corner of his satchel.

"Maybe if men are interested in you, it confirms who you are."

"I don't have that impression. Why should I need the interest of men to make me feel that I'm..." He hesitated about the word to use. "...complete?"

I bet it's the interest of men in you that makes her feel complete, Kaitling thought, stressing the word 'her'.

Peter shook his head. The strange, three-way conversation was getting too complicated.

"Why do you shake your head?" Fi asked.

"I have the impression this business with me and men has to do with you, not me."

"Wow! Pretty boy has a mind of his own. You really are not interested in men?"

"No. I'm fascinated by girls."

"Are you fascinated by me?" she asked shifting closer.

He wanted to move away, but he knew he couldn't do that. He was embarrassed by the turn the conversation had taken knowing that Kaitling heard not only everything that was said, but much of what he thought. He'd never taken the time to ask himself what feelings he had for Kaitling, but he certainly didn't want to upset her by admitting he really was fascinated by Fi.

Tell her the truth, Kaitling broke in.

Peter sighed, a sigh that was immediately misinterpreted by Fi who inched closer. "Yes," he admitted. "I have been fascinated by you ever since you first came to visit Sis. Any excuse was

good to be near you. It wasn't easy. Sis did everything she could
to keep you to herself..."

"That's lovely, my pretty boy," she said, leaning even closer
so she could run her outstretched fingers through his hair.

He was afraid she might cross the remaining inches and kiss
him. He wasn't ready for that. He felt himself blush scarlet and
drew back beyond reach.

"So what are we going to do with Witless?" he asked, banking on a change of subject to escape his embarrassment.

She chuckled and sat up straight. "My mother is working
at Our Lady of Grace this evening. She has to reclassify all the
girls' reports and she has agreed to let us help her move boxes
around."

"Great. What time?"

"Around five. Is that alright with you?"

"Sure. I'll hang around school and finish my homework.
There won't be enough time for me to return home. Where will
we meet?"

There's an emergency, Kaitling interrupted his train of
thoughts. *I have to go. Join me as soon as you can.* And she was
gone.

Fi must have noticed something was going on because she
said: "You are odd today, my pretty boy. Do you feel OK?"

"Maybe it was the fight," he said.

"It's more than that," Fi insisted. "It's as if you are period-
ically absent. Your face goes vacant, turned inwards on your
thoughts. What are you up to in your head?" she asked, chuckling at her own image.

"If I tell you a secret, can you keep it?"

Now that had her excited! She sat bolt upright, her eyes
gleaming, eager to know more. "Sure. Tell me all."

"There's an island called Drailong, and that island is ruled
by a group of twelve magicians..."

"I thought you were going to tell me a secret, not a tale."

"Patience. It's complicated. Are you going to listen?"

She nodded.

"One of the Twelve, as they are called has a daughter called Kaitling who is about my age." Saying her name out loud for the first time gave him a thrill that troubled him. "Well one day, I'm not sure how, I found myself in Kaitling's head."

Fi's face was incredulous. "What do you mean, you were in her head?"

"I suddenly found myself looking through her eyes, feeling her body, hearing her thoughts..."

"You see. I said you were a pretty boy!" And she hugged him.

He waited till she'd calmed and went on. "I admit, for a short while I thought I had become a girl. I often imagined that happening. But it wasn't like that at all. I was not her. I was separate. She had her own thoughts. I had mine."

"Good lord." Fi stared at him in amazement.

"It happened several times. I had no control over when and where. Then she was in my head here in this world and she spoke to me for the first time. Apparently she had been experimenting in travelling between minds and something about me made it easier for her to reach me, even though I live in a completely different world. She's an apprentice magician," he added by way of explanation. "Her father and other Master Magicians took time to train her."

"This is extraordinary!" Fi looked as if she would spring to her feet at any moment and start pacing the riverbank, such was her excitement. "Can I meet her?"

So much for Fi being jealous. "She just had to leave."

"You mean she's been here all this time, and you said nothing." She pouted. "I thought we were good friends. You might at least have introduced us."

"It's complicated. Her island has just been attacked by warrior priests called Syvans. She had to flee her home with a group of scholars, a cook and her daughter and the gamekeeper. They were chased by brutal soldiers and all her group were slaughtered except her."

Peter shuddered at the memory. "It was terrible." Tears

welled up in his eyes. "Kaitling is hiding in a shack in the Warsi Mountains. She almost got killed by a lion ... She has to hide and hunt her food..."

"Extraordinary! You must show me how to travel like that."

The whole unbelievable story didn't seem to unsettle her at all. If the tables had been turned and Fi had told him such a tale, he wasn't sure he would have believed her.

"I'm not sure how I do it," Peter told her. "It just happened. Then Kaitling taught me a lot of things." He decided not to boast about healing. He could tell her that some other day. "Maybe she could help you travel between minds too, but you would need someone to travel to and she's all alone."

He felt a tugging at his mind. He guessed it was Kaitling calling him. "I have to go," he told Fi. "Kaitling just called. Could you do me an immense favour?"

Fi looked cautious. "What?"

"If I travel to Drailong, I have to leave my body here. I can't take it with me. Could you look after it for me for a short while? If anything happens or I take too long, just shake me gently."

She looked disappointed. "I want to come."

"I know. We'll try to fix it so you can come next time. Ok?"

Fi nodded, still looking upset. He bent forward and kissed her gently on the forehead. "We'll figure out a way for you to come too."

She lay her back against the rock, pulled a book out of her pocket and began reading. He curled up next to her, laying his head in her lap, and closed his eyes. The last thing he felt as he slipped away were her fingers twisting in and out of his hair.

21.

Kaitling sat, her head cradled in her hands, her back leaned against the rough wall of her shack, sadness and anger vying for control.

What's the matter? Peter asked, worried.

Navigon has fallen. Many of the Twelve have been killed. The country is in chaos. Syvan soldiers and priests are everywhere while I am here, alone and unable to do anything.

Peter ignored the comment about being alone. *What about your father?*

He escaped and is leading the resistance.

How come you know all this?

I managed to speak mind-to-mind with father just now. He's on the run. He wouldn't tell me where he was, but said he would contact me as soon as he could. He warned me to be very careful and told me to hide as best I could. If the Syvans catch me, he thinks they will try to use me against him.

Let's look out back and see if there is somewhere to hide.

Kaitling agreed. *I'll bring my few belongings, just in case.*

She gathered up the weapons and supplies in a makeshift bag and slung it over her shoulder.

Behind the shack the ground dipped, forming a shallow hallow where digging must have gone on, then the cliff face rose abruptly to peaks hundreds of feet above. They scouted round the hallow, Kaitling taking them to a number of large rocks scattered at the foot of the cliff.

These must have fallen recently, she thought.

He quickly understood why she went there. Concealed behind one of the rocks was a low tunnel burrowed into the mountainside.

It's not going to be easy without light.

He felt Kaitling smile and a bright light burst into life in the palm of her outstretched hand.

Do that again so I can learn how you did it.

I doubt you'll be able to. It took me months of hard practice. Few magicians manage.

Well the more I learn, the more I can help.

She showed him again and then a third time while he studied the way her mind focussed energy and turned it into light.

Can you separate it from your hand?

She had never tried. With considerable effort she lifted the small ball of light a couple of inches above her palm.

Let me try. He went through the same motions as her, but nothing happened.

It's not the same, she reminded him. *You're trying to use my body and my energy to do magic. That must be much more difficult.*

Let me try again. Once more he was unsuccessful.

You are making took much effort. Think how you slipped into the lion cub. You did next to nothing. Make the ball of light with no more effort than that.

Effortless! What a paradox! It was almost as if he had to let the ball of light create itself. At the thought, a ball of light appeared in Kaitling's hand and rose majestically into the air.

Well done, she said, her pride at his success leaving him elated.

This kind of learning suits me perfectly. Apart from maths at school, I was never much good at anything.

I still have to visit that school of yours.

Kaitling set off down the tunnel with the ball of light hovering a short distance in front of her. After a few strides it began to dim. *You've got to keep it going,* Kaitling warned. *You created it. It's yours to handle. I can't simply take it over.*

She advanced cautiously till she reached a crossing. *I don't want to get lost,* she thought. Pulling a hunting knife from her bag. It had been the gamekeeper's. The memory made her sad. She'd liked the man and enjoyed their walks in the forest. Brushing away the thought, she scratched a sign on the rocks before taking one of the turnings.

Up to that point the tunnel had clearly been man-made, the walls showed signs of being hacked out of the rocks. Once they left the crossing, the tunnel curved and wound, its walls and ceiling smooth, as if it had been formed by the constant swirling of water, leaving treacherous holes in the floor where it must once have escaped.

Tell me how you communicate mind-to-mind, he asked. *I really need to know. Just in case.*

She shuddered, wondering if he meant she might die, but he immediately reassured her. *I want to be able to help you.*

It is similar to when you enter my mind, except you are not really inside, only your voice is. You can't feel the person's body in the same way and most of the emotions are masked.

How do you make the connection?

I generally picture the person in my head as strongly as I can and then reach out to her with my thoughts.

Can I try? I've told Fi about you and she's looking after my body at this very moment. Maybe it will be easier if she is physically just next to me.

Kaitling had mixed feeling about Fi being aware of her existence. Peter suspected she was annoyed but was masking the fact.

You remember what we said about apprentices who couldn't keep a secret, she nudged him mentally.

I know. They're a liability. But Fi is my best friend and I trust her. Without her I couldn't be here with you now.

As they talked they penetrated ever deeper into the mountainside.

Go on. Kaitling still sounded a bit peeved.

Are you jealous?

Who me? Why should I be jealous of a girl who knows next to nothing?

It struck him, but he kept the thought to himself, that she might be jealous of Fi for having him physically present when she could only have his thoughts.

I'll try. It'll only be a test.

Just don't use my brain to send sweet words to the girl, Kaitling said, sounding increasingly irritated.

Peter giggled mentally. *I have never ever said such things to her. I doubt I ever will.*

I know what boys are like, she scoffed. *The moment a girl bats her eyelids, they go weak at the knees and can't think of anything else.*

He decided to take the risk and tease her. *Of course,* he said, *I am lying there in her arms - well my body is - while I chatter here with you.*

She gave him a mental shove that almost drove him out of her mind.

Hey! I was only teasing.

Well don't. I don't like it.

He could feel that Kaitling's sadness was getting the upper hand.

I'm sorry, and he really was. He didn't want to upset her.

Try then, if you must.

Behind her words he could just make out a sneaking interest as to whether he would succeed.

He set himself to think of Fi, her short black hair, her slim face and figure, her high cheek bones, her sparkling blue eyes, her clothes an outrageous colour. Kaitling even generously added a few details. Then he spoke: *Fi.*

"Peter?" she asked. He imagined her looking around to see where his voice came from.

Don't be frightened, he tried to reassure her. *I'm talking into your mind. I'm still in Kaitling's world.*

"Say hallo to her for me," Fi said.

Hallo Fiona, Kaitling spoke, startling both Peter and Fi. *Nice to make your acquaintance.*

"Kaitling, isn't it?" Fi said intimidated. "Do call me Fi. I told Peter I wanted to come and visit you. I'd really like that."

It's not a very good moment, Fi. I'm being chased by a band of very unpleasant priests who have invaded my country and killed a lot of my friends.

"Peter told me some of your story. I'd still like to come."

Well, maybe Peter can teach you how to talk mind-to-mind even if you can't travel.

Peter sensed that Kaitling didn't relish the idea of having Fi in her head. *Is it time to return to school, Fi?* he asked.

"Oh yes!" Fi exclaimed. "We are going to be dreadfully late."

I'll be back in a few minutes, Peter said and he broke the communication.

Well you seem to have mastered that, Kaitling commented. *It's not fair. You realise it took me ages to learn to do these things and even now I can't always manage to contact my father, despite desperately needing to.*

I think it helps having you show me in your head. If I were standing next to you and you tried to explain, I don't think it would work so well.

Maybe, she muttered. *So you have to go?* He could hear regret in her voice. It was going to be lonely slogging through the tunnel under the mountain alone.

I have to. We are obliged to go to this pointless thing we call school. They will punish my mother and me if I don't!

Kaitling made one of those mental snorts she was so good at. *Poor you.* Her voice was heavy with irony.

Call me mind-to-mind if anything happens, and he withdrew.

He had been lying in an uncomfortable position next to Fi and his arm and leg were all pins and needles. He stretched and staggered to his feet with Fi's help.

"That was extraordinary," Fi enthused and she hugged him, almost knocking him to the ground in her enthusiasm.

They hurried along the path towards the bridge when Kaitling's voice resounded in his head. *Peter,* she called out. *This is terrible.*

He must have looked shocked because Fi asked: "What's the matter?"

"It's Kaitling." He grabbed Fi's hand, much to her surprise. Using that contact, he relayed Kaitling's words to Fi.

That tunnel we were walking down opens up into a horrible place, Kaitling said.

The full intensity of her horror hit him as if it were his own.

I can't come now, he said, desperate about what to do. *I'm in the middle of a busy street.*

"Let's go to my place," Fi put in. "It's near here and you can stay there while I go to school and say you are ill."

Peter wondered what Kaitling thought about having Fi listening in on their conversation.

Do it! Kaitling said, deciding for him. *I need you here.* With which she broke the communication.

Peter let go of Fi's hand as they hurried up the high street, heading for Fi's house. It wouldn't do for them to be seen holding hands. There would be too much gossip.

"Where were you and Kaitling?"

"In a tunnel that led deep under the mountains."

They reached Fi's house and the girl let them in. The place was deserted.

"Mum's visiting friends. She shouldn't be back for a couple of hours." She led him up to her room and set an alarm clock for an hour later. "You should leave when this goes off. It might be complicated explaining to my Mum what a pretty boy is doing on my bed." She grinned. "No wearing my clothes when I'm not here!" And she wagged her finger at him.

He had the uncomfortable feeling that her message was the opposite to her words. The thought made him blush.

"Will you come to school later?" she asked, ignoring his embarrassment.

"Yes. In just over an hour."

"Ok. I'll tell them the fish made you ill and that you hope to come when your stomach settles." She handed him a house key and left.

Peter looked around Fi's room. It hadn't changed much since he was last there. Her brightly coloured clothes hung from hangers just waiting to be used. He forced himself to look away. The bed had not been made, so he pulled the blankets into place, pulled off his shoes and lay down, resting his head on Fi's pillow.

As he closed his eyes, the smell of Fi was so strong he had difficulty concentrating. It was like he was a part of Fi, when he needed to become a part of Kaitling. The more he tried, the less he felt able to return to Drailong. It had always been so easy before. He broke in a sweat. What if he could no longer do it?

Are you coming? Kaitling asked in his head, startling him and in that moment he sped across the immense distance between them and was once again with the young magician.

22.

Peter could see nothing. It wasn't that Kaitling had her eyes closed. The place was pitch dark.

What happened to the light?

I was afraid it would wake them.

Who?

Them! Kaitling whispered as she created a small spark of light, just large enough to make out row upon row of sleeping men, each suspended inches off the ground. The moment he'd seen, she extinguished the light.

Peter was not sure if it was Kaitling or himself that was trembling with shock. She had hurried under the mountain for hours to get away from the Syvan priests and all the time she had been heading for the very place where an army of them were sleeping.

This is terrible, he thought. He strained to listen. He could hear nothing. No breathing. No snoring. Not the slightest movement.

I think they are like the one we killed, suspended somehow, waiting to come to life. I doubt the light will wake them.

Kaitling tentatively created a ball of light as she approached the nearest priest. His face was hard, his lips pursed in disgust, his eyes tightly shut. He made no movement as the light came close.

I think you're right. Kaitling enlarged the light, illuminating a much larger area. Peter counted. There were more than a hundred in the cavern, all alike. They wore the same deep blue robes that reached to their ankles, but it was the similarity between their faces that was the most striking.

They can't always be suspended like that, Kaitling thought. *I never heard of the priests floating around Syvatoy.*

It's some sort of protection, Peter speculated. *Do you think they might burn like the other one?*

Both of them shuddered at the memory of the flaming priest careening down the mountainside.

I bet they were put here ready to invade, Peter thought.

Which means someone will be coming to wake them up, Kaitling said, alarmed.

If it were me, Peter thought, *I wouldn't have put them all in one place, just in case anything happened.*

Let's hope these are the only ones. How could they possibly need more?

Have you explored this place? Peter asked. *Are there any other exits?*

I haven't had time. I called you immediately. She sounded defensive.

I wasn't finding fault, he thought, trying to reassure her. *I just wanted to know.*

I'm sorry. This place spooks me. To think these monsters have been sent to rule my people.

We need to destroy them, Peter said. *That's why I want to find another way out. What is on the other side of the Warsi Mountains?*

Ah, I see what you mean, Kaitling said, following his line of thought. *Yes, you're right there's the sea. They could have shipped them in that way. Nobody would have noticed. The tunnel must go to the sea.*

When this lot are awake, they'll probably leave the way we came in, Peter thought. *So if there is no third way, which one do we take? Shack or sea?*

Sea, I guess, Kaitling said. All this time she moved cautiously amongst the ranks of sleeping priests looking for the other exit.

It was a creepy experience. Peter couldn't help feeling that she would turn round and find a priest propped up on his elbow eyeing them. But no one moved. When they had crossed the complete length of the cavern, Kaitling began skirting the walls in search of a door.

If there is one, it's well hidden, she said.

Could they have sealed it up once the priests were in?

Too dangerous. What if the other exit was blocked?

They continued searching. *Could both exists be out the same door?* Peter asked when they had come full circle and found nothing.

Kaitling heaved open the heavy metal door and began searching along the tunnel. Sure enough, some ten yards down, a tunnel branched off to the right. They followed it as it curved around what must be the cavern and then headed in the direction of the sea.

Kaitling halted. *So what do we do? I can't see how we could possibly destroy a hundred of those priests. Look at the effort it required to burn one. We didn't even really manage that.*

Peter's imagination was chasing a wild idea. *How do you think that cavern was built? It would take years for men to dig it out of the rocks. What's more the walls are so smooth. Let's go back and look.*

Kaitling was following his train of thought.

So you think it was water that did all this?

Yes. If there's water, I wonder how those fire-spitting priests will react to it? If they don't drown in it, they might at least cook.

Despite her scepticism, Kaitling turned back and went to the large cavern in search of signs of water. Now they were paying attention to it, they noticed that the floor was not flat but was marked with large whirling patterns as if they had been worn out of the rock by the passing of water. The largest of these rock whirlpools lay on the other side of the cavern, farthest from the door. Carefully examining the roof, they found the place where water had once cascaded into the cavern. It had been sealed with a metal plate that was solidly fixed to the rock.

We'll never be able to move that, Kaitling remarked.

Let me think this through, Peter said. *If we can get the water to flow in here, there's a chance that the priests' bodies will react with fire and that will heat the water and produce steam. If we can close the door, the pressure of the steam will rise and with any luck all our friends here will be cooked. The only risk is that the pressure will blow the door off its hinges sending boiling water down the tunnel. If we take the other tunnel, the one to the sea, we must find a way to stem the flow of water in that direction so we can get away.*

What if they don't react with fire?

We can test that once we're ready. It didn't wake that priest when you tried to touch him with a stick.

Once again, Peter could sense Kaitling's scepticism. *I know, he was supposed to be dead.*

Fine, but how do we remove that metal plate? Kaitling asked. *And how do we block the other tunnel?*

Let's look at the tunnel first, Peter suggested.

They were in luck, concealed in the rock wall was a large round bolder that could be rolled out and used to seal the entrance. *I bet they made that deliberately,* Peter said. *If ever water were to escape.*

Kaitling tried to move the boulder but it was far too heavy. Back in the cavern they looked for tools. *Maybe there's a crow bar,* Peter thought. Kaitling had no idea what that was, so Peter showed her an image of one. But they found nothing.

Go back to the boulder, Peter said. He studied its shape and position. *You know what? I think this boulder will naturally block the entrance if ever there's any volume of water flowing around here. Look how the floor slopes. Look at these channels behind the thing. The water would flow in here.* He mentally pointed to one such channel. *That would force the boulder out. Judging from these marks around the entrance, it has already happened more than once.*

They hurried back to the cavern. The most difficult task remained to be done: the metal plate was just out of reach.

What about that long hunting knife, Peter asked.

Kaitling pulled it out of her bag and was relieved to see she could now chip away at the rock next to the plate.

Look, she said, *it's a bit damp there.*

Concentrating on that point, her work became a little easier as the rock crumbled when she hacked at it. A small piece of rock flew across the cavern and burst into flames above one of the priests.

Well, at least that much is clear, she said.

Her arms were beginning to ache from working above her head at the limit of her reach, when a first drop of water falling down her neck rewarded her efforts. The water was icy cold. It took quite a while before the occasional drop transformed into a steady stream. Then the pent up weight of water forced a much larger hole in the roof and a torrent of water cascaded into the cavern. Kaitling jumped back, almost bumping into one of the priests. Turning to flee, she saw to her horror that the water was rising rapidly and a thick cloud of steam formed as the water came into contact with the priests. It was very difficult to make out the way to the door.

Follow the wall round, Peter shouted.

It wasn't so easy. Sleeping priests surrounded by bubbling water and clouds of steam floated freely around the cavern bumping into each other and threatening at any moment to hit her. Despite her terror and her exhaustion, she waded through the rising water, pushing priests away with the point of the hunting knife.

When she finally reached the exit, water was already beginning to flow down the tunnel. She pushed her weight against the door managing to shift it slightly till the weight of the water snapped it shut with a resounding crash.

Run, Peter shouted.

The smooth rock face underfoot was slippery with the water but she made it to the turning without mishap and set off down the curving tunnel trying to get as far away from the cavern before the pressure made it blow up.

Peter maintained a bright light in front of her as she ran, dodging around the natural curves in the passageway. She couldn't run flat out because there were frequent holes in the ground where the water must have once seeped away. Her breathing was coming hard and fast. She wouldn't be able to run much further.

A sinister rumbling began behind her. It got louder, culminating in a high-pitched whistle. Then a tremor shook the walls of the tunnel and rocked the floor beneath her feet. She staggered forward and fell to her knees as the whole mountain shook. Aghast, Peter watched pieces of rock breaking from the walls and falling around Kaitling as she crawled forward on all fours.

A small piece of rock hit her shoulder sending a searing pain along her arm and across her chest.

I'll heal it for you, but you must keep going.

He didn't want to do the healing while she was moving so he spent his time dampening the pain.

Eventually, the anger of the mountain subsided and the tremors ceased. The path was strewn with rocks of various sizes, but Kaitling was able to continue. Finally she saw a growing light at the end of the tunnel.

Stop, he said. *The trembling is over and you will be safe here while I do the healing. Who knows what awaits you outside?*

Her collarbone was broken and the shoulder badly damaged. There had been some haemorrhage. He set the bone quickly and efficiently. He was glad the body knew how it ought to be. In fact, all he had to do was give Kaitling's body the encouragement and force it needed to put itself back together properly. He wasn't sure what to do with the haemorrhage but Kaitling gave him a few tips and soon he'd finished.

Eat something, he suggested, *and have a drink before you go outside.* She did as she was told.

You are my favourite personal healer, she said, smiling, albeit weakly.

Once she'd eaten, she got stiffly to her feet. Her knees and hands were grazed and she ached all over. Holding on to the wall of the tunnel for support, she eased her way towards the light.

At the entrance to the tunnel, once her eyes had adjusted to the sunlight, she was horrified at what she saw. In a make-shift harbour below, a dozen boats were moored, each teeming with Syvan soldiers and priests. It was at that moment that he was called urgently back to his body by a hand on his shoulder. *I'll be back immediately,* he thought to Kaitling, unsure if she'd heard him.

23.

As he came back to his body, Peter had only one thought in mind: return to Kaitling as fast as possible. Instinctively, however, he remained motionless and kept his eyes closed, trying to figure out what had brought him back. It had not been the alarm clock, of that he was sure. Then he felt it. Someone was sitting next to him on Fi's bed, a woman judging from the perfume.

Whoever it was held his hand and stroked his fingers gently, almost lovingly. The movement sent strange shivers down his back. He was sure it wasn't Fi. The hand was bigger, older, drier, with harder patches and longer, sharper nails.

He didn't have time to wait to know who it was, especially when there was a quicker way to get the answer. Making the most of her hand holding his, he slipped into the other person's mind.

Each new person would surely be a shock the first time, but being in this older woman's body was very strange. It was almost as if he'd entered the body of his own mother. It didn't seem right, as if he'd crossed a forbidden line. Not only were all her thoughts exposed, but every minute feeling was plain to feel. He kept his presence as small and as insignificant as possible, hoping she would not sense him in her mind. It was not easy. What he heard and saw sparked emotions that he was hard pressed to conceal.

I wish I'd been able to have a son, the woman thought.

Several sequences of images followed, memories presumably: Fi being born, a cute little baby; the woman's joy at her first child; the woman pregnant again. "It's a boy," a friendly doctor had told her. Then the birth and everything had gone wrong. She skipped the details. All she could think of was that she'd lost him the moment he came into the world. Tears ran down her cheeks as she remembered the doctor's words. "I'm sorry, Mrs. Tanner. It is very unlikely you'll be able to have another baby."

The woman's mind shied away from the suffering. Instead, she focussed her attention on Peter, on his face, his wavy brown hair, his full mouth. It was extremely disturbing to see himself in her eyes. He hadn't realised his eyebrows were so bushy and his nose had a slight kink in it. None of this mattered to her. She saw him as beautiful and he felt her body fill with intense desire. Not the sort of desire he imagined a woman might feel for a man, rather that of a mother for her long lost son.

Suddenly he remembered Kaitling stranded close to all those soldiers. He had no time to waste. He had to get away immediately. He could just drift off and leave his body at her mercy, but he sensed her concern. She wondered what was wrong and why he was lying on Fi's bed. She was contemplating waking him.

Speaking in her head would probably send her screaming from the room. Images, he thought, I need to send her images to help her understand. So he showed her a picture of him eating with Fi and waited to see how she reacted. He was relieved she took it to be a product of her own imagination, so he sent another image of himself being ill and ended up with Fi helping him to lie down on her bed.

She seemed satisfied with what she'd seen and decided to let him sleep. He was about to leave her mind when he realised that she had withdrawn her hand. The familiar panic at being stranded in someone else's body rolled over him, but he steeled himself and jumped, surprised at how easy it was.

As he prepared to return to Kaitling, he promised himself he would return one day, once he'd found out how to heal her so she could have the son she so much craved. Fi might also be delighted to have a little brother.

Peter found Kaitling lying unconscious. He immediately set about checking for damage: broken ribs, but no hurt to her lungs; a bad cut over her left eye that was swollen and very sore; bruises galore especially on her back, chest and legs; several broken bones in her right hand, she must have hit someone very hard; the skin around her wrists was chafed where she had struggled with whatever it was that attached her.

He set about healing her, hoping that no one would notice. The inner damage would surely not be visible, but when he came to her face and wrists he hesitated. Healing them would be too conspicuous. It wouldn't do for the priests to think she had magic and could heal herself. He opted to heal the deeper wounds on her wrists and above her eye but left the wounds on the surface untouched.

Once he'd finished, he felt tired. The healing must have drained him, he'd never noticed before, but then he had never had to do so much in one go. He sat back, as it were, and did something he'd never done before, he rifled through Kaitling's recent memories, hoping to find out what had happened.

A long column of soldiers marched up towards the tunnel, headed by a priest, their feet ringing ominously on the rock path. They must have heard the explosion, Kaitling thought. Fear gripped her as she realised she had scant place to hide. She crouched behind a tiny bush next to the entrance, holding her breath. The column marched by and disappeared into the tunnel. Relieved, she was about to get up when a heavy hand grabbed her shoulder and a blow hit the side of her head.

The wooden planks beneath her feet rolled gently from side to side as she staggered up. The place smelt of creosote. She must be on a boat. Her head ached where she had been hit. She struggled to clear her eyes, which refused to focus properly. When she finally managed, she found herself in a tiny cabin that was barely big enough for her to lie down.

Hands grabbed her, wrenching her from sleep as they pulled

her to her feet. She floored two of them before they realised what was happening. She fought bravely, Peter thought, but there were too many and they were much bigger than her. It was then that she'd got the broken ribs and a good deal of the bruises. The fight was short-lived. A beefy hand twice the size of hers shoved her back into the tiny room, sending her flying against the wall and the door was locked.

Peter was about to search for further memories, when he was startled by a deep and sinister voice rumbling in Kaitling's head: *You will no longer resist us when you wake up, woman.*

Peter scuttled into a tiny corner of Kaitling's mind trying inconspicuously to search for the origin of the voice. He could feel no other presence in her head. Someone must be talking mind-to-mind. Whoever it was believed in the value of repetition, rather like some of his teachers, because the voice repeated the same phrase over and over. Peter wondered how much influence such a message could have and whether he could help her resist it.

He toyed with the idea of erasing the memory of the voice, but the message might be engraved in other parts of her brain as well. What could be worse than obeying a command without knowing where it came from? He'd heard of hypnosis and suspected it worked in such a way. It was at that moment, he felt Kaitling's consciousness stir and she slowly rose to the surface. *Don't move,* Peter whispered. *Someone is trying to influence you while you sleep.*

You will no longer ... The voice repeated one more time.

Kaitling wanted to hit out, but Peter persuaded her to keep still. *They know how to talk mind-to-mind,* he told her, *but I don't think they can enter people's minds. I can find no other presence in you.*

Thanks for coming back, she thought. *You can't imagine how comforting it is to be able to talk to you, if only in my head. It gives me the strength and will to go on.*

I saw how you fought those sailors, Peter said, proud of her.

You were here?

No. I looked at your memories, he admitted sheepishly.

That's all right, although I hope you don't make a habit of it. There are things a girl has to keep to herself, a weak smile colouring her words.

He blushed mentally and changed the subject.

Would it help if you could strengthen the protection around yourself?

But then you might not be able to get in.

Maybe you can do it progressively.

A heavy hand shaking Kaitling's shoulder interrupted their discussion. When she opened her eyes she found a priest standing over her, his face harsh and sullen.

"Get up!" he ordered. "Follow me!"

Kaitling was led along a narrow corridor walled with varnished wood. The priests did not look back. He seemed confident Kaitling would follow.

Do you think he believes you have swallowed that nonsense he spoke in your head?

Maybe.

If I get a chance I want to get into his head to find out what they are up to.

Be careful. Remember that fiery barrier around those priests. His body and mind might be protected.

I doubt it. He touched you, so he can't be protected. Don't worry, I'll be careful. I'm getting good at making a tiny speck of myself.

The priest led her to a large room in which three priests sat behind a long table. She was required to stand opposite them. An unpleasant smell of burning flesh had Peter cringing at the thought of torture.

The explanation was quick to surface. A sharp snapping noise caught his attention. The priests' fiery barrier around their bodies was an efficient repellent against flies buzzing in the room.

Do you think that's why they use that? Peter asked grinning.

Shhhh! Kaitling thought, tense. *I have to concentrate.*

At first the priests sat in silence staring, as if they were trying to intimidate her.

Maybe they are talking mind-to-mind amongst themselves, Peter guessed. When Kaitling stared back at them, a voice boomed in her head: *Lower your eyes, woman.*

She did as she was told.

What were you doing in the mountains, the voice pounded in her head?

These priests are not very subtle in their attempts to dominate, Peter thought to himself.

"Trying to escape the people who have invaded my country," Kaitling replied, speaking out loud. She didn't want them to know she could speak mind-to-mind.

Did you see priests in the mountains? the voice asked.

"No. I was trying to avoid them." She couldn't help being amused at her response, although she did her best to conceal it.

Cease your impertinence, the voice insisted.

"My apologies," Kaitling said, doing her best to appear meek.

What do you know about the Twelve?

"They rule our country."

Your father is one of them?

Kaitling hesitated a second, wondering if she should admit who her father was.

I'm sure they know, Peter commented.

"Yes," Kaitling replied.

Where is he?

"No idea," Kaitling said, having no need to pretend she was worried as tears came to her eyes.

Then, as abruptly as it began, the audience was over. The priest, who had brought her, reappeared and led her away along a corridor. They climbed several steep stairs and Kaitling found herself on the deck of a large sailing boat. The sailors ignored her. The boat must have set sail while she was unconscious because she could just make out a smudge of the distant coastline low on the horizon.

"This way," the priest said. He led her to a narrow gangway that straddled the waters to another, smaller boat.

"We are going on a journey?" she asked, once they'd balanced their way across.

He ignored her question and indicated she should go below where he locked her in a small cabin equipped with a bench that presumably served as a bed. The cabin, which smelt strongly of urine, was otherwise empty and without a window.

First class, Peter commented. Kaitling did not understand his joke and he didn't bother explaining. *I'm going to have to leave you,* Peter told her. *Call me if you need me. If not I'll be back in a couple of hours.*

24.

Back in his own body, Peter found his hand was being held once again, but this time he was sure it was Fi. He slipped unseen into her mind and whispered huskily: *How was your afternoon?*

Startled, she dropped his hand and jumped up.

Surely you must be used to having voices in your head when you are around me, he said in her mind, trying to convey amusement in his voice.

"Stop that!"

Peter returned to himself and opened his eyes, surveying Fi who was standing pouting next to her bed in her school uniform, yellow trimmed with bottle green.

"You look lovely when you pout." He made a show of imitating her.

She aimed a playful swipe in his direction. He grabbed her hand and pulled, catching her off balance, she toppled onto him, her chest landing across his face, her legs straddling his waist. For a brief moment he was completely enveloped in her warmth and he thought he might smother in the pleasure of it as he savoured her softness and breathed in deeply the smell of her body.

Rather than scramble off him, she lay there, tightening her grip around his waist as she rocked her chest from side to side across his face. He could have sworn he heard her moan, her chest heaving in shuddering breaths. He wanted to fling his arms around her and pull her even closer, as if that were possible. He wanted to drown in her, to lose himself completely. Instead, he struggled to get free, embarrassed at the surging desire he felt at having her so close. He would have rolled off the bed, had she not held onto him.

After a moment, she shifted so she was lying next to him and looked at him, her lips slightly open, her chest still heaving. He was sure his face must be bright red from being so tightly pressed against her blouse.

"You are not getting away that easily, pretty boy." She grabbed his hand and licked the end of his fingers with the tip of her tongue.

"What you need is some serious punishment."

Peter was not one for pain, on the contrary, the thought made him cringed, but being punished by Fi sounded fun.

"So what do you propose?" He grinned, calling her bluff.

Fi thought for long moment, flinging one arm casually around his waist as if she was afraid he'd try to escape.

"How about you walking down the high street in Tallford dressed as a girl?" Her eyes were bright with excitement.

Peter's stomach did a back flip as he envisaged himself in Fi's uniform doing window-shopping with her down the high street. He struggled to breath normally as he sought a response. Further bluffing would be dangerous. Fi was quite capable of going through with her threat.

He was relieved not to have to answer as someone knocked. Not waiting for a reply, Fi's mother opened the door and stepped inside. Fi and Peter hurriedly sat up, putting some distance between them. He blushed and, out of the corner of his eye, he could see Fi's face redden too. Far from being upset or annoyed, Fi's mother grinned. What a strange woman! His mother would have been furious.

Apart from his brief excursion into her mind, Peter had never met Fi's Mum. For a mother, she was quite pretty, although it was a shame about the shadows under her eyes and the wrinkles forming around her mouth and eyes. Like his mother, she wore too much makeup, but having been in her mind, he found it easier to be forgiving. Life was not always easy. Maybe that much makeup helped her face the day.

"I didn't mean to interrupt." Her eyes sparkled with amusement. "But if you two want to come to Our Lady of Grace, it's time."

"Mum, meet Peter," Fi said, getting to her feet, straightening her skirt and tucking her blouse back in place. "Peter, this is my Mum."

Peter got awkwardly to his feet. "Good afternoon, Mrs. Tanner." He still felt embarrassed, although not so much for what they'd just done, more for what he remembered of her thoughts and preoccupations. She held out her hand and he shook it, resisting the temptation to slip into her mind. She lingered a long moment holding his hand as if not believing he was real. He searched her face for signs of her longing for a son. Yes. It was there as was all the pain that went with her unfulfilled desire.

"Are you two glued together," Fi asked, giving Peter a shove. "You can't have him Mum, he's mine!" Fi took hold of his hand and pulled him closer, adding to his confusion.

Fi's Mum chuckled. "I was worried Peter was still feeling a little weak from being so sick?"

"How did you know about that?" Fi asked, surprised.

"I came home early. Imagine my surprise to find such a handsome boy, one I'd never seen before, asleep on my daughter's bed. He looked so tasty, I thought I'd have him for breakfast."

Peter shuddered. Had he really escaped such a fate?

Fi snorted, furious, squeezing his hand so hard it hurt. "And you dare ask why I never bring boys home!"

Contrite, Fi's mother said: "Only joking."

Fi growled, clearly unsatisfied.

"In fact, he looked so pale, I guessed he'd been taken ill."

Peter felt a gut-wrenching sympathy for the woman. He certainly wouldn't go so far as let her make a meal of him, but, had it been feasible, he might have offered himself up for adoption then and there, if only to ease her pain.

"You should change out of your uniform, Fiona," her mother said. "You don't want to get it dirty at work. And don't throw any more dirty clothes on the floor. Peter can come with me while you change."

Fi continued to clutch his hand. "No he can't. I'm not letting him out of my sight when you're around."

Peter's mother would never have allowed such a thing, but Fi's Mum just shrugged. "Make sure you hurry. I don't want to be late."

"Turn around," Fi ordered, once they were alone.

He did as he was told.

She moved him so he couldn't see her in the mirror. "No cheating."

The house was silent. He listened as Fi pulled off her jacket, hearing the soft whisper of the lining caressing her blouse. A click of a hanger on wood told him she'd hung it up. Next came the sliding of silk on silk as she unknotted her school tie with its yellow and bottle green diagonal stripes. Then her fingers fumbled nervously at the buttons of her blouse. He imagined her working her way down from just below her neck to her navel and beyond till her blouse hung open and she shrugged it off her shoulders, letting it fall to her feet. The sound of a zip being undone came as a prelude to the faint whoosh of cotton of her skirt sliding the length of her legs. The bed creaked slightly as she sat to finish undressing.

He had long since closed his eyes, delighting in the scent of her near naked body so clearly visible in the sounds it made. As he listened, she rummaged noisily in her cupboards.

"You can look!" She had put on knee-length shorts and a loose fitting shirt, both of which were black. Round her neck she had loosely knotted a red tie and on her head she wore the green beret he liked so much.

She came over and, taking hold of his school tie that hung half-undone around his neck, she removed it and tucked it in his jacket pocket. In its place, she knotted one of her silk kerchiefs.

It was red, like hers, and cool against his skin. It smelt of her soap, a constant reminder that it was hers.

"Have you two finished?" Fi's mother called up.

Fi placed the flat of her hand lightly on his chest for a moment as if feeling the beat of his heart then pulled away and headed for the door. Breathless, he hurried down the stairs after her.

Our Lady of Grace stood in a large wooded park on the outskirts of town. Much of what must have been the front lawn had been sacrificed for an ugly car park. The main entrance was through a stylish mansion that had once been the residence of a rich family with its bay windows on the ground floor and the tiny balconies above. Behind, the school sprawled across the grounds amongst the trees, mingling brick and glass and steel to form classrooms, science laboratories, a swimming pool, a gym and a chapel. The playing fields lay beyond.

Fi's mother had no time for a guided tour, but she pointed out what she could as they made their way to her office which lay on the ground floor of the main building next to the entrance.

"These contain the reports of all the girls who have ever been to the school," she explained, unlocking row upon row of metal filling cabinets. "We are changing our filling system, so we have to stock all the records in boxes in the mean time."

She pointed to a pile of large cardboard boxes in a neighbouring room. "Your job is to transfer all the files to those boxes. The files are organised alphabetically. Keep them in order in the boxes and use this pen," she pulled one from her desk, "to write the name of the first and last person on the side of each box. Is that clear?"

Of course it was. Peter glanced at Fi. This was exactly what they needed. Now all they required was for Fi's Mum to leave them alone so they could do some serious exploring. Unfortunately, she settled at her desk and began typing.

Fi grasped Peter's hand and led him through into the room with the boxes. As she did he spoke into her mind, *We need to find Witless's report so when your mother is not looking I can put it in my satchel.*

They carried several boxes through into the office and, under the pretext of sizing up the job, they went from one filing cabinet to the next to identify the names. They discovered a number of boys' names in the files.

"I thought this school was only for girls," Peter said.

"It is. But we accept boys up to the age of ten."

They returned to their searching. The letter 'w' was predictably low down in the last cabinet. They decided to start there. If they began at the other end they might not reach Witless in time. Working together they began lifting the files out one at a time and placing them in a box.

To their disappointment, they found no file named Priscilla Wit.

Maybe she went under another name, Peter thought. Fi just shrugged. *Or maybe the files are muddled up.*

As they continued, it became clear that no files were out of order.

Not having to look for the lost Witless, they sped up, transferring a bunch of files at a time, working silently together. When Fi's mother said it was time for a pause about an hour later, they had already transferred most of the files.

She took them to the staff canteen and fixed them a drink. As they sat sipping their tea, it was Peter that broached the subject.

"Is that really all the reports, Mrs. Tanner? I can't believe there have been so few girls at this school."

Fi' mother laughed. "Call me Christina. Mrs. Tanner sounds so old and formal."

Peter saw Fi make a rude face. He ignored her. "Surely you have more reports elsewhere, Christina?"

"No. That's all of them, Peter. I can find you other work if you want," and she chuckled, only to become thoughtful. "Well, actually there are a few more reports, those of a few problem cases."

"Do those files have to be removed too?"

"I suppose they do. Yes. That way everything is done. But you should keep them in a separate box." She washed up the cups and led them back to the office.

"Let's do those special files." Peter felt he could get away with almost anything with Mrs. Tanner, although he probably couldn't nick Witless's file in plain sight.

Mrs. Tanner obligingly unlocked a separate filing cabinet and pointed to some ten files in one drawer.

"Are they in alphabetical order too?" he asked.

They were.

Fi went to fetch a box as her mother returned to typing letters. Peter pulled out all ten files and carried them across the office and entered the room next door with the files nestled in his arms. He knelt down next to Fi and slid the files into the box, one at a time. And there it was, the very last and by far the thickest, Priscilla Wit. He handed it to Fi who ducked back into a corner and hid it in Peter's satchel behind a pile of boxes.

Just at that moment Mrs. Tanner got to her feet and stretched, coming over to talk to them. Peter could have sworn she saw what Fi was doing, but the woman made no comment.

"Time to go," Fi's mother said. "Have you finished?"

25.

Witless's file, that lay hidden in Peter's bag, worked like a powerful magnet. Both ached to read it, so when Mrs Tanner invited Peter to stay for tea, he jumped at the opportunity.

"I'd love to. I'll call Mum to let her know."

To his surprise, no one answered. Both Mum and Sis were home, but surely they weren't that ill they couldn't answer. Maybe they were asleep. He gave up after a second try, thinking he'd phone later.

Mrs. Tanner kept them busy preparing high tea while she quizzed him about school and his family. She'd made potato bread, which she served with toasted rashers of gammon, grilled tomatoes and tiny fried mushrooms. It made a welcome change from beans on toast.

He offered to help with the dishes, but Fi tugged him away. "Mum doesn't need your help. She's got one of those dishwasher things." Peter would willingly have helped if only to use the contraption, but Fi was adamant and Mrs. Tanner said he'd already done his part. So the two bounded up the stairs to Fi's room.

"Mum shouldn't disturb us for a while," Fi said. "I'll make some room." She picked up an armful of dirty clothes and carried them down the hall to the bathroom. While she did, he straightened the cover on her bed and was about to sit down when Fi came back and tossed two large cushions on the floor.

"We'll be more comfortable there."

After some playful pushing and shoving, they settled on the cushions. Peter could feel their hips and shoulders touching and everywhere their bodies met he felt her warmth calling him.

Refusing to be distracted, he dragged his satchel onto his lap and was about to pull out the report when Fi put her mouth to his ear and whispered, "I like being with you, Peter McCloud."

It was the first time she'd used his name, rather than calling him Pretty Boy. That she liked being with him delighted him. He turned his head and was about to say that he liked being with her when she closed the gap between them and touched her lips to his, a fleeting contact that had him yearning for more. To his disappointment, she pulled back and looked meaningfully at his satchel.

"Are you trying to make me witless, too?" he asked, finding it hard to breathe.

"Witless?"

"Mad, crazy, nuts, bonkers, ... You name it!"

She grinned impishly. Apparently she was.

He pulled the wad of documents from his bag and opened it. A one-page typed text gave the bare details about Miss Priscilla Agnes Wit. Stapled to the page was a photo that, judging from the date on the back of it, was taken just before she entered Our Lady of Grace in September 1959. She looked strained and ill at ease, despite an attempt at a smile. Staring away from the camera, she held her hands clasped tight in front of her. Her blond hair was tied in a bun, just as it had been on her first day in Peter's class.

She was born on January 21st, 1948, the feast day of St Agnes, the virgin and martyr. Someone had scribbled on the page: Patron saint of chastity, gardeners, girls and virgins. And then added: Priscilla Agnes was hardly a lamb! She officially left Our Lady in May 1960 but had already ceased to attend the school a month earlier at the request of the Head of the school.

Peter noticed there was no mention of expulsion. Maybe the authorities had not wanted to call it that.

Her parents, Thomas and Ines Wit, were devout Catholics.

Her father studied theology but chose to marry rather than become a priest. The marriage took place in September 1947. Priscilla was their only child. She was born shortly after their marriage.

"Sounds like they were forced to get married," Fi said, pointing to the dates.

Peter's thoughts were elsewhere. "How come she came to our church if she's Catholic?"

"To see you, of course."

Disturbed, Peter turned to the next wad of pages. It was a neatly hand-written text, signed at the end by Ted Johnson, Detective. The man had written across the top: Confidential and then below, by way of introduction: This case was particularly complex given the unstable nature of several of the people involved, so it was decided to discreetly gather additional information using the services of a private detective. With the help of a psychiatrist, the following people were interviewed: Mrs. Ines Wit, Miss Priscilla Wit and several of the victims of Miss Wit.

"Sounds a bit like a detective story," Peter said, and read on.

Priscilla's early days were uneventful. The family was well off thanks to money inherited by her mother. Ines looked after her daughter and ran a number of local women's clubs in connection with the church. Mr. Wit worked as a divinity teacher in a large state school nearby. He too was active in different groups and associations, mostly involving men, although Mrs. Wit admitted she knew nothing of the nature or activities of these groups.

When Priscilla was nine, her father was sullied by a scandal with a number of other men involving young boys. The whole affair was hushed up and no official complaint was lodged. A year later, his wife caught him playing with a naked young boy in their bedroom. Once over the shock, she sought counsel from high-ranking members of the local church. She couldn't bear the idea of sharing her life with such a man, but, as a Catholic, she refused to consider divorce. Finally, she ceased all exchange with him and lived with her daughter in an independent flat in the same house. Priscilla continued to see her father on those rare occasions when he was home as she had the run of the whole house.

Several months later, shortly after the police had called to investigate complaints about further abuse of boys, Priscilla discovered her father in the stairwell. He was hanging by the neck from a rope attached to the banisters of the landing above. The girl was found seated at the foot of the stairs, unmoving, staring blankly at a wall.

Fi whistled through her teeth. "Extraordinary! No wonder she's cracked!"

Priscilla was taken to hospital in a state of shock. Despite medication and electroshocks, the girl sank deeper into depression, verging on catalepsy at moments.

"What's 'catalepsy'?" Peter asked.

"I think it is when people go all rigid and don't move anymore."

That state, the report continued, lasted five months during which her mother was also admitted for treatment. Finally the girl emerged from her inaccessible condition and promptly insisted on returning to school. Her doctors were sceptical, but finally agreed.

As her mother was in no fit state to look after her, Priscilla was trusted to a rich aunt living near Tallford. That aunt was on the board of governors of Our Lady of Grace and arranged for Priscilla to start immediately.

Boys were accepted at Our Lady of Grace till the age of ten. It was one of these boys that Priscilla singled out. The boy, who was small for his age and had unusually long curly hair, was shy and retiring. He spoke very little and had no friends. He was delighted when Priscilla befriended him.

She invited him over to her house, where, in the privacy of her room, she told him that some boys were possessed by a female devil. She convinced him that he was one of them and that it was her task to drive the devil out. The boy, who readily believed something was wrong with him, felt so guilty he told no one what happened at the Wit house. Priscilla devised a number of rituals to exorcise him. In one, she dressed him as a girl and stuck needles in his arms and legs.

Peter shuddered as he remembered Fi dressing him in her clothes. As if in echo of his thoughts, he felt her shift uncomfortably.

The boy took refuge in illness, the report went on, and attended school only sporadically. Finally, he left Our Lady for health reasons and no one thought any more of it. It was only later with the suicide and the subsequent investigation, that it became clear he had been Priscilla's first victim.

There was more, much more, but the gruesome details sickened Peter. He handed the rest of the document to Fi who read on, engrossed, while he sat staring at the rows of Fi's colourful dresses hung on hangers from the edges of her cupboards and bookshelves. What horrified him most was that the people Witless chose to torture had nothing to do with her. They were selected because they were weak or vulnerable and easy to bully.

"It's like I said," Fi told him, "the last boy committed suicide. That's why they were forced to carry out an investigation."

Peter wasn't surprised. For Witless these victims were mere disposable objects.

"Listen to the conclusion of the psychiatrist. It would seem that the trauma caused by her father's death and the implication of young boys in homosexual acts in her father's tragic end, led the girl to hate any suggestion of homosexuality in boys. Rather than find fault with her father, whom she revered, she punished effeminate boys for taking her father away."

They were both sitting in shocked silence, the documents open on Peter's knees, when Fi's mother knocked and entered. Adults seemed to have a knack of entering at the worst moments. Peter scrambled to hide the report, but not quickly enough.

"Now you've read that," Fi's mother said, taking the file from his hands, "I'll see it gets back to its rightful place. We wouldn't want anyone thinking it had got into the wrong hands, would we?"

Peter was astounded. "You knew! Why did you let us read it?"

"Fiona told me you were having problems with Priscilla. You having that information might avoid another catastrophe and I reckoned you were responsible enough not to tell anyone."

"Then why didn't you simply give it to us?"

"This way was far more exciting, don't you think?"

Fi groaned and made a face.

First Greengage, then the Headmaster and now Fi's Mum, Peter thought. What was wrong with adults that they were acting so oddly?

"It's getting late. You have school tomorrow. You should be going home Peter before your mother gets worried and calls the police."

Peter chuckled. "My Mum doesn't even notice when I'm not there," he said, regretting the bitterness of his tone.

"Well, just in case... And to avoid you having to cycle all that way in the dark, I'll drive you over." Fi was about to protest when her mother added, "You can come too, Fiona. To make sure I don't steal your Peter." It was her turn to chuckle. "Hurry up. It really is late."

"That's kind of you. But it might not be good to drive up to the gate. My sister is angry with Fi at the moment. If I were to arrive with you, I think you might be unwitting accomplices to a murder."

Both looked at him perplexed.

"Mine," he explained.

Mrs Tanner laughed and left them to get ready.

26.

A police car was parked in the drive when he arrived home. Surely they couldn't know he'd stolen Witless's report.

Inside, his mother was in tears, her head slumped on the kitchen table. A policewoman comforted her, while a police inspector watched on. It was the same one that had interrogated him at school, only now no headmaster was there to protect him.

"Where have you been?" the inspector asked sternly. "Your mother was worried."

"I had dinner with a friend. I tried to phone, but no one answered." He made no mention of forgetting to phone once they began reading Witless's report.

"Your mother called the police," the policewoman said. "She was very upset. Apparently you had an argument and she was afraid you might hurt yourself."

"We don't normally answer distress calls about teenage runaways, but we've had trouble with you..." the inspector added.

Peter was annoyed at the insinuation. It wasn't true. What's more, he couldn't remember having an argument with his Mum. It was so long ago. Why on earth would she imagine him hurting himself? He'd never dreamt of such a thing, let alone mentioned it. Turning to his mother, he saw her staring at him, bewildered.

You'd think she'd be relieved. Wasn't he back safe and sound?

"Where were you?" she accused, pulling at her hair. "Am I to put up with this? You're driving me mad."

Peter was flabbergasted. What was he supposed to have done? He was about to protest, but the look of greedy anticipation on the inspector's face warned him to keep quiet.

"Since your father died, you've been impossible."

More nonsense. His father had died seven years ago. How could that possibly affect what was happening now?

At that moment, Sis shuffled into the room still clothed in her nightdress. She looked uncomprehendingly at the police, then her attention switched to Peter. Her eyes flew wide open in disbelief and then she shrieked and flung herself across the room at him. He stepped back as she clawed at his neck. He braced himself for the pain, but her hands came away clasping the red kerchief Fi had given him. He'd completely forgotten it.

"You bastard!" Her face was distorted with hate. "That's mine."

Her lie made him furious. "No it's not. It belonged to Fi and she gave it to me."

Sis shrieked again and threw herself at him, her nails set to rake his face. Had Kaitling been there, he might have countered, but he'd heard nothing from her since she set off on the boat. Instead it was the inspector who caught Sis by the wrists.

"What an exciting life you lead, Master McCloud," the inspector said, tightening his grip on Sis, who strained to get free.

Peter looked from Sis to Mum and back. Both were wild and haggard, their faces tear-stained, their clothes in disorder, both restrained by the police. How had Witless wreaked so much havoc in such a short time? Or were his sister and Mum already tottering on the brink? Wracking his brain to remember, he could recall no warning signs.

"We should take you to the police station," the inspector continued, "for your own protection,"

Peter was horrified. He had no intention of going. Why was he always being punished for the folly of others?

"Unless of course, you have somewhere to go where you won't get attacked by angry women," the inspector added, his mouth twisted in what was meant to be a smile.

Peter thought of Fi's. Would her mother accept? It was worth a try. "Maybe. I'll have to phone first."

"No you don't!" Sis screamed, rearing up. "Not Fi's! She's mine, not yours!"

She struggled to break free, but was no match for the inspector. The man looked questioningly at Peter, clearly in serious need of an explanation. To avoid having to give one, Peter hurried to phone.

Mrs. Tanner replied, her voice cautious.

"It's Peter, Mrs. Tanner. Sorry to phone so late. I have a little problem and I was wondering if you could help." Her voice changed once she realised who it was and she was much more welcoming.

"Mum and Sis are not feeling very well," he said, glancing across the room at the pitiful scene around the kitchen table. He had to be careful. The inspector was listening to every word he said. "You were right, my Mum did phone the police. They are here at the moment. They suggested it might be better if I slept somewhere else. Could I stay at your place tonight?"

It was such a pleasure to hear Mrs. Tanner laugh. She hinted she understood he was not free to speak and offered to drive over immediately.

"It might be better if you honk when you arrive and wait outside." She laughed again and hung up.

His mood lifted briefly only to plunge again when he returned to the kitchen. An enormous rift had opened between his home and Fi's. The difference was even more striking than between his world and Kaitling's. How could such contrasting worlds exist so close to one another?

"It's all organised," he told the policeman, and hurried off to prepare some clothes.

The door to Sis's bedroom was open; inside the room was in chaos. Drawers and cupboards lay half open, clothes were strewn on the floor, books had been scattered here and there, and Sis's favourite nightdress was in shreds on her bed. The familiar magic that always awaited him in Sis's room had fled.

If anything, the room was dark and sinister.

He turned and hurried to his room, only to halt in the doorway. It too was in chaos. Sis had vented her rage on all she could. His shirts had been systematically torn and tossed to the floor. His trousers and jackets had been hacked at with a knife. Savage rents hung open in the cloth. Everything was ruined. She'd even left her mark on his underwear, scrawling obscenities with a black biro. He turned to take one last look at the ruin of what had once been his bedroom and headed heavy-hearted back to the kitchen his hands empty.

"I thought you went to fetch some clothes," the policewoman said.

"Ask my sister to show you my bedroom. You will understand why I leave empty handed. While you're there, ask her why she did that. On second thoughts, don't bother. She's not herself at the moment."

His words sparked fury in both Sis and Mum. They strained to get their hands on him. Luckily the police kept them at bay while he escaped by the front door.

Mrs. Tanner was waiting outside. So was Fi. Both looked anxious and curious to know what had happened, but neither questioned him. Fi opened the door for him to join her on the back seat. He climbed in and shut the door as Mrs. Tanner pulled away into the night.

The madness he'd just witnessed finally hit him: his sister unhinged, the tension with the police, their questions, his mother's wild accusations, the sheer violence of Sis and all his clothes destroyed. In the quiet, relaxed comfort of Mrs. Tanner's car with two women who cared enough not to badger him with questions, it was all too much. Tears welled in his eyes and overflowed down his cheeks. A shudder went through him and his body was wracked by sobs.

Fi gently put an arm round his shoulder and pulled him closer. He let his head rest on her chest as he continued to cry. She ran her fingers through his hair and planted tiny kisses on the top of his head. Contrasting emotions battled inside him, sadness and despair at the thought of his ruined family and relief and joy at the prospect of being with Fi and her Mum.

When he finally calmed, they had almost reached Fi's house. Mrs. Tanner asked: "Did you think to bring some clothes?"

A shudder shook Peter and he struggled to breathe as his lungs contracted with pain. "My sister destroyed everything. My jackets, my trousers, my shirts, even my underwear. Torn, cut up, scribbled on. Everything."

Both Fi and her mother gasped in horror.

They sat in Fi's tiny kitchen surrounded by a stunning array of shiny gadgets as Mrs. Tanner made hot chocolate. When she put the mug in front of him, he curled his fingers around it, welcoming its warmth. He was shivering. It was Fi that spread her school coat around his shoulders to keep him warm.

All three sat in silence for a while then Mrs. Tanner spoke. "Would you like to talk about it? Or would you like me to show you where you will sleep? It used to be my husband's study."

Peter thought of his father. Had his mother been right in putting the blame on the death of his father? Could a family not function correctly without one?

"What happened to your husband?" Peter asked.

Mrs. Tanner sighed. "When I lost my son at his birth, I was a little..." She paused, searching for her words. "...a little distraught. I was rather unkind to my husband and, in a way, I drove him out."

"That's a shame."

"It is indeed," Mrs Tanner said, her voice wistful.

"I miss my father," Peter said, voicing a feeling he was unaware he had.

There was a long thoughtful silence, then Mrs. Tanner said: "Tell us what happened this evening, Peter. We need to know."

So Peter told them the story. When he came to the part where Sis ripped the scarf from his throat, Fi promptly pulled off the scarf she was wearing and handed it to him. It was all he could do not to cry again.

"Thank you," he whispered.

Mrs Tanner was particularly interested in what the police had to say. Her questions led him to describe the altercation with Witless the day before and his interrogation by the police at school. He was surprised to realise how much had happened since then.

"The Headmaster is a good man," Mrs Tanner commented. "That inspector, however, sounds evil. I'll have to see what I can do to make your stay official, however short it is."

Peter was relieved to hear he wouldn't have to return home the next day. He had no wish to go back.

"I'll show you your room. You must be tired."

His bedroom lay across the hall from Fi's. The shelves that lined the walls were stocked with books and the desk was cluttered with papers.

"If I'd known you were coming, I would have cleared this away. But at least the bed is free."

Peter perched on the edge of the bed, which was invitingly comfortable.

"You'll be needing clothes," she mused. "We can go shopping tomorrow."

"I have plenty of money. My father left me an allowance. I hardly spend it. I can even pay you rent."

Mrs. Tanner chuckled. "We can sort that out another time."

"He'll need pyjamas," Fi pointed out. "I can lend him a pair of mine."

Peter wondered how Mrs. Tanner would react. His mother would have been furious.

"Well you must be about the same size," the woman said smiling, and that was that. He really was in paradise.

Fi hurried off to fetch him pyjamas and Mrs. Tanner gave him a towel and a toothbrush.

"Good night, Peter," she said kissing him on the cheek. "Good night Fiona," kissing her too. "No more adventures tonight," she said looking pointedly at Fi.

27.

Fi brought him a pair of light cotton pyjamas that were covered in tiny pink and blue flowers. He couldn't help smiling as he pulled them on and slid between the sheets. The pyjamas smelt characteristically of her, almost as if she were in bed with him. He was just about to switch off the light when the door opened noiselessly, and in crept Fi.

"How do you like the pyjamas?" she whispered, sitting down on the edge of his bed.

"They feel like you; soft and warm and inviting."

Fi blushed and looked away.

"I have to go," he whispered, suddenly remembering where he'd left Kaitling. His day had been so filled with wild adventures, he had hardly thought of the young magician.

"But you've only just arrived," Fi protested, placing a restraining hand on his shoulder. "Mum said you could stay as long as you like."

Peter smiled at the misunderstanding. "I am very grateful to both of you. But that's not what I meant. I have to go to Drailong, Kaitling has been captured and is being taken away by sea."

Fi's eyes lit up. "Can I come?"

"I'm not sure that's possible. I'll try to teach you how to travel to minds tomorrow."

Fi looked disappointed. "I'll remind you, all day long." Then she grinned. "So much for the no more adventures my mother asked for. Don't stay too long with that girl, I might get jealous and you've got school tomorrow." She lent forward and gave him a quick kiss on his cheek and was gone.

He lay enjoying the glow her lips had left on his cheek when a piercing scream wrenched him from his bed and catapulted him into Drailong and Kaitling's head.

What's up?

Priest, gasped Kaitling.

The man had one hand around Kaitling's throat choking her. His other hand pushed up her skirts, his body pressed hard against her.

Peter flung himself mentally at the priest, only to rebound. He tried a second time, without success.

Effortless, Kaitling gasped, amid her struggles.

Shrinking to a mere dot, Peter slipped into the arid world of the priest. Now was no time for hesitation. The priest's hand snaked ever higher up Kaitling's thighs. Peter tightened the muscles around the man's heart, causing the priest to cry out and let go of Kaitling. He almost blacked out.

Peter was horrified. He didn't want to kill the man. He loosened his grip, causing blood to rush painfully along the arteries. The man's hands flew to his chest, struggling to regain his breath.

Do that again, Peter growled in the priest's head, *and I will kill you. Now undo the cords that tie her hands.*

Peter had expected resistance and was prepared to stomp on the man's heart again, but the priest pulled out a knife readying to cut the cords.

From his position in the priest's head, Peter was surprised he could still talk mind-to-mind to Kaitling. He warned her the priest was going to set her free and quickly told her what had happened. *I'll send him to fetch food, and I'll go along to find out where we are.*

As the priest made his way to the galley, he puzzled about the voice he'd heard. Peter sensed the man's confusion. The priest was concerned that the voice might not be that of god.

He'd only very rarely heard the voice. Yet it had the same determination, compelling him to obey. Apparently priests received orders in their minds not from god but via the higher priests to whom god spoke mind-to-mind.

He discovered that they didn't call themselves priests. Instead they thought of themselves as the Chosen Ones, believing they were singled out as special because they could communicate with god. Peter had been lucky his voice had been mistaken for that of their god.

In the galley, the priest ordered a tray of food while he enquired about progress around Drailong. Apparently they were travelling north along the coast, heading for Navigon. From a snatch of thought the priest let slip, they planned to use Kaitling as bait for her father.

As he continued to rummage through the man's memories, he was intrigued to learn that one of the main tests to become a Chosen One was the ability to block outside influence from their minds. That might explain why he had had difficulties entering the priest's mind.

He found distant memories of training in mind-to-mind communication. They learnt to shield against anyone but their god and the higher priests. Judging from the emotions that tainted the memory, it had been a painful experience involving beatings and something like electroshocks.

He searched the man's memories for anything resembling travelling between minds, but found nothing.

The priest was about to leave the galley, when an older priest arrived. The priests looked very much alike, the same furrowed brow, the same tight lips, the same chiselled, rock-hard features. Something told Peter, however, this man was a superior. Maybe it was the fear he provoked in his host.

"What are you doing?" the higher priest asked, staring pointedly at the tray of food.

"Taking food to the prisoner. The god told me to."

Peter immediately sensed the man had lied. Deep down he was terrified it might have been the woman who spoke in his mind. Such a thing was unthinkable. No woman could speak mind-to-mind. Women were inferior beings, incapable of hearing the voice of god.

"I have heard nothing of this. Women don't deserve such special treatment."

"But, the god said I should."

"Give me that tray. I'll check."

Fearing what might happen should this dour figure get his hands on Kaitling, Peter prepared to jump to the older priest. He had a lucky break when the priests' fingers touched as they exchanged the tray. Sliding imperceptibly from one to the next, Peter braced himself against the shock of the change. To his surprise, there was very little difference between the two, both bathed in a sour mixture of obedience and pride and dour determination. If anything, it was only the inflated feeling of self-importance that distinguished them.

Peter wondered if imitating the voice of their god would work a second time, but he couldn't run the risk of alerting them to his presence. He sifted desperately through the man's memories in search of a clue, a lever he could use to get control. The higher priest had already reached the door to Kaitling's cell when Peter discovered a memory that fought not to be opened. He'd never encountered such a thing, as if it were imprisoned. Peter hurriedly tried to wheedle his way inside, coaxing and caressing, until the barrier finally let him through.

He was flooded with memories of a beautiful woman named Olga. The priest had been in love with her but his priesthood forbade such a liaison. He had continued to see her despite the ban, but the church had found out and the woman had been put to death. In this tiny corner of his mind he'd locked away his joy and grief, as well as his guilt and remorse.

"How dare you force one of our priests to bring you food," the priest accused Kaitling.

Peter sensed the priest was tensing his arm to hit Kaitling. Peter had to stop him. He caused the picture of Olga to surface in man's mind, flood him with love and despair. The emotions

were so strong the priest staggered, all thought of hitting Kaitling gone. He would have fallen to his knees had he not had
such cast-iron self-control. Instead he stood there, rigid, his eyes
closed, his fists clenched.

Peter spoke mind-to-mind to Kaitling, explaining what had
happened. He told Kaitling about Olga.

A raging argument was going on in the priest's head as
he struggled to regain control and shove aside his treacherous
memories. Peter continued presenting him with pictures of Olga,
getting buffeted in the process. He was confident he would win
because a part of the priest didn't want to forget, but the priest's
mind was strong and vicious and Peter was tired.

In a desperate gambit, the man slammed down a massive
wall around his time with Olga, catching Peter on the wrong
side. Peter panicked. He was trapped. Search as he would, he
could find no way out. The wall was rock hard and held in place
by red-hot hatred. Not even becoming tinier than tiny would
help. He was stuck in a sterile world with jaded memories of the
beautiful Olga.

Peter thought to attack the man's heart, but even that was
barred him. He shuddered at what the man might do to Kaitling.

Peter could always return to his own body, surely that must
still be possible, but he refused to abandon Kaitling. He examined his tiny mental prison. Without the guiding voice of the
body, he was unsure what to do. Conscious that Kaitling must be
suffering every moment he hesitated, he had to find a solution
fast.

A tiny red spot caught his attention. On closer inspection he
saw it was a knot of cells that were vibrating furiously. Surely it
hadn't been there before. Whatever it was, the spot was growing
rapidly, causing his tiny world to expand. He gave it a tentative
shove, thinking it might help him get free. The red spot resisted,
pushing back, then it flared, its growth accelerating.

A dull throbbing was seeping through the wall that enclosed
him and with it came the realisation that the priest was in pain.
The bigger the growth, the greater the pain and the more outside

feelings and thoughts filtered through. Peter let himself drift until he was able to pass through the wall only to discover to his horror that Kaitling lay unconscious at the priest's feet. Blood was flowing freely from the gash on her head.

Peter had some difficulty seeing clearly, the priest's vision was clouding over as the pain screamed for attention. Sinking to his knees, the priest clawed at his head as if he could wrench the terrible growth from his body. Peter couldn't leave the man like that, the priest would surely die and Peter didn't want to be a murderer. But Kaitling was wounded too and she was far more important. He jumped across the small space that separated Kaitling from the priest. Despite his overwhelming tiredness, he set about healing Kaitling.

28.

Kaitling emerged bewildered from the haze that had her stumbling through a thick fog and looked around troubled and confused. At her feet lay a priest. She nudged him with her foot, but he didn't move.

I did that, Peter informed her, sadness and guilt pervading his thoughts.

Is he dead?

I don't think so. I did something to his brain. Peter went on to explain what had happened. *I can't leave him like that but I have no idea how to undo it.*

It was there before you gave it a shove. You just helped. She struggled to her feet and tried to take a step but almost fell with exhaustion.

There's food outside the door. You should eat. You haven't done so for ages.

She crawled on all fours to the door and managed to open it. The smell of cheese and bread, however stale, had her mouth watering. She ripped off a chunk of bread and stuffed it into her mouth along with a piece of cheese. As she munched, she pulled the tray into the cell and closed the door.

You too are exhausted. I can feel it in your thoughts. You should get some rest. I can manage.

Peter was unwilling to leave. He was worried about Kaitling, but even more so, he was afraid the priest would die before he could heal him.

This is war, Kaitling reminded him. *I have killed several people over the last few days. I don't like it, but if I hadn't, they would have killed me.*

It's not the same. You killed someone from a distance with an arrow. I was inside him. I forced his brain cells to grow and develop. It was horrible. I saw it happening. I felt his pain. I could have screamed with him. Maybe I did.

He's not dead yet. Let's see what we can do. I'm feeling stronger now. I'll come with you.

She sat down on the floor next to the priest, her back against the wall and placed a hand on his shoulder. It was hard and cold and far from inviting. She closed her eyes and after several attempts she managed to follow Peter into the priest's mind.

Peter led her to a writhing ball that vibrated furiously. It seemed red and malevolent and enormous, but drawing back it wasn't much bigger than a tiny almond.

He was at a loss what to do. Normally he used the host's body to help in healing. The body generally knew best. But here, the cells were completely beyond the control of the priest's body. All contact was severed.

Is there no way we can stop it vibrating, Kaitling asked?

Hearing her voice next to him was a strange experience. He generally felt so alone and overwhelmed when healing. To have her there was comforting and reassuring. She knew much more about healing than he did.

Vibrating?

Yes. It is the vibrations that make the cells divide and grow. They have gone wild.

Peter looked closer at a small bunch of cells. It wasn't easy to locate an individual cell. Many seemed to have long tendrils that curled far out amongst the surrounding cells. A worrying thought crossed his mind. What if he were to touch one, would it infect him with its animosity and set him vibrating too?

That's very unlikely, Kaitling thought. *We're not here as cells. I'm not sure exactly what we are, but we certainly aren't cells.*

Peter stretched out mentally and tried to put a restraining hand on the cell. A sharp shock flung him back. If anything, his brief attempt had made the ball of cells even angrier, like a knot of writhing snakes.

Maybe images will work, Peter thought. *I used images on him earlier. He spread a soft blanket of calm thoughts around the enraged cells.*

That's not working, Kaitling pointed out. *Your images are not getting through. It's as if that ball was shielded. How about starving it?* She promptly cut off the blood supply to that part of the brain. The ball reacted immediately, burrowing into the surrounding brain with many tendrils.

Stop, Peter exclaimed. *That only makes it spread faster.*

Their efforts had further exhausted them. Kaitling wondered if they shouldn't give up, but Peter was unwilling. He roamed the priest's brain, not deliberately looking for anything in particular.

It's disharmony, he finally said, startling Kaitling who had drowsed off in her fatigue.

What do you mean?

My initial shove set off a growing disharmony. The cells are vibrating at odds with each other. A bit like music when people sing just off key. The resulting vibrations can become extremely violent.

I don't see how that helps. Kaitling admitted, confused.

Simple. I'm going to sing it to sleep. He smiled at the idea. *I mean, I'm going to imitate the natural vibration of his body and see if those cells don't realign. After all, that's where they came from.*

It was easier said than done. His presence was mute in the priest's mind. He had no voice with which to sing.

Let me listen for a moment. He concentrated on those cells that had not yet been set in motion. As he listened he was able to distinguish a faint, but distinct sound. Not just one note, but a complex mixture making up the body's harmony. He bent his mind to reflecting the sound until its volume grew and other cells in the brain responded. Soon there was a joyous concert under way that vied with the rattling and screeching of the angry cells.

It's less red, Kaitling said, delighted at his success.

It's not enough. I'm going to have to go in there and sing from within.

You can't do that. Kaitling trembled at the thought. *You saw what one cell did to you.*

She was right. He needed some sort of protection. On an impulse he started rummaging through the priest's memories in search of how the Chosen Ones shielded their bodies. Maybe that might help.

Understanding what he was doing, Kaitling began searching too. *Here,* she called out, *memories of the priest training younger priests.* Although the priest did not reveal how the shield worked, he thought it none the less and Kaitling and Peter were able to listen in.

That's not going to be enough, Peter mused. *I need to feel how he does it himself.*

Let's look at that memory again. I bet he thinks back to the first times he did it, Kaitling suggested.

Sure enough, the priest briefly thought of the first time he'd mastered the technique. Peter expanded the memory and replayed it several times. *I think I've got it.*

Test it first, she warned.

He called up the shield like the priest had done and stretched out to touch one of the angry cells. There was still a shock, but it was bearable.

That's not enough. Worry tainted Kaitling's voice. *There are hundreds of those blasted cells in there.*

Peter pulled the outermost layer of protection around him, like a tightly knit cloak, and stretched out to touch the glowing ball of cells. He felt nearly nothing. Not wanting to waste any more time - who knew when the priest might die? - he jumped into the middle of fiery ball thinking he would sing the song of harmony.

The shock was terrible. His own light wavered as a black abyss opened up in front of him leaving him tottering on the brink. Inexplicably a rush of love buoyed him up, pulling him back from the precipice.

The heart of the angry red ball was vibrating much more wildly than its periphery. Violent forces stabbed at him, trying to knock the life from him. Alone he would have stood no chance, but love continued to flood into him. Love was the only word for it. He marvelled at the warmth and brightness of it.

Sing! Sing, you fool! You can't bear this much longer. Drawing on the positive energy that cradled him out of harm's way, he began to echo softly that one complex chord, infinitely modulated, a vital thread of life in the body that was his current host. The memory of singing in the church last Sunday sprang to mind, his voice soaring above the rest of the choir, and he imagined himself singing the beautiful cantata that was life's essence and the church fell away replaced almost imperceptibly by a pulsing, living, giant body that sang along with him.

When his song came to an end, all was quiet, lest it be for a distant echo of his song that swirled around him and filled the priest's body. He didn't need to look to know he'd vanquished the fiery malady. He couldn't contain his elation. He wanted to fling his arms around Kaitling and kiss her fervently. *Thank you,* he told her.

But I didn't do anything. She sounded startled at his exuberance.

Did you not feel that wave of warmth and love that buoyed me up and saved me from certain death?

She shook her head.

I can still feel it now, all around me. Can't you feel it?

I think you are exhausted and need a rest.

You must be right. But I must do one more thing before I go.

He slipped back into the priest's mind. The man was beginning to stir, slowly regaining consciousness. The memories of Olga had been wiped out. Instead Peter replaced them with those of the wall the priest had tried to build round his former love. He showed how the angry red ball had formed and grown. He showed the battle against it and finished with singing the illness away with a choir of love. He borrowed from his own image of the body as a church and then returned to Kaitling.

That should give him something to think about. When he re-covers, get him to talk. Have him confide. There's a lot that he's never dared say. If you need me, call. I'll be at school so I may not always be able to come, but I will do my best.

Thank you. You not only saved his life, you saved mine too.

See you, Peter said, blushing. Thank heavens she couldn't see the colour of his face. Silly me, was his last thought, all my emotions are open to her.

Back in his bed he was astonished to find Fi cuddled up next to him, her lips pressed against his cheek, her breath playing lightly on his skin. She must have been asleep but coming back to his body awoke her.

"Ah, you're back," she whispered, relieved. "I was so afraid. You were shuddering and groaning. You seemed to be in pain. I was desperate. I didn't know what to do. So I wrapped my arms around you and sent you all the love I could..." Her voice trailed off, unsure, as she looked searchingly into his eyes.

"It was you," he whispered astounded and flung his arms around her, planting his lips squarely on hers. After a moment's hesitation, she returned his kiss with equal verve, tightening her grip around him. It was as if their two beings melted into one. He wasn't sure where his lips ended and hers began. He felt the full force of love that had saved him in Drailong wash over him once more and in the distance he could have sworn he heard their two life songs singing together.

"I love you," he mumbled, unsure if he only thought the words or if he really said them out loud, as exhaustion caught up with him and he slipped into sleep, cradled in Fi's welcoming arms.

29.

Fi stroking his hair awoke him. He cracked open his eyes, hoping she wouldn't notice. He didn't want her to stop. It was light outside and the birds were singing a riotous chorus to greet the day. Life was truly wonderful. Memories of the previous night came flooding back. Maybe he should have felt embarrassed or concerned to find himself in bed with Fi, but he didn't give a damn. Opening his eyes wide, he took hold of her hand and brought it gently to his mouth, kissing the tips of her fingers. He heard her sigh.

"You saved my life, you know," he said, speaking softly, not wanting to disturb the warm, fuzzy bubble that surrounded them.

"I did? Tell me."

"It was not all nice."

"How could it be, if your life was in danger?"

So he told her about saving the priest and how he'd almost died.

"That was so brave and wonderful."

Her admiration embarrassed him.

"Well you did something wonderful too. I don't know how, but across that immense distance you sent me strength and love without which I would have floundered."

"Floundered? You have an extraordinary vocabulary for someone who doesn't read."

"And you have an extraordinary ability for someone who

doesn't yet know how to travel between minds."

"You promised, remember."

"I know and I think it might be easier than I imagined."

They both lay back their arms intertwined, their heads touching, quiet and content, each in their own thoughts.

Neither of them noticed when the door opened and Mrs. Tanner peered in. They were startled when she spoke, but neither made a move, preferring to stay in each other's arms.

"I thought I said sleep, not adventures."

One glance at her face was enough to know she was not angry. She even looked wistful.

"Time to get up you two love doves. I've made you some breakfast and then it's off to school. Show Peter where he can have a shower, Fi, but don't take that as an invitation to have one with him."

At breakfast, Mrs. Tanner words were more serious. "Listen. What happens in this house is not like the world outside in 1960. You need to be careful what you say. Most people would be very upset, if not down right angry, if they knew you two had slept together. So there's a price for the freedom here, it is great caution elsewhere both in what you say, but also in what you do. Do you understand?"

They nodded. "I know what you mean. My mother would kill me if she knew and Sis has already tried. But they wouldn't stop there. They'd try to have you and Fi punished."

"People don't like to see others happy and the idea of someone getting pleasure is quite distasteful to most people. So be careful. Be especially careful around Priscilla Wit. She's just the sort of person who would do everything in her power to destroy what you two have."

Peter shuddered. Witless! He'd forgotten her. Maybe she wouldn't be back at school yet.

The first thing Peter saw when he walked into class was Witless sitting bolt upright in her seat, looking down her nose at him. His heart fell. He greeted Mrs. Greengage and went to his seat, not looking at his neighbour.

When he opened his desk, he found it stuffed full of pictures torn from a catalogue of girls' underwear. Witless burst out laughing, causing everyone to look. He blushed despite himself.

"Are you picking your new panties, McCloud?" Witless asked, loud enough for everyone to hear.

Peter felt anger bubble up inside him. He was not going to stand for this. "These are yours, I believe," he said, grabbing the glossy pages and thrusting them at Witless.

She shied away. "Why should they be mine? I'm not the pansy."

Peter was so angry he wanted to make a nasty remark about the girl's father being a pederast - he'd looked the word up in a dictionary - but fortunately he was able to restrain himself.

"If I were pansy, it would be much better than being a poor wallflower like you."

Witless swung at him with her right hand, catching him off guard, her fist connecting with his ear. The blow sent a violent ringing through his head as he staggered across the aisle bumping into another pupil's desk. The glossy pictures were scattered across the classroom, a bright array of tight flesh and pink cotton and nylon. His hand flinchingly fingered the side of his face, which stung red-hot.

"You're completely mad, Wit."

"You are a filthy pansy."

"So you said." He felt a steely calm settle over him. "What if I were, what does it mater to you?"

It was at that moment that Mrs. Greengage intervened. Any other teacher would have been on them immediately, but Greengage wasn't like other teachers. He was grateful to her. He felt strangely strengthen by the exchange. A couple of days before, he'd have cringed in guilt. His adventures with Kaitling and Fi must have changed him.

"Would you two step outside, please," Mrs. Greengage said. "The rest of you keep quiet and read the first chapter of Animal Farm. I'll ask you questions on it when I get back."

Peter was expecting Greengage to march them off to the Head's office. Hitting another student was a serious breech of school rules. Instead she led them to an empty office where the physics teacher prepared lessons.

"What seems to be the problem?" she asked, ushering them into the room.

"I'm not talking to you," Witless said, looking down her nose at Greengage. "You are biased. He's your favourite. I know. I see how you look at him."

"How do you see me looking at him?" Greengage's voice was even, but her eyes blazed.

"With filthy longing!" Witless screamed.

"I'm not sure I understand," Mrs. Greengage insisted.

"You wanna get your filthy hands on him..." Witless spat, her face distorted in a leer that was so grotesque it made her look inhuman. Instinctively Peter took a step away.

"I've heard enough," Mrs. Greengage said. "Follow me."

She strode out of the room with Peter scurrying after her. He didn't want to get caught alone with Witless. She was sure to kill him. Mrs. Greengage led them to the infirmary.

The nurse looked a little surprised, but once she saw Witless her surprise turned to a knowing look. How many people in school were aware of Witless's past?

"Miss Wit needs something to calm her nerves. She's a danger to herself and to those around her," Greengage said. "I'll inform the Head and we'll call your aunt, Miss Wit."

Terrified she'd leave him with Witless, Peter was relieved when Mrs. Greengage invited him to follow as she turned to go.

"Filthy cow, cock sucker, pansy..." the girl screamed as Mrs. Greengage closed the infirmary door. A crash rang out along the empty school corridor followed by the sound of glass shattering. Greengage stepped back and opened the door. Broken bottles littered the floor around Witless who stood bent over double, panting in the middle of the ruins of the infirmary. The nurse lay in a pool of blood at her feet.

Seeing the door open, Witless snarled, baring her teeth.

Kaitling, Peter called out s Witless advanced on them. Behind him he could hear voices, as more and more pupils flooded out of nearby classes to see what was going on.

Ah. I see, Kaitling said. *Let me take control.*

Witless lunged at them, letting out a furious battle cry. Kaitling pushed Mrs. Greengage to one side when the woman tried to step between Witless and Peter. Then she had him swerve to avoid the fist that was aimed at his face. With a wide sweep of his outstretched foot, she sent Witless sprawling on the tilled floor. Spinning round to face Witless, she settled Peter firmly on his two feet, flexing his arms. Witless lunged forward from a crouch, trying to grab Peter's legs in a rugby tackle. Kaitling had him sidestep, causing Witless to fall flat on her face. An appreciative roar went up from what must have been the growing crowd of onlookers.

Peter had no time to check. Witless had spun round and, rising to her feet, lunged at him again, her teeth bared like a wild animal, spittle forming around her mouth. *Let's finish this,* Kaitling told him. *I've got other things to do.* Side steeping slightly, she caught Witless's outstretched arms and, following through with her movement, sent the girl flying against the wall opposite with a resounding crash where she slumped in a heap on the floor, unmoving. Cheers went up and thunderous applause rang out.

Peter stepped forward cautiously, Kaitling having relinquished her hold, and laid his hand lightly on the girl's shoulder. He hesitated about entering such a person in such conditions, but he wanted to be sure she was not mortally wounded. Steeling himself against the girl's thoughts and feelings, he quickly checked her body. Her arm was broken and she was suffering from concussion, but otherwise she was remarkably free of injury. He stepped back.

"Return to your classes, immediately," a stern voice called out over the clamours of the noisy crowd. It was the Headmaster. Peter moved to stand next to Mrs. Greengage, who seemed completely shaken by what had happened.

"Sorry about that," Peter whispered. "Are you alright?"

Mrs Greengage shook her head, smiling weakly. "I know whom to get as my bodyguard next time there's any trouble in class."

Someone must have called an ambulance, because two ambulance men were already loading Witless onto a stretcher.

"You might do well to give her a strong sedative," Greengage said. "She's rather agitated and can be dangerous."

One of the ambulance men turned to Peter. "You should come with us. Judging from your face it might be a good idea to X-ray your head to see if nothing is broken."

The thought of being stuck at the hospital with a raging Witless had Peter shuddering. "It's only a bruise."

"We still ought to check."

Peter rapidly surveyed the state of his head from the inside. "I can assure you nothing is broken." He spoke with such authority that the ambulance man was taken aback.

"If ever your head or your jaw start to ache, I advise you to come to the hospital," the man said, returning to Witless, still unconscious on the stretcher.

Through the glass windows of a nearby class, Peter saw a police car drive up and the familiar inspector step out. He groaned. Yet another interrogation on the way.

"Come with me, McCloud," the Headmaster said. "You too Mrs. Greengage."

Taking Peter by the arm, the Headmaster led him away. Climbing several stairs, he brought them to the caretaker's flat and knocked on the door. The caretaker's wife opened.

"Good morning Mrs. Arne. Would you mind if we used your living room for a moment? We need a good place to hide."

"Of course. Come in," she said smiling broadly.

Peter had the impression it wasn't the first time the Headmaster had taken refuge there.

"Would you like a cup of tea?" she asked

"That would be wonderful." The Head led them into Mrs. Arne's living room. He clearly knew his way about.

"Take a seat. You look like both of you need to sit down."

"What an amazing demonstration of self-defence!" the Headmaster exclaimed once he too was seated. "Where did you learn that?"

So there was to be an interrogation of sorts, Peter realised. "A friend of mine is very good at self-defence."

The man chuckled. Turning to Greengage, his face became serious. "So what did Miss Wit do?"

Greengage was telling the tale when Mrs. Arne returned with the tea. She'd even brought chocolate biscuits. "My husband said the police are looking for you."

"Ask him to tell them I've stepped out from a moment. I will be back shortly."

Greengage continued describing what had happened.

"Is the nurse alright?" Peter asked.

"She'll be fine; just a bad bruise on her shoulder and some superficial cuts. Nothing that a couple of days rest at home will not cure. But tell me Mr. McCloud, how come you were so sure Miss Wit was not seriously injured?"

Now that question was going to be more difficult to answer.

"I can feel that kind of thing."

The Headmaster looked at him incredulous.

"Her arm was broken and she was suffering from concussion. That's all."

He immediately regretted having said too much. Both the Headmaster and Greengage were staring at him, a strange look in their eyes.

30.

"Tell me, Mr. McCloud..." The tone of the Headmaster's voice filled Peter with apprehension. "Did you have anything to do with those six older boys ending up in hospital the other day?"

Peter grimaced sheepishly. Here we go, he thought.

"Well..." he hesitated. "Yes. Sir."

"I've heard their version. I'd be intrigued to hear yours."

Peter took a bite of a chocolate biscuit to gain time. He immediately wished he hadn't. He had some difficulty swallowing. The Head and Greengage sat silently watching him, expectant.

"I was sitting under the trees across the playing field on my own, when those six saw me and ran to catch me. They threatened me..."

"How exactly did they do that?" the Head quizzed.

"One of them shoved me up against a tree and tightened his hands around my throat..." Peter said, turning pale at the memory.

"I don't see any marks around your neck."

"No you wouldn't, Sir." How should he put it? "I heal easily."

The Head looked surprised, but continued. "Why did they attack you?"

Peter had to wrack his brains to remember. He coloured with embarrassment when he did. "They said I was playing with myself. They called me a 'precocious wanker'." He'd looked the word up in the dictionary. Knowing the meaning added to his embarrassment. "I wasn't, I didn't, I mean..." he stuttered, feeling his face go bright red.

"Such words are meant as an insult," Mrs. Greengage said, as the good English teacher she was. "Not necessarily because of what they mean in the dictionary."

Peter couldn't believe he was having such a conversation. He wanted to crawl away and disappear.

"So you beat all six of them?"

"It wasn't so difficult, Sir. They didn't expect me to fight back and they were over confident."

The Headmaster looked dubious. "You had no outside help?"

"Apart from the advice of my friend," he said, deliberately being ambiguous, "no, I had no outside help."

"They said they were set on by a gang of thugs," the Headmaster informed Peter.

"I was alone."

"No wonder they lied. It can't be easy to admit being beaten by one so much younger and smaller," Greengage said.

"We've been having trouble with them for quite a while," the Headmaster admitted, more to Greengage than to Peter. "We knew they were bullying younger children, but we were never able to catch them. Seems like you have done our work for us, although I would have preferred it without the fight."

"So would I, Sir."

The Headmaster looked thoughtful. He picked up a biscuit and turned it over in his fingers. "How are things at home since that incident with Miss Wit? I saw your sister was absent this morning."

Peter groaned.

The Headmaster raised an eyebrow and Mrs. Greengage looked concerned.

"My sister has gone a little mad."

"Mad means so many things to people of your age," Mrs Greengage said. "In what sense are you using the word?"

"She destroyed all my clothes with a knife and scribbled obscenities on my underwear with a ball point pen."

No reaction showed on the Headmaster's face, but Mrs. Greengage whistled between her teeth. He had to smile. It was such an uncharacteristic sound coming from her.

"My mother called the police. Not because of what my sister did, I don't think Mum even knew, but because I hadn't come home. I was having tea with a friend and her mother. I tried to phone but nobody answered. My Mum told the police she was afraid I'd hurt myself. I think she meant..." He hesitated about using the word. It made him shudder. "...suicide." He took a deep, shaky breath and went on. "You'd have thought she would have been relieved to see me, instead she called me all sorts of names."

"Sounds like you've been having a difficult time," the Head said. "I guessed as much. When I heard your sister was absent I made some enquiries and found that both your mother and sister have been admitted to a psychiatric clinic."

Peter hadn't known. Maybe the news should have shocked him but it was a relief. At least someone was looking after them. He certainly couldn't.

"You can't stay at home on your own," Mrs. Greengage said, a worried look on her face.

"Don't worry. It turned out all right in the end. The inspector, the same one who questioned me here, seemed to think I was in danger and wanted to take me to the police station, 'for my protection' he said, but I refused. He finally agreed I could stay with a friend."

"And where would that be?"

"With Mrs Tanner and her daughter Fiona. They have been very kind to me. Mrs. Tanner said I could stay as long as I like. She's coming with me to buy me new clothes this afternoon."

"Fiona Tanner is a good girl," Mrs Greengage put in.

"Indeed," the Headmaster said, "You couldn't have found a better place to stay."

Peter agreed entirely, much more so than the Headmaster

could possibly know. An image of Fi in his arms kissing him flashed through his mind, making his stomach flutter with excitement. He quickly thrust it aside, doubting the Head would appreciate knowing how well he felt at Mrs. Tanner's.

The Headmaster looked at Mrs. Greengage for a long moment then he turned back to Peter. "We are responsible for our pupils. What I said to the police inspector the other day wasn't just empty words. I take that responsibility very seriously. All the more so when a pupil doesn't have the parental support he should."

He paused a moment and glanced at the English teacher. "Mrs. Greengage tells me you went to her house for help with your reading. I suggest you continue doing so. Maybe twice a week. I know Mrs. Tanner will help you a lot, but seeing Mrs. Greengage will give you an added pair of ears, someone else to talk to. How does that sound?"

Peter liked Mrs. Greengage and he had enjoyed his visit to her house. "Yes, I'd like that." He looked at Greengage whose eyes met his. Her face was full of concern. "As long as it's not too much bother for you."

"Not at all," she reassured him.

"Do you have any books about anatomy?" he asked, suddenly thinking of healing the priest. "What we learn at school doesn't always come at the right time. I'd like to know more about how the body works."

Both Greengage and the Headmaster seemed delighted.

"You are right," the Headmaster mused. "Having one curriculum for all students doesn't always work."

"My late husband taught anatomy at university. I am sure there are some things amongst his books that would be suitable."

Peter smiled. If only she knew what he was capable of. He would have loved to tell her, not to brag, but because he wanted to share his knowledge and joy at healing.

The caretaker's wife knocked at the door. "I just wanted to let you know the police left. They got fed up waiting," she chuckled.

The Headmaster thanked her and complimented her on her tea and biscuits. Getting to his feet, he said to Peter: "Good. That's settled. Of course, my office is always open if you want to talk."

It was already break when they left the caretaker's flat. He'd missed a double period of English. Not that it mattered as the teacher had been with him. Mrs. Greengage fixed him an appointment for late Wednesday afternoon and then Peter hurried off in search of Fi.

Fi, he thought mind-to-mind, *meet me out by the playing fields next to the school, where we met last time. I've got loads to tell you.* He'd have to teach her to speak mind-to-mind. It would make things so much easier.

Fi was impatient to see him. She jumped off the low wall on which she had been sitting and ran to fling her arms around his neck the moment he rounded the corner and came into view. How good it felt to be so welcome.

"My hero! I saw the fight. You were marvellous. Everyone has been talking about you. Our geography class was so abuzz, the teacher threatened to give everyone detention."

"It was all Kaitling. I could never have done that."

"How do you do it?"

Peter guessed it wasn't the details of the fighting itself she was after. "I step aside and let Kaitling take control. She uses my body, as it were."

The image of him stepping aside to let a girl take over was clearly giving Fi something to think about. She stood silent and thoughtful for a long moment.

"Don't you go getting any naughty ideas," Peter scolded playful, interrupting her reverie.

"I heard you weren't in class. Where were you?"

"Hiding from the police," he giggled. "With the Headmaster and Greengage."

Fi looked at him astonished. "You keep strange company."

"Not at all. They are great, both of them. We talked about the fight with those six bullies."

"That's another thing everyone is gabbing about. I even heard some pupils making up stories that it was you that beat the hell out of those six brutes, not a band of thugs as they pretended." Then Fi suddenly pulled away appraising him "It really was you, wasn't it? That's why you had blood on your nose on Friday."

"Maybe," Peter replied coyly, folding his hands behind his back and swaying his hips from side to side.

Fi stared at him, her eyes sparkling. "Just look at you. You are so modest and bashful, and the face you make with it. That's why I insisted you'd make an excellent girl."

"I've often wanted to be a girl. I even dreamt it was possible to become one. But I am a boy. I have that funny thing dangling between my legs," he said, not wanting to use it's name. Even saying it like that had him feeling embarrassed. He'd never, ever, spoken about these things to anybody. "But much as I'd like to be a girl, I can't imagine myself without that."

He looked up at Fi. She was engrossed in his words; her eyes encouraging, her lips delicious and inviting. He desperately wanted to kiss her, but he hung back. "Do you think I'm sick? I mean, like sick in the head?"

She shook her head, her face earnest. "No. Not at all. You're wonderful."

He laughed. "You're biased!" He gave in to the urge to kiss her and leant forward till their lips touched. She flung her arms around his neck and crushed her chest hard against his. Her lips parted and her tongue explored his...

Catcalls and whistles interrupted them. They stepped apart instinctively, Peter wiping his hand across his moist lips, feeling bereft. They must have missed the bell for the end of break, because the rugby team were trotting out onto the pitch, all of them leering at the young couple.

That's torn it, he thought into her head. *Now everyone will be talking about us.*

"Let them."

Hurrying to class, he said. "That won't do at all. The Head-master and Greengage know I am staying at your place. If they get wind we were kissing in public they'll put two and two to-gether and come up with a very large number. Maybe we should avoid each other, at least while we are at school."

"No way!"

"You remember what your Mum said about the price we had to pay for freedom, well, we haven't been nearly cautious enough. Witless may have allies or others will get it into their silly heads to try to expose us."

It was a sobering thought that left him feeling empty and anxious.

"At least let's go home for lunch," she pleaded, almost des-perate.

"Ok. Meet you by the library at twelve."

31.

Hip to hip, shoulder to shoulder, they lay holding hands on Fi's bed, looking up at the ceiling, silent. Peter's breath came in fits and starts and his heart was beating wildly in his chest. He could hear Fi breathing hard too. A pause had been indispensable. Their record broken, they had kissed solidly for more that five minutes. He was sure his lips must be swollen.

With one eye turned inwards, he watched his heart, intrigued. Although his body was excited by what had happened and pleasure coursed through his veins causing his heart to beat faster, it was plain that it made an effort to return to a more sedate pace.

"I can heal people," he said out loud.

"How do you do that?"

Most people would have reacted with disbelief or downright rejection, but Fi always responded with curiosity. He loved that in her. It was like a solid "Yes!" Not just to what he said, but to who he was. He felt strengthened by it and encouraged to go on.

"I enter people's bodies. The other day I healed someone in Kaitling's world that had what I think must have been cancer..." She knew it, because he'd already told her, although he hadn't gone into details.

At the mention of Kaitling, Fi perked up and propped herself on one elbow. "When are you going to show me how to travel to Kaitling's world? You promised. How about now? We don't have to leave for another hour."

Why not? But I want to ask Kaitling's permission first.

"Ok."

Think your answer to me, I will hear it.

OK, she thought, and giggled out loud when she sensed it worked.

Now try to send me a thought.

I love you, she thought, her thought accompanied by the same wave of well being that had saved him the night before.

I love you too, he thought, chuckling. *But that's a very big thought. If we are going to be in Kaitling's head, we'll need thoughts that whisper. Try again.*

If we are going to travel for any time, we should set the alarm.

That's better. Now what we have been doing is talking mind to mind. Travelling between minds is different. It means going into the person's mind, not just talking to them. He jumped over into her mind. *Now I am in your head. Try to feel my presence.*

It wasn't easy. Peter could see she didn't know what to look for. *Give me your hand.*

But I'm already holding it.

I mean mentally. Like this, and he took hold of her hand.

Ah! she thought, delighted and not a little confused. *It's so odd to be inside and outside at the same time.*

Now follow me. He gripped her hand mentally and led her across the barrier that lay around his body and into his own mind. *You are inside me now.* He felt a flutter of intense excitement go through her, which brought with it a good deal of confusion. When he next tried to speak to her, she was so engrossed in her emotions that she heard not a word.

Taking her firmly by the hand he led her back into her own mind.

Why did you do that?

He sensed the poignant loss she felt.

Some thoughts and emotions are so big and noisy they make mind-to-mind travelling impossible. When you were in my body, you completely lost it.

No I didn't. It was wonderful.

He could feel her pleasure. It was so intense and so yearned after that it eclipsed all else. If she could get used to being inside his head, things might be easier.

Listen, I've got a suggestion. I'm going to give you some practice. I'll help you back into my mind and then I'll go down stairs and clean up the mess we left while you stay in my mind and watch and feel what I do.

Ok, she said. Once again it was the lure of being in his body, the body of a boy that drew her out and excited her. He wanted to explore her thoughts and memories to understand why, but now was not the time and he wasn't sure she'd be very happy if he did.

He took her hand again and led her back into his body. He paused a moment as they crossed from her to him. *Do you feel that?* He moved backwards and forward across the line that separated them.

Fi giggled. *It tickles. What is it?*

He explained the second layer that encased the skin and protected against intrusion. He halted a moment and let go of her hand. *Try to cross over on your own.*

She bumped her metaphorical nose against his barrier as she tried to charge through.

Ow! That hurt. Why did you stop me getting in?

My body does in naturally. You need to approach that barrier more gently. You are trying to push through. It's made to resist. Instead of pushing try caressing.

She tried, but she was trembling both with desire and frustration. There was no way she could approach the barrier softly.

You want it too much, he said, quelling his growing irritation. Why had he not had such difficulties? After all, he too had very much wanted to be in the body of a girl. Maybe it was because he had been in Kaitling's head before he even knew he was there.

She tried again several times, but couldn't get through. He could feel her mounting frustration. How strange! A strong desire to do something acted as an impenetrable barrier to actually doing it.

Let's take a rest. It won't help if you wear yourself out.

I don't understand. I have no problem when you lead me across. Why can't I do it on my own?

One thing is sure, you have no problem talking mind-to-mind. I bet you forgot you were even doing it.

She chuckled out loud. *I did indeed.*

Let's see how you fare when I'm further away. He opened his eyes and got to his feet. *You lie there and keep your eyes closed. I'm going downstairs. Tell me the story about your little brother.*

He sensed her body go tense. *Is that too difficult,* he asked, making his way down to the kitchen?

It's not easy. My thoughts might be too 'big' as you put it.

Don't worry. Just tell the tale, however big or small.

My mother was so excited. She was convinced it was a boy. If it had turned out to be a girl I'm sure she would have been a good mother to it, but she just wanted a boy.

Peter knew something of her mother's desire. He wondered why Fi's Mum had wanted a boy so much.

I must have been four at the time. I remember talking to Mum about boys' names. We'd spend hours discussing. She wanted to call him Edward. I have no idea why. Every time I suggested another name, she always came back to Edward. It's a bit old fashioned, but it would have been a good name.

Peter had finished cleaning up in the kitchen. A quick glance at the clock told him they had another twenty minutes before they had to leave.

What happened at the birth? he asked, going through into the living room to admire Fi's painting.

During the entire pregnancy there had never been the slightest hitch. As it was her second child, the midwife expected the delivery to go easily. At least, that's what my father told me afterwards. But it wasn't easy. That cord thing that joins babies to their mothers was wound tight around its neck...

Peter felt her falter. Maybe this was too hard to tell mind-to-mind.

... It strangled him. Father told me the baby was born all blue and nothing they did could save the poor little thing...

Peter could feel she was crying, as the memories rekindled old emotions, but she laboured on.

Mum was devastated. She'd been so happy at the thought of her Edward and now he was dead. I had been looking forward to having a brother too. I think Mum's enthusiasm and desire rubbed off on me... I had imagined a whole future for us. Dad too was very upset although he kept his emotions to himself. I think he held himself together because the rest of us were falling apart.

Mum didn't come home from the hospital. She moved to another one, not a place to have babies, but one for people with problems in their heads. I didn't understand that at the time, but father explained later.

So there was just you and your Dad, Peter prompted as he climbed the stairs to return to Fi's bedroom.

Yes. He hired a woman to look after me, because he was often away on work. She was kind enough, but it wasn't the same. I think it made him sad to return and find Mum absent. Maybe that's why he stayed away so much. When I was alone I was so lonely I began imaging Edward was with me. At first I talked to him about my dreams and wishes. Then I began imagining I was him. If I could fill the hole he'd left, maybe Mum and Dad would return home...

She was sobbing now as Peter sat down next to her and laid a hand on her shoulder.

"Mum finally did return," she said out loud, grasping his hand in hers as she sat up, "but father was gone for ever."

Peter put his arms around her and hugged her. She continued to sob in his arms. "And Edward?"

"He's become a part of me, I suppose. When I kiss other girls, I imagine I'm him." She giggled amongst her sobs. "It feels good in a way, to give him life like that. But I'm pretty sure

I'd like girls anyway, even without Edward. They are so much more sexy than most boys."

"When you kiss me, do you imagine you are Edward too?"

Fi laughed, wiping the tears from her face. "I could be Edward and you could be Fi," she suggested, looking questioningly at him.

"We could indeed," he said, cautious about what he said. "But I want to spend time with Fi as well, lots of time with Fi, it's Fi I love," he said and kissed her gently on her lips.

He could sense she was mulling over his words. It didn't seem easy. Her face looked uncertain as if she were moving forward on unchartered ground. Several times she seemed about to speak, then she closed her mouth.

"You can be a boy if you want. That's OK with me, but it's the girl I love."

She suddenly burst into tears again and started pummelling his chest. He just stood there. Her blows had no force to them. It was more despair than rage. When she ceased, he pulled her closer and wrapped his arms around her, cradling her.

It was time to return to school. They were going to be late, but he didn't dare interrupt the moment. It was Fi that broke their embrace. She pulled a handkerchief from her pocket and blew her nose. "We are going to be late. I'll go and wash my face and then we can leave."

32.

Early afternoon was uneventful, were it not for Fi's constant mind-to-mind chatter. It was hard to concentrate. She told him about the delicious girls in her class: about Kitty Turner who was wearing pale yellow stockings under her uniform, despite the dress code, and who had put on eye liner, and Marlene whose breasts were so big they stuck out through her blouse, and how Ariana crossed and uncrossed her legs under her desk all the time, and there was the way Christine hung her head in thought or ran her fingers absent-mindedly over her luscious lips.

Listening to her you'd have thought it was an all-girls class, but Peter knew for sure that several of the third form rugby team were also in her class. When he'd got caught unprepared by Mr. Thompson's question in maths, Peter asked Fi to stop using mind-to-mind during classes unless there was an emergency.

In the protracted silence that followed, he worried she might be in a huff. But then, just as the bell rang, her voice called out urgently in his head. *Those rugby bods have me cornered outside class. They're taunting me about kissing a junior.*

Peter was about to hurry to her rescue when Fi announced that Mrs. Greengage had sent them packing. The gym teacher always told them that, unlike football, rugby was a ruffians' game played by gentlemen. Peter hadn't seen many gentlemen amongst the third form rugby team.

The afternoon was punctuated by a number of minor skirmishes, in which members of the rugby team tried to corner Fi.

Each time, the presence of a teacher or other pupils saved her.

I reckon they are trying to get revenge for you making fun of them, Fi thought as the final bell rang for the afternoon. *They are too cowardly to confront you face to face.*

Hurry to the library, Peter thought. *It was the safest place he could think of. I'll come and meet you there.*

Gym was Fi's last class of the day. When it came to hiding from the rampant rugby players, there couldn't have been a worse place. The whole area around the gym was riddled with dark corners and sinister places where the worst crimes could be committed unnoticed, outside class time.

When Peter reached the library, out of breath from running, Fi was not there. She hadn't spoken to him mind-to-mind either. He called, but she didn't respond. Something must be seriously wrong.

The gym was across the other side of school from the library. It would take him five minutes to get there. He'd be too late. Desperate, he glanced around the library. A small alcove table was free in the far corner. He dumped his bag under the table, sat down, laid his head on his arms, closed his eyes and jumped to Fi.

A wave of terror greeted him. Fi was trapped in an abandoned corner of the girls' locker rooms. Two oversized rugby thugs clasped her wrists from behind, yanking her arms back in a painful grip. A third one stood arrogant in front of her, fumbling with her breasts.

"Come on, tart!" the big one said as he struggled with the buttons of Fi's blouse. "You're not going to tell me you don't know how to do this."

The words had Peter in a rage. *I'm here,* he told Fi. *I'll deal with him. Kaitling,* he called out imperiously, *help Fi!* Then he jumped from Fi to the brute and slammed into his mind like a furious bull, not caring what damage he did. *Stop that immediately,* he shouted in the youth's head, mouthing each word separately. The youth did stop, alarmed at the voice he heard. He looked around perplexed but could see no one.

Do that again and I'll kill you, Peter snarled in the youth's head.

Peter saw his mistake immediately. The youth thought Fi was playing a trick on him and he turned on her with renewed ardour. "Don't think you can trick me like that, tart!" he spluttered and he raised his hand to slap her.

Peter saw Fi flinch through the eyes of the youth. He elbowed the youth aside and took control of his body. The slap missed and Peter carried it through, full force, to hit one of the boys standing behind her. The boys holding Fi stared at him, astonished.

"What are you doing, Mat?" one asked.

Peter had Mat punch the boy he'd already hit, causing him to bend over in pain. Then Peter smashed Mat into the second boy, freeing Fi who sank to her knees. Mat flung the boy on top of the first one and the two floundered, grappling with each other, trying to get to their feet. Peter had Mat fling himself onto the struggling heap, lashing out wildly with his fists.

Both must have realised this was no joke, for they began defending themselves. Punches and kicks were flying in every direction. Mat got a knee in the groin and someone tried to gouge out his eye. Peter released Mat's mind, for fear he himself would get stuck if the youth got knocked out.

Back in Fi's mind, he found no trace of Kaitling. Fi was slumped on the tiled floor, frozen in fright, her arms and legs trembling, her face wet with tears. He did what he could to calm her emotions and coaxed her away from the scene. She staggered along the deserted corridors, as Peter mentally guided her to the infirmary. Luckily the caretaker's wife, Mrs. Arne, was cleaning up the mess Witless had made.

"Oh my dear!" she exclaimed seeing Fi stagger towards her. The woman hurried forward and took Fi in her arms. "What happened to you, my dear?"

Fi was unable to reply. Her mutism worried Peter, but he had no time to deal with it. Seeing that Fi was in good hands, Peter spoke to her mind-to-mind. *I'll be with you in a moment. Mrs.*

Arne will look after you.

The attack had left Fi mute but he could feel she didn't want him to go. *The sooner I go,* he tried to reassure her, *the sooner I'll be back.*

Returning to his body, he was confused to find it wasn't where he'd expected it to be. Instead he was sitting silent and unmoving in a classroom with a number of other pupils, all in detention. Kaitling was there.

What ever happened?

A snotty young boy tried to wake you up, so I hit him. That had the place in an uproar. People screamed and ran for the door. I couldn't understand why. An old man came over; he seemed to be in charge. He said you had broken some rule or other and he would have to report you to a man called the Head. In the mean time, he said he'd give you detention. He ordered two of the older boys to escort you here. As you left, I heard the man muttering that the school had taken a serious downward turn since the new headmaster took over and that there was too much fighting going on.

I can't stay here, Fi has been badly hurt, Peter said, agitated.

"Keep still, McCloud. You are in enough trouble as it is," the prefect surveying detention said. He sounded delighted at Peter's punishment.

You could just walk out, Kaitling suggested. *He couldn't stop you.*

You don't have to come here every day. Peter glanced surreptitiously at his neighbour, a second year girl. *I have an idea. If I'm not back when the chaos breaks, get me into the corridor and hide.*

He sprung lightly into the mind of the girl next to him and conjured up the image of a large, black, hairy spider crawling down her back. The effect was immediate. The girl sprang to her feet screaming and tried to dash for the door. She overturned several desks in her mad rush and hurtled into the prefect who grappled with her, trying to stop her leave.

Peter jumped into another head. This time he thought of

snakes. The effect was the same. The boy screamed and climbed up onto his chair, flailing wildly around him. People were standing up to get out of his way, ignoring the prefect who ordered them to sit down.

One more person, Peter thought. Sure, the prefect. It was really a mean thing to do, but he was desperate, and the boy had been nasty to him. Peter whispered in the prefect's head that he was bursting to go to the toilet. The poor bloke hopped from one foot to the other trying to keep order as he struggled not to wet himself. Peter kept up the pressure till the prefect fled from the room.

Back in his own body, Peter hurried out of the door before anyone came to investigate. He dashed along the corridors, head down, making for the infirmary. It was as he rounded a corner that he hurtled into the Headmaster.

"Sorry, Sir," Peter said disengaging himself as he tried to edge round the man. The Head didn't look at all like the friendly or considerate man he'd been earlier.

"Stay here, McCloud. I want to have a word with you."

"I can't, Sir. I'll do whatever you want afterwards. But now I must go to the infirmary. Fi, I mean Fiona, has been hurt."

"What nonsense is this?" the Head asked, sounding like a typical headmaster.

Peter stood his ground and stared into the Head's eyes. "Don't force me to get round you," Peter said, more pleading than threatening. "Come with me, Sir. You'll see. She's with Mrs. Arne. Fi was attacked by a group from the rugby team."

The Headmaster stood there staring at him unbelieving.

Making the most of the Head's confusion, Peter stepped cautiously round him and hurried off down the corridor. He could hear the man following, but didn't look round. Instead, he quickened his pace, breaking into a jog.

Mrs. Arne had settled Fi on the couch in the infirmary and was sitting next to her holding her hand. The girl's face was deadly pale, her eyes were open, but they stared unseeing. Her blouse was torn and hung open revealing part of her chest.

Seeing him arrive, Mrs. Arne tried to chase him away, but Fi groaned and feebly held out her arms to him. He immediately sat next to Fi on the couch and took her in his arms.

"Oh my love," he said softly. "It's going to be alright."

She curled up next to him and laid her head on his shoulder while he ran his fingers gently through her hair.

"It's going to be alright."

The Headmaster must have arrived because Peter could hear Mrs. Arne talking quietly to him somewhere nearby. He didn't care. Fi was the only thing that mattered.

I will see if there is any physical damage, Kaitling said.

Peter had been so upset he hadn't even noticed that Kaitling had come with him. He continued to whisper reassuring words both directly and mind-to-mind to Fi, but she uttered no word of reply.

"Peter," the Headmaster said, addressing Peter by his Christian name for the first time. He no longer sounded angry, but rather concerned and perplexed. "Would it be alright if I phoned Fiona's mother to come and fetch you?"

"I think she's away on a trip. She'll only be back this evening."

"I still think it would be better if both of you were there rather than here."

Kaitling returned at that moment. *She's got some bruises and scratches and she's in a state of shock. I think you should take that man's offer and get Fi home. She seems to have lost the ability to talk. We can try and help her once she's home.*

"Ok," Peter said replying to both of them.

"Good. Mrs. Arne could you drive the two of them home. I will follow in my car."

Back at Fi's place, Peter made Fi a nest of cushions and blankets on the living room sofa, while Mrs. Arne tried her hand at the gadgets in the kitchen, making tea. Fi was comfortably settled when Mrs. Arne carried in a tray with a pot of tea and several mugs.

Fi didn't respond when they offered her a mug of tea, so Peter took it and sipped tiny mouthfuls as he cuddled Fi.

"It's good," he said to Fi. "You should try it."

Fi did not react.

Someone knocked and Mrs. Arne went to open the door. The Headmaster had arrived. He came in and sat in an armchair looking at Peter and Fi. Mrs. Arne handed him a cup of tea.

"I should get back," the caretaker's wife said. "It's a busy time. I can return later, if you need me."

"That's fine Mrs. Arne," the Head said. "Your help is very much appreciated, but I don't think that will be necessary. Fiona's mother will be returning soon, I believe."

33.

She's in a state of shock, Kaitling thought. *I have no idea how to deal with that.*

I want to check, Peter told Kaitling, *but I can't with the Headmaster here.*

Let's change places.

Just don't punch him on the nose. He scowled at the memory of having to do detention. He'd never had detention before.

Kaitling scoffed mentally. *I think I've learnt that lesson.*

Peter relinquished control of his body and slipped into Fi's mind.

It wouldn't do any good rummaging around looking for a label saying: ability to talk. So he drew back and pictured the whole brain, watching carefully to see if he could identify parts that were active. There were loads of them. This wasn't going to be easy.

Fi, I need to talk to you so I can figure how to help you speak again. I'm going to babble away until I find the place in your brain where voice is dealt with. You know, he began, *there was a time when I would have been happy to have a girl friend who couldn't contradict me.*

He felt her stir. Maybe he was getting through by another route.

Yeah. I used to find girls irritating because they never listened and just talked about themselves and things that interested them. You changed everything. It is so interesting to talk

*to you. I love to hear your voice and you have such surprising
things to say...*

He had already found the place he was looking for, but he
continued talking in the hope she would stir again. She didn't.

*I have to return to my body. The Headmaster is here and I
can't leave myself in the hands of Kaitling too long. The Head
will surely notice. I'll come back later. And I promised to teach
you to travel to other minds.* Once again he felt her stir, but it
didn't last.

"... Belladonna, probably," Kaitling was saying to the Head.
Peter had been so engrossed in his words with Fi that he hadn't
realised Kaitling was using his body to talk to the Head. *What's
going on?*

*We've been talking about medicinal herbs. The man seems
to know something about the subject.*

*He ought to, he teaches botany when he's not running the
school. Now I'm in a spot, he will think I know all about it.*

"Where did you learn all this, Peter?"

"From the same friend who taught me unarmed combat."

"I'd really like to meet him."

"It's a her, Sir. Her name's Kaitling, but she lives a long way
away."

"Kaitling? Sounds Chinese."

Peter kept quiet. It was safer. He hoped the Head asked no
questions about botany because Kaitling had had to leave.

Fi was still in his arms. It looked like she'd fallen asleep,
but when Peter tried to make her more comfortable she stirred
and groaned.

The Headmaster looked from Fi to Peter and back again.

"I'm not going to play the policeman, but I am perplexed.
Several inexplicable things happened today. Let me lay them
out like pieces of a puzzle. If you can help me fit them together
I'd be most grateful."

There was another long pause, as if he were collecting his
thoughts. "When I bumped into you in the corridor, you were
on your way to see Fiona. You knew she'd been attacked by a

group of rugby players. At least that's what you told me. You were so sure. Yet you couldn't possibly have known. You were in the library. According to the librarian, you caused a disturbance and were sent for detention. There's another thing I can't understand. I don't see you as one who would pick a fight. Then one of the teachers came to report a disturbance in detention. Apparently several pupils were in a panic, something about spiders and snakes."

Peter had a hard time not smiling.

The Head raised his eyebrows. "I see you know what I'm talking about. None of this fits. There must be some missing parts. Doesn't it irritate you when you can't finish a puzzle because pieces are missing? It does me. Maybe irritate is not the right word, let's say I'm puzzled."

He smiled at his little joke, but his face quickly turned serious. "Then there was the gym master who told me that three members of the rugby team were found beating each other up in the girls' locker rooms. If they had been the ones to attack Fiona, why would they be attacking each other? You see why I am puzzled."

Peter sighed. "I don't think I can help you, Sir. I agree it does sound strange." Peter didn't like lying, it made him feel uncomfortable, and people noticed. He was walking a very fine line with his replies.

"If I were not the Headmaster of the school you are attending, would it be any easier to fill in the gaps?"

Peter twisted his mouth in a grimace. This was all so tricky and the Head was a clever man. He didn't feel a match for him. "Probably not."

The Head got to his feet. "I'll go and make some more tea and see if there is something to eat. You must be hungry. Do you have any idea when Mrs. Tanner will return?"

"She said nothing about the evening meal. So I imagine she will be back soon. Unlike my Mum, I can't imagine her leaving us to fend for ourselves. She's such a caring person."

"As are you, Peter," the Head said, disappearing into the

kitchen.

The compliment troubled Peter, but he had no time to mull over it. Fi was much more important. He pushed her hair from her eyes and kissed her on the forehead.

"Come back my love," he whispered. "I miss hearing your voice."

He felt tears welling up in his eyes. It had been an exhausting day, what with saving the priest and the night spent with Fi. Then the fight with Witless, the talk with the Head and all the trouble with the thugs who wanted to hurt Fi. He let the tears flow. To hell! What did it matter? He closed his eyes, stifling a sob. He just wanted to be alone with Fi, to cuddle up next to her and to fill her with his love till she was whole again.

He remembered how Fi had saved him that night with her love. He had no idea how she had done it, but it had worked. Could it work the other way round? He conjured up all his love for her, till his body was brimming over. Then he let it flow warm and soft into Fi who lay cradled in his arms. *I love you,* he whispered in her mind. He felt her stir and something soft touched his eyelids, brushing the tears away. *I love you too,* Fi said mind-to-mind.

He couldn't help himself, the sobs broke through and he hugged her as tight as he could, feeling her lips soft against his cheeks. Her tears mingled with his.

"I see you have worked another miracle, Peter," the Headmaster said, startling them both. He was standing in the doorway from the kitchen, his look quizzical. "Glad to have you back, Fiona. This should tide us over till your mother gets home." He set a new pot of tea and a plate of bread and butter and jam on the table.

"What are you doing here, Sir?" Fiona asked, her voice croaky.

"Good question," he replied.

"Dr. Grant," Mrs. Tanner said as she entered the sitting room, holding out her hand to shake his. No one had noticed her arrive. "What a pleasant surprise." She glanced at Fi and Peter questioningly, then frowned. "At least, I hope it is."

Dr. Grant smiled. "We had some problems at school. I won't say it is all sorted out, but the worst seems to be over."

Mrs. Tanner looked at Fi. "Are you alright? You look pale."

"It's a long story," Dr. Grant said.

"Well you'll just have to stay to dinner and tell me all abut it," Mrs. Tanner said with a flourish.

"I don't want to intrude on your private life..." Dr. Grant began, edging towards the door. "I just wanted to be sure that both Fiona and Peter were safe."

Mrs. Tanner looked worried. "Safe? You really are going to have to stay. I insist." She smiled at him, a little embarrassed. "Just joking, of course. I'm not going to hold you hostage."

Peter saw the Head raise his eyebrows.

"That's alright," the man said. "The paperwork can wait till tomorrow. I'll tell my botany class I couldn't mark their work because a beautiful woman held me hostage. That is sure to set them gossiping."

Mrs. Tanner blushed, presumably at the word 'beautiful', and hurried off to the kitchen.

Peter chuckled mentally in Fi's head. *So that's why he stayed.* When Fi didn't understand, Peter added, *he stayed to be with your Mum.*

What nonsense.

Wanna bet.

"The more I look at you two," the Head said, sitting back in his armchair, "the more I have the strange impression you are having a silent conversation behind my back, as it were."

Both Fi and Peter blushed.

Dr. Grant laughed. "You see what I mean."

"You are far too clever and observant, Sir," Peter commented.

"Don't think flattery will get you off the hook."

"If some things are not said it is maybe because it is better that way." He immediately wanted to retract what he'd said. You didn't give lessons to your Headmaster. What's more, his words sounded pompous, even to his own ears.

"Indeed!" the Head exclaimed.

Peter did get off the hook though, because Mrs. Tanner asked him to lay the table and carry through things from the kitchen.

"Is Fi alright?" Mrs. Tanner asked when they were alone.

"She had a terrible shock. Some pupils attacked her..." He didn't get any further because Mrs. Tanner dropped a plate into the sink where it broke into several pieces.

"Maybe you should let me tell the story, Peter," Dr. Grant said from the doorway. Peter had not heard him arrive. "Then if Mrs. Tanner wants to throw a plate at me, at least you won't get hurt."

Mrs. Tanner went through the motions of throwing an imaginary plate at the Headmaster who ducked out of the way, laughing.

Fi's Mum made a salad and there was to be lasagne that she had prepared the day before. "We can eat the salad while it heats up. Would you like some wine, Dr. Grant?"

He declined. "I really do have correcting to do when I get home." Then he turned to Fi. "Can you make it to the table, Fiona?"

Peter liked the considerate way the man went about things. The Headmaster was attentive to details and careful about people, especially those who were vulnerable. It was one of the most surprising things about getting to know Dr. Grant.

"How do you manage to be so considerate and yet be a headmaster at the same time, Sir?" Peter asked. He liked to disarm people with questions that required deep thought. "I mean, aren't people in such a position generally distant and uncompromising?"

The Head chuckled. "Being in a position of authority does require you to keep a distance. Being friends with everyone doesn't work well when you need to give them orders, and there are some things that you really need to be strict about, like not attacking younger, more vulnerable people," he said looking at Fi. "But if you stray too far on the side of distance and strictness, you end up hard and unapproachable. So you need to be open to the unexpected and accessible to those who are honest and forthright with you, especially if they take risks trying to do what their heart dictates."

"The school is very lucky to have you, Dr. Grant," Mrs Tanner said, carrying in an enormous dish of lasagne.

Peter remembered the words of the librarian that Kaitling had relayed. Some people thought Dr. Grant's ways destroyed the traditional values of the school. He wondered if it was the same people that regretted admitting girls to the school. As a pupil he had very little insight into what the staff thought of the Headmaster.

"Grace?" Mrs. Tanner asked the Headmaster.

He lowered his eyes and said quietly: "For what we are about to receive and for all we have received throughout the day, whether it be good or bad, may the Lord make us truly thankful."

There was a tiny chorus of "Amen" then Mrs. Tanner served the lasagne and salad was placed on the side plate.

"Bon appétit," Fi said.

"Gé Bao!" Peter said. "I think that's how it is pronounced."

"What does that mean?" Fi asked.

"It means have a good meal in Kaitling's language."

"Ah" the Headmaster exclaimed. "Your elusive friend who taught you martial arts and who knows so much about botany."

"You must tell us more about her, Peter, but not now," Mrs Tanner said. "Now it's time to tell me what happened today."

34.

I think we should tiptoe away and leave them to it, Peter thought to Fi, delighted that Dr. Grant and Fi's Mum were getting on so well. The two were seated in adjacent armchairs talking animatedly about people they knew, as they sipped a coffee Fi's Mum had percolated.

Are you sure we can leave them alone? Fi asked, tongue in cheek.

Peter chuckled. *I told you there was something more to his visit!*

"We're off," Fi said, getting to her feet. "Do you think we dare leave you two alone?"

The Headmaster chuckled, but Mrs. Tanner looked embarrassed and aimed a playful swipe at Fi. "Impudent hussy!" her Mum said, pretending to be annoyed. "Off to bed with you and no lingering in Peter's room or vice versa."

"Good night, Sir," Peter said. "I'm glad we had a chance to get to know each other better."

"Me too, Peter. Good night," the Head said. Then turning to Fi, Dr. Grant added: "Good night, Fiona. I wish you pleasant dreams."

The goodnights over, they were off up the stairs two at a time and into their respective rooms to get ready for bed. Once all was done, they lay together on Fi's bed, cuddled in each other's arms, talking mind-to-mind.

I should check on Kaitling, Peter thought.

Don't forget you promised to teach me how to travel be-tween minds.

OK. Come with me to Kaitling's.

Fi was so excited she pulled Peter in a tight embrace, plant-ing a passionate kiss on his lips.

He was relieved that the horror of the rugby thugs had not soured her contact with him as a boy. They kissed fervently for several minutes till both of them were breathless and Fi remem-bered why she was kissing him.

So? Are we going?

I'm going to talk to Kaitling first. It might be rude to just arrive like that. I don't want to upset her.

He stretched out his mind in search of Kaitling and spoke directly into her head. *Hi Kaitling. How's that priest?*

I can't talk now. I'm having a complicated conversation with him.

Do you mind if I listen in with Fi?

She's listening in now, isn't she?

Yes, Peter admitted, feeling guilty. *How did you know?*

I can feel her eagerness. Ok. But don't get in the way.

Peter withdrew. *We will go then. You heard what Kaitling said. She's with the priest I healed the other day.*

So how do we do this?

He could sense her trepidation. *I'll guide you. I want you to get a feel for the thing. You can learn how to go on your own another time. Do you remember how to take my hand, mentally I mean?* She did, he felt her fingers firmly in his. *Ok. Off we go.*

Travelling was a little more laborious, maybe because he had a passenger. He could feel Fi's awe as she looked through Kaitling's eyes at the middle-aged priest squatting on the floor opposite her.

If we speak mind-to-mind, Peter told her, *Kaitling will not hear. But you must be careful to speak only to me. To be safe, perhaps you shouldn't speak at first.* He felt Fi nod her agree-ment.

"Why are you so sure your god does not approve of women?"

"The highest beings, the Chosen Ones..."

"Your priests?"

"Yes. Those of us men who serve god, we are the only ones who can hear the voice of god. No women can."

Peter could feel Fi shifting in indignation. *Keep your emotions quiet if you can,* he warned.

"Is that proof that women are inferior?"

The man seemed to think it was self-evident.

"What makes you think women can't hear your god? Maybe they can, but don't tell you."

The man laughed. Clearly he thought her words absurd. Peter wondered how the man would react if Kaitling were to talk into his mind, but she let the subject drop.

"How often does your god speak to you?"

"He speaks to the most important Chosen Ones regularly. Those who occupy a more lowly post hear him rarely. In fact, most of us only ever hear him when we are accepted into the order. Hearing the voice of god is the ultimate test we have to endure."

"So how do you know what the god says?"

"The most important Chosen Ones relay the words of god to the rest of us."

"How does that work?"

"We have a period of prayer and meditation at sunrise and at sunset. It is then that those who have heard the word of god pass it on to the rest of us."

Peter was fascinated. It was a bit like his church although a lot more rigid. The vicar spoke to the bishop and the bishop spoke to the archbishop and the latter spoke to god. And the normal man in the street believed what he was told.

"Has anyone ever questioned the word of god?"

Peter shuddered. She was taking a risk, but he understood why she wanted to know.

The look on the priest's face turned dark and foreboding and he remained silent for a moment. Peter wondered if it was a sin to question the word of god. He whispered the idea into Kaitling's head.

"I'm sorry. I didn't mean to offend. Is it a sin to question the word of god?"

"You must understand that the word of god is infallible. Questioning it is unthinkable." He hesitated a long moment as if weighing up how to go on. Kaitling kept quiet. "Your question pains me, because no one would dare think of such a thing."

If there had ever been a revolt against their god, it could happen again. It might provide the key to overthrowing the Syvan government and freeing her island.

"Can you tell me more?"

He snorted. "I have already said far too much. In doing so, I have committed a great sin."

The priest hung his head in despair and closed his eyes. Peter wondered if he was going to bury himself in remorse or, worse, warn his superiors. Peter was about to jump into the priest's mind, when Kaitling laid a restraining hand on him.

"What has happened to you must have left you confused and doubting. You were seriously ill. That illness was sparked because you were not allowed to love a woman."

The man flinched at the reference to Olga.

"Do you think your god would want you to be ill? Surely not! Yet his servants forced you to seal off those thoughts, planting the seeds of a sickness that would have eaten you up."

She paused but the priest did not respond. His hands remained clasped over his eyes, his head bowed. "Your body knows what is right. It knew that refusing those memories was not good. Yet the Chosen Ones forced you to turn a deaf ear to your body. They would have killed you."

"But sacrificing ourselves for god is the best thing we can do."

Peter was convinced that trying to provoke doubt was not a good strategy. For such a person doubt might be worse than death. He shared his thoughts with Kaitling.

You will not be able to change him, Fi added, speaking for the first time. *My mother worked with missionaries, some of whom were like him. They can't hear contradiction, even when it is obvious their behaviour is damaging both them and those around.*

You are right, Kaitling admitted. *I had hoped to wear him down, but it just makes him cling even harder to his beliefs.*

"You are tired," the priest said. "I will let you rest. We can talk another time."

I hope he's not off to warn his colleagues, Peter thought as the priest left. *Where are we, by the way?*

We are still headed for Navigon. We should arrive tomorrow, if the winds hold good.

A different train of thought distracted Peter. *I was wondering, if I could do away with their god, do you think it would stop them?*

Neither Fi nor Kaitling answered.

I mean, it might be possible to follow the voice back to its source. I bet its no god, but a man. If that were possible, I could put an end to the voice.

He was surprised there was still no reaction from the girls. *Kaitling?*

Sorry, she said, yawning, *I drifted off to sleep. What were you saying?*

Where's Fi?

I think she's fallen asleep. You'd better take her home. See you tomorrow.

Peter was about to look for Fi when the door of Kaitling's cell crashed open and a burly priest marched in. Neither he nor Kaitling had ever seen him before.

"Stand up in my presence," the priest ordered.

Kaitling struggled to her feet, while Peter jumped into the priest's head.

"You are accused of trying to pervert one of the chosen ones. You will be tried in Navigon and then put to death."

Peter rummaged hastily through the man's recent memories. The other priest had been sent away for what the man darkly thought of as 're-education'. Peter gathered that a lot of pain would be involved. Kaitling was to be taken directly to Navigon where there would be a show trial and she would be publicly executed.

Apparently they had abandoned their plans to use her as bait for her father despite the fact that he was still on the run. The resistance was not going well. A group of resistance fighters had been cornered near the town of Gao and only a few escaped. The Syvans were no longer so concerned about them.

"So much for justice," Kaitling said.

The priest raised his hand to strike Kaitling but Peter seized his mind briefly and had him smash his hand into the wall instead. Several small bones in his hand shattered. Peter immediately jumped back to Kaitling, not wanting the priest to search for an alien presence in his head.

Judging by his face, the man was in extreme pain, but he held his emotions in check, making no noise. He glared at Kaitling for a long moment, his eyes full of hatred but also doubt, and then he left, slamming the door.

Peter told her what he'd learnt. Kaitling was relieved to hear her father was still alive, even if the rest of the news was depressing. *Gao,* she mused, *that should be quite close to us. I'll try speaking to father mind-to-mind. You should take Fi home. I'm not sure it's good for her to sleep in someone else's mind.*

Peter had completely forgotten Fi. It took him a moment to find her sleeping presence. It was very faint. She was curled up, as it were, in a corner of Kaitling's mind.

Come on Fi, he said, cradling her in his arms, *it's time to go home.*

35.

It was almost midnight when they returned to their bodies. Fi was so drowsy she didn't have the strength to cross the corridor to her bed. She curled up next to Peter and went back to sleep. Travelling between minds must have exhausted her. Then Peter remembered she had been attacked that afternoon and regretted having kept her so long in Kaitling's mind.

He was going over his visit, wondering what he could do to help Kaitling, when she spoke to him.

I've managed to contact father. He's hiding nearby with a band of resistance fighters and is going to rescue me. I want to get as much sleep as I can. You should do the same. I might need you later. She wished him goodnight and was gone.

Peter was afraid the prospect of a sea rescue would keep him awake, but he too was exhausted and fell asleep immediately.

To his surprise it was gone six when Kaitling woke him. She sounded excited and happy. *We made it,* she exclaimed. *The priests were not expecting an attack. My father and his men climbed on board before anyone had any idea what was happening. Father was overjoyed to find me unharmed. I told him I had not been tortured, but I don't think he believed me. We sank the ship and returned to the marshes north of Gao with two rowing boats. That's where we are now.*

This is wonderful news, Peter told her. *How long can you hold out where you are?*

Father reckons it will take them several days to realise the boat has gone. Then they'll come looking.

Unless of course that priest sent in regular reports. In which case he'll be missed and you may have a visit sooner.

Kaitling brushed aside his pessimism. *Why don't you come over? It's really interesting here. I'll show you around.*

Does your father know about me?

No. I never told him about my experiments. I'm not sure he would approve. I suspect he would think it too dangerous. He'd say I wasn't properly trained. As if there was anybody who could teach me, she scoffed.

He might be jealous of his brilliant daughter.

She gave him a mental poke in the ribs.

He loved her when she was so playful. *Ok. I'll join you. I have at least an hour before I have to get up.* He quickly checked to see Fi was still asleep and jumped to the marshes north of Gao.

He found Kaitling alone, balancing her way along a narrow plank-covered path between head-high bulrushes. She carried a bow in her hand and a quiver of arrows slung across her shoulder. At her waist he felt a heavy knife pressing against her thigh. The air was humid and the sun already hot. Tiny insects buzzed around as she brushed the sweat from her brow.

Welcome to the Dar marshes.

Where are you going?

To meet my father. He went out in a small boat early this morning to steal supplies from Gao. He should be back soon.

Peter could hear the lapping of waves nearby and the screech of gulls overhead. The sea must be close. The path turned abruptly and then ran alongside a waterway just wide enough for a rowing boat.

Father told me to wait here, out of sight. But I want to explore further and see if we can spot them arriving. She ventured forward cautiously, moving from tuft to tuft. The planks underfoot had ceased some yards back and there was no guarantee the ground would hold her weight. Several times her feet slipped on a wet clump of earth and she almost slithered into the mud, but she was agile and managed to catch her balance. The sea was in sight when the tuft on which she was standing gave way and both her feet plunged into the marsh, sinking rapidly up to her calves. As she struggled to extract herself, she almost fell over backwards but just managed to keep upright.

If I get my bowstring wet, it won't be much use.

Peter was relieved to see she wasn't sinking any deeper. He didn't want to loose Kaitling to the mud.

Clinging to a larger clump of bulrushes, she struggled for several minutes and finally managed to drag one foot free of the mud, but lost her shoe to the sticky mass. Sitting on a large tuft of earth, extracting the other foot was a little bit easier although she lost that shoe too. Her hands were plastered with mud, so she rubbed them on her jacket just in case she had to use her bow.

Bent over double on the tuft she breathed deeply trying to regain her composure.

It was Peter that heard the faint splash of oars. Kaitling wanted to get to her feet and greet her father, overjoyed that he had made it back safe, but Peter cautioned her to remain hidden. To anyone entering the narrow channel by boat, the bulrushes largely concealed Kaitling. The fact that the people arriving were absolutely silent made her suspicious. If it had been her father, he might well have called out. Kaitling reached back and pulled an arrow from her quiver and fit it in her bow.

When she glanced round the bulrushes she saw several Syvan soldiers stealthily climb from a boat and make off down the path. She was unsure what to do. It was difficult to tell how many soldiers remained behind.

Let me go and take a look, Peter suggested.

But you can't jump into the minds of people you haven't seen.

All I need is a glimpse. But none of the remaining soldiers showed themselves or made a move. *I'll just have to jump blind.*

Don't be silly. That's far too risky.

Maybe there's some other way. Let me think. When I want to reach you, I stretch out till I find you. If I stretch out like that, maybe I can feel these people and then I can aim for one of them. He could feel that Kaitling was dubious, but neither of them had a better suggestion.

He sent out feelers in the direction of the nearby boat and immediately felt the presence of several people. He had the impression they were all men, but he could not distinguish between them.

Wish me luck, he said and jumped.

He was reassured to land safely in the mind of someone, but he was otherwise out of luck because the person was unconscious. He flicked through the person's recent memories and was surprised to find he'd chosen Kaitling's father. The man had been taken prisoner as he brought back the food he'd stolen. The Syvans had returned, hoping to round up the rest of the resistance fighters.

Peter quickly checked for any serious physical damage. Several ribs were broken and there was internal bleeding. Peter staunched the flow of blood and knitted the tissues back together. It was rough and ready work, but he had no time to fiddle about. He realigned the broken ribs and coaxed the body to fit them back as new.

As he did so, he called Kaitling mind-to-mind and told her he'd found her father. He then jumped into one of the other nearby presences. It was a sailor who had rowed them there. Not wasting time, Peter immediately took control of the man's mind. The man had no idea what was happening and offered little resistance. There were two soldiers in the boat. They were tense and vigilant, bows at the ready.

He described the situation to Kaitling. *I'll take one of the soldiers. You shoot the other one.*

But I might hurt you.

I'll take refuge in your father. I'll try to wake him. Ready?

She was.

He made the sailor get cautiously to his feet and then stumble forward, as if by accident, knocking over one of the soldiers. Out of the corner of his eye, he saw an arrow hit the second soldier who collapsed overboard into the muddy water with a noisy splash. The soldier he had been struggling with broke free and got to his feet, preparing to shoot an arrow. Peter heard the thud of an arrow planting itself in the chest of the soldier. The man keeled over falling next to the sailor. Peter released his hold on the man who scrambled to get out of the boat.

He jumped for Kaitling's father just at the moment an arrow sliced into the sailor's throat and the man fell back lifeless into the boat. As he sped across the short distance that separated him from Tyzi, Peter felt a dark shadow race after him.

Death, he thought, going icy cold.

Then he was enveloped in the warmth and security of Kaitling's father, and relief flooded over him.

Are you OK? Kaitling called out, anxiety in her voice.

I'm OK, but I nearly didn't make it. He shuddered mentally.

Sometimes you scare me, Peter McCloud! Kaitling exclaimed, her voice laced with tenderness and concern. *You take far too many risks. I really don't want to loose you...* Her words trailed off.

Her tone surprised him. Never had she expressed such affection before. It wasn't like Fi, with her heights of love and passion, but there was a sense of love and concern in her voice that troubled him.

I'm going to wake your father, he said, changing the subject.

Tyzi was already stirring. Peter whispered quietly: *Kaitling is here with you.*

The man opened his eyes and was abruptly wide-awake. *Who are you,* he asked? Peter didn't stay around for explanations. He jumped back to Kaitling.

As Kaitling came forward to hug her father, Peter could see he looked perplexed. But he said nothing.

"Let's round up those others before they do any more damage," she said, picking up a second bow from the boat.

They crept noiselessly along the path in the direction of the lean-to where the other resistance fighters were hiding. The Syvan soldiers had clearly hoped to catch them unaware, but the lookouts must have spotted them and they had managed to stall the attack. It was easy to pick off the enemy one by one from behind.

Sometime later, settling in to eat breakfast from the spoils that he had brought back, he confronted his daughter.

"I think you owe me an explanation." His tone was distant.

Kaitling tried to feign ignorance, looking at him as if she had no idea what he meant. *That's not going to work,* Peter pointed out.

"Tell me daughter, how can you explain that my ribs, several of which were broken, are now all healed?"

Kaitling genuinely looked surprised.

I forgot to tell you, Peter whispered. *I couldn't leave him like that.* And there it was again, a feeling of affection rolling over him, warm and comforting.

"And whose voice was it I heard in my head when I awoke? It sounded young and male. It certainly wasn't you."

"That was my good friend Peter," Kaitling admitted. "It was Peter that healed you. It was Peter that distracted the soldiers and saved your life." Peter felt her gratitude flow through him.

"I don't understand," Tyzi said, ceasing to munch on the piece of bread he had in his hand. "That isn't possible."

"Well actually it is. We have been experimenting. Not only is it possible to travel to the mind of someone else and see the world from that person's perspective, but also to heal people. Peter managed it while he was in someone's mind.

Better not tell him about taking control of the person, Peter suggested. *That might really frighten him.*

"He healed a lion cub that was about to attack me and he healed the priest that was guarding me. He was suffering from a growth in his brain."

Kaitling's father looked dubious.

I think we've turned his world upside down, Peter commented.

Kaitling smiled.

Her father must have noticed her reaction because he said:

"He's still here, isn't he?"

Greetings Master Tyzi, Peter said mind-to-mind.

Her father was used to communicating mind-to-mind but the idea of someone residing in his daughter's head talking to him had him gasp.

You should be careful with your ribs, Peter told him, *I had very little time to heal them so they may well be fragile for a few days.*

"Are you a magician?" Tyzi asked.

Peter laughed. *We don't have magicians in my world. Before I met your daughter I had no idea about such things.*

"But surely you have been schooled in healing!"

Not at all! I had learnt nothing of healing. Kaitling showed me many things. Others I have discovered for myself. But above all it is these bodies that have taught me most.

"What do you mean?"

If you listen carefully, the body knows exactly how it should be. It can guide you through almost every healing.

"That hardly seems sufficient," Tyzi commented gruffly. "Our healers spend years training before they are even allowed anywhere near someone who needs healing."

The tone of the magician had Peter worried. He had not imagined the man would be displeased, rather he expected him to congratulate his daughter. Peter was convinced the man was wrong about healing, but he had no time to think about it. Back at home, he could feel Fi stirring and she kissed him on his lips. She must have guessed he was travelling and it was her way of calling him back.

I have to go, Peter apologised to Kaitling. *Sorry to leave you in the lurch. I'll come back as soon as possible or why don't you join us for breakfast.*

36.

Both Peter and Fi were bleary-eyed as they trudged around the kitchen pulling open cupboards and drawers in search of breakfast. The second time they bumped sleepily into each other, they burst out laughing and pushed and shoved in mock battle for a packet of cereals, a battle that ended in a hasty hug and a not so hasty kiss.

They piled all the material for breakfast onto a tray and carried it through into the dining room. A note from Mrs. Tanner's lay waiting. She had left early for Our Lady of Grace. The meal sprawled across the table, as they used all the space. The whole, silent house was at their disposal.

"So what happened?" Fi asked.

Peter told her about Kaitling's rescue and how they had then had to rescue her father. "What bothers me was her father's reaction. I expected him to be pleased, but he was not happy."

You haven't heard the half of it, Kaitling said into both their heads.

Why? What happened? Peter asked, greeting her.

Father was furious. He went on and on about how irresponsible we were. We could have killed people with our incompetent meddling, he shouted.

Lucky you killed all the Syvan soldiers in the area, Peter interrupted with a smile. *Someone might have heard him.*

He felt Kaitling grimace. It was odd how he could know such things even when they were only speaking mind-to-mind.

I'm sure he would have liked to forbid me meeting you, but he's intelligent enough to know he can't stop me. That won't prevent him trying.

I think he's got it wrong, Peter mused, *but it isn't easy to explain.*

Of course he has. I'm fed up with him bossing me around.

I agree, but that's not what I meant. There's something wrong in his logic. Like our doctors here, your healers come at the body from the outside, Peter began, not sure where the train of thought would lead.

Not always, Fi pointed out.

Sure, Peter replied. *But they have to take a knife to the body to get inside. He shuddered at the thought. Or they use X-rays.* Realising Kaitling didn't know what that was, he briefly explained.

I suppose we can't blame them for looking at things from the outside, he went on. *That's all they've got, but they take it to the extreme. Do you remember what your father said about healers? 'Our healers spend years training before they are allowed near someone who needs healing.' Instead of trying to get closer to people's bodies and understanding their illnesses, they do the opposite!*

Suddenly things were becoming clear.

They bury themselves in a mass of books and lessons and keep away from the patient as long as possible, when all they need to know is already in each body, plain to see, if only they knew what to look for.

I don't think they are aware of that, Fi said. She thought of a recent visit to her family doctor. *Girls' stuff,* she said cryptically. *The way he talked to me, you'd have thought my body was my enemy!*

I doubt most of our doctors have confidence in the body to heal itself, Peter continued. *That's why they come at it with pills and knives...*

He didn't get any further because Kaitling had to leave. *My father's looking for me. I imagine he's not going to leave me any peace in the hope that will stop me travelling to you.*

Thanks heavens he has no idea what we can really do, Peter commented.

Speak to you soon, Kaitling said, and she was off.

"To anyone watching us," Peter said out loud, " we must seem very odd, the two of us sitting here in silence."

"We look thoughtful," Fi said smiling. She leaned closer and took his ear lobe gently between her teeth.

An imperious knock rang at the door. The two jumped apart, feeling guilty.

Who could that be? Peter asked mind-to-mind.

Neither wanted to answer the door.

I'm still in my pyjamas, Fi protested.

Realising that he was wearing Fi's floral ones, he was hardly presentable either. When the person knocked a second time, it was Fi that went to see who it was. Peter heard her open the door and he could just make out scraps of earnest conversation.

It's the police, she said mind-to-mind. *I tried to tell him you weren't here, but he insists.*

When the now too-familiar inspector stepped into the dining room, he made a show of surprise at the sight of Peter. At the thought of the man seeing the pyjamas he was wearing, Peter blushed.

"Did you know it was an offense to hinder the police in their duty?" the inspector asked pointedly, looking at Fi.

"Inspector," Peter said, trying to take the heat off Fi. "To what do we owe a visit so early in the morning?"

"Do you live here now?" he asked, ignoring Peter's question.

"We are in a hurry and need to get dressed for school, so, if you would excuse us, Inspector..." Peter said taking a step towards the door.

A look of intense irritation flitted across the man's face, only to be replaced rapidly by his habitual unyielding gaze. "Not so fast, young man." the Inspector said, moving to block the way. "What have you got against Miss Priscilla Wit?"

Maybe you should phone your Mum, Peter told Fi, mind-to-mind. *I don't like this situation at all. I'll try to distract him.*

"Ah!" Peter said, turning away from the inspector and walking towards the window. "She's quite a source of trouble," he said softly, too softly for the inspector to be able to hear properly at a distance.

"Speak up, boy! I can't hear you."

The force of the man's irritation surprised Peter. There was something more in his voice. Was it exasperation? Or possibly despair? Could the inspector be going deaf?

Keeping his back turned to the man, Peter leaned against the window frame for support and jumped into the inspector's mind. A brief second was enough to realise that the man did have difficulties.

Back in his own mind, Peter said: "Miss Wit does seem to make problems wherever she goes." He used the quietness of his voice to draw the inspector closer.

Fi was already out of the room and he could hear her dialling the number.

Backing away across the room as far as he could go, Peter said: "Did she tell you about the damage she caused at school yesterday?" He was pleased to see the inspector was following him, instinctively tilting his head closer to hear.

"She said you attacked her."

"Not before she had smashed lots of bottles in the infirmary and knocked the nurse over, cutting her with the broken glass. In a fit of rage, she went on to attack our English teacher."

Peter voice had sunk to almost a whisper. It was a wonder the inspector had not noticed. In the hall, Peter could hear Fi talking quietly on the phone.

"That's not at all what she said. Apparently you insulted her, calling her all sorts of rude names in front of the whole school," the inspector said, his words far too loud as if that would encourage Peter to speak up.

Fi had finished and was already back in the room. *She's coming,* she said, mind-to-mind. *She'll be here in about ten minutes.*

"Would you like a coffee, Inspector?" Fi asked.

The man jumped. He must have forgotten she was there.

"No thanks."

"Please excuse us, Inspector, we are going to have a wash and get changed," Peter said.

The man looked ready to stop them, but finally let them go.

The two took their time, coming downstairs only when they heard Mrs. Tanner's car slow to a halt in the drive.

"Hi Mum!" Fi greeted her mother at the front door. "We have a visitor," she said pretending her mother did not know.

"How can we help you, Officer?" Mrs. Tanner asked, seeing the man standing at the window in the dining room.

"Mrs. Tanner is it?" he asked.

Peter was astonished at the man's rudeness. Surely he should first tell Fi's Mum who he was. Did policemen always act like that?

"And who would you be?" Mrs Tanner countered.

"I'm Inspector Socal. I was about to take this young man to the police station for questioning."

"Do you have a warrant?" Mrs Tanner asked, standing her ground.

"He is not being arrested, Mrs. Tanner. Just questioned," he replied, a hint of exasperation in his voice.

"I cannot allow that," she said. "He is under age and current-ly in my care. If you want to ask him questions you may do so here, in my presence."

Three cheers for your Mum, Peter said mind-to-mind to Fi. He watched the inspector clench his fists and grind his teeth as he struggled to control his growing irritation. To his credit, he did manage to stay calm.

"Then I will question him here," he said turning back into the dining room. He sat at the table, saying: "Take a seat young man."

Mrs. Tanner remained standing, Fi stood next to her.

Pulling out a notebook from his jacket pocket, the inspector began. "Tell me what exactly happened with Priscilla Wit yesterday at school.”

Peter began with Witless provoking him in class and described the sequence of events up to his defending Mrs. Greengage, although he was careful to downplay his abilities in fighting. The inspector frequently interrupted with questions.

“Several older boys were savagely beaten up near the playing fields yesterday morning, do you know anything about that?” the inspector asked, once Peter had finished.

Peter was astonished by the word ‘savagely’. The inspector had got it all wrong; the bullies were being cast as victims.

“I heard about that.”

“But what do you know about it?”

“The group are renown for bullying younger children. Maybe someone fought back for once.”

The inspector looked at him in disbelief.

“You talk about bullying, is there a lot of fighting in school?” the inspector asked.

“I don’t know. I try to keep out of the way of the rougher kids.” The inspector turned to Fi. “I heard there was some trouble between you and a group of boys in the locker rooms.”

The man’s words annoyed Peter. They seemed to suggest Fi had been the cause of the trouble rather than the victim of it.

Fi blanched at the question. “A small group of third form rugby players cornered me in the girls’ locker room,” she said shakily, “and tried to force me to kiss them.”

“And you didn’t provoke them?”

“Come off it, Inspector,” Peter burst out, his fists clenched in anger. “Two brutes who were much bigger and stronger than Fi held her prisoner while a third one tried to rip open her blouse and touch her breasts.”

He couldn’t help it. He was just short of shouting at the man. “Do you call that encouragement? I call it assault. I thought the police were supposed to protect people against such things, not accuse those who need protection.”

“Well said, Peter,” Mrs. Tanner commented. “Your insinuations, inspector, are badly misplaced and totally unacceptable.

I must ask you to leave. You have asked enough questions and done enough damage for one day.”

Peter got to his feet and went to stand next to Mrs. Tanner. The inspector folded up his note pad, taking his time about it, and stood up, glaring at Peter.

“Rest assured I will get to the bottom of this,” he said through clenched jaws.

“I hope you do,” Mrs. Tanner said coldly.

“Good day,” the man said and Mrs. Tanner accompanied him to the door.

“What was all that about?” Fi asked when her Mum returned.

By way of an answer, Mrs. Tanner pulled a newspaper from her bag, unfolded it and laid it on the table. On the front page in large letters was the headline: Outbreak of violence at local school! And under it was a picture of Witless with a large bruise on her face.

37.

The school was abuzz when Fi and Peter entered the playground. Several pupils had the newspaper open and small groups read the article over their shoulders.

"You're a star, McCloud," a classmate called out, grinning.

"Can I have your autograph," one of the girls mocked. She blew him an exaggerated kiss and then glared at Fi.

Peter cringed and inched closer to Fi, gripping her hand even tighter. Life was so much easier when no one noticed you. He walked self-consciously across the playground heading for the back entrance, hoping to find refuge inside.

An elder boy intercepted him. Peter had no idea who the tall fellow was. It crossed his mind the youth might challenge him. He would look so stupid if some puny bloke gave him a thrashing.

"You wanna join the judo club, McCloud? I saw what you did yesterday. It was impressive." There was undisguised admiration in the boy's voice. "Our team could use someone like you."

Peter was unused to being admired, especially not when it came to sports. "Thanks. But I have a lot on my plate."

Next to waylay him was a group of fellow first years, each smaller and more inconsequential than the others.

"Did you do that to those bullies?" one of them asked eagerly.

"I heard they were beaten up by thugs from the town," Peter

replied, trying to continue on his way.

The group scuttled alongside like a pack of puppies. "I bet it was you," one of them said. "I saw you fight that girl! You were awesome!"

"Somebody had to teach those rugby players a lesson," another said.

"Could you show us how you do it?" one of the timid ones asked. "I'm fed up with being frightened all the time."

Peter squirmed at the admiration. He would willingly have helped, had he been able to, but, without Kaitling, there was not much he could do.

"I'm very busy at the moment," he told them, "but the judo club is looking for new members. Maybe they might help."

Their disappointment upset Peter. *I'm going to ask Kaitling to start teaching us today,* he said mind-to-mind to Fi.

It will take ages to be as proficient as she is, Fi pointed out soberly.

Maybe there's some way to learn faster like I did with healing.

You know what, Fi thought as they reached the door, *I reckon you had a gift for healing. That's why it was so easy.*

Well if I did, Peter thought opening the door for her, *I was totally unaware of it.*

Their mental conversation halted abruptly as a prefect barred the way. "School is out of bounds outside class time," the sixth-former said, pushing them back.

"Who says?" Peter asked, no longer intimidated by the big boy.

"That's not for you to question, squirt," the prefect said, blocking the entrance.

Outside, Peter pulled Fi against the wall. *Give me a hug,* he said mind-to-mind. *I want to jump into his mind and find out what is going on.* Fi planted her lips on his in a kiss that was hardly appropriate for a school playground.

Are you trying to lead me astray, Fiona Tanner? he asked mind-to-mind. *You almost made me forget what I was supposed to be doing.*

She snorted mentally and withdrew her lips, cradling him in her arms.

Like the school, the prefect's mind was abuzz with speculation about the latest news. Apparently an emergency meeting of the school governors had been called early that morning. They had decided to order an investigation into violence in the school. The Headmaster had spoken against what he called a hasty measure. As a result, the board had suspended him for the duration of the probes into laxity in school discipline. The Deputy Headmaster was to replace him.

Unlike Dr. Grant, the Deputy Headmaster, Mr. Sanson, fit the bill as a typical headmaster perfectly. He was distant, domineering and arbitrary in his decisions. As Sanson was his physics teacher, Peter had already had some brushes with him. The man, who was mean and petty, was hated by most of the pupils.

The prefect relished the chance to be an instrument of stricter discipline. Although Peter had never had anything to do with him, he could see the youth was a typical bully who picked on younger, weaker kids and got pleasure from it. Peter was tempted to deal a blow against these changes by hurting the prefect. To do so, however, seemed petty and underhanded.

He was back in Fi's arms just in time to hear the prefect say, "Cut that out. You're not allowed to make lurid displays at school."

He took Fi by the hand and they sauntered away, Peter describing mind-to-mind what he had found.

That's terrible, Fi thought. *Is there nothing we can do?*

Avoid getting into trouble. We'd be ideal targets for Sanson and his henchboys.

Fi giggled mentally at the word, although Peter could sense she was tense and worried.

Maybe we can gather information to help Dr. Grant, he suggested.

You mean our own private investigation?

Sort of. But we need to be careful.

The bell rang for class, but as they made their way to their respective classrooms, prefects herded them towards the assembly hall. A noisy mass of pupils, excited by the change, shuffled along packed corridors, speculating about what was going on. Prefects threatened detention or worse to those who made too much noise, but their efforts held little sway over the mass.

Peter and Fi were separated at the door by prefects, who insisted they go to their respective forms.

Don't do anything dangerous, Fi said mind-to-mind, as she laboured across the crowded hall to her form.

First formers traditionally sat in the front four rows and only one seat on the very first bench remained free. The staff sat stiffly on the raised platform a short distance from him. Mrs. Greengage looked very upset, although she tried to conceal it. Several other teachers also looked unhappy. In comparison, the librarian and the group huddled around him were joking with each other and seemed quite at ease.

A single, solitary chair, with a high raised back and proud armrests remained unoccupied several feet in front of the teachers. How unsettling to imagine someone else sitting in Dr. Grant's place.

Once all the pupils had found somewhere to sit, the buzz of conversation, which had persisted despite the prefect's efforts, abruptly ceased as Sanson climbed onto the platform. As one the assembly stood, including the teachers. It was a privilege reserved for the Headmaster, but no one hesitated about according it to Sanson.

He was not a tall man and his figure was unimpressive, but his face was stern and his eyes penetrating. Judging from his grey hair, he was a bit older than Fi's Mum. He placed a large wad of papers on his chair and turned to survey the assembly. Normally, the Head would invite everyone to sit down, but he kept the assembly waiting while he scrutinised the faces of the pupils.

Peter glanced at Mrs. Greengage. A look of irritation flitted across her face. She must have noticed him watching her because she winked almost imperceptibly. The tale of the emperor's new clothes sprang mischievously to Peter's mind and with it a compelling urge to unmask Sanson as an impostor.

"Sit!" Sanson ordered. He himself remained standing.

"Serious problems have broken out over the last few days. The lack of a firm response on the part of the Headmaster has led the school board to suspend Dr. Grant pending an official investigation..."

Peter was furious. He knew well enough the opinion Sanson expressed was his own and not that of the school board.

"I have been asked to take on the role of headmaster in the interim. Rest assured, I will do everything in my power to reinstate order in our school..."

Sanson stood unmoving, his hands clutching a paper, as he expounded his plans to redress the school, sounding more like an uninspired preacher than a future headmaster. Peter gave up trying to listen. Now would be a good time to tap into Sanson's memories, but Peter felt terribly exposed. Nothing stood between him and the man who was barely a yard away. From time to time, Sanson even glanced his way.

Peter supported his head with one hand and looked down at his lap, hoping Sanson wouldn't notice he had his eyes closed. Then he jumped into Sanson's head. He had to be quick, he couldn't leave his body unattended for long. Rummaging through Sanson's recent memories, he was astonished to discover the coup had been planned well in advance. Long before he'd had the trouble with Witless, Sanson had already drawn up a list of people to involve.

Peter was surprised to learn that Sanson knew Witless's aunt. They'd met the evening before. Could Witless have been part of the plan? He had no time to check. During their meeting Sanson and the aunt had finalised plans to evince Grant. It didn't surprise him to learn they had informed the journalist who wrote the article about the so-called scandal in school.

From time to time, Peter listened to what Sanson was saying, just in case there was any trouble for him personally. The man droned on about new rules and regulations to be enforced by an increased number of prefects that he would co-opt.

Searching further, he found that it was Witless's aunt who had called the emergency meeting of the school board of which she was a member. Several of her allies, mainly local businessmen who benefited from her patronage, moved to have Dr. Grant suspended.

According to Sanson's thoughts, he had a stack of plans for setting the school right and entrenching his hold on it. These included getting rid of a number of what he called troublesome teachers, including Mrs. Greengage.

Peter was alerted to a danger by Fi's urgent voice speaking mind-to-mind. *Careful Peter,* she said. *Sanson's noticed you and thinks you have fallen asleep.*

Peter readied himself to jump back into his body when Sanson broke into a tirade against him. "You are one of the worst offenders," he said pointing an accusing finger at Peter as he raised his voice. "You have been at the origin of a number of violent scenes in school."

Peter was furious, knowing what the man planned to do. Instead of jumping, he slipped words into Sanson's mind mixing them up in the man's sentences.

"You have been crapped..." A stir went through the assembly at the word that was hardly one you'd expect in the mouth of a Headmaster.

Startled at what had happened, the man steeled himself and blundered on. "You have been caught red hounded ... handed stirring up dribble ... trouble..."

Sanson looked desperately around the assembly, many students were smirking behind raised hands, a few even laughed openly. Peter could feel the man's fury mounting and didn't dare push him any further. He jumped back to his own body and raised his head to look at what was happening. In his confusion and anger, Sanson had completely forgotten Peter until he noticed the boy's grin.

"Come with me, young man," he ordered, pointing accusingly at Peter, "I'll teach you to make fun of me," and he abruptly left the room.

Peter glanced at Mrs. Greengage, wondering what to do. Behind him the assembly was in an uproar. Pupils had stood up and were exchanging anecdotes about Sanson's jumbled words. Some were having fun, noisily suggesting other words he might muddle up. Nobody knew what to do. The teachers looked just as confused.

Peter remained seated until one of the prefects approached.

"Didn't you hear the Headmaster?" the prefect said, grabbing Peter by the shoulder.

"He's not the Headmaster. Dr. Grant is the Headmaster."

The prefect shook him violently.

"That will do Smith," Mrs. Greengage said sternly. She had joined them, unnoticed. "I will accompany McCloud to see Mr. Sanson."

Smith was inclined to resist, but Mrs. Greengage was a teacher and her size was imposing. He turned and walked away, not disguising his irritation.

Once they were outside, Peter whispered: "You're not going to hand me over to that man, are you Mrs. Greengage? He's mad. He'll kill me."

"You are exaggerating, McCloud. I very much doubt he'll do that and I will be there should he try."

The thought of her accompanying him was reassuring but then he remembered that Sanson wanted to get rid of her. Defending Peter would give him a welcome excuse to dismiss her.

"It's really kind of you, but you had better not come with me."

"Why ever not, Peter?"

Peter hesitated over what to say. "Because he's looking for an excuse to get rid of you and this will give him just what he wants."

She halted and turned to look at him, astonished. "What makes you think that?"

"I am absolutely certain, but I can't tell you how I know.

Just like I know that he plotted with Priscilla Wit's aunt to get Dr. Grant revoked by the board."

Her mouth had fallen open. "These are serious accusations."

"I'm not accusing. I wouldn't do that. I have no tangible proof. Let's say, I just know. So that is why you must not go with me."

"All the more reason to accompany you, Peter. If what you say is true, the man really is dangerous."

"I wouldn't challenge him now," Peter said, worried by visions of Mrs. Greengage charging in and accusing Sanson.

"Don't worry. I won't do anything that will put us in danger."

38.

Sanson had requisitioned Dr. Grant's office. The proud tartan covered armchairs had been shoved against the wall, forcing visitors to stand. Sanson had also offloaded a large number of books from the bookshelves, leaving them in tottering piles around the room. He seemed absolutely sure his temporary position would be prolonged.

Sanson didn't immediately acknowledge their presence.

Mrs. Greengage nodded to the armchairs. They turned them round, pushed then back to their rightful place and sat down.

Sanson, who continued to ignore their presence, had obviously seen what they were up to because his face went white with rage.

"Who gave you permission to sit down?" he finally asked between clenched teeth, his fist raised in anger.

This gesticulating man reminded Peter once again of the emperor without his clothes, but this time he was cautious not to let his amusement show.

"You wanted to see McCloud," Greengage reminded him.

Peter admired the woman. She did not let an angry man intimidate her. He was glad she'd come, even if he worried about the consequences.

"I did not request your presence Greengage," he spat, distain in his every word. "I'll deal with you later."

The man was a bully, Peter realised, a grown-up bully. "Mrs. Greengage is here because I asked her to come," he said, refusing to be cowered. He remembered the Headmaster words to the inspector in that very office. "I have the right to be accompanied by an adult of my choice."

He noticed a hint of a smile on Greengage's face. Sanson, however, was scowling.

"You have caused enough trouble..." Sanson began.

Peter felt so indignant at seeing this man usurp the rightful place of Dr. Grant. It made him reckless. "What trouble do you have in mind?"

"Don't interrupt boy!" he fumed.

"McCloud's question is perfectly legitimate," Greengage pointed out calmly.

Apparently bullies were only at ease when confronted with someone weaker. Two determined people were enough to out manoeuvre him.

Suddenly Sanson rose to his feet, his face twisted in rage. "How d-d-did you do that?"

Peter was astonished to hear the man stutter. Could his messing with the man's words have sparked it off?

"Do what?"

"Twist m-m-my tongue in m-m-my mouth!"

"I have no idea what you mean." Peter struggled to conceal his guilt.

"Come off it, Sanson," Mrs. Greengage said. "As a scientist, how could you possibly imagine that McCloud could be the cause of your stutter?"

At the mention of the word, Sanson became even more agitated. He brought his fist crashing down on his desk, causing several papers to skid across the shiny surface and onto the floor. Peter bent forward to pick one up.

"Don't you dare touch that," Sanson screamed, scrambling round his desk, his hands out stretched to recuperate the paper.

Too late!

The list was headed with the words: Teachers and pupils to eliminate. His name and that of Mrs. Greengage were right at the top. When Sanson lunged for the paper, Peter ducked and passed it to Mrs. Greengage who stepped out of reach.

Sanson grabbed Peter's arm and wrenched him to his feet. If only Kaitling were there, but she'd been silent quite a while. Bluff, he thought. "Surely you saw what I did to Miss Wit when she attacked Mrs Greengage?" He struggled to keep his voice firm, but he was trembling with fear. "Would you like a demonstration?"

Sanson took a shocked step backward, releasing Peter's arm as if he had the pest. The man's eyes were wide with fear, but his mouth screwed up in hate and disgust.

"You filthy little queer. The world would be better off without the likes of you" he whispered, his voice full of venom.

Sanson and Witless must have compared notes.

"You'll end up like that Tuning fellow. Poison's too good for you. Even a bullet would be a waste." The man fumbled in his pocket reaching for a bulky object. Peter shrank back terrified he might have a gun. Instead he pulled out a cross and brandished it at Peter.

"The only person who's odd or out of place here, Mr. Sanson, is you," Peter said, struggling to contain his fury. "When the authorities learn that you conspired to have Dr. Grant dismissed, I imagine your cross will not protect you from the hell you'll find yourself in."

Sanson made a move to hit Peter with the cross, but Mrs. Greengage jerked him out of range. She placed her arm protectively around Peter's shoulder and the two of them stood defiantly staring at Sanson.

"You," he scowled looking at Peter, his voice now ice cold and hard, "are expelled, and you," he said turning to Greengage, "are dismissed. Leave school premises immediately."

"You do not have the authority," Mrs. Greengage pointed out.

Peter marvelled at her calm. It was as if the battle was already won, when Peter had the impression the bloodshed still lay ahead.

"As acting headmaster, I have every right," Sanson retorted, his face set in a grim mask as he strained to appear taller than he was.

The situation struck Peter as absurd. "You are naked," he chuckled, relieved he'd finally managed to say so.

The man's hand flew to his flies then he looked down at himself, to double check.

"Surely you know the story of Emperor's new clothes," Peter said, still smiling. "Well the costume of headmaster you've been sold is completely see-through."

He heard Mrs. Greengage chuckle. As for Sanson, his fury had reached such heights he was rooted to the spot, smouldering with rage.

"I think we're done here," Mrs. Greengage said calmly and, not removing her arm from Peter's shoulder, she led him to the door.

The moment they were outside, Peter felt completely deflated. What had he done? How dare he treat a teacher that way? Surely, if anyone was caught starkers in the story, it was him. He glanced at Mrs. Greengage who had removed her arm from his shoulder now they were in the school corridors. She still looked calm and had the remains of a smile on her face.

"You were remarkable, Peter. Few adults could have done better."

Despite her praise, Peter was miserable. "But I ruined everything. You promised not to put us in danger, but then I went and got us expelled." Peter could feel tears forming in his eyes.

"Don't worry about that. I am convinced this will all turn out for the best. What's more, you are not expelled. He doesn't have the right. No more than he can sack me. He will try, of course, but we will gather arms and defeat him."

"Who's Tuning?" Peter asked, curious.

"I believe there was a government scientist of that name. He poisoned himself with cyanide a couple of years back."

"Why ever did he do that?"

"Rumour has it that he was hounded because he was what Sanson called a 'queer'."

"Another one," Peter muttered, thinking of Wilde. "Will it ever end?"

Mrs. Greengage glanced at the clock on the wall. It was nearly time for lunch. The whole morning had been lost in this messy business. "Let's go and eat at my place," she suggested.

"Do you mind if Fi comes, I mean Fiona Tanner? We were supposed to eat together."

"No problem. Do you want to go and fetch her?"

"That's not necessary. She'll know where to join us." Peter realised immediately he'd revealed too much, but Mrs. Greengage made no comment.

Peter opened the door to Fi when she arrived at Greengage's place. "Sorry I took so long," she said, struggling to get her breath back. "I got mobbed by people wanting to know where you were. There's a rumour going round school that you've been expelled."

Peter laughed.

"Come in, Fiona," Mrs. Greengage called from the kitchen. "We were about to eat. We'll tell you the delightful story over lunch."

Peter stole a quick kiss and the two hurried hand in hand out to the kitchen.

They squeezed in behind Mrs Greengage's tiny table, not unhappy to have an excuse to sit so close together. Peter put his arm around Fi. She tried to shrug it off, embarrassed, no doubt thinking Greengage would object, but the English teacher made no comment.

It's all right, Peter whispered in her head.

From where they sat, they could see out over the long, narrow garden that stretched away behind the house. It looked more like a jungle than a garden.

Mrs. Greengage had prepared tomato soup, fresh slices of bread with cheese, pâté and a mixed salad.

"You should be in charge of school dinners," Peter said. "This is delicious."

Greengage laughed.

"The list of tasks I am to do, despite the fact that I have been sacked, seems to be escalating. What with encouraging pupils who refuse to read and saving hopeless cases from shipwreck and now surveying the quality and variety of school dinners, I wonder when I will get to teach English."

What an amazing woman, Fi said mind-to-mind, her thoughts full of admiration and affection.

She sure is, Peter replied. *You should have seen her with Sanson!*

"So what happened with the new headmaster?" Fi asked.

"He's not headmaster," Peter corrected, quick to get annoyed at the usurper's title, "and probably never will be."

"Touchy?" Fi said, tweaking the end of his nose.

"Sorry. He gets on my nerves."

"Your Peter," Mrs Greengage said smiling wickedly at her own words, "gave a marvellous performance. If it had been fencing, Sanson would have been peppered with holes."

"Stop playing with me and tell me what happened. Everyone at school thinks Peter has been expelled and you have been sacked."

"That's not exactly true," Peter said and they told Fi what happened. When they got to the part about Sanson stuttering, Fi was intrigued. "Did you do that, Peter?" she asked, not immediately realising what she was implying.

Greengage raised her eyebrows and shot a meaningful look at Peter and then at Fi, but she didn't ask any questions.

Peter wondered if he should tell her about their experiments. He wanted to. It would be good to share with an adult, but he was afraid she might react like Kaitling's father. He really didn't want to spoil their good relationship. There were so few adults he could count on.

Should I tell her, he asked Fi mind-to-mind?

You know her better than I do. I wouldn't. I don't trust adults. Look what happened with Kaitling's father.

Finally Peter decided against it, for the moment at least.

"What are we going to do about Sanson?" he asked.

"We need to gather evidence," Greengage said, pulling a folded paper from her pocket and holding it up.

"What's that?" Fi asked.

"You kept it!" Peter exclaimed, overjoyed.

"Our new headmaster," Greengage's voice was full of scorn, "has drawn up a list of people to get rid of..." She handed Fi the list.

"Hey! I'm on here," she said horrified.

Peter glanced over her shoulder to look. Many of the pupils he didn't know, but one or two of the teachers he'd already had.

"So what evidence do we go in search of?" Fi asked handing the list back to Greengage.

The teacher wasn't sure.

"Let me tell you what I know," Peter said. "This didn't just happen by chance yesterday. Sanson had been planning if for quite a while. He met Witless's aunt yesterday evening."

Mrs. Greengage raised her eyebrows.

"Sorry, I meant Wit's aunt. They informed the journalist and the aunt called an emergency meeting of the school board. She has several allies on the board, local businessmen who benefited from her patronage, and they moved to have Dr. Grant suspended."

"I'm going to assume you will tell where all this information came from, when you judge fit," Greengage commented, a wry smile on her face.

Once again Peter wondered if he should tell her.

"It's maybe better you don't know," Fi put in.

"I was afraid of that," Greengage said. "In the mean time, we need to keep an eye on Wit's aunt and the journalist."

"I wonder who those business men were?" Fi mused.

Peter knew he could probably find out easily by returning to Sanson's head, but he was loathed to do so. He certainly couldn't go with Mrs. Greengage around. Then he had an idea.

"Where's the toilet?" he asked. It was such a normal request, he felt sure it wouldn't arouse suspicion.

"Upstairs. First door on the right," Greengage told him.

Once the door was closed and Peter was seated, he jumped into Sanson's mind. The fake headmaster was in a meeting with the head prefect. Peter didn't bother to listen to their discussion, instead he searched for the names of the aunt's allies on the board. Unfortunately, Sanson knew only one, Brown, the director of the supermarket in town.

"... Yes!" Sanson was saying, annoyed. "Homosexuals, queers, misfits, whatever you want to call it..."

Peter didn't wait to hear any more, he jumped back to his body.

Back in the kitchen, Fi and Mrs. Greengage were washing the dishes. As he took the cloth to dry up, Peter said: "I've managed to remember one of the names of those allies on the board: Brown. He's director of the supermarket, I believe."

39.

With half an hour before they left for school, Fi and Peter lay down on Mrs. Greengage's sofa feigning to be asleep. In reality, they travelled to Drailong. To their surprise, all was dark, although Kaitling was clearly not asleep.

Kaitling, what's going on? Why is everything so dark? Peter asked.

Oh Peter! Kaitling exclaimed. *You made it.* She sounded relieved to have him back.

Sure, Peter thought, a little surprised at her emotions. *I'm here with Fi. Did you think we weren't coming?*

Kaitling burst into tears, her whole body shaken by sobs. Her behaviour was so uncharacteristic it had Peter worried.

Tell us what's the matter?

My father's gone mad!

Join the club, Peter thought.

He's convinced I've been taken over by a Syvan priest.

That doesn't make sense.

It was your voice that gave him the idea. He's got it into his head it was a priest. He's convinced the priest has taken control of me and is spying on him.

So why is everything so dark? Fi asked.

He's fixed a special cap on my head. It is supposed to prevent people getting in and out of your mind. It also makes it impossible to see or hear.

That's terrible, Fi said, shuddering at the thought.

How long ago was that? Peter asked.

I'm not sure, maybe an hour or two. I have no way of knowing.

Let me look where we are, Peter said, preparing to jump.

But he'll know if you go back into his head.

I doubt it. I don't think he understands travelling between minds.

But he stopped me travelling, Kaitling objected.

Are you sure? We travelled to you. Maybe the thought was enough to stop you.

With you here, I can hardly try, Kaitling pointed out.

We'll try later, once we've sorted this out.

Peter let out his senses, feeling several men not far away. He recognised her father and chose one of the others as his target, jumping into the man's mind.

They were still hidden in the marshes. The men were squatting around a small fireless hearth near a low, makeshift hut. Kaitling's father was talking. Peter could have described the scene mind-to-mind, but instead he sent what he saw to both Kaitling and Fi. He felt her surprise as the first pictures flooded her mind.

Extraordinary, she said, excited at the prospect and relieved to be able to see the world again. *I must try that as soon as I can.*

Peter had an idea, but he kept the gist of it to himself. He wanted them to learn to work together out of their bodies, gaining information and, if necessary, striking an enemy.

I'm coming back for a moment, he told them.

Once in Kaitling's head he explained. *I will take each of you with me, so you know how to do it. I'll take Fi first,* he said, *just in case your father tries to talk to you Kaitling.* Then he addressed Fi directly. *Make yourself as small as possible, like a tiny speck, so you pass unnoticed.* Then, realising it might be more logical to do something else first, he said, *But before we jump, why don't both of you feel out and identify the presences around us.*

This way of working pleased him. He could immediately

sense what the others managed to do and could show them what it felt like. They learnt so much more quickly. There were five men, one of whom was Kaitling's father. Peter pointed him out to Fi.

Taking Fi by the hand he jumped into the man he had visited earlier. Once Fi had adjusted to being in the man's head, Peter showed her how to send what she saw back to Kaitling. At the same time, he was aware he was also showing Kaitling how to do it, even if she couldn't practice yet.

Now jump back to Kaitling on your own.

She was unsure and hesitant, but with Kaitling's encouragement, Fi jumped back and was relieved and pleased to realise she could.

Now do it on your own, Peter told her. She did so, more easily this time. He made her go backwards and forwards several times before suggesting she jump to one of the other men. He could feel her trepidation about jumping into the unknown, but Fi had a lot of courage. With only the slightest hesitation she jumped into one of the other men and relayed the world from that perspective.

Kaitling in the mean time jumped into the head of a third man and they had fun comparing perspectives. Peter marvelled that they were skipping in and out of these men's minds without them having the slightest idea they were being used.

In many ways it was Kaitling's father's fault. He had given his daughter a perfect cover. With her head hidden, there was no way they could know she was absent. She might just be sleeping.

Let's explore the person, Peter suggested, *and see if any parts are out of tune.*

He quickly surveyed the man whose mind he was in. There was little wrong with him, lest it be an infection in his leg where an insect had bitten him. The man's body seemed to be dealing with the problem adequately. He let the others sense what that infection felt like, thinking the knowledge would help them search themselves. Kaitling had quickly found that her host had a stomach ulcer although it seemed temporarily dormant.

The task was completely new to Fi who had some difficulty. Peter jumped to join her. He also searched, but kept quiet about what he discovered. Instead, he showed her and Kaitling the body's blueprint, the one to be found in every cell. It contained the knowledge to heal the person.

Listen for this. Think of it as music, the body's base chord, the one it wants to return to. Now look for parts that are out of tune.

He followed Fi's presence as she flitted throughout the body, and was delighted when she discovered misplaced bones in the man's foot.

You see that, he said pointing to the area close by, *that's pain and there's also some infection.*

Should I heal it? Fi asked.

Not now. They would probably notice. I don't think he's in danger, he'll just limp badly and won't be able to run.

Now we know how to judge his health, let's see what we can find out from his memories. He returned to the person's mind and the others followed suit. *Memories are here,* he said showing Fi where to look. *You can leaf through them like this.* He quickly went though the mass of information, looking for those things that stood out. *If the person thinks a memory is significant, it will be conspicuous. Or you can stay with one memory and explore it more closely.*

Quite by chance he stumbled on a memory of the man in which he admired Tyzi's daughter. Admiration was a euphemism for the burning desire the man felt for the attractive young girl. Peter immediately felt Kaitling's embarrassment. *Sorry about that. Of course, being in someone's mind gives access to things it is not always good to know.*

It would be easy to give your presence away if a memory touched you too much, Fi thought. *If I were in Kitty Turner's head and I realised she wanted me, I don't think I could resist,* Fi said with a chuckle. Peter laughed. *You're hopeless, Fiona Tanner. Kitty Turner is one of the girls Fi drools over at school,*

Peter explained to Kaitling.

Aren't you enough for her? Kaitling asked, sounding sour.

I love being with Peter, Fi said, *we fit together so well. But I am attracted to girls. How about you?*

Peter noticed Kaitling struggling to conceal her feelings for him. They had always had such an adventurer's camaraderie, it had hardly crossed his mind there might be more. Luckily Fi, in her enthusiasm for Kitty Turner, had not noticed.

I don't know, Kaitling said, embarrassed. *I have hardly had any time for boys and the idea of liking girls never crossed my mind.*

Talking about being distracted by memories, Peter said, forcing himself to chuckle. *Why don't you check those of your host?*

They had a hilarious time digging into the men's memories, with Fi making them laugh at her outrageous imitations of the man who was momentarily hosting her. Kaitling laughed too, but Peter could feel her enthusiasm was half-hearted. It would be easy to dismiss her dejectedness as due to her troubled relationship with her father. But he couldn't help wondering if her affection for him and the bubbling presence of Fi didn't have something to do with her dispiritedness.

Let's try one last thing, Peter suggested. *Let's see if we can influence them. Such a skill could come in useful.*

Why don't we make a game of it, Fi suggested. *Each of us makes their man do something and the others have to guess what it is.*

Kaitling was not very enthusiastic. *If we make them do outrageous things,* she said soberly, *it is likely to make my life very difficult. My father will believe I did it, or rather the priest he thinks has taken hold of me. What's more, he'll know others can be influenced at a distance.*

You are right, Peter admitted. *I like Fi's idea though, so I suggest it is you that challenges us, Kaitling. You tell us what to make the person do and we have to try to do it.*

The idea was more appealing to Kaitling, who finally agreed.

She began with simple tasks: scratching his nose, pulling his earlobe, coughing and then progressed to more complex activities like whistling a song or going for a walk. Peter also gave tasks to Kaitling. All three of them managed to get the person to do what they wanted without taking over the person completely or having them suspect they were being manipulated.

You realise, Kaitling said, as they paused in their exploits, *how powerful but also how potentially dangerous these abilities are. We could do a lot of harm.*

But we don't intend to do harm, Fi protested, upset. She'd been enjoying their game immensely. Kaitling's warning disturbed her.

What is to stop you using this technique on Kitty Turner? It would be so easy to have her on her knees at your feet, Kaitling said grimly.

Peter could feel the prospect appealed to Fi. She might be tempted to use it. *Kaitling is right,* he said. *We need to set a limit, some form of code of conduct that would make us hesitate about misusing these abilities.*

What a shame, Fi said, pouting mentally. *There I was coaxing Kitty into my bed. It was so delicious I was drooling.*

You'll survive, Peter said. *So what do we swear?*

Not to harm others or to make fun of them or force them to do things against their will unless it is to stop them doing harm to others or possibly to themselves. How does that sound? Kaitling asked.

I agree, Peter said.

I agree, Fi said, mentally blowing a kiss of goodbye to Kitty Turner that made them all laugh.

I agree, Kaitling concluded.

<h1 style="text-align:center">40.</h1>

Back at school, pupils flocked to Peter and Fi, clamouring to know what had happened.

"Are you expelled?" one girl from Fi's class asked.

"Sanson tried, but Greengage said he didn't have the right."

"What happened?" several voices asked.

"He puffed himself up like a angry bird trying to intimidate us, but Greengage wouldn't having anything of it. Then he started to stutter..."

A number of people sniggered others chuckled openly.

"Wasn't that weird in assembly," Susan, a classmate, said. "People are whispering that you did it."

"That's what Sanson's thought," Peter commented. "Maybe he just stutters in tense situations."

Susan seemed doubtful.

"Surely now you will teach us to defend ourselves," one of smallest kids said. "Sanson's new prefects are bullies. One of them punched me." He pulled up his sleeve to show the blue-green mark on his arm.

Maybe we should help them, he thought to Fi, *if Kaitling could join us for a while.*

Their silent discussion was interrupted by the arrival of three overgrown youths, looking uncomfortable. Each was wearing a bright new prefect's badge on their hand-me-down blazer.

"Break it up!" one of them said, pushing the smaller kids out of the way. "The new school rules forbid gatherings of more than three."

"That's stupid! How are we supposed to go to class?" Peter asked, indignant.

"You've got an hour's detention for being rude to a prefect," the prefect said. "What's your name?"

Peter burst out laughing. The prefects might have been five or six years older, but they were puny, petty and pathetic. He thought of Kaitling fighting the Syvan soldiers, her head held high, her bow in hand. He was so much better and stronger than these bullies.

"I wouldn't touch him, if I were you," Fi said, a wicked grin on her face. "If Peter's takes a fancy to you, you might regret it."

Alarmed, the prefect took a step backwards, his hands flying to protect his crotch. Several people laughed, but some shifted uneasily.

It might not be wise to stress that pretty boy business, he said mind-to-mind to Fi, noticing their reaction. *The whole blasted business could come back and haunt us.*

The bell rang at that moment and the prefects moved away to police the return to class.

"Those who want to learn unarmed combat, join us beyond the woods across the playing fields after school," he said. "Take a roundabout route to get there and don't tell anyone you're coming." With Fi, they headed for one of the doors into the main building.

Inside, down one of the corridors, small knots of pupils were whispering together. Peter heard his name mentioned in the same sentence as the word queer before the group scattered, each pupil in a hurry to get away.

You see what I mean, he thought to Fi.

She groaned audibly. *They should get used to being with pretty boys and handsome girls. They are here to stay.*

She had said it in earnest, but he could hear her uncertainty.

Don't let them get to you. Call me if there's trouble, he added as she headed off to her class and he to his. He had history with Johnson.

On his way, he overheard several more small groups whispering about queers and pansies. A number of pupils looked at him as if he were soiled in some way. He tried to ignore them.

There was some comfort to be had in those people, many of whom he'd never spoken to before, who greeted him as a hero because of what happened after the assembly. It would seem that the story about Sanson trying to expel him had already done the rounds and came back grossly inflated. He heard one person saying he'd floored the Deputy Head in a spectacular judo hold. For another, Sanson had run screaming from the school.

It was a relief when they finally shuffled into class and the lesson began. Not that he was interested in history with its jumble of indigestible dates and pointless battles. Johnson excelled in making even the most exciting story boring. It was just that the whispering ceased, until an enterprising group at the back had the brilliant idea of passing scribbled notes around. Peter tried to ignore them, but the notes always found their way to him. Why give your soul to a pansy, one note asked unimaginatively. Another read: I'll let you touch my flower, if you'll give me your pansy. It had been signed 'Fiona'.

He shouldn't have been surprised, but he was angry all the same. They must have seen his reaction, because the clique stepped up its efforts to be crude about him and Fi. It was amazing that Johnson didn't notice, but the old fool just droned on.

Peter tried ignoring the notes, but the group at the back made sure the scraps of paper landed open on his desk. He clenched his teeth and tried to control his anger. He was tempted to use mind-travelling to put a stop to their taunting, but they had promised not to do such a thing. In any case, any retaliation would be taken as admission of guilt.

Let me do it, Kaitling said, arriving unnoticed in his head.

No don't. It'll only cause more trouble.

I know what we swore to do, but this is doing harm to someone. So it is justified to act.

Peter wanted to argue, but he sensed she'd already gone. He wondered whose mind she'd jumped to. He braced himself to withstand the onslaught once she'd done her worst. But nothing happened, nothing at all. There were no more notes and Peter was able to calm down and concentrate on the lesson.

You see, Kaitling spoke mind-to-mind. *You should have more confidence,* a trace of triumph in her thoughts.

What did you do?

You'll see.

When the bell rang, Peter gathered up the scribbled notes, meaning to throw them in the wastepaper basket.

Keep them. They could be evidence.

Peter stuffed the notes in his jacket pocket and headed for the door.

Judging from the teacher's angry words, something was causing a stir. It took a lot to get Johnson annoyed. Peter hardly dared look back, for fear of what he might see, but he was curious. Three of the oldest boys in his class, who always sat together at the back, had their heads laid on the desks fast asleep. He turned away quickly, not wanting anyone to see him gloating.

Excellent, he told Kaitling as he hurried to his next class.

Everyone knows that young boys need to get more sleep. I just helped.

He'd rarely felt Kaitling so playful. He wondered if she was trying to outdo Fi, but dismissed the idea. He didn't care, he was proud of what she'd done and more than pleased to be with her.

He chatted with Kaitling all the way to his next class. It was almost half way through when he realised that he'd heard nothing from Fi. Since she'd learnt to speak mind-to-mind, she frequently called him. Her silence was worrying. Peter called her, but there was no answer. Something must be wrong, but there was no way he could leave in the middle of a class.

I'll go, Kaitling said.

Can you find her? You've never jumped into her mind before.

Don't worry. I think I know her well enough.

Peter didn't make a habit of chewing his nails, but he was tempted to do so as he counted the minutes waiting for Kaitling or Fi to contact him. Ten minutes later, he was about to ask permission to leave class, when he heard Kaitling's voice faintly in his head, but her words reached him garbled.

What's wrong?

Someone used ... a drug ... on Fi ... Kaitling's words came in fits and starts as if the contact was being constantly interrupted.

Is she hurt? He was afraid the person had done her harm while she was unconscious.

Can't tell ... makes me drowsy too ...

Keep awake! Peter pleaded. *Talk to me and I will try and home in on you.*

He got to his feet and, not asking leave of the teacher, headed for the door.

"McCloud, where are you going?" McGill, the maths teacher asked, startled at Peter's behaviour. Peter was one of his best pupils.

Peter ignored him, much to the astonishment of the other pupils and McGill as well. Outside two prefects were waiting. They grabbed him and one of them cupped a damp cloth over Peter's mouth and nose. A pungent smell invaded his lungs. Feeling himself about to black out, he instinctively jumped to the mind of one of the two prefects.

The jump left him disoriented. He crouched tiny and trembling within the prefect's head, terrified he could not return to his own mind, fear threatening to drag him under. With a great effort he pulled himself together. They were lugging his body into the preparation room next to the chemistry lab where Fi lay unconscious on the floor.

The prefects let Peter's body crumple to the ground next to Fi and turned to leave. Peter had to act quickly, he might not have another chance. Shoving aside the presence of the prefect, he took over. Putting all the prefect's weight into his clenched fist, he swung it upwards and connected with the chin of his unsuspecting colleague, sending him crashing into a wrack of bottles. The blow hurt terribly, but at least it had worked. The prefect lay unconscious on the floor.

Peter could feel the prefect raging to get free.

Shut your gob or I'll silence you for good, he growled.

The prefect shut up and kept deadly still. Peter locked the cowering presence away in a tiny corner of the prefect's mind.

He bent down and touched Fi's hand, calling out to Kaitling. She was there, if only faintly. He didn't dare jump into her body. He would probably succumb like Kaitling had.

Try to move towards the finger touching Fi's brow, he said. He coaxed her all the way till she crossed the boundary between the two and collapsed in the prefect's mind. Peter kept up a steady flow of encouraging words as Kaitling gradually recovered.

How do we wake these two bodies? Peter asked, once she'd almost recovered. *We have to hurry. Who knows when other thugs might turn up?*

Let me take over, Kaitling said and she wandered unsteadily around the small room studying the bottles aligned on the shelves. She finally halted in front of a tiny flask. *This should do it.* She unstoppered the bottle and took a cautious sniff. The pungent odour stung the prefect's nose.

Yes. This will do the trick. Then bending down over Peter she wafted the open flask under his nose.

Peter could feel his body beginning to respond. He wasn't sure he dared jump back, but if he didn't, there would be no one there to open his eyes.

Pull me out, if I succumb.

Back in his own body, he felt groggy, his eyesight was blurred, there was an incessant buzz in his ears and his stomach heaved unhappily. He gently moved his head trying not to throw up, as he struggled to focus on Fi. She too was shaking off the effects of the drug with the help of Kaitling. Peter gingerly got to his knees and then pulled himself up on his feet. He staggered a moment, his knees threatening to give way.

Let's get out of here, Peter said. *They could come back at any minute.*

What about this boy? Kaitling asked.

Hold on to him, he might still be useful.

He peered cautiously out, but the corridor was empty. They hurried to the back door that led to the main road and stepped out into the fresh air. Both Fi and Peter were beginning to feel better when a shout went up behind them. Several of the new prefects emerged from another exit and came running in their direction.

Run! Kaitling shouted in their heads. *I'll deal with them. I'll join you in a short while.*

Peter and Fi clasped hands and ran across the main road then through the park beyond. Once in amongst the trees, they paused to look back. The single prefect was making easy work of the others.

Thanks Kaitling, they said mind-to-mind, then turned and hurried away. Her laughter rang out in their heads. She was enjoying herself.

41.

Fi and Peter took refuge in Tallford's only supermarket. They wouldn't be able to stay long, school would soon be out and it was a favourite haunt for many pupils.

Fi was exhausted and extremely fragile. Would she go to pieces like his Mum and Sis? He couldn't bear the thought, but what could he do?

We should call your Mum. If anybody knows what to do, it'll be her. She's so solid and resourceful.

I'm worried how she'll react, Fi replied.

Peter was sure Mrs. Tanner could take it in her stride. Fi wasn't convinced.

I'd preferred to go home and wait there, Fi said. *Mum'll be back this evening.*

That might not be a good idea, Peter pointed out. *They could be watching your place, waiting for us.*

Fi didn't have the strength to argue, so when Peter found a phone box, Fi dialled the number and it was Peter that spoke.

"Hi Mrs. Tanner. Please don't panic, but Fi and I have had a serious problem at school and we need your help."

Of course Mrs. Tanner wanted to know everything.

"I can't tell you over the phone."

Fi's Mum was worried and she wanted to be reassured.

"Neither of us has been hurt, but we've both been badly shaken, Fi in particular. Could you come and fetch us?"

"No we are no longer at school. We are in the supermarket,

but we should meet somewhere else. Too many people from school come here."

She suggested a tiny teashop that only old ladies used, adding, "I'll take you home. We can talk there."

"I don't think that's a good idea. Your house may not be safe. We need to go somewhere no one will expect to find us."

Mrs. Tanner balked at the idea, but didn't insist. "I'll be there in ten minutes. That'll give me time to find a place to go."

Peter told Fi what her mother had said as they headed for the teashop. It was one of those quaint little buildings down a narrow alley that looked like it had strayed from another age, with its tiny bay windows and old-fashioned lace curtains.

Peter entered first with Fi close behind. The place smelt strongly of roses and toasted buns. The teashop was empty apart from the serving lady who polished cutlery behind the counter. She raised her eyebrows at them. Indeed very few young people must come there.

"Good afternoon," Peter said amiably as he went up to the counter. "We are waiting for our mother." It gave him a quiet thrill to call Mrs. Turner his Mum. The woman smiled. An explanation wasn't necessary, but he didn't like to make people feel uncomfortable. He ordered a pot of tea and a couple of scones, paying from his allowance. Thanks Dad, he thought, in a silent prayer.

To an outside observer they sat in silence, buttering their scones. Mind-to-mind they discussed what had happened.

A few days ago, we went to a normal grammar school and led a simple life, Fi thought. *And now look at us. We've been sucked into a weird world that sprouts nightmares.*

I don't think the change was so sudden. Sanson has been planning this for quite a while. I bet he already had those fake prefects lined up. Even without Witless's wild behaviour or me toying with Sanson's words, it would still have happened sooner or later...

A group of old ladies entered chattering noisily about their respective illnesses and people they'd visited in hospital. When they saw Fi and Peter huddled in one corner, their conversation broke off and several of them gave the children a filthy look.

No wonder no young people come here, Fi thought.

You're right. What kid would brave the evil eye of those witches?

The tiny bell over the shop door rang again and this time it was Mrs. Tanner. Fi and Peter rose to meet her and she flung her arms around them, pulling them into a reassuring hug.

I really like your Mum, Peter whispered mind-to-mind to Fi.

Not more than me I hope, she retorted.

It was a relief to hear her spirits pick up. Fi without her sense of humour and her joyfulness would not be Fi.

Mrs. Tanner greeted the ladies present and then led the children out, her arm thrown loosely over Fi's shoulder.

"So?" Mrs Tanner asked, once they were in the car and out of earshot.

Peter, who sat at the back, leaned forward and told her about the attack on Fi and himself, without mentioning Kaitling. Instead, he had them recover and escape on their own.

"This whole story doesn't make sense," she exclaimed once Peter had finished. "Why would they try to drug you?"

"Sanson believes I'm a homosexual," Peter explained. "If I were unconscious, maybe I wouldn't be able to seduce him."

"That's a bit far fetched," Mrs. Tanner said. "And Fi?"

"She was the bait."

"Thanks for the role!" Fi complained.

"Unless of course they thought you were trying to seduce Sanson too," he retorted.

"Bah! That's disgusting!" Fi retorted.

He sat back and pulled the screwed up ball of papers from his pocket. Searching through them, he found the one he wanted and handed it forward to Fi.

She gasped. "Who wrote this?"

"A small group of charming boys in my class."

"What does it say?" Mrs. Tanner asked.

Fi refused to read it, so Peter took the scruffy paper back and read, I'll let you touch my flower, if you'll give me your pansy, signed 'Fiona'.

"How poetic! Those boys have a lot of imagination," Mrs Tanner said chuckling.

"It's not funny, Mum! They are suggesting that I'm offering myself to Peter because he's a homosexual. It's not true and it's downright mean."

"You are right, but I doubt they thought that far," Mrs Tanner said, as she turned the car into a narrow drive lined by a tightly knit wood.

Peter and Fi starred out the window wondering where Mrs. Tanner was taking them. The drive, which was surprisingly long, finally wound to the right and halted in front of a large mansion surrounded by lawns and carefully tended flower beds.

"Who lives here?" Fi asked.

"You'll see," Mrs Tanner said with a grin.

They climbed the four steps to the main entrance and Peter rang. He could hear a distant bell chime and then footsteps approaching. When the door opened, Peter and Fi were surprised to discover Dr. Grant standing in front of them.

"Headmaster!" Peter exclaimed, "Delighted to see you, Sir."

"Headmaster no more, Peter," Dr Grant said inviting them in. "Former Headmaster, if you please."

"Not for long, if I have anything to do with it."

"Sir Peter, the fearless," Dr Grant said, no hint of irony in his voice. Then he turned to Fi. "Hello, Fiona. I see you brought your Mum with you. A wise precaution."

The immense relief Peter felt at seeing Dr. Grant surprised him. He felt so light-headed, he could have skipped and danced around the large table in the dinning room.

"Make yourself at home. I'll go and fetch some things from the kitchen. You two must be starving."

Peter was about to protest that they had just eaten when Mrs. Tanner offered to help and hurried after Dr. Grant. Catching Fi's eye, Peter gave her a wink. She just shook her head.

Once tea and warm crumpets and jam and cream and marmite and more scones and marmalade and chocolate were laid out on the table, they all sat down and Dr. Grant said grace.

As he savoured the crumpets, Peter pondered what was to come. There would be questions, difficult ones, questions he might not want to answer. Their futures might depend on the answers they gave.

We might have to tell them what we have discovered, he thought mind-to-mind to Fi, who was curled up in her mother's arms.

Fi sighed by way of response. She was happy and Peter was happy for her.

Since the attack earlier that afternoon Fi seemed younger and more vulnerable. He too felt vulnerable and longed to curl up in the welcoming arms of a mother. He felt tears forming in his eyes and tried to conceal them, but Mrs Tanner saw. With her free hand she waved him over and put her arm around him, pulling him closer. His tears flowed freely as he turned and buried his face in her shoulder.

All was silent in the house bar the distant tick of a clock. When Peter finally looked up, his eyes still blurred by tears, Dr. Grant smiled at him and offered a handkerchief.

"So," Dr. Grant began, once Peter had blown his nose and wiped his eyes. "You two have been having adventures I hear."

Peter grimaced. "You won't believe half of it."

"We are open-minded," Mrs. Tanner said, brushing his hair out of his eyes. That little gesture almost had him crying again. He swallowed hard and concentrated.

"It's not an easy story to tell. We will tell you everything, well almost everything, but you must hear us out."

"Go ahead," Dr. Grant said.

"It began not so long ago, rather like the story of Alice, with me dropping off to sleep, but unlike Alice I didn't fall down a rabbit hole. I ended up in another world called Drailong. I found myself in the head of a girl called Kaitling."

"Ah!" said Dr. Grant. "The mysterious botanist and expert in unarmed combat."

"Exactly. Kaitling's the same age as me. Where she lives she's being trained as a magician or should one say a sorceress. At first I thought I had become a girl..." He laughed embarrassed at the idea "... but I quickly realised I was just a visitor in her head. I travelled to her place several times having no idea how I managed it. Then she came to visit me and we spoke for the first time."

He went on to explain how he'd learnt to speak mind-to-mind and then to travel to another mind. He described his first experiments with healing but downplayed his ability to take control of another person.

"I told Fi about it and she wanted to learn, so with Kaitling we practiced. It's not easy for Kaitling because she is on the run. Her country has been invaded and she has been captured once. She's in hiding with her father, who unfortunately has turned against her. He thought she'd been possessed and was being manipulated by the enemy."

"Now I have to track back and begin with Witless, I mean Miss Wit." He told them briefly about their first encounters and her threats, followed by Witless's violence in the street. Then he recounted the scenes at his home and the shattering of his family. He kept quiet about Fi's involvement as the lover of his sister. He took them quickly through all the events up to the prefects drugging him and Fi and how they managed to escape with Kaitling's help.

"So you see, that beast Sanson is a real danger and we need to get rid of him as soon as possible."

Peter looked up at his audience. Dr. Grant looked astounded, almost incredulous. As for Mrs. Tanner, she was looking at Peter with unconcealed tenderness and affection.

If you have any doubts, Peter spoke mind-to-mind to the two adults, *I can show you.*

We can show you, Fi amended.

Both adults gasped.

"I don't think that will be necessary," Dr. Grant said, still amazed. "I believe you, Peter, even if it's hard. I find it difficult to stop my mind racing after the implications of what you two, or rather three, have discovered."

Hello, another voice spoke into their minds. *My name is Kaitling. I can vouch for all Peter has told you.*

"Can you hear us if we speak out loud," Dr. Grant asked.

Yes. I can hear you through Peter's ears and see you through his eyes.

"When I said adventures," Dr. Grant chuckled, "I had no idea how adventurous you really were!"

42.

"There's one thing I want you to promise Christina and I," Dr. Grant began.

Peter was delighted at the use of Mrs. Tanner's first name. He was more worried about what the Headmaster was going to say.

"I want you to promise never to enter either of our heads."

He's just like my father, Kaitling said to Peter and Fi.

Peter looked from Dr. Grant to Mrs Tanner. Fi's Mum looked concerned. Peter remembered what he had learnt of the woman the one time he'd strayed into her head and he thought of the promise he'd made himself.

No he's not, Peter replied to Kaitling. *His concern is legitimate.*

Still looking at Mrs. Tanner, he replied: "I understand your concern, Sir. I too have my secrets. But I cannot promise you that."

Mrs. Tanner's face creased in displeasure. Dr. Grant was more composed. "Why do you say that?"

Peter was embarrassed. He didn't want to admit he'd already been in Mrs. Tanner's head and, above all, he didn't want to talk of what he'd seen there. It was far too personal, and he wanted to keep that secret.

"I want to be free to heal either of you, if ever that should be necessary." It was true enough but it wasn't the main reason.

Apparently neither of the adults had thought of that. A look of hope flashed cross Mrs. Tanner's face then she turned to Dr. Grant, masking her feelings.

"I still want you to promise not to mess with out heads, Peter," Dr. Grant insisted. "How can we possibly be with you if we are constantly wondering what you are doing to our minds?"

"It's not like that," Fi said. "I am with Peter all the time. It's more like a conversation."

"But you are in love with Peter, my dear," Fi's mother said, matter-of-factly. "That changes a lot. Whereas, I am your mother and Dr. Grant is a good friend, but we are adults and have our own lives, our own thoughts, our own secrets." She continued looking at Dr. Grant, her affection for him plain to see.

The answer is simple, Kaitling spoke in all their minds. *You two need to learn how to shield your thoughts and memories.*

"Of course! You're brilliant, Kaitling!" Peter exclaimed. "I don't need to know your thoughts. That could be very embarrassing," he went on, chuckling mainly out of relief. "It's easy. I can teach you."

It would be better if I taught them, Kaitling pointed out. *I come from a completely different world, so your secrets are nothing to me. I will promise not to reveal anything I might see.*

"What if we can't do this shielding business?" Mrs. Tanner asked nervously.

"Don't worry, Kaitling is an excellent teacher," Fi said.

Peter was glad to hear her praise Kaitling, relieved their mutual attachment to him had not led to animosity.

"I accept," Dr. Grant said.

"I accept, too," Mrs. Tanner said.

"Kaitling could you do it right away?" Peter asked, looking from one of the adults to the other. "Then they won't be continually wondering if we are peeking at their thoughts."

You're forgetting the young ones waiting for you at your school, Kaitling reminded them.

"What's this about?" Dr. Grant asked.

"A number of the younger kids wanted me to teach them self-defence. Sanson's new prefects are bullying them."

"It's a good idea," Dr Grant said. "But it might not be wise to stay so close to the school. Those prefects could wreak havoc. How about the church hall? I'm sure it's free. I'll check."

"Let me drive you to school. I can take everyone on to the church hall," Mrs. Tanner offered.

"It's free," Dr. Grant told them when he returned. "You can use it for the next two hours." Then he turned to Mrs. Tanner. "I think it might be too dangerous for you to stay at your place. Why don't you stay here for a couple of days until this is sorted out?"

It was Mrs. Tanner's turn to look embarrassed. "I don't want to put you to so much trouble, John."

"It's no trouble at all," he insisted.

Peter wanted to say he'd love to be there, but he was afraid it would seem like blatant matchmaking.

"Ok. I invite you all to dinner this evening. We can talk about it then," Dr. Grant suggested and everyone agreed.

When Peter, Fi, Kaitling and Mrs. Tanner reached the wood they found ten pupils cornered by four prefects who were taunting them.

"Your saviour ain't coming," jeered one of the bullies.

One of the first year boys had a bloody nose, a girl was cradling her arm as if it hurt and all the children were clearly scared.

Kaitling you help me, Peter said. *Mrs. Tanner keep back with Fi so you can support her body if she has to jump into one of those bullies to disarm him. Fi will explain. Once we've got rid of them, we can look after the injured.*

Kaitling, your turn. He felt her grin.

"You lot still haven't learnt your lesson," Peter said in a loud voice as he approached the prefects.

The bullies spun round, their eyes suddenly wide with fear. They had clearly heard what Peter was capable of.

"We are going to teach these youngsters to defend themselves against the likes of you. Please stay. We were looking for people to demonstrate on."

Several of the prefects took a step back, but the largest held his ground. "I'm not scarred of you, squirt."

"You're making a big mistake," Peter said as he mentally stepped aside and let Kaitling take over.

One of the prefects turned and ran. He didn't get far. He tripped over his own feet and fell flat on his face, provoking timid laughter from the beleaguered pupils. Peter guessed Fi was at work. Despite his efforts, the prefect couldn't seem to scramble to his feet.

Kaitling made fast work of the big bloke. He was over confident and completely unused to the speed of an opponent like her. When she had finished, he couldn't even crawl away.

The two remaining prefects helped their two colleagues to their feet and ran.

Let them go, Peter said mind-to-mind, *and spread the good news.*

Peter turned to their cheering protégés. "Don't expect to be able to do that immediately," he said chuckling. "Now let's see those of you that are hurt."

The boy with the nosebleed was OK. Fi helped him clean the blood from his face. Peter looked for the girl with the broken arm. She was sitting with her back to a tree, her face twisted in pain.

"Explain where we are going and take them to the car," Peter said to Fi and Mrs. Tanner. *I'm going to have a look at this arm but I prefer to have no one watching,* he added mind-to-mind.

He sat down next to the girl, whose name was Lilly, and placed his hand gently on her arm. "I'm just going to see what's wrong with your arm. It will help if you close your eyes."

He ran his mind over her arm. The arm wasn't broken, but it was bent at the wrong angle and was pulling painfully at the muscles and tissues around. He could have asked Mrs. Tanner to take her to the hospital in Tallford, it would be the sensible thing to do, but, from personal experience, he knew that might take hours and the girl would walk around with a plaster on her arm for quite a while.

"Lilly, your arm is not broken, but one of your bones has shifted. That is what's causing you so much pain. If you agree, I can heal it. If not we can take you to the hospital."

"Heal it?" she asked in a whisper.

"I can shift the bone back to its right place."

"Will it hurt?"

"A little, probably, but above all it will feel strange."

"Ok," she said, still hesitant.

"Let me show you. Feel that?" He helped the body shift the bone back to its place. "Can you feel it moving?"

Lilly nodded, tears flowing down her cheeks. She was putting on a very brave face. He could feel how much it hurt.

"There. The bone is where it should be. I'm sure that feels better."

Lilly nodded, wiping tears from her eyes with her free hand.

"All we need to do now is help the muscles and body tissues get over the shock. If you concentrate hard on you arm, you might feel the muscles sighing as they recover."

The girl giggled. "It tickles."

"That's it, finished."

"Already?"

"You'll need to be a little careful for a few days." He helped her to her feet and was surprised when she flung her arms around his neck and hugged him.

"That was wonderful," she said, stepping back as she gingerly flexed her arm.

He wondered what she was referring to, the fight, the healing or the hug.

"People are so used to how doctor's work, they can get quite upset when someone does it differently. I need you to promise not to tell anyone."

"I promise. How did you learn to do that?"

"Healing, you mean?"

She nodded.

"A very good friend of mine helped me learn."

"Could you teach me? I've always wanted to be a doctor, but this seems so much better."

Peter had known that healing her would cause problems or at least raise questions. He would willingly teach others, but he was worried about the consequences. Most people would probably take it for sorcery or black magic, causing trouble for him and those he taught.

"Healing people is tricky. It requires care and concentration, but it also involves a risk."

"You mean that you might hurt someone?"

"No. That is not possible. It's rather what people think. As I said, people can get very upset if you don't follow the usual procedure, even if you heal successfully. For the moment, I don't want people to know and I can't teach anyone else."

"That's a shame. What a silly world!"

Mrs. Tanner came back and drove Peter and Lilly to the church hall where the others were grouped around Fi. She was explaining how to find their right balance. Apparently Kaitling was using Fi to teach them. Peter found a chair in one of the darker corners of the hall and sat down to watch. He knew he should have joined in. He had a lot to learn, but he relished getting out of the spotlight.

Kaitling ran through a series of exercises on balance and movement then she showed them ways to fend off common attacks.

They were nearing the end of the lesson when the Vicar poked his head around the door. He looked irritated to find both boys and girls wrestling in the church hall. He was about to say something when he spotted Peter. His face suddenly twisted in fury.

"Get out of here, boy," he shouted, striding towards Peter, waving his fist as he did. The lesson with Fi came to an abrupt halt as all the children turned to see what was happening.

Peter was getting used to being threatened by adults, although it didn't get any less unpleasant with practice. He made no move to leave.

"Get out!" The Vicar repeated. "No peeping toms on church property."

Don't either of you jump to the Vicar, Peter warned Fi and Kaitling mind-to-mind. *I have to handle this.*

"I organised this course at the request of those pupils who were being bullied," Peter said, starring pointedly at the Vicar as he spoke.

The Vicar glared at him, then turned and stomped out of the hall.

"What's wrong with him?" one of the boys asked.

Peter shrugged. "Maybe he's the only one allowed to watch."

43.

When they returned from the church hall, Dr. Grant gave Fi and Peter free run of the attic. Mrs. Tanner had brought a suitcase of clothes for them from her house. They carried it up when they went to explore. Deciding which room would be theirs was easy. They chose one with a comfortable double bed. Accustomed as they were to sleeping in Peter's narrow bed at Fi's place, the prospect of having a large bed thrilled them.

They tumbled onto the bed with squeals of glee and rolled over and over wrestling. Out of breath, they paused in each other's arms and then kissed passionately till they were out of breath again. Lying on their backs hip-to-hip, shoulder-to-shoulder, holding hands, they both starred up at the ceiling.

He would never have imagined he could be happier than at Fi's, but he was. What with Mrs. Tanner and Fi and now Dr. Grant, it was as if he'd found a new family. The sort of family he might have dreamed of, had he ever let himself imagine such a possibility.

His mind turned to Kaitling. In comparison, she had lost what remained of her family and her home. He wished there was some way she could be a part of his new family.

"Maybe we should check on Kaitling."

Fi agreed, always game for an adventure.

Their friend was still confined to the soundless dark and was glad to have them join her.

What's going on with your father? Fi asked.

No idea, Kaitling said, voicing her frustration. *I used to see my father as an intelligent man! I wanted to be a magician like him. He had no failings for me. How blind can you get?*

Don't be too hard on him, Peter said. *He's trying to do what he thinks is best. You should see the mess my mother has made! The only one of our parents who is in any way sane is Fi's Mum. Let's hope she doesn't go overboard running after Dr. Grant.* Kaitling chuckled, but Fi was embarrassed and gave him a mental prod.

Let's give you some eyes and ears, Peter suggested.

Both he and Fi prepared to jump, but to their surprise they found only one person present and it was not Tyzi. They jumped all the same. The man was seated on a flat rock near the low shack. Fi relayed what the man saw to Kaitling, while Peter rummaged through his memories.

Your father and the other men have gone to Navigon, Peter told them. *They hope to liberate several members of the Twelve. They left about three hours ago. This man is worried it might be a trap. If you hadn't been under his care, he'd have fled to a fishing port called Bei.*

Now might be a good time to escape, Fi mused. *Maybe we could convince him to take you with him.*

Do it, Kaitling said, delighted.

Peter set to work whispering in the man's mind that the best way to protect Kaitling, but also himself, would be to take her with him to Bei. Convincing him was not hard. He was waiting for an excuse. It was a little more difficult persuading him to remove the Kaitling's hood. He was superstitious. That Kaitling might take over his mind terrified him. If only he knew!

Peter gently floated images of Kaitling stumbling along the path with him having to lead her. The man finally decided to risk it and removed the headpiece.

The light was blinding and Kaitling had to rely on images Fi sent her till her eyes adjusted.

You're going to have to find some pretext if you want to teach Dr. Grant and Mrs. Tanner to shield their thoughts, Peter said.

Don't worry, it's easy for us girls to pretend we're weak and tired. Isn't that what men expect of us? She and Fi chuckled, but Peter protested, annoyed at the caricature.

We still have time before dinner, Fi said, changing the subject. *We can accompany you part of the way.*

Peter was pleased the two were becoming friends. It was hard to be otherwise when you spent so much time in each other's minds.

Fi jumped back into Kaitling's mind, but Peter remained with the man, just in case. Once they left the marshes, hiding became more difficult. They travelled westward hugging the coast, as all villages and towns lay inland.

The man was taciturn, trudging tip-lipped a few yards behind Kaitling.

He's hungry, Peter said. *Find him something to eat and he'll be more forthcoming.*

If he lent me a bow I could bag a gull or two.

Peter reminded the man that Kaitling was an excellent shot. At the same time, he made the man feel even hungrier.

"Could you shoot down one of them gulls?" the man finally asked, his tone surly.

"Yes."

He reluctantly handed her a bow and arrows and she shot down several gulls that circled above. They found a cove nearby and made themselves a makeshift shelter among the rocks. The man built a fire of driftwood and Kaitling plucked the birds. The meal was almost ready when Peter and Fi had to leave.

See you later, he said to Kaitling. *Call us if you need help.*

Back in the mansion, they stretched and rubbed their eyes as they tried to adjust to being back in Tallford.

"Peter, Fi," Mrs. Tanner called out. "Dinner's ready."

"You look like you've had a nap," Mrs. Tanner commented when they settled at the dinning room table.

"Not at all," Fi said. "We were visiting Kaitling trying to help her escape."

"Did you manage?" Dr. Grant asked, as he placed a tureen

of soup on the table.

"Yes. She's on her way to a small fishing port at the north-west tip of the island."

"She'll join us later," Fi explained. "She's shot some gulls with her bow and they were roasting on the fire when we left."

"We'll I can't offer you such a delicacy," Dr. Grant said with a chuckle, "but I did manage to catch a chicken in the forest and it's roasting on a spit in the garden!"

Fi looked incredulous at her mother, who burst out laughing. "He's pulling your leg. There is a chicken, but it came from the butcher's and it's cooking in the oven."

"Come on," Dr. Grant said. "Let's eat. The pumpkin soup will get cold." He invited Peter to say grace then he ladled out generous helpings of soup. It was rich with cream and tiny pieces of what must have been fried bread.

"Croutons, the French say," Dr. Grant explained.

Once most of the chicken had been dispatched, the conversation turned to Sanson.

"What should we do with the pretender?" Peter asked.

"If we could gather proof of his plot and misdeeds," Dr. Grant said, "we might be able to convince the board they'd made a mistake. We will need allies amongst the governors, though."

"I know several people on the board," Fi's Mum said. "I'll sound them out once we've got the evidence."

"We already have Sanson's handwritten list of people he wants to eliminate," Peter said. "Mrs. Greengage has that."

"It would be good to have something that links Sanson to the journalist," Mrs. Tanner suggested.

"We'll have to discredit Witless's Aunt and her allies," Peter said.

"But how are we to get the information we need, supposing it exists in a form we can use?" Fi's Mum asked.

Nobody had a suggestion.

Peter had a pretty good idea. If it had only been him and Fi with Kaitling there would have been no problem. But he hesitated suggesting manipulating the minds of the aunt and Sanson.

He was sure the adults would be against.

"We could use our mind skills," Fi suggested, enthusiastically.

Peter wished she'd consulted him before mentioning it.

"What do you mean?" her mother asked sounding wary and worried.

Let me explain, Peter said to Fi, mind-to-mind. *They're not going to buy this on enthusiasm alone.* Fi was peeved that he take the spotlight, but she kept quiet.

"We can suggest options to people and, if we do it well, those options appear difficult to resist," Peter said, realising immediately that he might be able to sway minds but he could not do it now with his spoken words.

"That's manipulation!" Mrs. Tanner exclaimed, shocked. She was an easy-going person, and Peter like her immensely for it, but she had just reached her limit.

"But Mum!" Fi said. "These people abducted us using drugs. Goodness knows what they would have done if we hadn't escaped. All we are proposing is to encourage them to give us the information. They probably won't even realise what's happening."

Peter was concerned how Dr. Grant would react, but the Headmaster was keeping out of the fray.

"We are aware that working with people's minds raises problems," Peter said.

Suddenly he felt centuries old and, although he enjoyed all they had learnt, he would willingly have been free of it. "With Kaitling, the three of us have drawn up and sworn a pact. It goes as follows: We will not use travelling to minds to harm others or to make fun of them or to force them to do things against their will, unless it is to stop them doing harm to others or possibly to themselves."

He paused, thinking someone might object, but no one spoke. "Both Sanson and Aunt Witless are doing harm to a lot of people. The four of us are their main targets, but many of the other pupils at school, especially the younger ones, are also hurt or in danger."

He thought for a moment. "Think of our work as a lie detector. We are simply going to make them divulge the truth. If they have done nothing wrong they will not be hurt. If they have done wrong they will probably be punished, but not by us."

"I see why you get such good marks in maths and logic," Dr. Grant said chuckling. "You should join the school debating team, you'd be a real asset. Compliments apart though, I believe you are right and I find your proposed acts morally acceptable. Can you live with that, Christina?"

She looked uncomfortable. "I hate the logic of battle that condones an eye for an eye. When the battle is over, the winners find it very hard not to pursue their violence. If you are strong enough to hold true to your pact, then you have more moral fibre than most adults. What you three are capable of is frightening. It can be used to take away people's free will. Free will is one of the pillars of being human."

She looked at Fi and then at Peter, searching long and deep in their eyes. "Ultimately we have to believe that people are capable of doing good rather than the contrary," she continued. "I love both of you, like a mother loves her children, and as a mother, I am always afraid my children will get hurt or be tempted by wrong doing. Yet ultimately I must let you chose and be confident that your choice will be the right one. So I accept your choice."

She stepped forward and pulled Fi and Peter into her arms and hugged them. Peter was moved by her speech. He asked for nothing more than to be considered as her child and to be respected for what he was.

Out of the corner of his eye Peter could see Dr. Grant standing alone, watching them. There was yearning in his face, but sadness and joy too. Peter wanted to call out, Join us! But they were not his words to say.

As if reading his mind, Fi's Mum beckoned Dr. Grant over. The man took an uncertain step in their direction. Mrs. Tanner took hold of his hand, pulling him gently closer, put one arm

round his shoulder and kissed him on the cheek. He returned
her kiss, fleetingly, unsure of himself. Then Fi's Mum pulled
him even closer and he put his arms around Peter and Fi as well,
until all four were one big embrace.

44.

What a happy scene! Kaitling said wistfully as she arrived. *I wish I had such a reception to return to. It's not for that reason, though, that I have to break up your little gathering. I need Dr. Grant and Mrs. Tanner, if I am to teach them how to hide their thoughts.*

"I have to go to choir practice," Peter said. "Why don't you come along, Fi?"

"You know the Vicar is not fond of girls hanging round," Fi's Mum said.

"He's not fond of me," Peter commented. "When he saw me at the hall earlier he started shouting. He's nuts."

"Well, you were sitting in a dark corner staring at us pretty girls and boys throwing each other's bodies around," Fi said, a hint of malicious glee in her voice. "I reckon he thought you were a voyeur."

Fi's Mum spluttered. "I have no idea where you young people get such outrageous ideas." She turned to Dr. Grant, trying to conceal a grin. "Is it at school, Headmaster?"

"I sincerely hope not," Dr. Grant said, making a good attempt at appearing shocked.

Don't mind them, Peter said to Kaitling. *They're making fun of us!*

Kaitling was confused. *My father, for all his shortcomings, would never do that. What he says is what he means. He would never play a role like an actor. How do you know when people are being serious and when they're 'joking', as you call it?*

"There are many parents like your father," Fi's Mum said.

"You have happened on a rather unusual family," Dr. Grant added. "Most parents do not behave in such a way with their children. Your worries may be justified, though. Maybe this is the beginning of the end."

"He's joking again," Peter said.

"Maybe not, Peter," the Headmaster said.

This is all too confusing, Kaitling complained. Let's get on with what I came for. I'll teach you first Dr. Grant, as Mrs. Tanner is taking Peter and Fi. For this to work, you are going to have to accept me in your mind, even before you can shield your thoughts. I cannot teach you from Peter's mind. I can talk to you from here but I need to be in your mind for this to work. I have to show you what to do.

"It's not like at school where you read a book to learn," Peter said. "It has to be felt to be understood, and it has to be felt from inside. Once you've felt it and you can see how it works, doing it is easy."

"If this sort of thing were to catch on..." Dr. Grant began.

"Which I hope it won't," Fi's Mum interjected.

"... We'll have to rethink our teaching methods."

Peter thought of Johnson teaching history. "I'm not sure our subjects at school would work with such a method. I certainly wouldn't like to have Johnson droning away in my head!"

"Peter!" exclaimed Mrs. Tanner, shocked.

"The man's a bore," Fi said in Peter's defence. "I can't imagine anyone who could make history less interesting."

Dr. Grant chuckled. "If ever I return as Headmaster, I'm going to have to talk to pupils more often, or I'll have a revolt on my hands."

"They probably wouldn't tell you what you want to know," Peter said candidly. "You're the Headmaster!"

Dr. Grant was about to reply, but Kaitling interrupted. *I thought you had a choir to attend!*

"Come on Kaitling," Dr. Grant said with a sigh, "teach me

how to keep my secrets."

The others choristers were talking to the choirmaster when Peter and Fi arrived. He suggested she sit somewhere inconspicuous in case the Vicar turned up. The building was shroud in shadow. Only lights near the organ where on. Peter left Fi in the obscurity and took a side aisle, heading for the light. St. Mary's was not one of those high churches with services in Latin, but they did use incense from time to time. He relished the faint scent that curled around the pillars and lingered in dark corners. It was like a familiar signature.

He nodded a greeting to the other boys who were huddled around the organ console near the choir stalls. He had no particular friend in the choir. He wasn't much interested in spending time with boys. Their conversation was often stupid and their pursuits bored if not scared him. But, after so many years in the choir, and now as head chorister, he knew the members well enough. What with choir practice once a week and church on Sunday and parish breakfast, they met quite often. A few of the older ones even went to his school.

When the choirmaster had finished explaining what they were going to sing, Peter apologised for being late. He was pleased to hear he had a solo on Sunday, one that he knew well.

They were busy practicing a difficult descant to the anthem, when their singing was interrupted by a shout from the darker part of the nave. Everyone turned to see the Vicar stomping along the aisle, red faced and furious, towing Fi by the arm.

Stop him, Peter, she said mind-to-mind. *He's hurting me.*

"Let go of that girl immediately, brute!" Peter said taking several steps in the Vicar's direction. "You are hurting her."

Rather than let go, the Vicar shook Fi as if she were a rag doll. "Is this yours, Peter McCloud?"

"I said let go of her! You're hurting her. She has done no wrong,"

"I won't have you talking to me like that, boy. Nor will I have you bringing your girlfriend to choir practice. This is a church not a bordello."

"I warn you one last time," Peter said, his voice deadly quiet. "If you do not cease hurting this girl, I will be obliged to hurt you."

The Vicar suddenly let go of Fi, causing her to fall to the ground at his feet, and took a step backwards, fear on his face. "Get out of God's house! I knew those rumours about you were true. Filthy pansy! You stink of Sodom and Gomorrah. Get out and never come back!"

"You can't do that..." The choirmaster began to say, no doubt wondering who would sing the solo on Sunday.

"I will not tolerate this boy a moment further in my church," the Vicar spluttered.

Peter wondered what to do. No point in arguing with the Vicar, the man had gone crazy. Another one! But he didn't want to leave the choir. He loved singing and he enjoyed going to church. It was a magic place where he felt himself unfold.

He stepped forward and helped Fi to her feet. She was trembling. He examined her arm and the large bruise forming there. Putting an arm round her, he pulled her closer and she laid her head on his shoulder. Their position reminded him of a picture in one of the stained glass windows depicting Mary pregnant in Joseph's arms as they searched for a place for the night.

"Get out!" the Vicar continued, pointing to the door.

"Is that what you would have said when Mary stood before you in the arms of her man, in search of a haven for the night?" Peter asked.

The Vicar halted, perplexed.

"Are you so sure of yourself that you can divide the good from the evil and turn away the poor and weak and needy?"

The Vicar's face turned purple with rage. "How dare you talk to me of the Mother of God?"

It was then that a very strange thing happened. Pianissimo at first, then mezzo forte, the choir began to sing the anthem. Peter had no idea whether the choirmaster had encouraged them or if the boys had spontaneously broken into song. In the half-light of the church, unaccompanied by the organ, the boys' voices were ethereal, almost eerie.

When they reached the point at which Peter should begin his solo, he took a deep breath, pulled himself up straight and sang. As his voice soared above the choir, a calm filled him and he let himself go with the music. Fi was still in his arms, her hand clasped in his. He felt the warmth of her body against his chest and the rise and fall of her breathing. At the same time, it was as if there were thousands of other people around him buoying him up.

When the anthem came to an end, he looked around in wonder, expecting to see all those people he'd felt. Instead there was just Fi and the choir and the choirmaster. The Vicar had gone.

"Sing like that on Sunday," the choirmaster said, clearly moved as he wiped his eyes, "and you'll have the whole congregation in tears." There was a long pause then he spoke again. "I think that's enough emotion for one day."

Animated chatter broke out amongst the choirboys that rippled out through the nave. The pipes groaned and sighed as the choirmaster turned off the organ and closed the console. To Peter's surprise, several boys gave him a friendly pat as they left.

Beautiful, Fi whispered mind-to-mind. *How could that silly man think that an angel like you could be in league with the devil?*

Maybe devils are beautiful too, Peter mused.

When Mrs. Tanner arrived to fetch them, she was not her usual talkative self. Instead she drove with her eyes fixed on the road and asked nothing about choir practice. If anything she looked disappointed, if not worried.

Fi didn't seem to notice. Instead she bubbled over with news about what had happened in the church. "You should have heard Peter sing, Mum. His voice was so beautiful even the choirmaster had tears in his eyes..."

Dr. Grant was nowhere to be seen when they arrived at his place.

"Where's Kaitling?" Peter asked.

"She had to return to her world," Fi's Mum said, her voice surprisingly toneless and resigned.

"What happened?"

"I have no idea, she just had to leave."

"I don't mean in Drailong, I mean here between you two and her. Something's wrong and I want to know what it is."

Mrs. Tanner sighed and sat wearily in an armchair in the living room. "We couldn't do it."

"What?" Fi asked, alarmed.

"We couldn't shield our thoughts. No matter what Kaitling tried, there was no way we could manage."

"That's not all, is it?" Peter quizzed.

Mrs. Tanner laid her head in her hands, bowed her shoulders and closed her eyes. "I told Dr. Grant that I didn't think we should stay if you two could read our thoughts..."

A wave of wretchedness washed over Peter. He would be forced to return to his own empty house, or even worse, to live with a foster family. He would probably be expelled from school. He might not see Fi again and the timid beginnings between Dr. Grant and Fi's Mum would be over. Tears welled up in his eyes as the feeling of loss and despair gripped him.

Fi was furious. At first he thought it was at him. After all, he had brought this about. If he had not gone to Drailong, none of this would have happened. The moment Fi spoke, however, it was clear she was not mad at him, but at her Mum.

"What have you done with my mother?" Fi exclaimed.

Mrs. Tanner looked up, alarmed. "I don't understand."

"My mother would never react like this. She would never give up so easily. My Mum's a champion, a fighter, but she's also a very sensitive person. She would never hurt so many people like you are doing now."

Fi's Mum was staring at her daughter, her mouth fallen open. It looked like she wanted to say something, but no words came.

"I want my Mum back!" Fi said staring hard at her mother's frozen face.

"It's complicated..." Mrs Tanner finally said in a whisper.

"You wouldn't understand, you are only a child."

"You see what I mean! My mother would never say such a thing!"

"Don't be too hard on her, Fi," Peter said, feeling sorry for Mrs. Tanner. "She's only trying to do what she thinks is best."

"Don't you start," Fi said, turning on him. "Go get Dr. Grant. He's not going to slink away either."

Peter called out in the stairwell, not knowing where the Headmaster had gone. "Dr. Grant? We need you!" Above, he heard a door open and the sound of footsteps down a corridor.

"Yes, Peter?" the Headmaster asked as he descended the stairs, his face creased with concern.

"Fi wants to talk to you," Peter announced then he added "Sir", thinking he might have been disrespectful.

Back in the living room, Fi stood with her back to the fireplace, her hands on her hips, her eyes blazing like some warrior queen leading her troops into battle.

"You two are worried that we will poach secrets from your minds," Fi said, direct as ever. "Are you prepared to ruin all our lives to protect those thoughts, despite the fact that we swear we will never do that to you?" Turning towards her mother, she continued. "Are you going to sacrifice the very best side of yourself to stop us learning you are in love with Dr. Grant when it is plain for all to see?"

Mrs. Tanner blushed, but said nothing.

Fi turned to Dr. Grant. "How about you? Is your feeling safe in your thoughts worth more than the happiness of all four of us?"

Peter could see that the fire was going out of Fi's anger. As it did, she appeared less like an imposing warrior queen and more like the young girl she was. He went to her side and put his arm around her waist. Both of them stood silent in front of the unlit fire, waiting for the adults to respond.

"I..." Mrs Tanner began, tears in her eyes. "I'm sorry, Fiona. I'm sorry I disappoint you. Sometimes it is hard to be the kind of person you see in me." Then she turned to Dr. Grant. "I'm sorry John. I didn't mean to push you away. The children were really only a pretext. I was afraid. I've been alone for a long time now..."

Peter was embarrassed at being witness to such an intimate scene. It didn't seem right. He took hold of Fi's hand and pulled her towards the door. "If we are to promise not to riffle through your thoughts, maybe we can begin by giving you some privacy now," he said.

As Peter and Fi headed up the stairs to their room, they heard Dr. Grant and Mrs. Tanner laugh. Everything was going to be OK.

45.

Fi raised herself on one elbow propping her head on her hand and ran the index finger of her free hand over his high cheekbones and traced a fine line down his nose.

"I wonder why they couldn't shield their thoughts?" she mused.

"Maybe the older you get, the more difficult it becomes."

"Or maybe Kaitling wasn't the right teacher."

"Well she managed to teach me easily enough."

Leaning forward, Fi planted her wet lips in the middle of his forehead.

"Is that how you read my mind?" he asked, wiping the saliva from his forehead.

"Yes," she giggled. "I saw you had an irresistible desire to kiss me."

"Would you be trying to manipulate me, Fiona Tanner?"

"Never," she said grinning, then kissed him firmly on the lips.

"Talking about manipulation, we have some work to do."

"Whom should we begin with?"

"Sanson." Of that much, Peter was sure. "I have been in his mind several times, so I should be able to jump there easily."

"What are we looking for?"

"Written proof of conspiracy."

"But how are we to get it? We can't move objects with our minds."

"No. But we can get him to move them for us."

"You mean have him give them to us?"

"Something like that. Shall we go?"

Sanson was slouched at a desk, the room a blur. A large bottle reared out of the gloom amid a jumble of papers. The man popped the cork and poured himself a generous glass, taking a greedy swig. Peter shrank from the heady aroma and cringed as the whiskey hit the man's stomach.

Can we get drunk from being in a drunkard's head? Fi asked.

Probably. We need to be quick. The feeling of reality slipping away was alarming. *This must be the best deterrent against drinking alcohol,* Peter thought, disgusted. *Keep an eye on him while I rummage through his memories.*

He was disappointed to find nothing on the meeting with Aunt Witless. He began skipping backwards rapidly through insipid memories and vague thoughts, till he stumbled on an exchange of letters with Witless's aunt.

I may have something. He focussed in, trying to get a better picture but, to his frustration, Sanson didn't recall them well.

I'm going to have to make him dig out those letters, Peter said. *His memory is pathetic. I wonder how he ever got to be a teacher.*

Peter brought the memory of the letters to the forefront of Sanson's blurred thoughts. He troubled Sanson with the idea that he might have missed something important until finally the man got up and staggered in search of what he called 'the damned letters'. It took him a while to remember where he'd hidden them.

This place stinks, Fi commented. *I wonder when he last opened a window?*

Or had someone clean it, Peter added. The more he saw, the more the man disgusted him. He couldn't help comparing this place to Dr. Grant's well-kept house.

Sanson almost gave up several times. Peter had to egg him on, plying him with doubts and fears. Finally Sanson found the letters in a shoebox under his unmade bed on the first floor.

Remind me to take some disinfectant if I ever have to deal with Sanson face to face, Fi muttered.

Shhh! Peter said. *I need to concentrate.*

Sanson shoved a screwed up pair of pyjamas onto the floor and brushed aside a pile of smelly socks and some filthy underwear. He smoothed the ruffled sheets with an unsteady hand then up-ended the contents of the box.

A number of things tumbled out, but Peter was only interested in the letters. He wanted Sanson to open each in turn. But as the man threatened to flake out, Peter was forced to make him gather up the contents and carry them down to the kitchen where he prepared himself a strong coffee.

The kitchen was as much a pigsty as the rest of the house.

Fi could contain her disgust no longer. *How could he ever have been be considered a Headmaster?*

Peter shared her disgust and anger, but he had to concentrate. Once Sanson had swallowed a large cup of coffee and prepared himself a second, he cleared a space on the kitchen table and poured out the contents of the box. He opened the first letter, in search of whatever it was he'd forgotten.

One was from Aunt Witless confirming their appointment and suggesting ways to oust Grant. She mentioned she had a number of board members who would willingly follow her lead if they were to act. Another letter was a first draft of one written by Sanson, expanding on Witless's ideas including provoking violence in school as if Grant were at fault. A third letter was from the journalist thanking Sanson for all the information he'd sent about the problems in the school. The journalist requested a meeting and said he hoped Sanson could provide concrete proof of the Headmaster's incompetence.

We couldn't have asked for better, Fi said as she followed what Sanson was reading.

Now comes the tricky part, Peter said. *We have to get him to give us the evidence.*

Sanson was still reading the letters, unable to find the illusive idea that troubled him. Peter began by knotting the man's stomach with deep-felt anxiety. He floated visions of people trying to break into his house in search of just these documents. Sanson sprang to his feet, his immediate reaction being to burn them. Peter struggled to stop him.

Give him a phobia of fire, Fi suggested.

Sanson was already on his way to the fireplace in the living room, the letters grasped in one hand, a lighter in the other. Peter beset him with images of fire ravaging his house. Only a spark would be enough. He completed the picture with a searing pain in the man's hands and arms and face as if he were burning. Sanson screamed, halting mid-step. With exaggerated care he placed the lighter on a table and retreated to the kitchen, his head swinging desperately left and right as if in search of flames.

Peter breathed a sigh of relief. *That was close.*

He had Sanson put the letters back in the box with the rest of its contents and wrap the box in a plastic bag. Then he suggested hiding it outside, somewhere no one would think to look.

Shoving on his slippers, Sanson unlocked the back door and looked warily into the darkness. He was trembling with terror. To Peter's horror, Sanson doubled back and headed for the fireplace, but a quick look at the man's thoughts showed he was after the poker. So armed, he ventured out into the back yard.

We need somewhere accessible, Fi whispered.

Peter had the man search the whole garden for a suitable hiding place. It was Peter that picked the spot, an unused metal box behind the front wall concealed below a mound of dried leaves. Then he coaxed Sanson to put his packet inside, relieved when the man finally returned to the house leaving the box behind.

I have just one more thing to do, Peter told Fi.

Sanson let out a deep sigh of relief once he'd locked the back door, but Peter didn't want the man to get off so easily. Reigniting the man's fears of fire and burglars, he drove his anxiety up several stops. Sanson scurried into his study and shakily grabbed for the bottle. Taking several large swigs, he lurched into an armchair, the bottle still in his hand.

Time to let him sleep, Peter said, satisfied. *I wouldn't like to be in his dreams tonight.*

Returning to their bodies both were profoundly shaken and horrified at what had happened. They were not immune to the emotions that coursed through their host's body, or his drunken stupor.

"I don't think I'll ever do that again," Peter said, his voice trembling.

"Me neither."

Peter felt as cold as if he'd been out in his pyjamas in a snowstorm. Fi too was shivering.

They hugged each other, desperately trying to get warm.

"Do you think Dr. Grant has some hot chocolate?" Peter asked.

"What a wonderful idea!"

Downstairs they found Mrs. Tanner and Dr. Grant in deep discussion in living room. Looking up, Fi's Mum exclaimed, "You look so pale. What's the matter?" She got to her feet and walked over to them. "You are trembling!" she said, worried. "My dears," Fi's Mum exclaimed and hugged them both.

"Your hugs work wonders, Mrs. Tanner, but I think we need something to warm our insides," Peter said, shakily. The thought that his words might be misconstrued to mean alcohol almost had him throwing up. "Have you got any hot chocolate, Dr. Grant?"

Settled next to each other, a mug of hot chocolate clasped in their hands, Fi and Peter finally returned to normal.

"I think you owe us an explanation," Dr. Grant said, a look of concern on his face. Mrs. Tanner sat next to the Headmaster and had one hand lightly resting on his arm. That sight did as much to warm Peter's heart as the hot chocolate.

"We went in search of the proof you need," Peter began wearily.

"And we found it," Fi added. She seemed to find it easier

to recuperate than Peter. Of course, she hadn't had to handle Sanson like Peter had.

"That Sanson bloke is..." Peter didn't know what words to use. "If I said he was a tramp, it wouldn't be fair to tramps. He's a miserable specimen who lives in squalor. We left him in a drunken stupor, terrified of his own shadow."

"But how are we to get this proof," Dr. Clark asked.

"That's not difficult," Peter said. "He put it out for us."

"We should leave immediately, in case he changes his mind," Fi said, getting to her feet.

"I doubt he'll change his mind tonight," Peter countered. "But you are right. The sooner we get that stuff to safety the better. Do you know where Sanson lives?" Of course Dr. Grant did.

Dr. Grant let the car coast to a halt some fifty yards from Sanson's house. Peter donned the gloves Dr. Grant had loaned him and jumped from the car. He couldn't reach the box from across the low wall and was obliged to climb over to remove it from its hiding place.

Back at Dr. Grant's place, Peter emptied the contents onto the dining room table. When Mrs. Tanner went to pick up one of the letters, Peter stopped her. "Better not touch them. You never know. Fingerprints and all..."

With gloved hands, he opened each letter and laid it out so they could be read. The final envelope was considerably thicker and heavier than the others and was dirty with stains and creased as if it had been frequently opened. It was crammed full with what looked like photos. He had some difficulty pulling one out, wearing gloves as he was. When he finally managed, he gasped to find a picture of a boy his age, naked on a settee, his legs spread-eagled, his hands cupped over his crotch.

Hearing him gasp, everyone grouped round to look.

"Put it back in the envelope, Peter. We've seen enough," Dr. Grant said. "It would seem that Sanson had more than one dirty secret."

Witless's father was not alone it would seem, Fi thought to him, mind-to-mind.

How many adults are like him? Peter asked, troubled by what he'd seen.

As Fi and the adults returned to the letters, Peter examined the other objects in the box. There were three balls of wax paper slightly smaller than his thumb. He undid one and found what looked like a lump of greenish, black rock inside. "What's this?" he mused.

Dr. Grant leaned closer and sniffed the rock. "That's cannabis resin!" he said surprised. "Our new Headmaster really is a paragon of virtue."

46.

Kaitling crouched on cold stone, her head rested on her knees. "I'm useless," she whispered.

"Incapable and worthless," intoned the black-robed priests.

"Even my father has abandoned me," she wailed.

"A traitor," intoned the priests.

Kaitling hesitated, uncomprehending then continued. "My friends have turned away from me! It's unfair."

"Against you," the chorus of priests chanted.

Peter struggled to object. Of course they hadn't turned against her. They'd just been busy.

"Oh Peter," Kaitling sobbed. "Why have you forsaken me?"

I haven't, he shouted, striving to break through Kaitling's nightmare, to no avail.

"Your only friend is us," the priests intoned.

What nonsense! Peter screamed. *They're the enemy! Can't you see?*

Kaitling stared at the black-robbed figures, through tear filled eyes. "Friends?" she asked, dubious.

"Friends!" chanted triumphantly the priests.

"I don't have friends," Kaitling continued, lowering her head.

The rustle of heavy cloth on cloth had Kaitling's look up in alarm. The block of the black-clad priests took a step forward.

"You're not my friends!" she screamed.

They shifted one step closer.

Kaitling struggled to her feet and raised her fists.

The priests closed the gap.

If only he could reach her.

Inches away now, the priests stepped one final pace swallowing Kaitling in the dark.

Peter awoke in a sweat, the horror of the dream clinging to him. Could Kaitling have been so downhearted? The adults may not have noticed she was upset the evening before. They had been so frustrated and disappointed.

It was dark outside. By the dim light seeping under the door, he could see Fi fast asleep, curled up next to him. There was no alternative, he had to visit Kaitling and set matters right.

All was dark and silent. Had his dream come true? His terror threatened to fling him out of Kaitling's mind, but he clung on. Letting out feelers he found that Kaitling was asleep and unhurt. Further afield he sensed a considerable number of men, but their minds were shroud. Priests, he thought.

He roped in his attention and focussed on Kaitling's recent memories. She and the man had pushed on to Bei, walking swiftly, despite the failing light. She looked forward to shelter, sustenance and a good night's sleep. Maybe that was why she hadn't spotted the patrol concealed behind the rocks. The ambush caught them just as Bei came into sight. The Syvans seemed to have known they were coming.

Her fellow traveller had defended her bravely, dealing out deadly strokes of his sword, but an enemy arrow had got the better of him. Alone and heavily outnumbered, Kaitling had quickly been overpowered. Apparently they wanted her alive.

They had marched her to the road, tied her up in a cart and packed her off towards Navigon. Soon after, a priest had arrived and coiffed her with a headpiece identical to the one her father had used. Unable to hear or see, she had drifted off to sleep.

Two soldiers dragging her roughly from the cart awoke her. They pushed her along interminable stone corridors and down many flights of stairs, till she was finally locked in a small room. It was on the floor of that room that she now slept.

Peter didn't want to pry, but he was intrigued to know what had happened with Dr. Grant and Fi's Mum. He raced back over the recent events till he reached the time Kaitling spent in Dr. Grant's house. He had been right to think Kaitling was upset about her failure. She felt both sad and incompetent.

He replayed her attempts to help them create a shield. The adults had quickly become flustered and confused, their minds forming a natural barrier to protect them from experiencing what they saw as a failure. The more they tried, the less access they had to the workings of their minds. In a way, they shut themselves out. Kaitling in turn had been frustrated and irritated, not understanding why they couldn't feel what was going on. She pushed them even harder, unaware she was producing the contrary to what she wanted.

When they finally gave up, everyone was sure they'd failed. Kaitling returned to her world miserable, convinced Peter would not visit her again. He didn't need her anyway, he had Fi. Seeing where Kaitling's thoughts were leading, Peter hastily pulled back, not wanting to pry into her feelings for him.

At least there were some things he could set right. He whispered her name softly in her mind, his voice full of tenderness and concern. Stirring, she searched for the source of the sound and, feeling Peter in her mind, she hugged him fervently. *You came,* she exclaimed, her voice trembling with emotion. *I was sure...*

Well you were wrong! I would not abandon you. Neither would the others.

But I failed!

Do you seriously think I would turn away from you because of that? If you do, you misjudge my affection for you. He felt her tremble at the word affection.

We need to find out what's going on, he said, shying away from any thought of attachment, and stretched out his senses to feel for people nearby. As he'd noticed earlier they were all heavily shielded. *This isn't going to be easy,* he told Kaitling.

If he were to enter a warrior priest's mind, guarded as it was

by an iron will, grim determination and years of gruelling practice at warding off mental attacks, he would have to shrink to
minuscule proportions. Being so tiny, the slightest puff of wind
or the most insignificant of vagrant thoughts might hurtle him
off course.

Stop doubting, he told himself sternly and jumped.

Fearing that travelling directly would cause him to use too
much force and automatically spark opposition, he attempted to
hover just short of the barrier, something he'd never tried before. What if he fell short and lost himself in limbo? The thought
had him terrified. To his surprise a faint force held him in place.
From there he was able to slip unnoticed into the priest's mind.

Sight and sound flooded into him as he connected with the
man. They were in a large meeting room devoid of any decora-
tion. Several priests were seated around a table. Peter rapidly
scanned the priest's recent memories. Kaitling's father was held
prisoner nearby. He was to be tried that day. Their god would
pronounce the final judgement. There was no doubt in the man's
mind that Tyzi would be found guilty and condemned. Kaitling,
being a girl, would not be tried. She would be executed alongside her father.

Peter plunged into the priest's memories a second time in
search of information about the place. Maybe there was some
way Kaitling could escape. To his disappointment, he saw only
interminable corridors and locked doors. Try as hard as he
would, he could not get a clear picture of the layout. He did get
a glimpse of the room where the trial was to take place, a giant
hall with many narrow glass windows that ran from ceiling to
floor. From what he was able to see, the hall had a high rostrum
at one end and rows and rows of benches placed in semi-circles
before the platform.

They've got your father, he told Kaitling the second he was
back. He let her know all he had learnt including details of the
trial. *You will be taken along with him, although you won't be
put on trial.*

She remained completely level headed at the mention of her

death. As for him, the thought had him on the verge of tears. He was ashamed when she consoled him. It should have been the other way round.

Tell me everything you know about their god, Peter insisted, his voice urgent in Kaitling's head. She tried, but recalling was not easy. *If you allow me, I will search your memories. It will go much quicker.*

So there is one distinct Syvan god, Peter said. *I wonder how I could influence his decision.*

How could a mortal influence the voice of a god?

In my world I attend church. It's a house where people are supposed to be able to communion with god.

And do you?

Yes, Peter said, his voice trembling with emotion. *Not often. When I sing solo in the choir and the music lifts me up and carries me away, I have the most intense feeling of being connected to everything and everyone. At that moment I know I am in contact with god.*

I have once heard this voice the people here call god. It is nothing like the experience I had. That voice has authority, it is true, but it is the authority of a general on a parade ground, not of a god.

As he spoke, Peter discovered his own thoughts and was as surprised by them as Kaitling. *I don't believe that voice comes from a god. It comes from a man. I am sure. If I can trace it back to its source, maybe I can force the man to spare you and your father.*

Kaitling had begun to cry softly. His words had undone her, releasing a flood of pent up emotion.

I love you, Peter McCloud, she said through her tears. *I loved you long before you knew I existed. Even if today is the last day of my life, I will carry you in my heart and mind forever.*

Confronted with the sweet tenderness of her feelings and the strength of her emotions, a deep-seated struggle in Peter ceased and he let go, feeling himself dissolve. There was no fear of loss in that dissolution. Instead, he was at one with Kaitling, two and one together, united, intertwined in a bliss that overflowed in every direction.

Peter had no idea how long the moment lasted. He didn't care. He was at one with Kaitling and the two of them were at one with the whole universe. Then, with a sigh, he felt himself draw slowly back and he was once again separate from both Kaitling and the universe, although that tripartite union had left an unforgettable mark.

47.

Fi slumbered on when Peter returned from Drailong. The blissful look that lit her face touched him deeply, as if his heart were raw and vulnerable. He needed to be alone. Any more emotions and he might burst. He slipped noiselessly out of bed and pulling on a pullover, he headed down the stairs and out into the garden.

Under his bare feet, the grass was cold and wet with dew. It sent shivers of delight coursing up and down his spine. Birds were stirring in the trees, shaking out their feathers. Here and there they began their dawn chorus until all joined to greet the new day. In the east, through the trees, Peter could see the first rays of breaking day drive back the night.

The joy he had felt with Kaitling surged anew, threatening to rip him apart. He knew of no better way to appease the intensity than to sing. Softly at first so as not to shock the birds or wake the neighbours, then with more verve, he sang the solo he had sung the day before in church. Who needed churches, a tiny part of his mind muttered? He ignored it. Once again he was at one with the universe. He could feel the love of Kaitling. He felt that of Fi too. He felt the love of Fi's Mum and Dr. Grant and he was complete.

When his solo was over, he stood a while savouring the chorus of the birds that continued, then he turned, intending to return to bed. To his surprise, there in the open French windows stood Fi, her Mum and Dr. Grant, their eyes fixed on him. He was happy to see them, if not a little embarrassed to be out in an old pair of Fi's pyjamas, barefoot in the garden.

"Sorry. Did I wake you?"

"You can wake me like that every morning, if you like." Dr. Grant said. "I thought I heard an angel."

"I believe you did," Peter said, smiling shyly.

As they sat around the breakfast table, Peter was relieved no one asked why he had been singing in the garden. Talk centred on what to do with Sanson's treasure trove. Mrs. Tanner was to contact the people she knew on the board and show them the letters, but only if she felt they could be trusted. There was some talk about what to do with the drugs and photos. Fi suggested returning them to Sanson and then tipping off the police, but in the end they decided Dr. Grant would get rid of the filthy evidence.

"I will not be going to school today," Peter announced.

"Are you afraid of reprisals?" Dr. Grant asked.

"I doubt Sanson will be in a state to badger anyone. No. I have to return to Kaitling's world." Peter paused a moment, striving not to drown in the rising tide of sorrow and despair. "Kaitling is to be executed today..."

Everyone round the table gasped in horror.

Mrs. Tanner got to her feet, her face ashen. "How did this happen?"

Fi pulled her chair closer and placed one arm around Peter's shoulders. She was crying.

"She was caught yesterday evening. They'd already captured her father. He is to be tried today, but there is no doubt he'll be found guilty and Kaitling will suffer the same fate as him."

"What do you plan to do?" Dr. Grant asked, his voice grave.

Peter paused a moment, unsure if he should explain. "The final decision lies with their god."

"How can that be?" Mrs Tanner was shocked. "Surely god would not let such a horrible thing happen."

"This is no real god. It's a voice that speaks in the heads of their priests. I am sure it is no more than a man. I intend to track him down and convince him to undo the damage he has done."

"I will come with you," Fi offered.

"It is too dangerous. I don't want you hurt."

"But we can do so much more together."

"Not this time."

"How can you possibly find that man alone, if you have no idea where he is?" Tears streamed down Fi's cheeks.

Peter brushed away her tears. "Don't cry. It'll work out." He tried to sound convinced.

"You have done some wild things, but you have never done anything so risky."

"Please don't make this difficult for me. I know it's dangerous. I know I might not come back. I'm scared witless." He smiled weakly at the word that had long been a source of loathing. "But I have to try."

He looked at each of them in turn. In Dr. Grant's eyes he saw the man was intensely proud of him, just as he was proud and pleased to know the Headmaster. Peter stepped forward and hugged him fiercely. *You would have made a wonderful father,* he thought. Turning to Mrs. Tanner, she looked at him with all the love of a mother for her son. Should he return, he would keep his unspoken promise. They embraced. Finally he turned to Fi. Her eyes were red from crying, for Kaitling, for him, for herself. He took her in his arms and kissed her forehead. *I love you,* he said mind-to-mind. *I love you too,* she replied. Then he pulled away.

"I have to make a quick trip to find out when the trial will take place. I reckon I'll only be able to pinpoint this god of theirs during the trial."

"Then I will come with you, if only to speak briefly to Kaitling, maybe for the last time," Fi said.

"Please be careful," Mrs. Tanner said, tears welling up in her eyes. "I couldn't bear to loose either of you." She wiped her cheeks dry, straightened her back and continued: "I have to phone my acquaintances on the board. With any luck I may be able to get them to convene a meeting this morning."

As Peter and Fi lay on their bed and prepared to jump, they kissed briefly. It was a timid kiss full of restraint. Neither wanted to release the pent up emotions that threatened to carry them away.

Kaitling had not moved. She was still crouched on the cell floor, although someone had removed the hood. She welcomed them both warmly. Like earlier with Peter, it was Kaitling that consoled Fi who couldn't stop crying.

You two talk for a moment, Peter said. *I want to find out when the trial is to be.*

I can tell you that, Kaitling said. *The trial takes place at the end of the afternoon and culminates at sunset with a ritual during which their god joins them. It is he that announces the judgement.*

Do you know anything about the ritual? Peter asked. *It could be very important.*

On rare occasions their god speaks to all the priests, not just the chosen few. Tonight is to be one such occasion.

Good, Peter said, relieved. *I was banking that he would be present so I could trace him. I have a suggestion.* He hesitated about how to go on. *It's difficult and will only work if you both agree. I will understand if either of you refuse.*

His words had both girls worried.

If the worse comes to the worse... His voice faltered. He had to steady himself before going on. *If Fi will have you, I suggest you jump to her mind at the last moment. It may not work ...* He didn't have to go into details. Everyone knew what he meant.

Can't I jump to your mind? Not that I wouldn't be delighted to spend time with Fi, but...

I may not get out, Kaitling. I want you to have a safe haven.

You are welcome to join me, Fi said. *Two girls are better than one!*

Then I will jump to your mind if this turns out badly, Kaitling promised.

Will you be all right if I leave you for a while? Peter asked. *I have some things to sort out.*

Go. I'll talk to you later.

Fi and Kaitling hugged mentally then Peter and Fi left.

Back in the kitchen at Dr. Grant's house, Mrs. Tanner was describing her conversation with one of the board members. "They weren't surprised. I'm meeting them in half an hour. They'd like to see the whole content of the box."

"Is that wise?" Peter asked, moving into the kitchen.

"They insist. They think it will sway people against Sanson and the Wit woman."

"What about the trial?" Dr. Grant asked, his face creased with concern.

"It's late this afternoon. I will go to school in the mean time. I don't want to miss this."

"I phoned the clinic where your mother and sister are staying," Dr. Grant said. "I wanted to enquire about their condition. The Head of the clinic is concerned about their health. He told me he would like you to visit your family this morning. He thinks it might help. I said I would pass on the message, but couldn't guarantee you would go."

Peter really didn't need yet another tense situation. He wanted to ignore the request, to keep his mind free to save Kaitling, but he knew he wouldn't let the two women flounder if there was anything he could do to save them.

"I'll go. When is the appointment?"

"I don't know. I'll ring back. If you agree, I would willingly accompany you. This kind of thing can be taxing and you might need support. I'm sure Christina would accompany you too, but from what I've heard, her presence might spark an explosion," Dr. Grant said with a chuckle.

Peter smiled weakly. "It might indeed."

A few minutes later, Dr. Grant returned. "The Head of clinic suggested we go immediately. That way you won't miss the fireworks at school, if you still want to see them.

Better to get it over with.

"Apparently your mother requested you bring a pullover or two for her. She says she's cold," Dr. Grant added.

Peter had been away only a few days, but the house on the hill reeked of abandon. The air hung stale and uninviting, flies buzzed around the kitchen. Dust had formed on the floors, on the work surfaces and on the tables and chairs.

A pitiful miaow greeted him.

"Oh Jenny!" he said, getting on his hands and knees to search for the cat. "Poor thing! I'm so sorry girl."

He found her cringing under one of the armchairs and coaxed her out. Cradling her in his arms, he returned to the kitchen. The milk in the fridge had gone off, but he found a solitary tin of cat food and dolloped its contents in her bowl.

Leaving the cat to eat, he went in search of his mother's pullovers. Contrary to his expectations, her door was not locked. A faint smell of perfume greeted him as he stepped inside. The place needed airing. The curtains were drawn, but there was enough light to see the room was impeccably tidy. The bed looked unused. No objects littered the bedside table and the dresser was free of any clutter. It was eerie, as if no one had ever lived there, more like an unused hotel room or a museum, a soulless place. He shivered.

Pulling open the wardrobe in search of his mother's pullovers, he found neat rows of plastic bags hanging in perfect order, each with its dress or skirt or blouse, all pressed and ready to wear. In the drawers of the dresser, every article of clothing was carefully folded and placed in regimented piles. He hardly dared touch anything for fear his mother might charge in, screaming at him for misplacing something.

Of course, the pullovers were in the last drawer he opened, right at the foot of the dresser. He lifted two out. They were already wrapped in a see-through plastic bag, as if waiting to be taken away. He placed them at the bottom of his bag and prepared to leave. Dr. Grant would be waiting. He hurriedly closed the drawer and was relieved to shut the door on his mother's lifeless room.

Jenny came to greet him as he crossed the living room, miaowing as she did. He scooped her up and slung her over his shoulder.

"I can't leave you here girl. Goodness knows when someone will come to look after you. You'll have to come with me. Let's hope Dr. Grant will agree to take you home."

48.

The clinic was a fair drive from Tallford. Dr. Grant took the back roads, driving at a leisurely pace along the country lanes. Peter sat with Jenny curled up on his lap, asleep, snoring softly. He gently stroked between her ears as he watched the hedgerows glide by.

"I'm really grateful you can take Jenny. Fi will look after her if ever anything happens to me."

He could have sworn he heard the man wince, but neither said anything.

"What are you going to do with the cat while we are in the clinic?"

"I don't know. Maybe I'll carry her in my arms."

"As long as she stays quiet, I suppose that will be OK."

The receptionist made a sour face at the sight of the cat. Animals were against the regulations. Only when Dr. Grant intervened did she begrudgingly give way. They were to follow the green markers on the floor till they reached a small waiting room. Someone would come and fetch them.

The tense atmosphere and the muffled silence was suffocating. Madness was a daunting prospect that both intrigued and frightened. Witless had spent months in that place trying to piece together the shattered fragments of her mind.

Peter stared at the many closed doors imagining inmates jumping out, grabbing Jenny and running away cackling down the corridor. Dr. Grant must have sensed his uneasiness, because he offered him his arm and Peter took it. The two of them walked arm in arm to the waiting room, Jenny slung over Peter's shoulder.

"Peter McCloud," a nurse asked.

"Yes."

When the nurse saw the cat draped over Peter's shoulder, she pointed at Jenny. "You can't take that?"

"Why not? This is a family reunion and Jenny is family."

The nurse sighed and gave him a look of disgust. "Come with me."

When both Peter and Dr. Grant got to their feet, the nurse halted. "Only Peter."

"I will accompany Peter," Dr. Grant said firmly.

"That's not a good idea. Patients are often disturbed by outside observers."

"Either Dr. Grant comes with me, or I leave," Peter said wearily.

The nurse raised her eyebrows, but said nothing. She led them to a large room where a number of chairs had been placed in a semicircle facing a mirror.

"Take a seat. The doctor will be with you shortly."

Peter found the mirror disturbing. He shifted his chair so he had his back to it.

The door opened and a tall man with a gaunt face marched in, his white coat tightly button across his chest.

"Good morning. You must be Peter," he said, his voice strangely squeaky. "I'm Dr. Drang. And you are?" he said turning to Dr. Grant.

"I am Dr. Grant."

The man must have deemed Dr Grant unworthy of attention, he promptly turned his back on him.

"Could you please put that chair back where you found it," Drang ordered Peter.

"I prefer it here. I don't want to see myself in that mirror all the time."

The man frowned, then continued. "We need you to sit opposite the mirror so the people behind the mirror can see you clearly."

Peter glanced at the mirror, perplexed. Why would people spy at them from behind a one-way mirror? "I came to see my mother and my sister, not to put on a show for people hidden behind a mirror." Out of the corner of his eye, he saw Dr. Grant smile.

Drang was clearly exasperated. Had Dr. Grant not been there, he might well have tried to force Peter to obey. Instead he pulled out a notebook and wrote a few words in it.

The door opened again and an old lady wearing a green dressing gown shuffled in accompanied by a nurse. They must have got the wrong room, Peter thought. Then the woman glanced up. Despite her bewildered look and exaggerated stoop, he recognised his mother. He got to his feet, in shock. What had they done to her?

She did not recognise him at first, then a faint light lit her eyes and she took a tottering step forward. "Peter?" she asked, uncertain.

Peter handed Jenny to Dr. Grant and held out his arms to his mother. She came to him hesitatingly, like a frightened child. She laid her head on his shoulder and cried. It was all wrong. Who were these monsters that had reduced his mother to this?

He pulled a chair next to his, with its back to the mirror, and helped his mother sit down. He was beset by questions and accusations, not for her, but for Drang. His mother sat meekly, her hands clasped in her lap, looking distractedly at her fingers.

"How are you Mum?" It was a silly question, but he didn't know what to say.

"Tired."

Jenny struggled free of Dr. Grant and jumped up onto Peter's lap.

"Jenny has come to say hallo," Peter said, trying to smile.

His mother stretched out a trembling hand and stroked the cat. Her movements were clumsy and hesitant.

"I heard you were cold, so I've brought you two pullovers,"

he said extracting the packets carefully from his bag.

The nurse, who had remained standing silently next to his mother, stepped forward and took the clothes. His mother looked disappointed. Had she wanted to take them herself? He had an idea. He fished his school scarf from his jacket pocket and wrapped it around her neck.

"If ever you feel cold, this will keep you warm and it'll remind you of me when I'm not around."

Reaching out, she took hold of his hand, uncertain, crying quietly as she did. She pulled it shakily to her lips, and kissed it fleetingly, then laid her cheek against his hand. He stroked her hair and was shocked to find it greasy and dirty. Anger flared. Did they not help her wash properly, she who treasured cleanliness? How humiliating!

When Mum began to cling to him, clearly desperate he would leave, the nurse firmly unclasped her hands, guided her to her feet and led her, resigned, to the door.

"Good-bye, Mum," he called out as the door closed on her.

Furious, he spun round to face Dr. Drang. "What have you done to her?" he asked. "She was not like that the last time I saw her."

The man brushed aside Peter's accusation with a wave of his hand. "There are things that someone of your age cannot understand."

"Are your responsible for this clinic?" Peter asked.

"Yes," Drang replied, surprised at the question.

"Then you are responsible for any hurt or damage caused to the people in your care. My mother always prided herself on being spotlessly clean and well dressed, yet she came to us filthy and ill-clothed."

Drang looked furious and was about to say something but Peter continued. "My mother was a proud woman, one who set up her own business and made a success of it, but she came before us here like a wretch, uncertain, frightened even, as if she had been beaten. My mother was no sportswoman, but she was fit and agile, yet here she is, after only a few days in your company, and she can barely walk unassisted. Her movements are hesitant and uncoordinated. You," Peter said pointing at Drang, "are responsible for her state and you will have to pay for the harm you have done her."

"Are you threatening me, boy," Drang said icily, getting to his feet.

"I do not need to threaten you," Peter said, inhabited by a force and an intelligence that surpassed him. "Clearly your methods, whatever they are, are not working. If you are not sanctioned in this life for the pain and suffering you have caused to helpless people like my mother, you will suffer for it in your next life."

Drang scoffed. "Cease your bluster, boy."

Dr. Grant interrupted him. "As an independent witness, I too am shocked by the degradation of his mother's condition. You can be sure I will see that an enquiry is carried out."

The doctor braced himself to reply, but the door opened and in marched Sis flanked by two male nurses. She seemed to have weathered her stay in the clinic much better than her mother. She was dressed in her normal clothes and didn't seem drugged. A crooked smile twisted her face at the sight of Peter.

"Has your whore sent you to gloat over my condition?" Sis asked.

"Come now, Maryse," the doctor snapped, clearly annoyed. "What did I tell you about anger?"

Sis ignored the man, taking a step towards Peter, closely followed by her two guards. "She must be disappointed. I bet you're not as good in bed as I was," she leered and spat on the floor. "How could a boy," she curled up her lips in disgust at the word, "possibly know how to pleasure her?"

She meant to hurt him, Peter realised, but instead her words disgusted him. His love for Fi had nothing to do with Sis's sordid imaginings. Being in hospital didn't seem to have helped her. She was still as hostile as she had been at home. It made him sad.

They had never been close, despite all his secret fascination with her, but there had been times when there were less fights. On holiday with Mum on the south coast, they'd spent several happy weeks dressing up in old clothes and costumes, inventing wild stories.

"How are you, Sis?" he asked.

"Better without you around to mess with my clothes."

"Your clothes are feeding the moths at home," he retorted, unable to hold back his annoyance at her accusations.

"If you dare touch my things while I'm away, I'll kill you!"

One of the nurses put a restraining hand on her shoulder. She shook it off angrily and took another step towards Peter.

"Jenny!" she cried out, suddenly noticing the cat. She surged forward, her arms outstretched to pick up Jenny, but the cat hissed violently and lashed out, raking the back of Sis's hand with her claws.

Sis screamed as blood spurted from the scratches. Ceasing her screams abruptly, she stared at her hand in dismay. "You've even turned the cat against me!" Then she lunged at Peter, her nails outstretched. Jenny struggled free and escaped to the floor. Peter dodged.

The two nurses finally sprang into action, grabbing Sis by her arms. She struggled wildly as they forced her to the ground at Peter's feet and one of them ripped down her skirt and pants, baring her backside, while the other plunged a syringe into her white skin. Peter looked away, shocked by the brutality.

When he looked back, Sis was a limp heap on the floor. Her skirt had been roughly pulled back into place. One of the nurses helped the girl to her feet and supported her as she staggered to a chair. No one seemed bothered that blood was still seeping from the wounds on her hand. Sis herself stared uncomprehendingly at the gashes, as if they were someone else's.

Carrying Jenny in one arm, he pulled up a chair opposite his sister and sat down facing her. "Behave, Jenny," he ordered. Then he tendered the cat to Sis, but she shrank away, terrified. "Dr. Grant," Peter said. The Headmaster came to his side and took the cat.

"Sis. Show me your hand."

One of the nurses stepped forward to intervene.

"Get back," Peter said firmly. "Leave her alone. "

The man hesitated, glancing at Drang, then withdrew a pace.

Sis was wilting like a flower. Whatever had been in the shot, it looked likely to knock her out pretty soon. He would have to hurry. "Give me your hand," Peter insisted softly, as he held out his own hand palm up. Cautiously she laid her hand on his. Just as cautiously he laid his other hand over hers to conceal the wound and immediately set to work healing, all the time keeping his eyes on her face. The damage was only superficial, but he did a thorough job.

Her eyes drooped and closed, her head sank forwards. Keeping her hand in his, he leaned close and kissed her cheek. *Look after yourself, Sis,* he said mind to mind, something he'd never done before. Her eyes flew open, wild and alarmed, and locked on his. *Concentrate on getting out of here as fast as possible,* he continued. *This is not a good place.*

He released her hand and her eyes closed as she sagged forward snoring gently. The two nurses caught her arms, heaved her to her feet and dragged her to the door.

Good-bye, Sis. I love you, he said, mind-to-mind.

Recuperating Jenny from Dr. Grant, he headed for the door intent on leaving as fast as possible.

"How did you do that?" Drang asked, disbelief clear on his face.

Peter pretended not to understand.

"What you did to her hand. I saw it. I'm not blind, boy!"

"I don't know what you are talking about."

Drang shook his head, a look of alarm on his face and reluctantly let them go.

Peter couldn't resist one last word. *Be careful what you do, Dr. Drang,* he said mind to mind. *We'll be watching.*

49.

"I'm sorry about that," Dr. Grant said, once they were in the safety of his car. "I would never have suggested you come had I known."

"I'm glad you did," Peter said, his tone grim. "Now that we know, we can do something."

"What was that doctor ranting on about? I didn't understand."

Apparently Dr. Grant had not seen the healing. Peter hesitated. He'd been foolish. The fewer people who knew he could heal, the better. Sis's life had been in no danger, but he was sick of seeing his mother and sister suffer.

"I healed her hand."

Dr. Grant chuckled.

He really wasn't like other adults. "Why do you laugh?"

"As head of such an institution, surrounded by people beset with hallucinations and crazy ideas, seeing a miracle must be a very frightening experience."

"You mean, he might worry he's going mad?"

"Exactly. I reckon that must be his greatest fear."

"Then I have done him great harm," Peter said sheepishly.

"I doubt one miracle will push him over the brink."

"But I did more."

Dr. Grant glanced at him quizzically.

"I spoke mind-to-mind. I couldn't resist. He'd been so nasty. It made me angry, so I spoke to him with the voice of god..."

"And what did god say?"

"Be careful what you do. We'll be watching."

Dr. Grant burst out laughing. "If he survives, I imagine he will be more careful in the future!"

Dr. Grant left him a few streets from school. They'd agreed it wouldn't be good to be seen with the former headmaster.

At the gate, a prefect barred the entrance, demanding his name.

"If you lot don't know who I am by now, you really don't belong in a school like this."

The prefect raised his hand to hit Peter.

"You really are slow to learn. I'm the person who beat up several of your mob yesterday."

The prefect's eyebrows shot up and his hand fell limp at his side. He'd finally realised who Peter was. "Take an hour's detention, McCloud, for being late and an additional hour for being rude to a prefect."

Peter shrugged and walked by. No point in arguing, he might not be alive to do his detention and the prefect would probably be gone too.

The first period was over, so he headed for history with Johnson. Down one corridor he spotted a group of second formers standing with their faces to a wall, their hands on their heads. Two prefects were pacing up and down behind them.

Peter sighed. He was fed up saving people. Couldn't he have a quiet moment? A part of him wanted to walk by, but he knew he wouldn't.

"Sanson wants to see you," Peter told the prefects. "He said you should let these people go."

The two prefects looked at him incredulous. "Who asked your opinion?"

"Sanson sounded pretty upset to me. He's not going to be very happy if you disobey."

A look of doubt crossed their faces. "We'll take you along," one of them said, "just in case you're making this up."

Turning to the second formers, the prefect said: "Get lost.

And be quiet about it!"

Peter shrugged his shoulders. He didn't care. School was just one whirl of chaos after another. He might as well be at the centre.

I'm back in school, he said mind-to-mind to Fi. *A couple of prefects are taking me to Sanson. Bring an army if you don't hear from me in half an hour.*

A group of prefects milled nervously in front of the door to Sanson's office, waiting for orders. The two accompanying him pushed through, dragging Peter after them.

"Get out!" Sanson said, not looking up from the papers on his desk.

"Excuse me..." one of the prefects began.

"Don't bother me with your problems," Sanson snapped, his hair dishevelled, his jacket creased as if he'd slept in it.

The prefects backed towards the door, relinquishing their hold on Peter who stood his ground. You're getting reckless, he told himself.

"Close the door after you," Peter said to the prefects, then, turning to Sanson, he asked amiably: "Did you sleep well, Headmaster?"

Sanson looked up, startled. "How did you get in?"

"By the door," Peter said. He had nothing to loose. If he were to die, why not have some fun.

Sanson blinked twice, not believing what he heard, then he struggled to his feet.

"You needn't get up for me," Peter said, battling with a heady feeling of unchecked impertinence. "With your headache, you'd be better off seated. Would you like me to have someone fetch an aspirin?"

Sanson slumped back in his chair, his mouth fallen open.

Peter was tempted to taunt Sanson with what they'd found in the box, that would surely scare him stupid, but doing so would be foolish. It might even be to Sanson's advantage.

The man closed his mouth with a snap and sat up straighter.

"I thought I expelled you."

Peter took a seat in one of the armchairs. "I'm like one of those bad dreams that keeps coming back."

The phone rang. Sanson looked at it as if he couldn't grasp what it was.

"Your phone is ringing, Headmaster."

Sanson stared at him uncomprehending, then back at the phone, but still didn't pick up the receiver.

"Whoever it is, seems to insist." Peter had to struggle not to laugh.

Finally Sanson picked up the receiver. "Sanson here."

There was a long pause as he listened. At first he looked perplexed, learning towards the phone as if that would help understand. As the call continued, he slumped further back into his armchair and scratched his head with a curved index finger. Little by little, a frown formed and deepened on Sanson's face, and creases of worry gathered around his eyes. His lips tightened and the muscles of his jaw clenched.

On and on went the person at the other end. Sweat began to form on Sanson's brow and trickled down his face. His hand shook slightly as he tried to wipe it from his eyes. He clenched the receiver so hard, Peter worried it would break.

Several times Sanson looked to be on the verge of speaking, but the words stuck in his throat. He even shook his head as if to clear it, but remained speechless. Anger gave way to fear. Sanson's eyes spread wide, his mouth went slack and hung open. With a shaky free hand he reached forward, pulled open a draw and drew out a bottle of what looked like whiskey. Taking a slug, then a second, he replaced the open bottle on his desk.

The call must have ended because he finally returned the receiver to the phone and sat there staring blankly for a long moment.

"Bad news?" Peter asked, worried the man had finally slithered over the brink.

Sanson looked up at Peter, his eyes unseeing, and said nothing. Then he took another swig from the bottle and pulled a packet of cigarettes from his pocket. With the cigarette between his lips, he began searching for a light. He rummaged through his jacket pockets, then those of his trousers, but found nothing. He pushed aside the piles of papers on the desk, a number of them falling to the floor. In his agitation he managed to knock over the bottle, spilling whiskey on papers and desk alike. The smell brought back bad memories of the night before.

In the mean time Sanson found a box of matches. He broke several before he finally managed to get one alight. But rather than light his cigarette, he held the flame up to his eyes, a look of terror on his face.

"Be careful," Peter called out. "You're going to burn yourself."

Sure enough, the match burnt down to his finger. He let go of the burning stub, which fell to the desk, setting off a wild blaze of paper and whiskey. Peter got to his feet and stepped away driven back by the heat. Sanson struggled to get up, but must have caught his foot in the chair, because he tumbled over backwards and hit his head against one of the many piles of books littering the floor.

The fire had already spread to the floor where paper and books lay scattered. *Fi, get help! There's a fire in the Head's office,* he shouted mind-to-mind, as he ran round the blazing desk in search of Sanson. The man lay unconscious amid a pile of books. Peter slapped him hard, but nothing could awaken him. The flames were jumping from pile to pile of books, getting closer all the time.

He couldn't die now! It was not time. He had to rescue Kaitling first. He glanced around for an exit. The fire blocked the path to the door. He heaved Sanson in the direction of the windows. Some were high set. He could never lug the heavy man out those, but there was a pair of French windows.

He was soaked with sweat and began to cough as smoke filled the air. Getting down on all fours he inched backwards towards the windows, pulling Sanson after him. To his dismay, the windows were locked and there was no key. Abandoning Sanson a moment, he got to his feet and rammed his shoulder against the windows. On his second try they gave and burst open, shattering as they did. A searing pain shot through his arm, his hand instinctively going to the wound. It was slick with blood. He must have cut himself on the glass.

It was no time for healing. He hurried back, dragged Sanson's unconscious body free of the fire and halted at a safe distance in the garden. To his horror, the man's trousers were on fire. He ripped off one of his shoes and used it to beat out the flames.

It was then, as he slumped to the ground exhausted, that he heard the sirens and the noise of a crowd gathering nearby. He closed his eyes and went inside, examining the damage. He felt weak with blood loss and lack of oxygen. It was difficult to concentrate, but he steeled himself and persevered. He helped the wound seal over. He would have a scar but it was the best he could do. He lay back and let fresh air chase smoke from his lungs.

"Peter?" he heard Fi call out, desperation in her voice.

"Over here," he croaked.

"Oh, my love, you're covered in blood."

It's all right, he said mind-to-mind, not wanting bystanders to hear. *I cut myself on the window, but it's healed.*

With Fi's help, he got to his feet and looked around. Behind the cordon set up by the fire brigade, a large crowd had gathered. Firemen were moving here and there carrying hoses. Water was already streaming into the headmaster's study and the nearby rooms.

Peter searched for Sanson. The man was where he'd left him, a fireman kneeling at his side giving him oxygen.

"How is he?" Peter asked.

"He'll survive. He stinks of whiskey," the fireman said.

Peter nodded. "He knocked over a bottle of the stuff."

"So how did the fire start?"

"He dropped a match on his desk. He was trying to light a cigarette but he burnt his fingers."

"So he dragged you out?" the fireman asked.

"No," Peter said, annoyed at the misunderstanding. "He stumbled and fell, knocking himself out. It was I that dragged him out."

"Well done youngster," the fireman said. Noticing the blood, he asked: "What happened to your arm?"

"It's nothing. I cut myself breaking the window."

The fireman checked the wound. "There's hardly a scratch," he said, surprised. "Do you think you can walk?"

Peter nodded.

"Then go get yourself some hot, sweet tea. I'm sure there's a kettle and a tea pot in the staffroom. I'll send a doctor to see you and the police will probably have questions. Go get your strength back."

Fi and Peter went to the staffroom, knocked and entered. Several staff were astonished to see two pupils enter their room and were about to turn them away despite Peter's bloody shoulder and arm and the black smut all over his face and hands.

"Is that how you treat a hero who has just saved a man's life?" a familiar voice asked. It was Dr. Grant. "Get out of the way!" he ordered, helping Peter to a chair. "What are you doing here, anyway? Shouldn't you be out seeing that all the pupils are safe when there's a fire in the school."

The teachers scurried away leaving them on their own as Fi's Mum entered. "Your arm!" she exclaimed horrified.

"It's OK. I healed it."

Mrs. Tanner hugged him fiercely. "Stop giving me frights, young man!" she scolded. "I can't stand it." She bustled off to make tea.

A doctor came, as they were sipping tea. He left, astounded at the speed of Peter's recovery. The policeman stayed longer. Peter told him the whole story from the moment he entered Sanson's room.

"Why were you there when you had classes?"

"Two of the prefects bought me to Sanson."

After many more questions the policeman finally left.

"So?" Peter said, turning to Dr. Grant. "Is it all sorted?"

"Yes. The board has reinstated me and they've fired Sanson. There is to be an enquiry."

"I guessed as much," Peter said, feeling exhausted. "I was there when he got the call."

"Had you not been there, he would surely be dead," Dr. Grant pointed out.

"How ironic that it should be you to save his life," Fi's Mum mused as she got to her feet. "Anyone for more tea?»

50.

When Peter awoke, Fi lay cuddled up next to him under the covers, one hand lightly laid on his bare chest. They had slept on and off most of the afternoon. The morning's adventures had left him exhausted and he wanted to be fit for the evening's ordeal.

Mrs. Tanner insisted they both eat before they slept. They'd had a quiet lunch. They could have celebrated Dr. Grant's reinstatement, but the atmosphere was subdued. Peter's coming trip to Drailong weighed heavily on them.

He glanced at the clock on the bedside table. Five, time to go. Turning to face Fi, his movement awoke her. She kissed him, then slid an arm round his waist and pulled him in a tight embrace, her breasts crushed against his chest, one leg wound around his thigh. He ran his hand down her back. She was dressed in only her pants and a bra and her skin was warm and inviting. His fingers came to rest on the elastic of her pants. What had Sis said about pleasuring Fi? The thought troubled him, but not as much as the image of the nurse yanking down Sis's skirt to bare her buttocks while the other nurse plunged a syringe in her skin.

Peter drew back from Fi's reluctant arms. "I have to go." Another image assailed him, his mother clinging to him, desperate, unwilling to let him go, as the nurse wrenched her hands free. He didn't want Fi to feel rejected, but there were too many goodbyes, too much suffering. He wanted to get it over with.

He got out of bed and pulled off his pants, for once not bothering that Fi was watching him. There were tears in Fi's eyes as she got up and pulled on her shorts and blouse.

"I love you," he said.

"I love you, too," she said, her voice catching on the words.

She kissed him one last time, hastily, then tucked him in like a little child and said: "Please be careful."

Alone at last, Peter close his eyes, took a deep breath and jumped to Drailong and Kaitling.

The headpiece was on again, masking her sight and hearing.

Surely they could let you see and hear as you go to your trial, he said, intensely angry at the priests.

Hello, Peter, Kaitling said, calmly. *They must be afraid I will attack them.*

Peter marvelled at her stoicism. His own nerves were close to snapping.

Hearing his thoughts she replied: *It's easier for us. We believe in reincarnation. So even if this is the end, I am not afraid, for I will go on in another form. Maybe I'll be a brave and courageous boy like you.*

His love for her surged so strong he had to hold on to himself to avoid shattering in a thousand tiny pieces. *I love you,* he said, his words a pale reflection of his feelings.

I love you too, Kaitling echoed.

Calming himself, Peter reached out to feel those nearby and jumped to the priest closest to Kaitling. They were in the giant audience hall with its row upon row of narrow vertical windows. A dais with a large table and a number of vacant chairs stood before them. Not far away sat Kaitling's father, his hands attached behind his back, his head covered like that of his daughter. Nudging the priest to look around. Peter was surprised to find the hall full of priests. Of course, this was not just a trial. There was to be a special ceremony.

Using what he called the 'voice of god', he ordered the priest to remove the headpiece from Kaitling. When the man stalled, Peter sent a searing pain through his chest. The man gasped and hurried to remove the hateful thing from the girl's head.

Peter returned to Kaitling. *I have to go in search of this god of theirs. Remember what you promised: if this looks like finishing badly, you jump to Fi and no hesitating!*

Ok boss! she said, a smile in her voice.

He jumped back to the priest. Rummaging through his mind he found that the Syvan priests were organised in a strict hierarchy. Ordinary priests were at the lowest level. Then came the deans who were responsible for a group of priests. At the higher echelon were the bishops, who reigned over a large number of groups. Finally there were five archbishops, who took their orders directly from the voice of god.

Priests rarely saw the archbishops, except from afar at major religious ceremonies. Peter learnt that several of them were to make the trip from Syvatoy. Unfortunately his current host had only a very vague idea what they looked like. Peter would have to climb the hierarchy if he wanted to reach their god.

Thanks to his priest, Peter found a nearby dean and jumped. He had to hover longer than with ordinary priests as he tried to wheedle his way in. He'd got over the alarm at being outside a host, but it was still very uncomfortable.

The dean knew little more than the ordinary priest. Peter had him look for a bishop. There were few of them and none were currently in the room. Aware that time was running out, Peter had the dean search for someone who was close to a bishop.

He had to be careful. The higher he went up the hierarchy, the more carefully the minds would be guarded. Finally the dean pinpointed a fellow dean whose job was to aid a bishop. He jumped to the new man and began sifting through his memories for images of the bishop, for the sound of his voice, for anything that would give a feel for his presence.

Peter had never jumped to a memory before. It was frighteningly risky, but at any moment the trial might begin and he still had to find the god and convince him. Bathing in all he knew of the bishop, he let out his feelers in search of the man. He found nothing, no matter how far he stretched his awareness. The effort left him weak and dispirited.

He withdrew and tried to collect his thoughts. Maybe he could find someone, whoever it might be, who was physically close to a bishop. He reached out amongst the many strong forces present for the slightest echo of the man he sought. It was difficult, some people's presences blared like trumpets, masking all else. He was about to give up, when he caught a faint scent of the man. Honing in on the source, he jumped.

It was just an ordinary priest alone in a corridor, carrying a bottle of wine and several glasses on a tray. Bitterly disappointed, Peter prepared to jump back to Kaitling, but the man knocked at a door and inside sat an older man still and silent in a high backed chair. He was wearing brightly coloured robes and had a strange five pointed hat on his head. The priest bowed and handed the tray to the older man. When the priest's hand brushed the older man's hand by mistake, Peter seized the opportunity and jumped.

Had the men's hands not momentarily touched, he would never have managed the crossing. The bishop, for that's what he was, was guarded like a fortress. If the archbishops were as well protected, he would never get near them.

Peter hurriedly looked for memories of archbishops and their god. To his delight, two archbishops were waiting in the next room.

Rummaging through the man's memories he collided with a wall. Secrets? What could the man be hiding? Intrigued, Peter wheedled his way round, only to discover a plot to assassinate an archbishop so the bishop could replace him amongst the ruling five.

As for their god, the priest knew only the god's voice. He had heard it often. Using those memories Peter searched for the corresponding presence but found nothing. The god must be far away, beyond the reach of ordinary mortals.

A voice in his head ordered the bishop to enter. Two men stood before an open log fire warming their trembling hands. They looked old and frail. A strong man, like the bishop could have killed them easily.

They wore no hats. Their hair was thin and gray and reached almost to their waists. Unattached, it floated cloud-like over their colourful robes. Their wrinkled faces were as gray and flimsy as their hair, their lips thin and mean, but their eyes were alert and sparkled. On their long slender fingers they wore several large rings set with gems that flashed in the firelight.

Bishop Zing, a voice greeted the man in his head. *How convenient that it should be you to bring us wine.*

Although the voice was old, it sounded rich and strong, not at all the voice of the trembling old men that stood before them. Could this be an illusion, a subtle form of protection? Surely the bishop would not be fooled. He must see them often. Or maybe someone else was speaking. Could it be their god? Peter quickly compared it with the voice of god he heard in people's memories. It might be.

So you think you can replace one of us? the voice went on, amused. *How were you thinking of doing it?*

Bishop Zing was terrified. How had his secret got out? He'd shielded his thoughts and spoken of it to no one. He took an involuntary step back, steeling himself against the pain he knew would come.

Peter was terrified. He might not escape if they killed the bishop. His chances of jumping to one of the archbishops seemed slim. They were much more powerful than they appeared.

When one of the two archbishops pointed an accusing finger at the man, Peter fled, clinging desperately just beyond the man's outer skin, buffeted by the many shields that sought to drive him away. He could no longer see what was happening but he felt the shock as the blow hit the man and he crumpled to the floor. Peter was relieved that the shields immediately ceased their work, but he was also cut free. Death must have destroyed the faint force that normally held him close to a host's body.

Adrift in the room, all Peter could sense were the living forces at play. He was naturally drawn to the two archbishops, unable to resist that pull. If they were protected he was going to get fried.

The voice of the god spoke again. The words were incomprehensible, but they shook his being to the very core. Could the voice be transmitted through the faint fields of living energy that he was floating in? He clung with all his force to the voice, riding its rise and fall. When the voice paused and air rushed in, Peter let himself be sucked up and away toward the presence that was the source of the voice.

51.

A sharp metallic twang like a taught spring snapping back into place startled Peter. He no longer floated, but was firmly anchored in someone's mind. This was surely no god, the man's eyesight was watery, his joints ached and there was a dull pain in his chest.

He sat at a desk in a dimly lit study, his fingers grasping a fountain pen. Several leather-bound books lay neatly piled on the side of the desk. A thick notepad lay open in front of him, the current page blank. The man put down the pen, scratched his head and got unsteadily to his feet, crossing the room to pour a cup of tea from a large earthenware teapot encased in a fluffy brown tea cosy.

To Peter's surprise, on the wall hung a large portrait of Her Majesty the Queen at her coronation with Prince Philip at her side. Under the photo read the inscription: Queen Elizabeth II, 1953. Peter had been only five at the time but he remembered the excitement and the flags. It was shortly after his father died. So he must be in England, in his own world. How strange! Someone from his world was controlling Drailong.

Balancing the bone china cup and saucer in uncertain fingers, the man shuffled back to his desk and sat down.

"This is not a good time for a visit," he said, shaking his head.

Peter had seen no one else in the room. Could the man be talking to himself? Or had he gone mad?

"I have a lot to do. Couldn't you come back another day?"

Troubled, Peter had the feeling the man was talking to him, yet he couldn't possibly know he was there.

"Yes. You. What is your name?"

Peter's instinct was to remain silent. Unseen and unheard, he could work better.

"Hurry up. I have to attend that tiresome ceremony."

Peter, he replied in the man's head.

"Peter? I don't recall there ever being a Peter in my story."

Story? It was Peter's turn to be puzzled. Had this man invented the whole thing?

"How old are you?" the man asked.

Twelve.

The man took several thoughtful sips of his tea.

What do you have to do with Drailong? Peter asked.

"I invented it!" the man exclaimed. He stretched out his shaky hand and drew the pile of books closer. Opening the first book to the title page, Peter was able to read: The strange history of Syvatoy and Drailong by Arthur W. Yong.

But it really exists, Peter protested. *I've seen it. People live there.*

"Of course it does. Every world that people dream up exists somewhere. They are just as real as this one. Don't they teach you anything at school?"

They teach us that stories are not real, that they are invented and the worlds they describe do not exist.

"How disappointing. I wonder why we waste so much money on the places."

Do you realise those priests from Syvatoy think you are god?

The old man chuckled, setting off a violent bout of coughing. When he finally regained his breath, he said: "Well at least they give me that much credit."

It's more than that. Their priests do what you tell them.

"I sincerely doubt that. They are a most undisciplined lot."

You have to stop them! Peter insisted, remembering why he was there and how little time he had. *They are going to kill my best friend.*

"What's her name?"

Kaitling.

"Ah yes, the magician's daughter. She has a lot of promise that one."

Not if you don't tell them to stop the execution! The dithering old man annoyed him.

"What's this about execution? I didn't write anything like that."

Peter explained about the invasion and the mock trial of Kaitling's father.

The old man hardly seemed shocked. "That's really too bad."

Is that all you have to say? You started this. Aren't you going to do something about it?

The old man sighed. "You wouldn't understand."

Try me!

"Writing a story about a place calls that world into existence. Sometimes, as the author, you accompany it a while. But even as you write, the characters have minds of their own. Their unpredictable acts surprise you. The more the story moves forward, the less control you have."

I don't believe you. You make regular excursions to their world. You influence them through the words you put in the priests' heads.

"My dear Peter..."

Don't patronise me! Can't you grasp how desperate this is? Someone I love most is about to die. I came to you thinking you could save her. I expected a fight. I did not come prepared for resignation. You've got to do something.

"I am sorry for the misunderstanding. But there is nothing I can do."

Yes you can. You can tell those priests to spare Kaitling and her father. You can tell them to return to Syvatoy and free Drailong.

"I wish it were that easy. I could do as you say, but there is no guarantee they'd listen to me."

But they call you their god and are sworn to obey your words.

"Are you a believer? Do you go to church?"

Peter had no time for a discussion about beliefs. *I hardly see what that has to do with saving my friend.*

"Ah, but it does."

I am, sort of.

"But do you believe in god?"

Peter thought about it. I don't 'believe' in him, as you put it, but I have experienced his presence.

"Good. But if god spoke to you, would you obey?"

Peter was irritated with the conversation. The execution was getting closer and closer. *God doesn't speak to me. If he did I would be astounded and probably terrified. I don't know if I would obey.*

"Can you imagine why Syvan priests are delighted to hear the voice of god?"

Peter pondered the idea. *Well, it's only those at the top, the archbishops and sometimes the bishops, who hear your voice.*

"Exactly. Being at the top means hearing the voice of god, and hearing the voice of god means being at the top."

Ah! Hearing the voice of god gives them power, power over others. Then Peter remembered the scene with the two old archbishops. It had been the god's voice he had heard. He recognised it now. Had it not been the god who had killed Bishop Zing? A nasty suspicion crossed Peter's mind.

Whose side are you on?

His question caught the old man-god off guard.

"Don't ask silly questions. Surely it must be obvious."

It was indeed. Of course the man would say he couldn't intervene to save Kaitling. He sided with the Syvans. Why hadn't he seen it before? This old man god had no interest in Drailong except as a place for his people to invade.

I have had enough of your stories, Peter shouted. *I'm going.*

"Why don't you stay a while? You might still manage to

convince me."

Peter flung himself from the body of the man and hung suspended just outside his presence. There he shrank to the most infinitesimal size he could imagine before slipping back into the old man-god. He couldn't be sure, but he hoped he'd passed unnoticed.

He hurried to the man's memory and quickly turned the pages, confirming his suspicions. The old man had planned the attack on Drailong and was masterminding the dismantlement of the Twelve. Tyzi was the last remaining member, all the others were dead, and old man-god was delighted to finally get rid of him. It irked him that the people of Drailong had refused their allegiance. Kaitling too had defied him, but, like his priests, he had no time for females. She was just a nuisance he was pleased to get rid of.

Peter urgently needed to take control of the old man. But how? Time had run out. The old man god was already talking to his priests, welcoming them, as they lay prostrate at his feet.

This is an important day for all in Syvatoy, he announced, smiling. *The last of the Twelve cringes before us awaiting our axe. These barbarians have resisted our will far too long...*

Peter remembered how he had out manoeuvred Sanson. He prayed it would work again.

I created them in my image just like you. There is no reason why we should be fighting them ... The old man-god broke off, realising that the words he said were not those he intended. He struggled to root out whoever was tampering with his words, but Peter kept constantly on the move and was so tiny, the man could get no hold on him.

The priests must be wondering what was going on. The old man-god clenched his teeth and continued. *I see no reason why these two people should be executed...* He stopped again, his fury boiling over. He knew full well Peter was playing with him. In his frustration, he lashed out with his hand meaning to send the cup flying across the room, but with his clumsy gesture, he knocked all three of his precious volumes about Syvatoy to the floor.

Tears formed in old man god's eyes. "No! Not after all the work I've done." He struggled to his hands and knees in search of his books. Peter had only one more sentence for the man to say to the priests. Preoccupied by his books, the old man offered no resistance.

Set the prisoners free and quit Drailong immediately! On those words, the old man-god fell unconscious amongst his books a violent pain in his chest. It was not Peter's doing. The old man-god's heart had been weak and an attack had been waiting in ambush for ages.

Peter jumped back to Kaitling, overjoyed at his success.

Did you hear that, he asked?

What? she asked, alarmed. *I heard nothing.*

I got their old man-god to tell them to spare you and to quit Drailong.

You are wonderful, my hero! You've saved our lives.

Peter let success buoy him up. He had never been sure he would succeed. He'd prepared himself for the worst... But neither he nor Kaitling would have to die. Life was truly wonderful.

Peter! Kaitling called out, fear in her voice. *Listen!*

The archbishop was talking. "In accordance with the will of our god, this man and his daughter are sentenced to death. They will be executed at sunset today."

Peter screamed. *That's not what he said. I was there. I heard it.*

Suddenly Kaitling's head was like a prison. He wanted out. He wanted to confront them face-to-face. To tell them they lied. To show them up for what they were: bigots and traitors.

Kaitling was crying. She had bravely held out so long. To believe that she was saved, only to discover it was not true, finally broke her. Fury boiled over in Peter. He jumped like a deadly warrior into the heads of the lower priests, moving from one to another at lightening speed, spreading doubt and chaos. The archbishops lied. They might hear the voice of god but they didn't listen to it. It was all a fake, to keep control. It was time for the priests to take over.

Murmurs went up as priests began to voice their misgivings, the crowd at the back of the hall stirred and, as it grew, it began to push its way forward. Fights broke out. The deans that tried to intervene were knocked down and trampled under foot. Peter continued to win supporters to his desperate cause.

One of the archbishops got to his feet. Shedding his mask of the feeble old man, he stood there, full of youth and authority. "Stop immediately!"

The crowd trembled and came abruptly to a halt, then began pushing forward again.

"Your minds are being manipulated by this girl." His voice was twisted with hatred. "Kill her!" he ordered the executioner who sat nearby.

The man got to his feet, his axe in one hand, and grabbed Kaitling by the hair, causing her to scream in pain. He dragged her forward and forced her head on the chopping block.

A roar went up from the priests, whipped into frenzy by Peter. "Stop!" they shouted as one. To no avail. The executioner brushed the girl's hair free and raised his axe.

Blind with despair, Peter threw himself at the executioner. Brawn met him with grim determination as the man steeled himself to kill. At his feet lay Kaitling moaning softly, her head on the block, her lovely hair pulled back to bare her neck. Peter fought with all his strength to gain control, but muscles flexed, despite him, preparing the axe.

No! Peter shrieked, flinging himself into Kaitling's body. He reached out to grab her hand, to flee with her, but no hand was there to hold, her body was empty.

She'd gone. Yet her body moaned and shook in terror.

Panic seized him. He gathered his thoughts to jump. She'd be waiting for him at home. He saw her face, her brown ringlets, her sharp blue eyes and her infectious smile, calling him.

Kaitling's moan abruptly cut off as the axe did its work. Life rushed out of her with a sudden whoosh and darkness fell.

Epilogue

Christina leaned forward and kissed the boy's cold forehead.

"Don't leave me," she whispered through her tears, words she'd repeated hundreds of times. "I have lost one son. I don't want to loose a second."

She had sat there by that hospital bed on and off for just over a month, taking turns with Fiona and John, one of them always present, none of them willing to let Peter go. From time to time a nurse would come and silently check the drip feed, then leave. Once a day a doctor made his rounds. This morning the doctor had tarried, his face gray and grave.

"I realise this is hard," he'd begun. She knew what was coming and didn't want to hear. He went on, despite her. "After such a prolonged period of unconsciousness there is bound to be a price. What's more, the longer the coma, the less chance there is of survival. You should talk to your husband and daughter. Maybe the kindest solution would be to let him go."

Tears had welled up then too. She knew the doctor was right, but she clung to the hope the boy would make it through.

She remembered seeing Peter for the first time, asleep on her daughter's bed. She looked at him and tried to recall the angelic face she'd seen. She had held his hand, like she did now. At the time, the bond between them had immediately been apparent. Like love at first sight, only this was son at first sight.

She felt a hand, warm and comforting, settle on her shoulder. No need to look up, she knew it was John, back from school. He had been reinstated and the school board had issued a public apology. Shortly afterwards they had been married, quietly, with Fiona's consent. They'd held the ceremony next to Peter's bed so he could be present.

John pulled up a second chair and sat next to her.

"Any...?" he began.

She shook her head.

He laid his hand on hers, that in turn held Peter's, and lapsed into silence.

"The doctor came by," she finally said, the words slow and heavy in her mouth. "He..." She couldn't bring herself to say it.

John put his arm around her and pulled her close. She buried her face in his shoulder and let her tears flow. "I can't. I won't," she spluttered.

"Are you alright, Mum?" she heard Fiona ask.

Glancing at her daughter's face through watery eyes, she saw a look of alarm and terror there.

"Is he...?" Fiona began, tears brimming up in her eyes too.

"No," Christina said. "He's still with us."

She beckoned Fiona over and all three of them stood in a silent, tear-filled hug.

A faint groan nearby had them turn as one to the bed. Peter groaned again, louder this time.

It was the first sound he'd made since she'd found him unconscious by his bed. Taking his hand in hers, she bent closer, brushing the long hair out of his eyes. He would be pleased. In one month his hair had grown considerably.

His eyelids fluttered and then struggled as if trying to open.

"Peter," she said. "We are all here with you."

"Maybe his eyes are sealed shut," Fiona said, "like they sometimes are after sleep."

The girl moved round to the far side of the bed and leaning over Peter, she gently licked his eyelids. It was such an intimate gesture, so profoundly sensuous, unashamed and full of love and tenderness.

Peter's eyes fluttered again and this time they opened. Not

moving his head, he looked at Fiona then at her.

"Greetings Peter," John said. "Welcome back."

The boy looked bewildered. Had the doctor been right? No. She wouldn't think of that.

"Your throat must be dry," she said. "How about some water?"

He nodded almost imperceptibly.

With one hand under his curly head, she lifted him gently till she could bring a glass to his lips and poured a few drops of water into his mouth. He coughed then swallowed with difficulty.

"Not too much to begin with," John cautioned.

"Oh Peter," Fiona said, bubbling over with joy and relief. "You should see yourself! You have long hair like a girl now. I've been combing it for you everyday. You are lucky, you have such natural curls."

Her daughter had told her all about their games, about Peter wanting to be a girl. She'd wanted to be a boy briefly herself when she was young. Why not? She'd rather that than loose him.

"Kaitling?" Peter asked, his voice barely audible

Both she and John turned to look at Fiona. Peter did too.

The girl's face twisted in pain as she shook her head. "She didn't make it," Fiona said quietly, tears flowing anew down her cheeks. "She can't have jumped."

All of them knew that if Peter had been in a coma it meant that Kaitling had died and he had not been able to return.

"But she wasn't there..." Peter croaked.

Well at least he wasn't amnesiac.

He closed his eyes and one solitary tears formed in his eye and rolled down his cheek.

"Oh!" he said startled, his eyes flying open, searching the room. "Is that you?" he asked, unbelieving.

"Who?" Christina asked.

"Kaitling," he whispered, a look of wonder on his face. "She spoke to me. She seemed so far off."

"This is wonderful," Fiona said, excited. "She must have

jumped to you instead."

"I can't feel her," Peter said still croaking, a perplexed look on his face. "I could always feel her when she was in my mind. But she's there now, I can hear her." He smiled. "She says hallo!"

Fiona grinned. "You see, my pretty boy. I was right all along. You are both boy and girl."

Annexes

344   Alan McCluskey

The Author

Alan McCluskey lives amid the vineyards in a small Swiss village between three lakes and a range of mountains. Nearby, several thousands of years earlier, lakeside villages housed a thriving Celtic community. The ever-present heart-beat of that world continues to fuel his long-standing fascination for magic and fantasy.

Whether it be about Sally, Brent and Keira in The Storyteller's Quest or Peter, Kaitling and Fi in Boy & Girl. In Search of Lost Girls or We Girls, all Alan McCluskey's novels tell the story of young people who, despite the immense difficulties that abound, discover and develop their own astounding talents and manage to do the exceptional.

We Girls is the third in the Boy & Girl Saga. The other two books are Boy & Girl and In Search of Lost Girls. Alan McCluskey has published three YA novels in The Storyteller's Quest series: The Reaches, The Keeper's Daughter and The Starless Square. The fourth book in the series, World o'Tales is awaiting publication. In addition, he has published two other novels, Chimera and Stories People Tell. The sequel to the latter, Local Voices, is awaiting publication.

Boy & Girl Saga Book 2
In Search
of Lost Girls
2020 edition
Alan McCluskey

In Search of Lost Girls
The Boy & Girl Saga - Book 2

Listen carefully. You can just hear the mournful tolling of a bell over the shuffle of girls' feet as they traipse to Mass, nursing bruises and numb despair. No one cares. No one is there to stem the torrent of injustice and abuse. They are lost and forgotten. In another world, the cathedral still reverberates to the melody of angelic voices as the mourners file out, heads bowed, words hushed. If only they knew that the two girls whose music delights them so were really boys in disguise, sanctity would flee in the face of raging indignation. Then a gunshot threatens to put an end to the girls' lost cause. The scene is set. The author picks up his pen with trembling fingers and begins to write. Time to tear Kate and Peter apart. The thought of making her life hell has him dribbling in anticipation. Age is no excuse. He ought to know better. Things rarely turn out as an author expects.

Boy & Girl Saga Book 3
We Girls
2020 edition
Alan McCluskey

We Girls
The Boy & Girl Saga - Book 3

Peter is beset by an existential choice, retain his androgynous ambiguity or say goodbye to his girlish self. Circumstances, however, force both him and Kate to take up other challenges. By straddling the line between child and adult, between carefree creativity and weighty responsibility, between play and work, they find imaginative ways to confront far-reaching problems on which adults persistently turn a blind eye.

Secret Paths Editions presents
Stories People Tell
A novel by Alan McCluskey
"We raise our fists in salute, not in threat but as a sign of
solidarity. In those fingers held tight we embrace everyone
however different they may be. Gay. Trans. Straight. Black.
Brown. Yellow. White. All colours of the rainbow.
All are welcome in our London."
Annie Wight, London Whatever

Stories People Tell

Stories People Tell is a tale about Annie Wight, a shy schoolgirl who, despite sustained, cruel treatment and personal doubts, blossoms into a major voice in the grassroots movement 'London Whatever' celebrating gender diversity while struggling to end violence against women and care for the weak and marginalised.

Annie wasn't expecting to fall in love with a girl or to shoot to notoriety when she got swept up in 'London Whatever'. Nor could she have known that, right from the outset, she would become the number one target of Nolan Kard, the homophobic Lord Mayor of London. who was campaigning to 'Keep London Straight'. She bore the brunt of attacks from his rogue police, not to mention from a sinister gang of ghostwriters, the nightmare of all Kard's enemies.

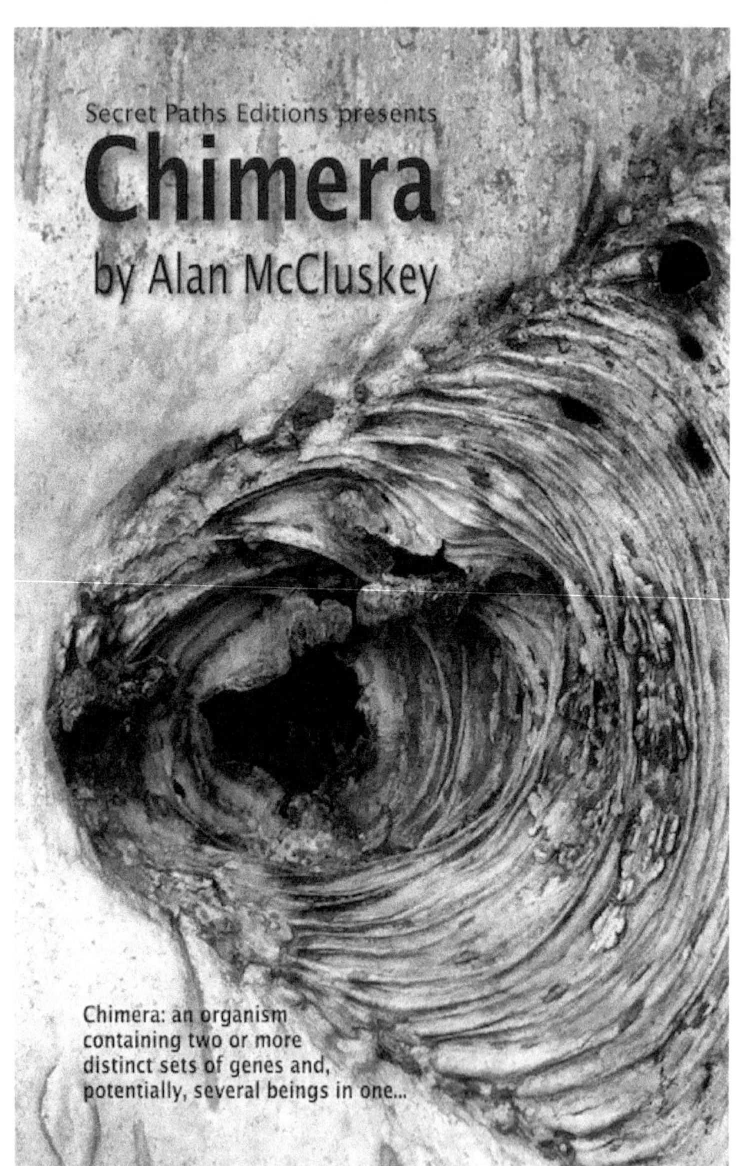
Secret Paths Editions presents
Chimera
by Alan McCluskey

Chimera: an organism
containing two or more
distinct sets of genes and,
potentially, several beings in one...

Chimera

A chimera is an organism containing two or more distinct sets of genes and, potentially, several beings in one. Sami and Sam are a chimera, two people in one, a girl and a boy, a leader and healer of people sharing a body with a brilliant but autistic child.

Sam talking to himself on discovering he is one half of a chimera...:
:: not being able to speak, to move - such was the price I had to pay - to cut out the chaos and confusion from a world run wild - a raw satisfaction - being barricaded in my head these past twelve years - all for nothing - that blasted girl has ruined everything - surging out of nowhere - pirating my body - bridging the gap between me and the others - letting chaos rush in - beguiling everyone with her codswallop - not me - I'm not impressed - some say she's destined to be our saviour - as if the block-head could save a fly - I just want her gone

Sami's first ever words to her teacher and her father...:
"I ... need ... to explain. Words come with ... difficulty. I must ... be brief. Sam and I are a ... chimera ... there are two of us... Sam is the boy you know. New things terrify him. He cannot speak ... out loud. He stumbles. He falls. I am new. I just awoke. I am a girl. I play piano I talk. I walk. As for that violence you just saw, that was Sam trying to kick me out"

The Storyteller's Quest ~ Book One
The Reaches
Alan McCluskey

The Reaches
The Storyteller's Quest - Book 1

The quiet town of Avan with its port, its provincial university and its conservative seafaring folk would hardly be the place you'd expect to run into an adventure and frankly neither Brent nor Sally nor Keira were going out of their way to have one. At least nothing more than the occasional torrid love affair and the awkward self-questioning typical of many young adults like themselves. Sally was finishing her studies in the Theosophy Department of the University hoping to become Professor Rafter's assistant, Keira, Sally's best friend and lover, was a young librarian who occasionally sang in a popular folk group and Brent was a would-be writer who couldn't quite get his act together and who spent hours wandering the streets and lanes of the town in search of inspiration. Yet unbeknown to them forces had long been at work that would throw them together in a series of adventures that were going to tax them to the extreme forcing them to develop abilities that went way beyond what would seem possible during a voyage from the real world to the realm of dreams and on into another world called the Reaches that at first sight looked deceptively like their own.

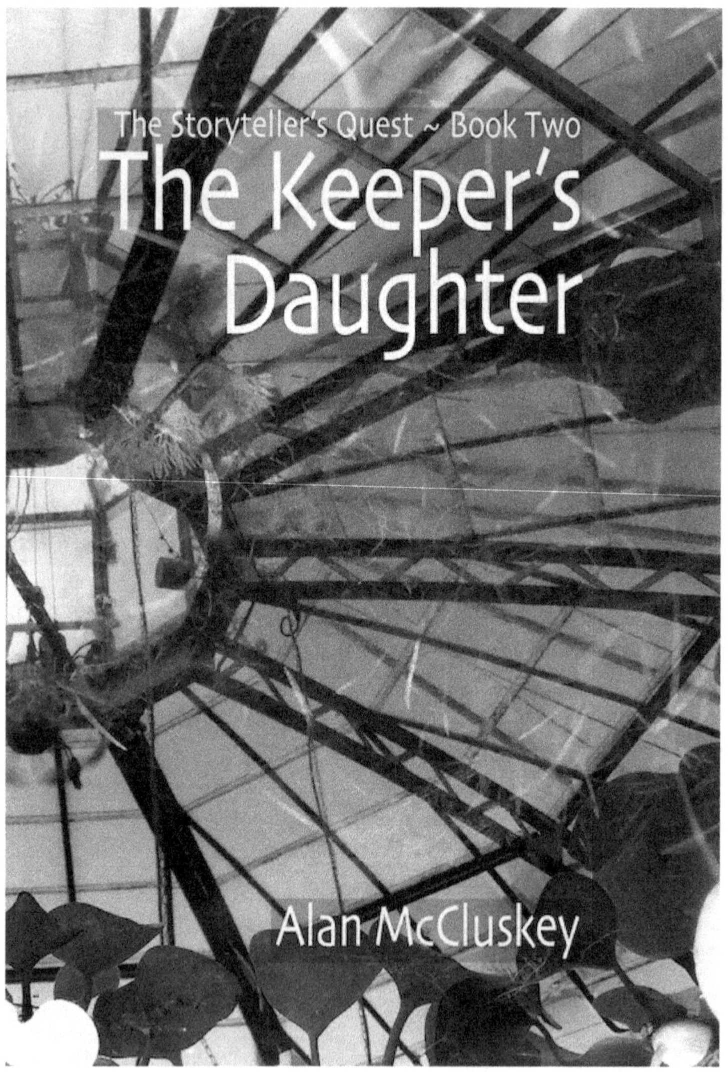

The Storyteller's Quest ~ Book Two
The Keeper's Daughter
Alan McCluskey

The Keeper's Daughter
The Storyteller's Quest - Book 2

It wasn't Brent's fault if he was stuck in the form of Jake the Owl, at least he didn't think it was as he sat on a branch preening despondently. The threads of all his stories had become inextricably muddled in his owlish head. To think that he'd once prided himself on being a storyteller. His stories had become adventures and some of those adventures had become nightmares, and now he was stuck with them. He'd flown in search of his friend and lover, Mia. She'd been dragged off by a band of thugs just when it was time for them all to return to their world. Only Sally, their mutual friend and lover, had made it back from the world of the Reaches to their hometown of Avan. Hearing her story, despite the dangers she'd had to face, her friends suggested Sally teach them to travel to the Dream Realm and beyond to the Reaches. The idea appealed to everybody. Not that Sally knew how to get back to the Reaches, but the idea of a 'dream class' as they called it pleased her and, above all, she wanted to return to the world where her newly-found half-sister lived and where her two friends had so abruptly disappeared.

The Storyteller's Quest ~ Book Three
The Starless Square
Alan McCluskey

The Starless Square
The Storyteller's Quest - Book 3

A weekend of joyous festivities! Such was the Theosophy department's response to a group of fanatics bent on destroying their reputation and having them shut down. Theosophy? Professor Rafter, head of the department, calls it "the study of our direct relationship with that which is beyond and above the normal range of human experience". He could just as well have been describing the adventures of a group of young friends who have been called back from their travels in another world to defend their department with their new-found abilities. But how could entrancing singing or breath-taking storytelling or exquisite cooking possibly stand a chance when pitted against the evil black cloud that threatens to obscure the Starless Square?

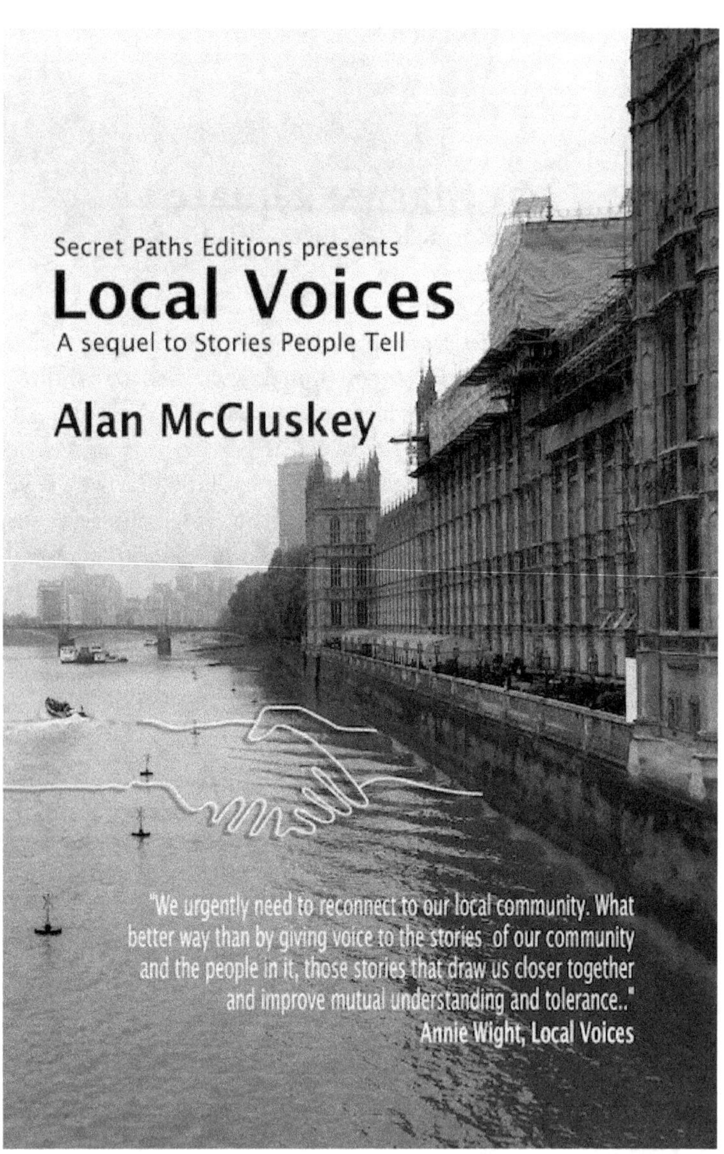

Secret Paths Editions presents
Local Voices
A sequel to Stories People Tell

Alan McCluskey

"We urgently need to reconnect to our local community. What
better way than by giving voice to the stories of our community
and the people in it, those stories that draw us closer together
and improve mutual understanding and tolerance.."
Annie Wight, Local Voices

Local Voices
Coming soon: a sequel to Stories People Tell

In her campaign to re-assert and strengthen the role of women at the heart of hearthside healthcare, seventeen-year-old Annie Wight finds herself pitted against Health England, a conservative think-tank backed by pharmaceutical giants and private healthcare providers. Pretexting the defence of the National Health Service, they stop at nothing to stamp out Annie's efforts. They target not just her but those close to her, wreaking havoc in friendships and affairs of the heart. As part of her response, Annie launches a project to share the stories of those that never figure in the spotlight. By celebrating local voices, the project fights against isolation and disempowerment.

Online

Secret Paths: https://author.secret-paths.com
Facebook: https://www.facebook.com/Secret.Paths
Instagram: https://www.instagram.com/secretpathseditions/
Twitter: https://www.twitter.com/Almacme